ETERNAL

THE INFINITE SERIES: BOOK 4

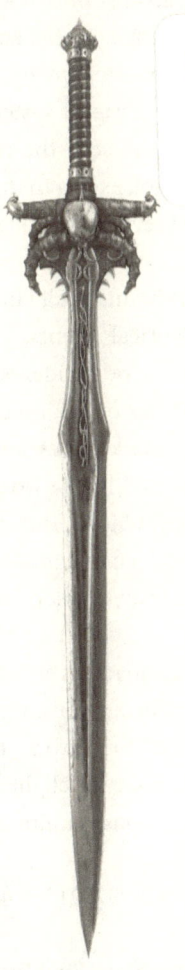

NICOLE
CORINE DYER

ISBN-13: 978-0-9970212-6-4 (Paperback)

First Edition First Printing
Editing by Jennifer Tovar at Gypsy Heart Editing
Cover Design by Michelle Preast
Formatting by Stacey Blake at Champagne Book Design

DEDICATION

To my granny, Doris Lee Dyer. All these books are dedicated to you, without a doubt. You were my number one fan. I tried to get this finished for you in time but couldn't. Hopefully, you can read this in Heaven.
Love you to the moon and back.

PROLOGUE

RYAN WATCHED AS TEARS poured down Julia's cheeks. There were no words to say to her as the body of Grace burned in the pyre next to Ahmose and many others. If there was anyone in this world Julia loved the most, he knew it was Grace. She was the mother Julia needed after her mother had passed. Grace was her confidant. Her rock.

Now, her body was reduced to ashes that blew away as the wind wound its way through the flames. A life so precious, reduced to nothing but memory.

The only solace was that Michael the Archangel had come to retrieve her soul as Zeus did with Zee. Ryan was thankful his second father did not make the trip himself. He more than likely would not handle the reunion well.

Everyone had left the funeral except Ryan and Julia. Damian had whisked Anna off to bed—he was already being a cautious father, while Cato remained in the healer's quarters.

The nighttime sky twinkled above, pure and calm. There was no trace of the horror it was a few days prior.

"What will I do?" Julia asked.

Ryan didn't have an answer for her. There were no answers. All he could give her was the comfort of his presence. "I don't know, but we will get through this together."

"When is my trial?" She stared at the flames instead of at

Ryan. Her face was set in stone as the light of the fire danced across her pale skin and a never-ending cascade of silent tears streamed down her cheeks.

"Tomorrow, but don't worry about it." Ryan had reluctantly become part of the Council of Command since the other members were murdered. He would be damned before Julia received a punishment for acts she had no power to control.

"They will execute me, I know it."

"If they try to lay a hand on you," his tone severe, "I will kill them all."

"You can't kill everyone, Ryan."

"Watch me."

CHAPTER I

Ryan

Six Months Later

TIME GOES BY FAST when you are in a constant battle with the world.

Ryan sat in the C-17 aircraft with Damian, Cato, and a group of United States Army personnel.

During the past six months, the Immortals had been doing nothing but leading, commanding, and recruiting mortals that opposed the Risen. It wasn't hard to convince the Americans given most of them were hell-bent religious believers to their very core.

Some people wouldn't change their minds no matter what proof you gave them. He had to admire that.

The entire world was a battleground now. Nowhere was safe from the religious war. Children were spared, their innocence their only savior but some would become orphans. It was a fact that infuriated Ryan.

There was no clear winning side as of now. Both seemed equally matched in their forces. How the Risen had gained such a following so quickly was beyond him.

Every Immortal alive that remained on their side was now spread across the world in command of the Resistance's troops.

They now called this World War III. It was in fact a literal world war. Nowhere has been unaffected. Some have even called it the War of the Followers. It was fitting for both sides of the equation.

"We are nearly there, sir," a young private yelled across the aircraft. He was hunched over from the weight of his rucksack hanging in front of him. "I just wanted to say it's an honor to be in your presence, sir."

Ryan, Damian, and Cato stood out from the rest of the men. Their gear all black as opposed to the dark camouflage the army personnel wore.

Ryan nodded to the man and faced his friends.

"Ready?" Ryan adjusted the straps on his parachute. The harness of his chute was crushing his balls.

Cato tapped his feet anxiously. Ryan remembered he loved jumping out of planes. "Yep."

He'd healed surprisingly well since his fight with his father. The General was merciless with his son, nearly killing him for his own ambition.

Ryan stood up, the rucksack between his legs heavy. "Alright boys." The cargo area grew as silent as it could with the hum of the engine. "As soon as we reach the target head to the base. Do you all remember where that is?"

Everyone nodded so he continued on, "We might come down with some fire but more than likely the area is secured by our guys. Once we get to the base you will be assigned your different duties."

All the men, and a few women, prepared themselves for the leap out of the aircraft.

"You fuckers ready?" Ryan looked at Cato and Damian.

Damian shook his head. "You've been around the Americans too much."

"I like it," Cato said. "They have colorful language."

"No, they curse. Hardly colorful," Damian countered.

"Back to my original question, are you fuckers ready?" Ryan asked.

The two side doors of the C-17 opened and Ryan's ears were consumed with the fury of the wind and the massive plane engines. Their troops stood in lines ready to jump.

They waited for the red light on the plane to turn green, signaling for them to jump. Ryan placed the first man in front of the door and as soon as the light turned, he smacked the man's ass letting him know to jump. He continued this until everyone was off the aircraft.

"Don't even think about smacking my ass," Damian yelled at him over the near deafening wind.

"Come on, baby, for old times' sake?" Ryan grinned.

With a roll of the eyes, Damian, Cato and then Ryan leapt out of the door. Ryan kept his body tight as he was sucked out of the aircraft. His chute opened and he plummeted down to earth. The city of Rome glistened in the night sky as he soared through the air.

He was glad everyone seemed to be untangled and a decent distance away from one another. Last thing he wanted was for someone to get tangled up in a chute and crash down to earth.

Just as the Vatican came in view, Ryan guided his parachute to St. Peter's Square. Some of their crew had already landed safely. Ryan dropped his rucksack once he neared the ground and bent his knees slightly. His feet hit the ground hard and he rolled his body over. As soon as he landed, he ripped off the parachute pack, tossed his rucksack on his back and ran towards the entrance of the Vatican.

Ryan could hear gunfire off in the distance and thundering sounds of larger ammunition being used.

They climbed up the steps as bullets collided with the building's walls.

"Get in!" Ryan yelled to the crew as they piled inside. Damian, Cato, and Ryan covered them as they squeezed into the entrance, shooting at the men propped on the columned walls that curved around the St. Peter's Square.

He fired his gun in their direction, hopefully killing them, at the very least he wanted the enemy to cease fire long enough for them to get in. His plan worked and once the doors were closed Ryan let his M4 Carbine hang from its strap.

They made their way to the rest of the group who stood around anxiously waiting for instructions.

"Everyone good?" Ryan asked. They nodded they were.

"I'll go get Fredrick." Damian made his way to a tall thin man with dark hair and bags under his eyes.

"Ladies and gents', this is Frederick. He will be your commanding officer here," Ryan started. The group nodded and Ryan shook hands with the man. "Good to finally meet you in person."

Frederick nodded. "You look smaller on TV." The both stared at each other and laughed after a beat. "A pleasure, Ryan. It is nice to finally meet the leader of the Resistance."

"I'm hardly the leader," Ryan said. He held his hand out to show his troops off. "They are ready for your orders."

"Do any of them speak Italian?"

Ryan frowned. He had forgotten about the language barrier. "Do any of you speak Italian?"

The group looked among themselves and a female with a dark complexion raised her hand. "I speak some, Sir."

"Good. If any of you have questions the three of us will be around, but if Frederick can answer them then ask him."

The group followed Frederick to an area filled with papers

fluttering about. Ryan had finally convinced them to quit saluting him. It was their own tradition and he felt as if he didn't deserve it.

Damian had told him it was a sign of respect, but Ryan could not take it that way. Every soldier had their traditions and as much as it made him happy that they saw him in such a manner, he had his own ways.

Cato and Damian followed Ryan down the extravagant hallway towards the tall black throne centered below the Vatican's dome.

Ryan sat down on the seat and reclined in it. The pope had life made.

Damian cleared his throat loudly. "Don't you think that is highly disrespectful?"

"What?"

"Sitting in the Pope's throne like that." Damian gave him the look Ryan knew was only ever used with himself. A look of annoyance mixed with amusement.

"First off, don't you think it is weird that a man of God has a throne? Odd. Whatever, not my business." Ryan winked at Cato who was hiding his growing smile the best he could. "Second, the guy is in his room. Hanging around doing who knows what. I doubt he cares where I sit. If he were to come down here and say, 'Hey Ryan, can I have my chair back' I would oblige."

"I remember a time when you spoke in a dignified manner. I miss those days." Damian yanked Ryan by the front of his vest causing him to almost tumble to the floor as he got off the damn chair.

"We have spent too much time around the generation that killed language. I am full of L.O. L's and W.T. F's and going hard in the paint, as well as being savage," Ryan said. "Still not sure what being hard in the paint entails exactly."

Damian draped his arm around Ryan's shoulder. "Will you please quit talking like that?"

"Next I am going to grow out a beard and my hair enough to where I can do a man bun." Ryan felt the urge to tease Damian further. "Maybe wear extraordinarily tight pants, start smoking an electric cigarette and drink a soy latte in a reusable eco-friendly cup," he said as he took his helmet off.

Damian was rolling his eyes while Cato looked to be deep in thought. "I had a mental image of you like that, it isn't pretty. Sort of annoying actually."

"More than he is now?" Damian asked. "Is that even possible?"

Ryan scratched the scruff on his cheek. He had grown a liking to having a beard. It wasn't long by any means. He kept it clean and short. Julia said it made him look rugged. Cato said it made him look more like a man, than having a smooth babyface.

They all seemed to have adopted a fondness for having a light scruff on their faces. Cato's was slightly longer than his buzz-cut hair, but Damian followed Ryan's example of short and clean.

"So, when can we leave?" Ryan asked.

"We just got here. We're sticking around for a few days, remember? Getting everything in order." Damian had that look again. "I know you think it is stupid to be here, but this is one of the religious meccas of the world. The Risen is surrounding the Vatican and the Pope's life is in jeopardy."

"I am well aware of that, but our time needs to be concentrated on taking the General down. Nothing is going to be solved until he is dead." Ryan avoided eye contact with Cato. His father, the man that raised him was long gone. Replaced by an evil monster, hardly recognizable to anyone that really knew him.

The mortals that follow the Risen think of him as a literal god. How Marc managed to pull that off, Ryan would never know. Smoke and mirrors probably.

"Where do you think he is?" Cato asked.

"The Smithsonian was his main fortress. My guess is he is there," Ryan said.

"What if he is setting up shop in Urbs? Since most of the Immortals are out in the world. It would be easy to take," Damian said.

Ryan had given the order for every Immortal on their side to join the fight against the Risen. Only women with children were allowed to stay behind but they were moved into the Domus for protection. Urbs was on lockdown until the threat was cleared. He didn't want any more of their people harmed.

It was about time every Immortal fulfilled their duty to their existence. Even the ones that had never fought before were trained and sent into the world. This is why the gods created them. Not to live forever in Urbs in peace, but to keep the peace.

"There is no need to take it over. No one is there," Ryan said. "We need to hurry along with this. The past six months has been nothing but war waged on the entire planet. It needs to stop. Too many are dying."

"Tell us something we don't know," Cato grumbled.

Anna

Waddle, puke, eat, and repeat. That was what her life consisted of now. Anna hated being pregnant. From what the healers gathered she was about seven months along and sporting a huge bump protruding from under her shirt. She refused to wear maternity clothes, mainly due to stubbornness but also her inability to fully accept her larger stature.

Julia seemed more excited about their future addition than Anna was. Even though the alien feeling creature was obviously inside of her, she still couldn't wrap her head around the idea that she was going to be a mother.

It was scary. Probably one of the scariest things she would ever face in her lifetime. Then there was Damian. He was so excited he could hardly function around her.

He always put his hand on her stomach and talked to the baby. Could the thing hear him? She had no idea, but it was weird. Part of her was glad he was out with Ryan and Cato. It gave her some peace from him doting on her every need.

Sure, it was nice at first but there came a point where she had to put her foot down. She could still tie her own damn shoes, but she had to admit the continuous massages were a plus.

Anna looked down at her stomach and splayed her hands out over it. Although everything about this was crappy, she loved the little creature growing inside of her. This baby was part of her but mostly it was part of the love of her life.

"Will you concentrate?" Julia snapped her back to the task at hand.

"Sorry," Anna sighed. They were in Damian's room, which was now their room. Since Cato's room was right by Damian's, he gave it up so they could have a bigger space for the baby. The wall between them had been recently knocked out and their expanded living space was complete.

She'd moved what little possessions she had into his room along with her cat Calypso. Damian insisted on them living together in the Domus as a couple. There really was no point in living apart anyway. Ever since she found out about her little fetus, he hadn't left her side unless he went on a mission.

Julia crossed her arms, tapping her toe in obvious frustration. "Have you decided?"

Anna looked at the color Julia had picked out for the baby's room. Honestly, the room was far too massive for such a small child but who was she to deny the best for her kid.

"Blue?" Anna asked. Julia made a look of disgust. "Okay, yellow?"

"You need to take this seriously Anna, honestly."

"It's the color of its room. I really doubt the thing will care." Anna sat down on the gliding chair Julia had purchased just the other day. Stupid thing was annoyingly comfortable.

"Will you stop calling the baby 'it', 'thing', and 'alien'? It is a baby. A precious little life given to you as a gift and you need to treat it as such."

Anna was really getting sick of this conversation or maybe it was just the hormones. "It's a freaking color."

Julia threw her hands up in frustration. "You have no concept of glorifying the atmosphere for the perfect amount of Zen to raise a happy healthy baby."

"I have never felt dread for Ryan as much as I do now when I think of you two having children in the future," Anna said deadpan.

Julia's cheeks blushed and she continued to fold the soft white baby blanket and place it on the completely extravagant dresser fit for royalty. "We are still working things through right now. You know that. We're not even near the conversation of children."

"Do you really think I was near the conversation of children?" Anna laughed. "Yet here I am, knocked up and picking out nursery colors in a fortress made for professional killers."

"My point is that Ryan and I are still in rough patch." Julia sighed. "He is still having trouble with the Zee incident, as am I."

Anna hated that conversation. She could hear Ryan and Julia fight through the wall next door where Ryan's room was. The fight usually consisted of Julia not being able to accept what she did and Ryan trying to convince her it wasn't her actual self that did it.

She could understand both sides. Julia had been drugged and brainwashed into committing those crimes. If she were in Julia's shoes it would be difficult to get rid of the guilt as well. It was a terrible situation, even if Ryan had made sure Julia was forgiven by the council for her crimes.

Not everyone could forgive her though, especially Zee's family. Anna couldn't say she blamed them, but after knowing the real Julia, Anna realized she would never do anything like that. Her heart was too pure.

Anna decided to change the subject. "Which color do you think?"

"Mint, gold, and grey." She was obviously about to explode with her color scheme idea as she jumped on the balls of her feet for approval. She was by far the most ridiculous woman Anna had ever known, but in a good way.

"Really?"

"Trust me. It will be calming, fit for prince or princess and perfect for you two." Julia clapped her hands together, her blonde hair flowing behind her as she scurried to design the baby's room.

She started to mumble about paintings and what types of equipment Anna may need. Julia left no stone unturned as she began to squabble on about breast pumps and how useful they are these days. She even suggested Anna throw a baby shower as soon as possible for guests to give their 'blessings'.

"Whatever you want, crazy lady." Anna thumped her fingers against her belly. "When are the guys going to be back anyway?"

"Who knows with them. More than likely they are knee deep in danger facing horrible circumstances." Anna's eyes widened and Julia must have realized what she had said and backpedaled to try and calm Anna's nerves. "They are fine. Always are."

Anna took a deep breath. "Yeah, okay."

Julia grabbed hold of Anna's hands, giving her that motherly look Anna grew to become impatient with. "Damian will be fine, I promise. That man would kill anyone in his way to get back to you."

"Really? A pep talk that includes death?"

"I forget how sensitive you are to that." Julia shook her head smiling to herself. "One day it will be normal for you. It's a part of life."

"It's pretty sad how numb you all are to death." *Except with their families and Zee.*

Julia stiffened for just a moment. "Never numb. We never forget. We accept." Shaking her head, she made her frown into a smile. "Sorry, didn't mean to get serious."

"Death is a pretty serious topic," Anna said.

"It is."

"At least all of us will see our loved ones in the end." Anna smiled but Julia's face was sullen as ever. "What?"

She gently rubbed the top of Anna's hand before letting it go. "It is much more difficult for us Immortals. We could live forever without seeing the ones we lost ever again. I may never see my mother once more. Ryan may never see any of his family, as well as Damian. Everyone in their lives are dead and gone."

"Nathan was all I had." Anna hated that her mortal life was practically a big ball of loneliness. "At least I have Damian now though. And you have Ryan and your brother."

Julia merely nodded and the tension in the room grew far too serious and frankly uncomfortable.

"Can we go back to talking about room colors?"

"No, because it's already been decided. You just sit there thinking of names." She winked and all seriousness left the air as she sashayed her way towards the ornately carved crib. "Don't you dare think about naming that boy Maximilian, I don't care what Damian says."

"Believe me, that isn't a problem."

Chapter II

Ryan

JUMPING FROM THE LEDGE *with blades in both hands, he thrust a dagger deep into the man's neck and rounded about on another man. His dagger was soaked with fresh blood. Hidden behind a dark cloak that masked his true identity, he pressed forward. He was a shadow of death, wreaking havoc upon those who threatened his life, his mission, his purpose.*

He was attacked from all sides. He needed to escape the burning castle as wood planks fell from the rafters hitting the stone floor. Heat intensified within the room quickly, but more men entered the room to end his life.

He managed to find a spear, twisting it in his hands as he thrust it into one man, then two. Continuing this onslaught until finally it broke leaving shards of wood that he thrust into the men with ease. The sickening crunch of their bones breaking from impact vibrated through his hands, but his attack didn't stop. It couldn't.

His daggers appeared just as quickly as they had left his hands. Slicing into flesh before his victims knew what happened.

Fire raged around him threatening collapse, yet he remained in battle. Killing every man that entered his realm of death until no more entered. He looked around at the carnage before him.

Bodies, limbs and swords lay useless around him. Nothing moved but the dancing fire around him.

Standing there, he breathed heavily, his hood still covering his face. He sheathed his daggers soaked in blood. This… this is what he does best.

"We are under attack!" someone in the Vatican yelled, waking Ryan up from the little catnap he felt he deserved.

Sleeping in full gear was never all that comfortable, but somehow he'd managed to fall into a deep enough sleep that made waking up difficult. His eyes fluttered open, Damian and Cato were already pulling themselves up from sleeping against the wall. Grumbling, he tried to rotate his neck but the kink in it was protesting.

"Get up," Damian grunted as he pulled Ryan up to standing.

He thrust out his chin to give Damian the go ahead to slap him awake, which he did happily with a smirk on his face. "I haven't gotten to do that in a while."

"Don't get so excited," Ryan said. "Alright, what's going on?"

He heard gunfire and explosions going off outside the Vatican. Although it wasn't his religion, it bothered him deeply that they were destroying a religious hub. Catholics had their problems as did all religions, but he knew they were a deeply faithful people. Losing the Vatican would be a major blow.

"You can hear what's going on, why ask?" Cato rubbed the sleep out of his eyes after he put his helmet on.

Deciding to ignore Cato's pissed off attitude, he strapped his helmet on and jogged to the front of the Vatican along with a large group of people. Everyone was buzzing with worried comments and a few looked on the verge of passing out. Most of these people were civilians. It was obvious compared to the seasoned soldiers standing stoically. Still, their courage was commendable.

Ryan pushed his way through the crowd until they realized who he was and they parted to let him pass easily. He had forgotten what it felt like to have a silent command over people. A familiar feeling of power started to rise within him, but he mentally pushed that feeling down. Different time. Different people. Different circumstances.

Peeking out the door, he saw their guys were hiding behind large bags of sand shooting at the offenders perched on top of the columned walls. Two helicopters were coming their way from afar and he was very certain it wasn't their men.

"Fuck," he muttered under his breath.

"What's happening?" Cato asked.

"Why ask?" Ryan mimicked his earlier comment. Cato glared. "We have shots being fired from up top and two choppers coming our way. I want two groups on the outside of St. Peter's Square. Shoot them from behind while our guys out front distract them. We will take care of the choppers."

Two women handed out earpieces to the groups that Frederick was relaying Ryan's orders to. Once the groups were wired up, they ran to exit through the back of the Vatican and surround the square. The group that remained with Ryan and his team stood nervously in the entryway waiting for instruction.

Ryan checked his equipment, made sure his guns were loaded and bounced on the balls of his feet. He was pumping himself up. The rest of their group looked at one another as if questioning if they should do the same. One guy in the back apparently thought so because he started to hop until he realized no one else was doing it.

"You good?" he asked Damian and Cato.

"Yeah, now let's get out there before our guys get slaughtered." Damian cracked his neck.

One man stood at the entrance to the door, ready to open it quickly for them as they scurried out into the conflict and shut it immediately behind them. Ryan, Damian, and Cato joined the soldiers that were already engaged in the frontline action. As Ryan's back hit the sandbags, he tucked his head low to avoid fire.

"Thank fucking God," said a woman with blonde hair pulled back into a frizzy low bun. "Thought you guys ditched us or something."

"Never, sweetheart." Ryan winked at her, but she just rolled her eyes.

She shot off a few rounds. "I'm gay. Don't even think about it."

Ryan had to laugh at her. Apparently calling a woman sweetheart and winking at her meant attraction. Well, probably but that wasn't his intent.

"I bet I could change that." He shot off a few rounds himself. Screw it, might as well make light of the situation.

"You wish, dickhead." The woman grinned now. Apparently, his newfound fame didn't faze this woman as it had others.

"So many dirty comments, so little time." Ryan patted her on the back, aimed at a man through his scope and took him down. "The choppers are here."

"Alright, you get on out there, Cap' and kill em' all." A man next to frizzy lady showed off his crooked grin when he looked at Ryan. With a salute and a wink to Ryan, the man continued to shoot his rifle towards the enemy.

Ryan turned to face Damian and Cato hiding grins behind their gloved hands.

"You heard the man. Go get em' Cap!" Cato waved him forward with an over exaggerated wink.

"Let's just shoot the birds down," Ryan grumbled. Once the helicopters came closer, they let off rounds into the air. With any luck they would hit the gas line and blow the things up sending shrapnel at the men stationed on the wall rather than crash it into the Vatican. There was no such luck.

The helicopters turned around, circling back with gunfire raining down on Ryan and his crew. They ducked as low as they could behind the sandbags, bits and pieces of stone scattering around them. White dust from the marble filled the air making Ryan cough as he inhaled.

"Shit!" Cato yelled once the helicopter went past.

Gunfire rang out in the distance. Ryan snuck a glance over the bags to see members of the Risen falling from their perches on top of the stone walls like sacks of flour. Bodies began to outline the bottom of the wall.

"Our guys are in position and they took out the front line on the columns. Let's get out there." Ryan waved Damian and Cato towards the right, while he went left. The helicopters were making their way back around for another go but they didn't shoot. Instead, both the birds flew directly overhead with ropes falling to the ground. Ryan hid behind the tall columns of the square, aiming at the people that cascaded down the ropes.

Letting rounds off, he killed two men before their bodies even hit the ground. Shots whizzed past him and he hid behind the column again. Once the firing stopped, he faced the helicopters again, a few boots were already on the ground.

A rocket sped out from the Vatican's entrance and hit one of the birds. It blew up in the air, and the heat could be felt from where Ryan stood.

From the sounds of it, the other helicopter flew off but when Ryan dared to face the destruction before him, he was met with two members of the Risen with their guns pointed at his chest.

Ryan quickly knocked a weapon down. A second later a bullet hit the ground by his foot while he maneuvered the other man's gun from his grasp. He shot the man with his own gun while the other man raised his arms up in defeat. Ryan grimaced, sickened by this man's pathetic resolve to surrender.

"Die like a man," Ryan hissed between his teeth to the masked man.

"Please," he begged. Something sparked in the back of Ryan's mind about the man's voice but he was too far gone in his battle rage to figure out what it was.

"I don't think so."

"Then make it quick." The man hung his head low. "Have mercy."

Ryan wanted to shoot out the man's kneecaps and then shoot him in the stomach and let him bleed out, but he took pity on the soul before him. "Turn around and kneel." Doing as he was told, Ryan aimed between his shoulder blades to sever the man's spine. "Pray to your false god."

Before he could pull the trigger, the man reached back and grabbed both of Ryan's legs from behind and toppled him over. He jumped onto Ryan's chest and started to punch him, taking Ryan completely by surprise.

Ryan blocked most of the hits until he finally found an opening and grabbed the man by the throat. Choking sounds came from the masked figure as he held his neck and Ryan reversed their positions. Ryan unstrapped his knife from his leg but before he thrust it into his assailant's chest the man lifted up his mask.

Ryan grimaced but didn't loosen his grip on the dagger. "Well, fuck me."

Julia

As she got ready for bed, combing her hair while listening to her record player, Julia hummed softly to the tune being played. There was something so pure about records compared to other listening devices.

The little things like the soft crackle before the music started and the soulfulness of it. She couldn't explain it, nor did she really need to. Anna called her ancient. Said she was stuck in the old days. But what Anna seemed to forget was that it spoke levels about Julia.

She was ancient.

Her eyes were closed as she combed through her hair for much longer than needed. It was soothing just being in the moment without a thought of the world. Humming along to the sound of Etta James's "All I Can Do Is Cry" felt almost therapeutic.

In her meditative state she must not have heard her door open as two arms gently wrapped around her from behind. It was a touch she had become accustomed to and had ceased to catch her by surprise. She rested her head against his shoulder and received a kiss against her temple.

Setting down her comb, Julia placed her hands over his and allowed him to tenderly pull her to standing. As she turned around, she looked into the adoring gaze of the only man she'd ever loved.

With one hand around her waist and the other gently pressing her hand to his chest, their bodies began to sway as they danced. He was dressed in dark jeans and a black cotton shirt, smelling of soap and spices. His bearded cheek pressed against the top of her head making her smile from its tickle.

Ryan started to sing along with the song, "I saw my love, walk down the aisle." He kissed her forehead again and the small touch made her weak at the knees. "Till death do us part." She grinned at the choice words he picked from the song. "All I could do was cry."

They danced along to the heartbreaking song that he'd turned into one of her favorites in an instant.

"Well, hello." She kissed his lips gently once their eyes managed to meet.

Ryan pressed her body closer to his. "I missed you."

She wriggled her body against his. "I can tell." The man seemed to always be in a constant state of arousal around her. "How was your trip?"

His forehead touched hers. "Can we talk about that later? Right now, I have plans for you." His voice was almost a demanding growl and her body became putty in his hands. In normal circumstances she didn't put up with a demanding man but when Ryan used that voice she obeyed.

"What sort of plans may I ask?" Her voice was barely above a whisper.

"You will just have to be surprised." He grinned as he swept her feet out from under her and carried her to the bed. He laid her tenderly against the pillows, kissing her all the while and positioned his body on top of hers.

After moments of sensual, soft kisses he drew back to look at her. Julia's eyes fluttered open, still in the trance he had her in.

"What's wrong?" Her breaths were quick.

"You are so beautiful," he said. "Inside and out."

It was a phrase he'd repeated over and over to her after she was brainwashed by Aden to reassure her that she was good. No matter what Ryan said, she still felt guilty for everything her alter ego did, regardless of her being in control or not. Ryan made a point to remind her of who she really was on a daily basis.

"Okay." It was all she could ever say. No matter how long she lived, the blood on her hands would never wash away. She would always feel guilty. "Tell me about your trip."

"Really?" His hips ground into hers. "Now?"

"Yep." He needed a little teasing occasionally.

"Persistent little thing, aren't you?"

"You know it."

"Can we please talk about this later, Julia? I've missed you and before I left, we fought."

She placed her hand against his cheek and watched his eyes close at her touch. He was so different than she ever expected. Ryan went from a womanizing jerk to a soft romantic that wouldn't give another woman a second glance anymore. Sweet, kind, and willing to do anything for her, it was a drastic change from the past.

Something in the way she looked at him must have made Ryan give in because he said, "Aden is downstairs in the dungeon and I don't want you to go near him."

"What?" Her eyes went wide. Her breathing grew quicker and not in a good way. Ever since their big battle she seemed a little less strong and a lot more fearful when it came to Aden. Ryan took notice of her change right away.

"He can't get out, but as I said, I don't want you going near him. You aren't ready for that yet."

Her brows knit together at his assumption and she tried to reign in her anxiety. Perhaps she needed to finally face her fears instead of running away.

"How would you know if I am or not? What do you think I will do? Run off and kill more of our people?" She covered her mouth as soon as she said it. The look of hurt on his face was apparent. "I am so sorry."

"It's the past."

"But Zee—" she started but he silenced her with a finger to her lips.

"My love, this is about us. You are my soul. My life. I will never give up on us ever again. All of my doubts are gone, baby."

"Ryan—"

"No, you need to hear this, Julia. Every breath has been wasted in this life until you became mine. I thought all my time here would be spent around the company of death, but you gave me a chance to see the good in the world, Julia. You are the purest blessing a man could ever hope to receive."

"There is so much blood on my hands."

Ryan grabbed her hands, bringing her knuckles to his lips. "These hands? These hands are small." *Kiss.* "Sweet." *Kiss.* "And mine. Pure, safe, and loving."

"You are so full of it." She couldn't help but grin.

"Couldn't be a truer statement." He kissed her lips, trailing them along her cheek down to her neck. "Now, let me show you how full of it I am."

"You are so idiotic sometimes."

"You like it."

"And you are an expert at changing subjects."

He started to kiss her neck. "Yes, ma'am. I am."

Julia was going to ignore Ryan's command to stay away from Aden. Everything in her body told her to listen, but she had to know why he did what he did. She felt violated by him. He raped her, drugged her, turned her into a completely different person—an evil person who did evil things and there was no changing that. She had to know why her? Sure, her father was the mastermind of the most evil plan known to mankind, but there was something off about it.

Cato wasn't dragged into the mess. Just her. Only her. Why?

Most importantly, why the hell did her father allow him to use her body like that? Was she just a prize given to Aden for good service? It made her feel even more unclean just thinking about it. She must be nothing more than a piece of property to her father. Her body was a toy for his ally to play with.

She shivered at the thought of Aden touching her. He wasn't ugly. Far from it in fact, but that didn't mean she wanted him. She really never did but there was no taking those actions back. What was done was done and although she would never forget, perhaps she could find some sort of peace by facing him.

Tip toeing her way to the torture chambers, the eerie cold drifted around her legs, washing her in the uncertainty of her actions. Ryan would be furious if he found out what she was doing but she intended to keep it to herself. As for Aden, he might spill the beans, but it was a risk she had to take.

Groans could be heard as she made her way down the halls. The last time she was down here Sven was being tortured for the attack at the Great Temple when Anna was made into a Warrior. It seemed like so long ago.

So many of the rooms were now filled with prisoners since the start of the war. Some were simply locked up whereas others weren't so lucky, suffering the same fate as Sven. Fortunately, each door was labeled with who resided inside and Aden's was the very last one.

She knocked but no sound came from within. Either he was alone, passed out, or dead but that didn't deter her from finding out. As she slowly opened the door, Julia peeked inside. It was dimly lit by a single light that hung from the ceiling and sitting in the center of the beam was Aden, his wrists strung up in the air by chains.

The faint glow of the single light reflected off his damp, dark hair and shadowed his face from being fully seen. His body had wounds but nothing too terrible. She had expected him to look near death, especially since Ryan had gotten his hands on the man, but that wasn't the case. It almost bothered her.

"Aden?" she whispered but didn't know why. No one was down here but criminals.

No movement came from him, so she whispered louder, "Aden."

Slowly he pulled his head up to look at her. He had a cut on his lip and a black eye but otherwise he was fine. His hair was getting longer than normal and scruff was forming along his jaw.

"Julia. What a pleasant surprise." That familiar smirk danced across his dry lips. Even tied up he could maintain his attitude. "To what do I owe the pleasure?"

"I wanted to see you." She inched forward. His eyes squinted in confusion. "I wanted to ask you some questions."

"Get in line sweetheart, everyone does." He pulled himself up by his wrists. They were raw and bloody, but it didn't seem to bother him.

"Are they hurting you?"

Aden's laugh was scratchy and it quickly turned into a coughing fit. She went to the sink and filled a small bowl up with water. Aden greedily sucked down the liquid even as a vast majority of it dripped down his jaw onto his bare chest.

"I didn't expect kindness from you but then again that is your fatal flaw. Kind, even to the worst of souls."

"You have me pegged all wrong, Aden." Merely being this close to him made her nauseous. "I want answers from you. If that means I need to get you some water to make you talk, then so be it."

"Take your false pity somewhere else then," he hissed.

She had to choke down the lump in her throat from being so near him. "Will you answer my questions, Aden?"

"Depends on what they are."

"Why did you choose me? I get that my father wanted me by his side but what doesn't make sense is the fact he let you get close to me. Too close." She couldn't bring herself to say what they actually did. It felt vile to form the actual words on her lips.

Aden cocked his head to the side. "Do you mean, why did your father let me fuck you? Let's just say that wasn't part of his plan. I kept that part to myself." His smile was unnerving. Without thought, she slapped him across his face.

"Why would you even want to?" She couldn't mask the anger she felt through her voice.

"You're kidding right?" He appeared confused and she just stared blankly at him. "You're not kidding. Okay then. First off, I have always wanted you, Julia. You are gorgeous, talented, and everything a man could hope for."

"And second?" she pried.

"Second, I am surprised dear old Dad hasn't told you."

"I thought my father didn't know about you and I like that?"

"I don't mean your father, Julia. I mean mine." That evil grin was back on his face. Aden used to be sane. She knew he had been at a time, but it seemed that any semblance of his humanity was gone. Replaced with a demon so hideous he could never be saved.

He started to laugh at her. It reminded her of the sadistic laugh of a clown at an amusement park she went to with Grace.

Even as an adult, clowns terrified her, and Aden's laughter was hauntingly similar.

She took a step back without meaning to. "I don't even know who your father is."

His head rolled back, laughing even harder. He picked up his legs and swung on the chains causing his wrists to bleed more. "Oh Julia, you really don't know, do you?"

"Know what?" She edged away.

Aden ceased moving. After a moment, he looked her in the eyes, his face serious as he moved as close to her as the chains would allow. His presence and his lack of mental stability was unnerving. Frightening.

"My dear, dear Julia. What better way to hurt my father, than to sleep with the one woman he loves more than life itself?"

Her eyebrows knit. "What?"

"My father was a womanizer. Little did he know his seed implanted my mother. She was a disgraced Warrior—pregnant out of wedlock in a time where that was not allowed. I believe you lost your virginity to him. I tried to get it. I knew that would drive him mad, but it seems even in your altered mind you couldn't resist him."

She grimaced in disgust. Just the thought of her sleeping with a father and son was unthinkable. "You're lying."

Aden's grin appeared again. "No. I am afraid Daddy didn't even know about me. He was too busy sleeping around, saving the world, and not giving a damn about any woman he stuck it in."

"No…"

"I imagine it will be the same for you."

"Stop." She closed her eyes.

"How does it feel to have made it around our family tree?"

"Enough!"

The voice behind her was the last thing she wanted to hear right now. She kept her eyes closed but she could feel Ryan's presence behind her. Julia felt numb.

"Long time no see Daddy-o." Aden's singsong voice gave her chills. He was insane. There was no doubt about it.

Julia opened her eyes and dared to look at Ryan. His mouth was set in a tight line. He wore only sweatpants, not even a pair of shoes on his feet. He must have left bed in a hurry.

"Go to my room, Julia," Ryan's voice lacked any emotion. Julia felt like her feet were incapable of moving. "Now."

"That's no way to talk to my ex, Dad. I don't care if you are banging her now," Aden laughed.

"Aden, that is enough."

"Oh, the look on both of your faces. So priceless."

"Julia, leave." Ryan's voice grew louder but his face was void of emotion.

Julia turned on her heel, making her way towards the door when Aden called out, "Come back again, Julia. We can have another go for old times' sake."

Ryan

"You bastard," Julia's voice rang out in his room.

Ryan couldn't blame her for getting angry with him. He should have told her the moment he knew Aden was his son, but he just couldn't admit it. It was difficult even for him to process. Blood tests had been done and Aden was confirmed as his own flesh and blood.

"I'm sorry," he said and he meant it. "But you shouldn't have been down there in the first place."

Judging by her growing anger that was the wrong thing to say.

She walked up to him, poking him in the chest with her finger.

"How could you not tell me?"

He took a breath, then one more for good measure as he tried to reign in his own anger. "I wanted to tell you on my own when I was ready. I'm still having trouble dealing with this. The guy is my son. Do you have any idea how I treated him?"

"I know perfectly well, but that isn't the point." Her voice started to waver. Julia's heart was too big, and he could see in her eyes how bad she had begun to feel for Ryan instead of herself.

"I've broken his arm, his leg... Hell I stuck his face in shit! There hasn't been a good moment between him and I, not ever. I would never treat my child the way I have treated him. If I knew, I would have raised him to the best of my ability. Showed him the love he deserved, but that wasn't the case."

She was fighting with her own demons about this realization. Ryan knew that and he couldn't blame her for her anger. It wasn't every day that a woman found out the only two men that knew her body were father and son.

"The worst part is that he won't tell me who his mother is. I have no idea. Something in his eyes reminds me of someone, but I can't figure it out." Ryan ran his hand through his hair. It had started to grow back but he decided to keep it at a decently short length. "Do you have any idea how that feels?"

Julia looked at him like he was an idiot. He felt like one, but she didn't need to point that out. "Really?"

"Okay, I get it. I slept with countless amounts of women. It could be anyone. Hell, the kid looks exactly like me. How could I not have known?" He rested his hands behind his head. He tried so hard to push down the thoughts of Aden being his child, but it was forced to the surface.

"He knew. He knew all along, Julia. I bet all he could think about was how cruel of a man his father is. No wonder he is evil. No wonder he is a killer. I ruined him."

Julia slowly got closer to him. He could see her hesitation, her nervousness to be near him after his rant. Instead of backing away she came to him, wrapped her arms around his waist and hugged his body. She was such a petite little thing but it made him feel safe, secure and loved even though they were fighting.

Ryan dropped his arms down and wrapped her up in an embrace as if to shield her from his own troubles. He clung onto her but felt strength rise in him. His life was on unsteady ground, but she was his rock. After all they had been through, he still couldn't shake the love he felt for her.

"Ryan?"

"Hmm?"

"I don't mean to bring up your problems. I really don't and I know you wanted to tell me in your own time."

"But?"

"But," she sighed, "if you feel so terrible about this, why is he hanging by his wrists in the dungeon?"

Ryan closed his eyes tight. It took him a moment to speak because he didn't want his voice to crack with the weakness he felt. "There is nothing I can do for him."

She pulled away only enough to look him in the eyes, but Ryan kept his grip around her. "He is your son."

Pressing a small kiss against her forehead he spoke, "He has done unthinkable things. Regardless of him being my blood, I cannot show him any more mercy than any other man or woman."

It was mostly the truth. Ryan had refused to torture Aden and he was still doing his best to keeps those who wished Aden harm at bay. The only way people could see getting information out of him was torture. Ryan agreed but he couldn't do it. He wouldn't allow it.

"You are a good man, Ryan." Julia pressed her hand to his cheek. "I hope you know that. I can tell how much this hurts you."

"Knowing what he did to you, it feels wrong wanting him to live. If it were anyone else, they would be dead in a minute. A slow, painful death."

"It's a difficult situation and I understand. I don't think any less of you for wanting your son to be alive. I won't lie though, he still haunts my dreams, but time will hopefully heal it."

"He should be dead for all he has done though." Ryan knew it to be true. Maybe it was his own guilt that wished Aden to remain alive. "For what that piece of… for what he did to you."

Ryan closed his eyes as she wrapped her arms around his neck. He loved having her against him. They fought so much lately that her gentle touches were his addiction. The stress of the world consumed him and he knew she got the brunt of his wrath.

"When this is over, I want you to be my wife." He placed a kiss on her neck, feeling her body shiver at his touch. "We will do this right. Marriage and children. My heart is entirely yours and I will never take you for granted ever again. You are my eternal love, Julia."

Julia's grip tightened. "I'll hold you to it."

Chapter III

Anna

"HOW ARE MY TWO loves doing?" Damian rubbed his hand along her stomach.

She understood his excitement but honestly it gave her a complex. "We are fine."

He crouched down, now eye level with her belly and placed his hands on either side of her waist. "Daddy missed you little one."

Damian was so sweet that she felt her hormones kick in gear and tears welled in her eyes when he kissed her stomach. She took deep breaths trying to control her current state, but it was no use. Damian sensed her mood change and brought himself up to her eye level and kissed her gently on the lips.

"Baby, what's wrong?" His forehead touched hers and he soothingly ran his hands up and down her arms.

"Just emotional." Anna took a deep breath still trying to contain the tears that spilled over her eyelids. Damian brushed them away with his thumbs. "I hate feeling this way."

"I know."

"You do?" She felt horrified. He was so excited to have a child and he knew how much she hated being pregnant. She was going to lose him. He would hate her. The negative train of thoughts wouldn't stop. "Oh my god, you hate me, don't you?"

His eyebrows scrunched together. "Baby, I could never hate you. This is your first child. You are scared. Your body is changing. We haven't been together that long but believe me I get it. This child is a blessing to us though."

"What if we split up for some reason, Damian? This is so new between us and adding a kid to the mix is insane and irresponsible."

His stance seemed to be planted in front of her as if he were talking to a child. Ready to tell the scared kid reasons why the boogeyman wasn't real.

"If we were to split up, heavens forbid, I would never abandon you or our child. You will never be alone in this. I will be there every step of the way and yes, we should have taken precautions to prevent this but it's too late for that. Those thoughts no longer matter because the fact of the matter is, that you are pregnant with my child and I love you both more than I have ever loved anyone."

Anna was filled with warmth from how amazing this man was. He was everything to her and perhaps this child was a blessing after all.

"I still hate how I can't do what I want though." She wanted to complain. Hell, she was pregnant, it was a right.

Damian grinned as he kissed her forehead. "Darling, you have less than two months until this little bundle of joy is in our arms. Two months is nothing to how long I have waited for the both of you. It will pass sooner than you realize."

"I hate how calm you are."

"I adore your tenacity."

"I hate throwing up."

"I love taking care of you."

"Why do you have to be so perfect?"

"I am only becoming the man you rightfully deserve."

Anna rolled her eyes. He was calming her down just like he always did. "You don't hate me for being rude and hateful towards this pregnancy thing, do you?"

"As I said before, this is a major and quick change in your life. You are allowed to have doubts even if I don't." His hands made their way to her stomach once again. "I cannot wait to see our child. I hope it's a girl. Tough and stubborn just like her mother."

"I thought you old school dudes always want boys?" She laughed at the thought of Damian putting a little girl's hair in pigtails.

He shrugged. "A time long forgotten."

"You are one cheesy bastard, you know that?"

His laugh seemed to echo throughout their room and it made her smile. "I am well aware, but every word is true. Do you need anything?"

Anna shook her head. "Not right now. Julia has been doing nothing but following me around asking the very same question."

"She means well." Damian led her to their bed and the next thing she knew, he had her feet in his hands as he massaged them. "I am sure it's to make up for what her other self did."

"I bet. Evil Julia was a bitch." Anna smirked. "I love the real one though. She doesn't need to try so hard."

"With time she will realize we've all forgiven her. That wasn't her and we know it." His fingers dug gently into the arch in her foot. "I have a surprise for you. I hope you don't hate me."

"What now, Damian?" Anna could hardly take more news, but the foot rub was definitely making her less agitated.

"Well, Julia and I have been talking and—"

"Surprise!" Julia's voice rang throughout her room.

Anna sunk further back into her pillows. The woman was

suffocating her, but she was so sweet she couldn't help but love her for it.

She turned her head to see Ryan and Cato pushing in a large cart with some sort of medical equipment on it and a large flat screen TV.

"What are you people up to?"

Julia clapped her hands together, hardly able to control her excitement. "We are going to look at the baby. Aren't you excited? I bought this 4D ultrasound thing and learned how to use it from this sweet old lady in Texas who does it for a living. Who knew they had such things?"

"I guess Immortals don't usually have sonograms done?" Anna laughed.

"We haven't had a baby in our family since I was born so this is unchartered territory. Besides, I want to know what this little bundle of joy is." Julia's voice was so high pitched that Anna had to smile at her. The woman was more excited than she was. "So, boys, set up the equipment and up goes that shirt."

She glared at Damian.

"A little warning would have been nice." She knew she was pregnant but, in all honesty, she dreaded seeing her baby. It made it that much more real.

What if I am a terrible mother?

He shrugged as if it were no big deal. "I was getting to it, but Julia obviously was far too excited to do this. I am sorry. If you don't want to do this, we don't have to."

Anna looked to Julia who stopped in her tracks. Her lip was caught between her teeth, probably preventing her from arguing with Damian. Damn woman had Anna wrapped around her little finger.

"Alright, let's do this."

Julia literally jumped up and down, her long blonde hair

trailing behind her like some sort of model. "I cannot wait to see our newest addition. She will be perfect."

"She my ass," Ryan spoke up from behind the flat screen. "That baby is all boy."

"Wanna bet?" Cato grinned as he finished doing whatever he was doing with the medical cart. "Five says it's a girl."

"I'll take that bet." Ryan sat down by Damian on their bed, reaching over him to rub her stomach gently. "A boy. I just know it."

"Five bucks? Big spenders." Anna laughed but was quickly silenced by Cato and Ryan's raised eyebrows. "What?"

"Five dollars? Squirt, we're betting five thousand," Ryan laughed. "Couldn't do much with five dollars."

Her eyes widened. What she wouldn't give to have five grand to toss around like it was nothing when she was mortal. That was a big chunk of change for the poor girl she used to be. Here they were, just betting it away like it was nothing.

"Alright, we are all set up." Julia sat on the other side of Anna, along with the medical cart and everyone stared at the huge screen in front of them.

Whatever Julia was doing, Anna had no idea. All she knew was a warm gunk of jelly substance was squeezed onto her bare stomach. Julia rubbed a large white hockey puck-looking thing connected to a cord along her belly and a black and white picture popped up.

Julia moved the thing around her stomach some more and Anna felt her heartbeat racing. She could make out a baby, just barely. It was hard to see but she could tell there were legs and a head.

"It's adorable!" Julia squealed in excitement.

"How can you tell?" Ryan's eyes squinted at the screen. "It's just a black and white picture."

"That's just regular 2D. Just wait." Julia clicked some buttons on the machine and up popped a skin colored picture of a baby.

Anna felt her eyes widen as she could see the features of her child. Its little nose looked like hers, but who could really tell with a baby. They never looked like anyone, but she swore it had her nose. It was sucking its thumb in her stomach. It was unbelievable to see her little alien so clearly.

She couldn't take her eyes off the screen as Julia continued to show Anna her baby. She moved the hockey puck thing around her stomach until it came to the area between its legs. "It's a..." Julia muttered as she moved the puck around.

"Yes!" Ryan yelled.

Anna jumped at his sudden outburst making the baby kick her hard in the ribs. "Dammit, Ryan!" she yelled at him.

"I knew it. It's a boy!" Ryan tackled Damian to the bed and ruffled Damian's hair. "You are having a son!"

Anna watched with amusement as Damian's grin didn't dissipate in the least. The excitement in his eyes was apparent and it warmed her heart to see him so happy. Tears spilled over her eyelids, running down her cheeks until it wet the bed sheets below.

"A boy!" Ryan hopped up off the bed and hugged Cato so tightly she thought she heard his back pop. "What will his name be? Something regal and strong. I'm a fan of William. Or perhaps Helios."

"What about Alexander?" Anna blurt out. The air in the room instantly shifted and was filled with silence. Everyone looked to Ryan who had his eyes narrowed at her. The man's celebration seemed to end so quickly with just a few words. "What?"

"Anna," Damian held her hand, "baby, you know that bothers him."

"So?" She didn't take her eyes off Ryan nor did he with her. "Ryan is family, your brother and it is a strong name from a strong man. It would be an honor to have that name for our son."

The room was silent until Ryan spoke, "Why?"

"Because you are everything to us all. The reason I am alive. Hell, you're the reason why all of us are alive and because I like the name. Got a problem with that? Well too bad buddy." Anna crossed her arms over her chest daring him to yell at her.

Instead she was surprised with something that was a rarity with Ryan. Silence.

Ryan

"You don't have to let us name him that." Damian walked up the steps to the Great Temple with Ryan.

They were having another meeting with the newly appointed Council of Command. Ryan was appointed on the council and as the leader of the Warriors he was required to be there.

"It's fine." Inside he screamed at Anna when she suggested they name their child after him, but he had to get past his demons. This was a step towards the acceptance of who he was so he could become the man he wished to be.

"I know you don't like it. I could see the look on your face when Anna said it. I will talk to her." Damian started to make his way into the temple when Ryan pulled him back by his arm to look into his friend's eyes. "What?'

"It bothers me." Sadness washed through Damian's eyes. Ryan continued, "But I want you to name your child whatever you wish. Yes, it will be a transition for me, but I know why you two are doing it and it warms my heart."

Damian pulled him into a one-armed hug. "You promise it's okay?"

Ryan held his friend out at arm's length, giving him a reassuring smile. "Not really but I will be fine." Ryan slapped Damian's shoulders and led him into the temple. "Let's get this over with."

The council were all seated in modest leather chairs forming a circle within the room. The Great Temple had nearly been destroyed and they were still in the process of bringing it back to its former glory. Statues were being made by the artists in Urbs to replace the broken ones from when the Risen had destroyed them, but not all of the gods could be remembered. Some were long forgotten by dead civilizations.

Ryan took his seat next to Damian's, looking out among the men and women that watched him warily. A conversation had obviously been in full swing before their entrance. One Ryan wouldn't like to hear judging by their faces. So, he sat back in his chair casually and waited for whatever nonsense came out of these people's mouths.

"Ryan, Damian, thank you for joining us on such short notice. We know you have been busy. Damian, we must congratulate you on your child once more. It is said to be a son," Alois, the man Ryan was annoyed with most, spoke.

His high cheekbones were emphasized in the torchlit room along with his long nose that cast a shadow over his cheek. He was a pretty man, without experience in the heat of battle. A reborn with no talent to be seen and yet he had the audacity to speak to Ryan however he felt.

"Thank you." Damian felt the same as Ryan about the man. They tried their best to maintain their tempers but it was becoming harder to do so the longer these meetings continued.

"We have called a meeting to discuss a very important

issue upon which you have stood on firm ground about." Alois fidgeted in his gear. Ryan thought it was amusing that these people dressed in their ceremonial gear for these meetings. They weren't doing anything but arguing and it was a waste of his time to get ready for it.

Instead he wore dark jeans with a white cotton shirt. "If this is about Aden, you have had my answer. We will not torture him. It is unjust and even under strenuous pain he will most likely give false information."

"You have never had a problem before." Alois' nostrils flared. "Lives are being lost every day while we waste valuable time with this man. I don't know why you are so against it. Hell, all of us would have thought you would jump at the opportunity given your past with him. We have made a collective decision that Aden is to be tortured for information."

Ryan's blood boiled. He squeezed the arms of the leather chair. He knew his knuckles were turning white from the pressure. Alois was well aware of how he made Ryan feel. Just the look in the man's eyes told Ryan he enjoyed this. He enjoyed whatever power he could take.

"No."

Alois looked among the rest of the council. "It is not up for discussion."

"Are you the leader of this council now, Alois? You seem to be the only one speaking up," Damian growled.

"Damian." Brianna bit her lip. She had barely made it out of the ambush her brother had set up for Damian and Anna before their trip to Shambhala. The woman was a force to be reckoned with. "We didn't come to this conclusion lightly. Aden was one of us. We knew him well and what he did cannot be forgiven. A lot worse has happened to our own people and if he has information, we need it."

"Not like this." Damian glared at her. "This isn't going to happen."

"It will happen. Just as it did with Sven and countless others. Aden will receive the same treatment." Brianna sat back in her chair. The little woman looked to age right before Ryan's eyes. He could see she wasn't in line with the decision, but it was out of her hands.

"So, who is going to be doing this exactly?" Ryan asked. "Whoever you wish to harm Aden will have to go through me first."

"Dammit Ryan, this isn't a dictatorship!" Alois' face turned red. "The council has made this decision. It will be followed through. We have elected that you perform the task under supervision. Be it inside or outside of this room but you will do this."

"I won't." Ryan knew there wasn't a choice in the matter once the council made a decision, but he couldn't do it. Not to his own child. "I will not harm Aden."

"Then find yourself under investigation. Actually, your entire team and your mates will be under investigation. You have such a hard time torturing a traitor to our cause, it raises questions of your loyalty."

"That is absurd!" Brianna's voice rose. "They are the most loyal to the gods."

"Julia was within their ranks as well. Ryan refuses to torture a known member of the Risen. Damian is in cohorts with Ryan as well as Cato. By default, Anna and their child are also up for treason if Ryan doesn't do this." Alois raised his eyebrow, daring Ryan to argue with him. "Prove your loyalty, Ryan. We wouldn't want a pregnant woman to stand trial, now would we?"

The training arena was the only place he could blow off some steam. He threw knives, flawlessly hitting their targets with ease, dummies were punched, and arrows were shot. Right now, he was at the punching bag hitting the bag as hard and as fast as he could while his anger spilled over the brim of his sanity.

Could he torture Aden? The thought would have been easy had he not known the truth, but the man was his child. His son. Flesh and blood. Despite all that Aden has done it didn't change the fact that Ryan felt responsible for his upbringing. Had he been there, perhaps this would have been avoided.

Music blared in his ears as he continued his beat on the defenseless bag. The men singing, or at least that is what they called it, sounded just as angry as he felt.

He punched fiercer and faster until the bag broke off its chain and landed hard on the floor. He stared at it in disbelief. He had never done that before.

Dragging the bag to the corner of the room he felt a tap on his shoulder making him jump. His ear buds were plucked out before he could do it himself and he came face to face with Cato.

"We must get going."

Ryan unwrapped the tape from his wrists. "I can't do this."

"We don't have a choice." Cato seemed rather upset by their circumstances as well. "Alois is waiting for us to begin."

Ryan's fury only seemed to heighten. Alois had insisted the entire council watch Ryan torture Aden from behind a two-way mirror. Apparently, the man didn't trust him to get the job done without a babysitter.

"Why can't they get someone else?" It was a question he kept asking over and over and the answer was always the same.

"You know him best and you are trained in this," Cato said with gritted teeth. They had heard it for days from the council and Ryan constantly needed reminded of it. "Let's go."

As soon as they made it to the torture chambers, Ryan was handed scrubs and an apron to wear so he wouldn't get messy. He couldn't care less if blood got on him, but he was thankful for the surgeon's mask that covered his face. Maybe Aden wouldn't realize it was him.

Cato was dressed the same but the scar down his face gave his identity away. "Just breathe, he will get through it. Pain is only temporary."

"For me it will be infinite." A man could never heal from such an act on his own child.

Alois and the council strolled up the hall towards them. Most wouldn't look Ryan in the eye as they walked past him into the viewing room, but Alois almost seemed pleased with himself. "Do not hold back on the traitor. We must know of their plans."

"Fuck you," Ryan spat.

Alois grinned widely showing off his crooked teeth. "Enjoy." He shut the door to the viewing room behind him.

With a deep breath, Ryan entered the newly furnished torture chamber. There were things in there that would make even a sadist's skin crawl. All the implements were new, gleaming and crafted maliciously to cause as much pain as possible.

His heart raced when he saw his son strapped to a padded cross staring straight ahead with dead eyes. He knew what was going to happen to him and showed no emotion. There was no way Ryan would get information from him like this. It was as if he were bored.

"Well now," Aden was the first to speak. "Get on with it, boys. We don't have all day for you to gawk at your new toys."

Neither Cato nor Ryan said a word. His feet didn't want to budge but Cato placed a hand on his back to guide him further into the room. Every step he took felt heavy, dragged down by his own grief and guilt.

"Are you scared?" Aden laughed. The amusement dancing in his eyes was the only sign of emotion since they entered the room. "Clearly my reputation must be horrifying if my torturer is scared of a confined man. Not to mention having an audience hiding behind a mirror. Yes, I know you all are there. Hope you enjoy the show."

Ryan turned his back to Aden and closed his eyes to try and gather his wits. He had to do this. Not only for the sake of his friends but also for the sake of the world. Any information would help. It had to.

His trembling hand reached out towards a knife, but Cato beat him to it. "Let me," he whispered. "Just guide me along."

Ryan silently thanked his friend. Damian couldn't leave Anna's side tonight to be with him. She was having false contractions and was in pain. Cato was Ryan's only other support system capable of doing this and there was no way Ryan would ever be able to repay him.

"We need information," Cato started. "It can either be given freely or taken. Your choice."

Aden rolled his eyes. "You already know I won't answer so get on with it. Cut into me all you want. It won't change the fact you will receive nothing from me."

"We shall see." Cato's voice was surprisingly even. The knife hovered over Aden's bare chest. "Last chance."

Aden leaned towards Cato as far as he could, a grin spread across his lips. "Bring it on, Cato."

He knew. Of course, he knew who they were. This was going to be even more difficult.

Cato ripped off his mask, the knife hovering against Aden's neck. "Look, I don't want to do this but if it means saving our people, I will skin you alive."

Aden spit in Cato's face and a smile danced on his lips. "Better get started then."

Ryan turned away at the first cut Cato made on Aden's chest. His holler of pain filled the air followed by maniacal laughter. The sanity of his son was tainted and replaced with something darker. With all his heart Ryan wanted to save him but it seemed to be a battle he would never win.

More slashes were made and Ryan still couldn't face Aden. His screams and laughter echoed in his mind until Cato placed a hand on his shoulder making Ryan jump.

"I need to know what to do next. Knives aren't working." Cato breathed heavily.

"I don't know, just pick something up that hurts and have at it," Ryan grumbled.

"Except I could hit a major artery and kill him and I really don't think you want me to do that. Also, I am trying to avoid making him handicapped for the rest of his life."

Ryan cracked his neck from side to side. He needed to get a handle on this. Aden was his son, that was a fact, but he was also killing innocent people and hurt Julia beyond repair. He needed to man up. To do what was right and quit thinking with his heart.

"He can't die in this enchanted room, remember." Ryan picked up a hand drill. "I've got this." He squeezed the trigger a few times to see if it was charged. It was.

Cato was right. They needed to avoid possibly making Aden handicapped for the rest of his life. There were so many ways Ryan had tortured a person before, but their future was never on his mind. He'd hurt them badly. So much so that death was a gift to them. Now he needed to find the balance between harm and mutilation.

"Is that dear old Dad?" Aden grinned widely when Ryan turned around to face him. Cato had cut into his chest multiple times but it wasn't enough to break a man, not by any means. "I knew you were a supporter of parental abuse."

Ryan inched forward, the drill bit turning loudly. The instrument hovered in front of Aden's thigh, but he couldn't force himself to do it. His hand trembled so badly he almost dropped the drill.

"Hand it over." Cato snatched the nearly fallen instrument from Ryan's hands. "Where at?"

Ryan had to turn away from Aden's prying eyes. "The meat of his leg. Don't hit the bone."

"What Father, too weak to do it yourself? After so many years of torturing me and breaking my bones, now you shy away? Pathetic!" Aden yelled at him. "You don't have the stomach to win this war. You will die and so will that little bitch of yours."

"I say again, give us information." Cato's tone was more aggravated at this point.

Aden obviously refused to answer because the drill sounded once more followed by such a powerful scream that it tore through Ryan's soul like a shard of glass. Six times Aden's scream peaked along with the quickening of the drill. He couldn't take this.

"Stop!" Ryan ripped off his mask as he stood in front of the St. Andrew's cross.

Blood seeped down Aden's legs, his complexion became ashen from the agony of his wounds. His body began to shake from the pain sending Ryan into a panicked state. He held his son's head between his hands, praying that Aden would look at him.

Aden's eyes fluttered but couldn't remain open for long. "It's your fault."

"What is?"

"She is gone because of you. Hated me because of you." Aden drew in a ragged breath. "Now you do this. I hate you."

"Aden please," Ryan begged. "Please just give them something. Anything. This needs to stop." A crushing weight of helplessness overcame him. It wasn't something he was used to experiencing.

After all the years of hatred towards this man, knowing that he was his child washed it all away. If Ryan were there for Aden, he would have never done the things he did to Julia and countless of his friends wouldn't be dead. Everything was Ryan's fault. There was no one to blame but himself.

"After we made ourselves known to the mortals, our next course of action was to conquer the world's strongest military powers. Some fell to us, some didn't."

"I know this."

"Yes, but while we battle for power, our next step is to completely destroy the mortal's faiths. Especially their places of worship."

"Churches and mosques are burning everywhere, Aden. This isn't anything new." Ryan watched Aden's eyes grow heavy.

"I mean the big places." Aden winced trying to shift in his restraints. "Rome was the first on the list, but your presence wasn't known to us. Had you not been there, we could have taken the Vatican."

"Where is the General?" Cato asked.

Aden tried to laugh but it came out weak. "He was with me there. He wants the mortals to see how he is the king of the new gods. How he destroyed them all himself, but I imagine he got away."

"Where will he be next?" Ryan cringed at the thought of every place of worship, every sanctuary for religious believers, destroyed.

"I can't tell you that."

"Please, Aden."

"No."

"Enough asking," Alois came over a speaker. "Make that traitor speak!"

Ryan glared back at the window that held the council. Alois was going to get what he deserved one day. He swore to Zeus he would make it so.

"Don't make me do this. Tell me or I will have to get it out of you." Ryan forced his voice to be steady.

Aden's mouth formed into a hard line. He refused to say anything more and was forcing Ryan's hand. Was he punishing him in his own way? Making him hurt his child to be forever haunted by that fact?

He turned, sulking away from Aden with Cato at his heels.

"What now?" Cato asked.

"I have to think," Ryan grunted. "I can't cut his fingers or toes off or saw off an arm or leg. I definitely refuse to hang heavy weights from his manhood until it breaks off."

"How decent of you. So, then what?"

He couldn't do this. It was wrong. "Nothing. We will do nothing."

Alois came over the speaker. "You will do this Ryan or so help me—"

"What will you do?" Ryan interrupted loudly. "Make your threats but I guarantee I have far more leverage than you amongst the Immortals."

Ryan made his way towards the door to leave. He couldn't stand another second listening to Aden's moans of agony. Alois was going to have to find another puppet to do his dirty work or so help him, Ryan would make that man suffer worse than his son.

As soon as he opened the door, Ryan felt a prick in his neck. His hand went instinctively to his pierced skin, but his body grew too heavy to hold himself up. As he fell to his knees, Ryan could barely force his tired head to look up at Alois who was holding an empty syringe.

"Just a little something to calm your nerves. You know, while I take over from here." Alois grinned maliciously down at him. "Enjoy your rest."

Before Ryan could even reply his eyes grew too heavy to keep open and he was forced into darkness with the sound of Aden's moans echoing through his ears.

Chapter IV

Julia

"You should have seen him, Julia," Cato softly spoke. "I have never seen him like that before. He was so conflicted on what had to be done. He refused to hurt him."

Julia placed a fresh, cold cloth on Ryan's head as he slept in his bed. The medicine in the needle was still working its magic rendering Ryan unconscious. He was so peaceful this way, which was a big relief given the stress the poor man had gone through as of late.

He moaned once the cloth hit his skin and Julia grinned to herself. It was nice taking care of him like this.

"Can you blame him?" she asked. "After what we know now about Aden?"

"He would never be able to do that to his own kin. I get that but with all the evil Aden has done to us, especially you, it pisses me off he couldn't handle it. He chose to be merciful to a monster."

"Ryan blames himself for Aden's upbringing," Julia spat. "He believes that if he were there for Aden, he would have turned out differently."

Cato rolled his eyes with a deep breath, not out of annoyance but of pity. "That man will never understand his worth."

There was nothing to say to that. She fully believed her brother's words, as would a lot of people. No one would consider Alexander the Great to be humble. Yet Ryan remained unable to realize how magnificent he really was and how no one could ever compare to his genius. Hell, even her own father had once revered him as such.

Ryan's breathing grew heavy, and he started to turn his head from side to side but when she made eye contact with her brother, he seemed unaffected.

"Does this happen a lot?"

"I figured you'd be used to it by now." Cato joked but in reality, she only had a few experiences of Ryan's demons appearing at night.

"He usually just mumbles, which even that doesn't happen much."

"This used to happen all the time." His eyes filled with sadness. "Memories of his past mostly. At least that's what Damian told me when we were on missions and Ryan would have fits at night. He would be kicking and screaming in his sleep but when he awoke, we'd pretend to be asleep. Damian didn't want him feeling self-conscious about it."

Her heart hurt for this man even more than it already did. His past wasn't for the weak of heart. Being the bringer of so many deaths and heartaches had to have taken its toll on his sanity.

"I think he is waking up." Cato nudged her arm bringing her out of her thoughts.

Ryan's eyes fluttered open slowly. He was obviously feeling groggy because when he tried to talk his speech came out as nonsense.

"What?" she asked.

"Aden?" It was the only coherent word he could form.

Julia smiled weakly at him. "He is alive. Barely, but Cato had nothing to do with it." She looked to her brother for confirmation.

"What can I say? I listen to my leader more than a small, pretty man that could easily be a eunuch if I didn't know better." Ryan's mouth smirked, but it didn't meet his eyes. "Alois took it upon himself to finish the job. We will head out as soon as you are up and ready."

Julia watched Ryan carefully as he processed the information. There wasn't any sign of emotion on his face and it worried her. Silence and Ryan were a scary combination capable of the most damaging consequences.

"Ryan?" Caution filled her voice.

He closed his eyes, inhaled deeply and pushed himself to sit up. Julia wanted to tell him to lie down, but it was pointless to try and convince this man of much when his mind was set.

"Where are we going?" His voice was tired but whatever was in that needle seemed to be wearing off quickly.

"Nowhere until your strength returns." She tried to smile but he gave her a sharp look.

"Last I remember, Aden said they were taking places out one by one. We have to go now or it may be too late. My strength is not important if we can't protect our most sacred relics."

"It's somewhere that is important for Islam." Cato jumped up to help Ryan swing his legs over the side of the bed. It seems even Cato knew when to give up. "It's the Sheikh Zayed Grand Mosque. It's not an easy place to defend so we better get to it."

Ryan nodded, standing up as if drunk yet somehow he managed to gain his balance. "Why the fuck did Alois knock me out?"

"Apparently to 'calm' you down." Cato did finger air quotes. "I think he just wanted to be a dick, to be honest."

"Get dressed. We head out as soon as we can. Damian will come, tell him if Anna is unwell that I am sorry, but we need him. Julia will look after her."

"Or I could just go?" she suggested.

"No. I need you to look after Anna." Ryan's demeanor was demanding but Julia wasn't going to back down.

"Look, I know that I wasn't myself for a long time, but I need to get out there and do something to redeem myself. You have kept me locked up in here ever since you defeated the Brahmastra and I am sick of it. Like it or not, I am going and you damn well better deal with it!"

Before he could answer back, she stormed off towards her room to get ready. She was sick of being dictated to and watched over. Didn't they understand the only reason she turned evil was because of the tonic Aden had given her? It wasn't as if she would just jump back suddenly into evil Julia mode.

Busting into her room she prepared herself for battle. After she dressed and armed herself with weapons she boldly walked back into Ryan's room. He was shirtless and alone, struggling to pull up his pants. Cato must have been ordered to get himself and Damian ready.

At the sound of her entrance, Ryan looked over his shoulder at her with a smirk. She loved that damn look on his face, but she wasn't about to swoon over the man that tried to boss her around. So instead, she crossed her arms, locked her legs and asked, "What?"

"I think you have come back to me finally." He finished fastening his pants as he made his way over to her. The jerk had the nerve to look like a god as he did so.

"What do you mean by that?" The lump in her throat started to grow thicker as she took in the sight of his bare chest. He was doing this on purpose.

His hand went under her chin, pulling her eyes up towards his. "That sass of yours. I missed it. It's one of the many reasons I fell in love with you." His lips brushed lightly over hers sending goose bumps down her entire body. "You've been so set on pleasing me, trying your hardest to make yourself how you were before, but you forgot one thing, my love."

"What's that?" She managed to sound stronger than she felt.

"You don't take shit from anyone and you certainly don't try to please them." He grinned against her lips. "You take what you want and you never say sorry about it. And you certainly don't listen to commands."

Despite trying to look tough and angry with him, she grinned. He looked so delighted that she couldn't help it.

"Damn straight. Better get used to it." She nodded. "Who will look after Anna?"

"She is doing fine. Colette decided she could give it a go." He took another step towards her, the space between them disappeared and the heat from his body radiated against hers. "Are you ready to get back into the world, my love?"

"You bet your sweet ass I am." Julia grinned when he cocked his head to the side. "I've been hanging around Anna too much."

"That seems to be a problem for us all. Especially when our language is involved."

"Whatever. You love that girl."

"She makes my best friend happy. It's been a long time coming."

Julia bit her lip. "And a baby in the mix. What could be better?"

His eyes narrowed at her hinting. Had she wanted children? Of course. For a long time actually but her purity was something she treasured. She wouldn't let sex make a woman out of her and certainly wouldn't use it to her advantage like most powerful women. She wanted to make a man fall for her strength, not her body.

Still, a child was something she'd thought long and hard about for hundreds of years. She never thought it would actually happen, that a man would love her for more than her looks. That a man would love her for her soul but Ryan, of all people had managed.

"What are you saying?" He treaded carefully.

She cleared her throat, but he was no fool. He knew what she was talking about. "Just that… it is a blessing beyond belief to have found your soulmate and to have a baby boy on the way. No better happiness."

Ryan silently nodded but she could see those wheels of his working in his head. Had she pushed him away with such talk? He talked about marriage and children with her before, but they'd never decided when exactly that would happen.

"Did I say something wrong?"

The grin that appeared on his face was of a mischievous nature. "Not at all."

"Dear Jupiter, what is going on in your mind?"

"Not a thing, darling." He kissed her lips and continued to get dressed in a hurry.

Before she could reply, Cato and Damian came rushing into his room. They both helped Ryan finish getting ready. Once they were done, Damian threw a crystal in front of them, muttering their destination. Instead of rushing into the portal, the three men stood unmoving in silence.

"What's going on?" She tried to peek around their bodies that covered the scene.

"See for yourself." Damian stood aside from the portals entrance revealing massive white columns clouded by smoke as fire bellowed from colossal domed roofs.

She lunged through the portal and found herself in the Sheikh Zayed Grand Mosque. The portal brought them to the large white-marbled courtyard surrounded by open columns with delicately painted vines of flowers crawling up them. At each point of the square shaped yard, a tall white and gold minaret rose into the sky, looking down upon the carnage in their once peaceful home.

The entire mosque was built purely white except the occasional gemstones that were embedded in the marble to create complex floral designs. It was a sight out of the ages, built in modern times and beautiful beyond measure.

Yet when Julia looked at the scene around her, she nearly dropped to her knees and prayed. The white marble was clouded by thick smoke and black ash from weapons fired within the walls. Bodies lay scattered around the courtyard, some burning, others simply draining their lifeblood out onto the once pure stone.

She took a step further towards the center of the courtyard and nearly slipped in blood until Ryan caught her arm. She looked up at him but his eyes were on the scene before them, his gaze drifting as if looking for some type of sign.

"We are too late." Damian lowered his gun as he looked out towards the structure. It was so damaged and littered with debris that it threatened to collapse.

"Obviously," Cato muttered as he walked ahead of their group. His shoulders looked tense even through his gear as he checked the bodies of the fallen. "Most of these aren't soldiers. They look as if they were worshippers."

It was a massacre. Women, men, and children lay motionless spread throughout the mosque. Some of the bodies where charred, others were riddled by gunfire. The rancid smell of burning hair and flesh enveloped her sense of smell.

"They ran for their lives." Damian observed. "Looks as if they were herded in here and cut down."

"How do you know?" Cato placed a woman's hands over her chest and used his fingers to close her eyes.

"Men and women pray separately in different areas of the mosque. Yet they are all here together."

They all cautiously moved forward. Julia nearly screamed when a man stuck his hand out, grabbing Ryan's leg as he walked by in front of her. Unlike Julia, Ryan wasn't the least bit surprised and knelt down towards the victim. His face was burnt so badly that his features were distorted and whatever clothing he wore had melted into his skin.

"You…" the man seemingly smiled up at Ryan, "you are him? Aren't you?"

"Who?" Ryan asked gently, pulling the man's grasp off his leg only to hold his singed hand in his own.

"Leader of the Resistance. The un-killable man. Our savior… Ryan."

Smiling weakly, Ryan nodded. Tears threatened to spill from her eyes as she watched relief pass over the man's entire frame. It was as if all the pain he felt was replaced by hope just from being in Ryan's presence.

"May Allah bless the savior of mankind."

"And you." Ryan hung his head when it was apparent the man's spirit left his body.

Ryan placed the man's burnt hands over his unmoving chest, then rose slowly and strode ahead of them towards part of the courtyard still lined by columns. Fires continued to blaze on the other side of the pillars, but it didn't stop Ryan from walking right toward it. Julia cautiously followed behind along with Damian and Cato who looked just as concerned as she felt.

Immediately through the archway they were met with pools

of water. What was once so clear that it could reflect the clouds above, was now forever tainted by evil. Bodies floated on the surface, some looked towards the sky with eyes frozen in fear while others faced down in the ponds of crimson.

"Are you okay?" Damian placed a hand on her shoulder.

Thankful for him pulling her out of a state of shock, her attention immediately went to Ryan. Like a statue, he stared down at a pool of bodies with a barren expression. The very air around him seemed to change as she cautiously walked closer to him.

Just as she was about to place a hand on his shoulder, he turned away from them making a beeline back to the courtyard. With worried glances, they ran after him but he had already walked through a portal back to the Domus.

Damian

Aden continued to lead them to more sacred sites the Risen were after and every time they got there it was too late. The basilica of the Sanctuary of Fatima was toppled over, crushing the bodies of its believers that gathered for worship below. Ryan became distant when he saw only parts of bodies sticking out from under the heavy stone.

Their next destination fared even worse than the previous. The Temple of Borobudur was bombed from above. The step pyramid that was meticulously shaped into a giant mandala had crumpled in on itself filled with Buddhists seeking refuge and prayer.

Once their team arrived, they could hear the screams of the victims buried under the heavy stone. Ryan dug at the blocks vigilantly trying to get the innocent out, but it was no use. The four of them pushed their bodies to the point of collapsing trying to dig through the wreckage until they passed out. Once they had come back to consciousness, the screams were no longer there. Ryan yelled at the rocks, desperately trying to find even one survivor but there was no answer.

The Great Mosque of Mecca was filled with bodies reaching the top of the walls that surrounded it. Canterbury Cathedral had been demolished into rubble. Jerusalem was wiped off the face of the planet as if by a nuclear blast.

Each place took its toll on their leader. Damian regularly spoke of his concern about Ryan, as he always did but this was different. Not even Julia could pull him out of the temper he was in. She said her touch was always pushed away. That she tried to make him smile by being silly but was met with disdain. Nothing worked.

Damian watched Ryan's face turn gaunt, his body becoming thinner by the day and his jaw constantly tensed. He was haunted by the people he couldn't save and the hell the world had turned into. They were losing their greatest weapon to a guilt that wasn't his burden to bear alone.

"We need to have scouts out watching these places!" Cato yelled during one of their many fights between blown up sacred sanctuaries. "We could get a jump on the situation better."

"How to you recommend we do that?" Ryan glared at the table in front of him. "I have already sent our forces to protect Rome and the Americas. Those are our strongholds. If we lose them, we'll lose it all."

"There are enough men to cover both. Keep enough there and send small groups out." Cato looked on the verge of pulling out his hair.

Damian kept quiet. Ryan's mind wouldn't be altered. He had a plan and rarely deterred from it even when others couldn't see the possibilities. It's what made him who he was.

"If we try to remove our forces from there, the Risen will pounce on us with all they have. We cannot lose either or we are done for."

"Fine then, what about the stragglers in China or Japan?" Cato had a point.

"There are too many that believe they have seen actual proof of a god in the General. They won't follow us until we prove otherwise." Ryan had a point.

"Then prove yourself to them as well, Ryan."

Damian looked at Cato in confusion. "Are you suggesting we represent Ryan as a living god?"

"Fight fire with fire." Cato nodded.

"I will not stoop to their level. Nor will I lie to our people." Ryan's voice was firm.

Cato growled as he spoke, "Then what do we do? Let them all die? Let our most sacred monuments crumble on themselves and let the Risen wipe out all our hopes? Is that what you want, Ryan? Because if it is, you are doing a damn good job at it."

Ryan's fist hit the table in front of him at the same time he stood up to face Cato. Both men stared each other down. A familiar discomfort swept over Damian as they glared at one another.

"There are thousands of places of worship on this planet. The Risen is attacking them one by one. Why do you think that is?" Ryan's nostrils flared as his cheeks began to turn red. "This isn't to just destroy our religious abodes. If they wanted them all destroyed it would be in the hundreds per day. Not one. They have enough men. So why are they doing this? That is what we need to figure out."

Damian followed Cato's eyes down to the large crack Ryan made in the table with his fist. With a forceful calm to his voice Cato asked, "So, your plan is to do nothing until we figure out their game plan?"

"In order to defeat your enemy, you have to understand them. Marc isn't an idiot. He has something bubbling in his mind. The question is, what?"

"I'm not confident Ryan knows what he is doing anymore," Damian confided to Anna as he rubbed her growing belly. This was his happy place with his hand upon the two dearest people in his life, his wife to be and a son to show the world to. "He makes sense and yet he doesn't. He won't divide our resources to catch the Risen, but he wants to stop them. He's waiting to figure out their game plan."

"Maybe he is right?" Anna suggested as she ran her fingers through his hair. He loved the feeling. "I mean, they do have enough people to destroy hundreds of places at a time, but we only hear about one every day. They have enough followers in the world, right? What do they care about our beliefs anymore?"

Damian closed his eyes. In truth, he had never thought about that until Ryan mentioned it. Praises of the General were plastered over every town and every television showed him as a living god. Mortals ate that stuff up. They always did so why give a damn about religious meccas?

Yet on the other side of things they had Ryan. Over the past few months nearly every mortal knew who he was. Calling him by name, proclaiming their loyalty to him and forever pledging their faithfulness to their gods. Ryan made a point to get to know those who still believed. It was what made him so popular.

Perhaps Cato was on to something. Maybe, just maybe,

their followers felt as if Ryan was a god or at least an angel of God. The ultimate avenger of faith and humanity sent to deliver them from evil.

"I need a change of subject. How is Alex doing?" Damian kissed her belly and nearly jumped off the bed when he felt a kick on his lips. "Not liking his name apparently."

Anna laughed, making Damian laugh at the sight of her belly shaking in her joy. "I don't think he does either."

"I've been meaning to talk to you about that actually." Damian sat up on his legs, holding her hands between his. "Ryan told me it was fine to name him Alexander, but I have been second guessing the decision."

"Huh?" Anna crossed her arms, observably annoyed making it difficult for Damian to keep a straight face.

"Let me finish." She pouted pathetically at him. "Instead of our son living up to the name Alexander, a burden I wish upon no man, how about we name him after someone his mother loves very much."

Anna tried to sit herself up straight, but her weight made it difficult. He of course kept his mouth shut about that fact and let her try and sit up as much as her belly allowed. "I'm waiting."

"Owen."

"Are you serious right now?"

He bit his lip. "Pretty sure."

"Why would you want to name him that?"

"Because he mattered to you."

"It doesn't bother you?"

"Not in the least." He kissed her knuckles.

"It doesn't bother you to give our son my dead boyfriend's middle name? The man that I was going to marry."

"I would love to honor the memory of a man that kept

you so close to his heart. The man that protected you while in foster care and brought joy to your life before I could do so myself."

Tears welled in her eyes as she nodded her head. "Fine, but it's going to be Owen Alexander. I don't care what you guys say." She smiled while he leaned in to kiss her lips. "You are annoyingly perfect."

"I do my best."

Chapter V

Ryan

"I NEED YOU TO TALK to me." Julia sat down on his bed, looking to him for some sort of confirmation he was remotely present in mind.

Of course he was, but he was stressed. No, beyond stressed. He was without a doubt defeated in mind, body, and soul. So many dead and for what? Personal vendetta.

"There is nothing to talk about," Ryan grunted.

"You won't talk, you're getting thin, and there are bags under your eyes. You need to eat, sleep, and for god's sake take a shower."

"If you are unhappy with my current state then perhaps you should go somewhere else." Was he being rude? Without a doubt but he was in no mood to listen to her complain about him. People were dying at an alarming rate and a damn shower wasn't even in the realm of his concern right now.

He lingered over the map of the world covering his room's floor. The paint was starting to peel off from his constant pacing, but he didn't have the energy nor care to reapply it. He knew it by heart anyways, even if the paint were gone the picture remained clear in his mind.

Julia stood up from his bed and wrapped her arms around

his waist. He tried to look over her, but she remained in his way. "Move," he grumbled.

"No."

"Now."

"Or what?" She raised an eyebrow at him.

Normally her tenacity would amuse him but as of now he had a job to do. There wasn't time to waste with small talk, showers, or even sleep. He should have locked his door.

With her arms wrapped around his waist she pushed him backwards towards his bed. He put his foot down to stop the progress, but when she pinched him on the leg it made him jump in surprise giving her enough time to gain the advantage on him. She was being relentless as they got closer to the bed.

"Will you stop?" he growled at her. "I need to work."

"What you need is rest."

Although right, he didn't care. There would be time for sleep later. "Julia, don't make me carry you out of this room and lock the door on you."

"You wouldn't dare." She smirked.

"I wouldn't?"

"No, because you are too weak to do it."

Now her persistence was a little amusing. She was challenging him. The woman knew how to get to him.

"Am I?" He picked her up by her backside and carried her to the bed. Instead of gently lying her down he chucked her on the bed and walked away.

Before he got too far, she jumped on his back and his knees almost buckled from under him. "What the hell are you doing, you spider monkey?"

"Talk to me, you jackass!"

"You're cute when you cuss."

What wasn't cute was when she put him in a choke hold.

His body was being pulled back towards the bed by a very strong blonde and he was too caught off guard to balance himself. This was getting ridiculous.

Julia's back hit the bed and he unwillingly toppled along with her. With her legs wrapped around his waist, she kept her grip tight around his neck. He could get out of it but that would require hurting her and that wasn't going to happen.

"If you won't willingly go to sleep, I guess I will just have to put you to sleep, you big baby," she muttered from underneath him.

Screw this.

Ryan reached behind him and grabbed her hair. She squealed in protest, but her grip didn't release until he yanked harder to get his point across. As soon as she let go, he turned on his stomach and pressed her angry body back down to the bed with his own. His hips dug into hers and the anger from her face changed in an instant to arousal.

"What if I don't want to sleep quite yet, Julia?" he growled.

Her eyes fluttered closed as he continued to tease her body with his. Running his hand from her thigh to her waist, he heard her sharp intake of breath. He couldn't help but smirk. Her reactions to his touch were an addiction.

Grasping her hair once again he tugged making her chin tilt up. Her eyes studied him but didn't protest. *Good girl.*

"Does my love like this?" When she bit her lip, he got his answer. "Interesting."

He pulled a little harder to hear that glorious sound of her quick breathing. Her body squirmed under his and made his amusement increase. This woman was beyond anything he could have hoped for, she was becoming adventurous.

"Why interesting?" she panted.

"Never thought my sweet girl would like it rough." He

pulled again. "But hearing that hitch in your breath tells me you do."

"News to me." Her nails raked down his back, probably drawing a small amount of blood but this type of pain was most definitely welcome. "It seems you do as well, judging by that deep bear growl of yours."

"You are a distraction." He nuzzled her neck. "I need to keep working."

"You've been working and suffering and distant to everyone around you. I think you need a break."

"I don't have time for this." He kissed her neck, leaving small bites along the way to her collarbone. This time she pulled his hair forcing his head back and somehow maneuvered herself on top of him.

She straddled his hips and raked her nails down his chest this time. His eyes couldn't help but close at the feeling. This damn woman was starting to figure out how to push his buttons in a good way.

"Sure you have time." Her hand skimmed up his chest. Delicate fingers wrapped around his throat putting the slightest of pressure on it.

Words couldn't form even if he wanted them to. The pressure on his neck slightly increased even as the fingers of her other hand wound through his hair caressing his scalp. His eyes were growing heavier by the second until the word turned black.

"Well, that was embarrassing." He sat up from his bed realizing Julia had just tricked the hell out of him. That little minx seduced him to sleep. He hated to admit it, but she was right, he undeniably needed rest. Ryan had no idea how long he was out, but his mind felt clearer and his body was less tense.

Sitting on the edge of the bed he rubbed his hands over the scruff on his face. He contemplated shaving but it wasn't long enough for him to really give a damn. To be honest he was just being lazy.

Looking around his room he noticed it was cleaned up but empty of anyone but himself. The night sky was out, and the moon shone through his open windows. Julia was probably airing out the place. He really did stink.

He decided to listen to the love of his life and take a shower. Damn did it feel good. The warm water cascaded over his body and the sting from Julia's scratches made him smile.

"That woman, I swear," he said ruefully.

Once he was clean, he finally took in his appearance in the mirror. The person looking back at him wasn't what he was used to. He was much thinner and dark circles rimmed his eyes. He looked like hell and a half.

Ryan ran his hand over his protruding hip bones and grimaced. This was a new look for him, without a doubt. His ribs were more visible, but he didn't look sickly, it was just totally different from his regular body build.

"Finally realizing your ass needs to eat and sleep?" Cato smirked from the doorway.

Ryan didn't even care that he was butt ass naked. He turned around and flipped Cato the finger before grabbing a towel to dry off. "What are you doing here?"

"Julia said she knocked your ass out. You've been asleep for almost an entire day, so I figured I'd come check on you." His sly grin didn't go unnoticed.

"Amused?" Ryan's eyes rolled.

"Oh, for sure. When you find out your sister puts her

boyfriend in a choke hold it's always funny." He looked Ryan up and down. "And apparently you were mauled by a tiger."

His cheeks flushed, not really wanting to talk about the things Julia did to him while in bed, so he changed the subject.

"Well, I am up so is that all?"

After their last exchange he wasn't really in the mood for Cato. They always butted heads, but the occurrence was becoming too frequent. At this point he had to wonder if they would ever go back to being on good terms.

"I ordered you some room service. I was told to make sure you eat." Cato left the bathroom with Ryan following behind. "No one likes an emaciated leader."

"I'm not that bad." It was still shocking how much his body had changed in such a short time.

"Well, you sure are on your way. So, deal with my sister's insistence and bossy attitude and just do it. Otherwise, both of us are gonna get our asses kicked."

A small knock at the door came followed by the appearance of a sheepish woman with a blonde pixie haircut carrying a tray. He couldn't really see her face as it became obvious she was trying to hide it from them. Ryan figured she was just nervous being around them like most of the staff appeared, until he caught a glimpse.

"Emma?" Ryan uttered.

Quickly she set down the tray of food by the bed and scurried back towards the door. Before she could make it, Ryan had her gently by the arm. She tried to pull away, but he didn't let go.

"Leave me alone," she stammered nervously trying to avoid eye contact.

He couldn't help but hold her head between his hands.

"What happened to you?" Ryan grimaced as he got a closer look at her.

Her once long blonde hair was chopped off and fresh cuts cascaded down her cheeks. A long gash along the side of her head was stitched up but that wasn't the worst of it. She was missing fingers on her left hand which was still bandaged.

"Got a little rough in Texas. They are disorganized." She wouldn't look him in the eye and he couldn't blame her. Their last meeting was anything but civil. Another cascade of guilt crowded into his already filled resume.

"What's going on?" Cato came from behind and when he saw Emma his face twisted to anger. "What the hell happened, Emma?"

She quickly looked away from him and tried to back out the door again, but Cato wasn't having it. "Please, just let me go."

"Talk to us." Cato added, "Please."

"There are a lot of mortals on our side in Texas, but most are just civilians. We were sent there to train a leader to take over the camp but while scouting we were ambushed. The mortals with us didn't make it. My team and I barely managed to get out."

She still wouldn't look at them so Ryan crouched down to where her line of sight was until she looked at him.

"We will take care of this. I am so sorry. For everything."

"You shouldn't be delivering food either." Cato rubbed her arm awkwardly. "You are a Warrior, not a damn servant."

"I doubt I will be much use as a Warrior anymore after this." She held up her hand. "So, I am keeping myself busy doing what I can. I need to go." She practically ran out of his room and Ryan let her. He didn't need to add to her misery any more than he already had.

He was fuming. Sure, he didn't ever see Emma like he did Julia, but he would never wish something bad to happen to her. She was obsessed with him at a point and it was annoying.

Nevertheless, seeing her so timid and defeated made his blood boil.

Ryan punched the wall from his frustration and watched as bits of stone trickled to the ground. He needed more than just a wall to hit. He needed to end the General.

"Have you noticed you are getting abnormally strong as of lately?" Cato inquired.

"What do you mean?"

Cato shrugged. "I mean, I suppose it is natural to break off stone with your bare hands, put a crack in a table with your fist, and completely smash a punching bag off its chain. Super normal."

Ryan looked down at his bloody hand. The knuckles were scraped up but otherwise it felt fine. "Curtesy of my father probably."

"Right." Cato's eyes narrowed. "Well, what is your next plan."

"Eat. Then head to fix that damn problem in Texas. That shit isn't going to happen to anyone else."

CHAPTER VI

Damian

"RYAN, WE NEED TO talk."

"Not now, Damian. I have to figure out a strategy." Ryan was bent over the wooden table in their tent that held a large map. They were camped with their troops on the outskirts of Austin, Texas which was right in the middle of the conflict with the Risen. Canada remained loyal to them but was stripped of their resources while the northern part of the United States was taken over by the Risen and advancing on the south.

"I thought we were here to train a leader not to take over."

"Sort of hard to train someone when they are in the middle of a shit show."

"I'm serious, Ryan. We need to talk about what's going on with you."

"I don't need your concern right now. Our forces are holding the Risen from entering Kansas, but their numbers are growing by the day. Colorado has fallen and Missouri is about to follow. If we don't act, we lose Kansas and then Oklahoma and then the entire country."

"It won't happen."

"It's about to unless I can figure out what to do and for that to happen, I need you to be quiet." Damian stood opposite of

71

Ryan at the table and crossed his arms. Ryan's build still had muscle, but he could see stress was weakening him. He was growing thinner than he had ever seen him, but according to Cato he ate before coming here. "What are you looking at?"

Damian shrugged his shoulders. "Not a damn thing, Ryan."

"We not only have to defend here but the Risen's troops in Germany are moving through Switzerland into Italy. Rome is their prize so I had a general in Austria move some of his men to keep them at bay along the border. I need to enforce them before Norway crosses the sea into Germany to strengthen their troops."

"Have they set sail yet?"

"No. Sweden is making their stand, but it doesn't look good."

Damian looked down at the map. It reminded him of times when they were mortal. Black pieces from a chessboard made up the Risen's occupation in certain countries while white ones were theirs. Needless to say, black was outnumbering the white, but just barely.

"It seems your dream of conquering the world has resurfaced." Damian watched Ryan's eyes dart over the map. Back and forth, up and down. "You almost did then, I imagine you will be able to now."

"This is different."

"In what way?" Damian knew how to reach Ryan while his mind worked on war. The only way to get into that head of his was to keep calm. Ask questions. Wait for answers. Ryan would come to a solution through that process.

"This is modern war. Guns, airplanes, and instead of conquering I am defending. Which is vastly different from when we were mortals."

"Then why don't you conquer instead of defend?" Damian asked quietly. The flaps of their large tent slapped against itself while Ryan continued to stare at the map as if waiting for it to suddenly change.

He took a step back, then forward, to the side and back to the center. His little dance brought back memories of their camp in Greece. His habits never changed, not even after all these years.

"Conquer," he muttered to himself. "Not defend."

"Precisely."

"We are outnumbered." Damian remained quiet. "But if Canada used their remaining resources and we marched towards the north from here, we could trap them."

"Destroying their entire force in North America."

"If the UK sailed to meet Norway there is no way they could survive a naval attack from them along with the ground troops in Sweden."

"Giving Germany no back up to take Rome."

"Yes," Ryan muttered. "Yes. I've been looking at it wrong. Conquer, not defend. How didn't I see this before?"

"Your head was too far up your ass to see a simple solution." Ryan looked like he was about to make a smartass comment, so Damian went on. "Do we leave for the battle in Europe?"

"No, we give the orders to our generals. This will work easily, especially here in the Americas. We just need to find the right people to lead these men in Austin."

"And then what?" Damian picked up a white pawn off India on the map.

"We will go after the main source of our problems." Ryan's hands gripped the sides of the table. "Marc needs to be shown to the world for what he really is—a mortal being capable of dying. He is no god. We will capture him and execute him on television for the world to see. To prove how mistaken they have been to follow a fraud."

Ryan

"Sir, they are attacking!" A female soldier came running into their tent, her hair disheveled and specks of blood sprinkled her face.

"How many?" Ryan checked his gear for extra clips and Damian did the same.

"I'm not sure."

"Then use you damn brain and guess. How many?" Ryan's patience was thin.

She cleared her throat but the strength she was trying to portray wasn't working. "Maybe two to three hundred."

"Why so little?" Damian strapped on his helmet. "We have over five thousand men here."

It had to be a ploy. "Marc would never send so little men here against our numbers. There has to be another reason. Extinguish them quickly, make no attempt to advance on them."

The female soldier remained in the tent and she looked on the verge of exploding.

"What?" he barked.

"Sir, most of the men are still asleep, they caught us by surprise by using knives instead of guns. They made it within the camp and we are holding them back as much as we can."

Ryan wanted to scream. He had put scouts out around the camp for a reason, this very reason in fact, and yet the mortals managed to screw the simple command up. *No wonder Emma had been hurt.*

"Why weren't the scouts—You know what? Never mind." Ryan growled. "Let's take care of this."

He pushed past the soldier and out into the night air. He saw the camp coming to life before him as his 'soldiers' rubbed the sleep out of their eyes. Suddenly, on the far end of camp, shots were fired and short bursts of light pierced the night. Screams were becoming louder by the second as more gunfire went off.

"Oh no, by all means take your time waking up. We are only being attacked!" Ryan yelled at the men and women who were more interested in looking towards the commotion than helping.

As he and Damian sprinted through the camp, Cato appeared at their side and remained close at their heels. "Sorry, I was taking a sh—"

"Never mind, Cato," Ryan groaned.

"You need to understand you are commanding mortal civilians not mortal soldiers," Damian said.

"Some are soldiers so there's no excuse."

Ryan knew he was demanding too much out of these people, but he couldn't help it. His forces were made up with all types. Commanding them was a challenge. The actual military personnel from these countries were on the front lines of the conflict where the Risen was strongest. This was just backup.

They came up behind the line of conflict and the ground was already wet with blood. The mud that had formed pulled his feet down with each step, but it didn't stop his momentum. Men were falling to the ground left and right of him.

The Risen were wielding swords and daggers while his troops were struggling to get off shots and reload their guns. They were caught off guard and completely unprepared for an attack in the middle of the night. He needed to give them more time to get their shit together.

"You take the left, Cato. Damian, the right." Each man nodded to him and scrambled to pull their troops together.

Ryan unsheathed his sword in his right hand, a pistol in his left. He sliced, shot, and dismembered any member of the Risen that he encountered. The carnage around him begun to build, forcing him to move from his spot in fear of tripping over the dead.

He spun around, ready to attack before realizing it was one of his own men whose eyes widened in fear.

"Pull yourself together! You can do this!"

"Thanks, Ryan." The man had a spark of determination in his eyes that wasn't there before. "Sir."

He was starting to get used to the mortals knowing his name. It was still an odd concept after being virtually unknown by them for so long. Still, the burden of their expectation began to weigh on him. Living up to the reputation he inadvertently created would be difficult to maintain.

Out of nowhere, a man jumped at him with a sword in hand. The bastard was experienced and managed to cut Ryan on the arm, but his victory was short lived. With an obnoxious grin Ryan brought down his blade on the man's head, severing it in half.

The satisfaction he felt was terrifying. He missed combat like this. It was euphoric being able to know the very moment a life was taken by his hands as his blade dragged through flesh and bone.

Before long, the body count had piled higher in their favor. The Risen was maybe twenty men strong at this point and they turned to retreat. His troops began to follow but Ryan yelled as loud as he could, "No! Do not follow!"

He knew the end game. Marc wanted to pull them into his own camp and divide Ryan's forces from those tired from fighting and those who were uselessly still waking up. Thankfully, it didn't take long to gather his men back to camp.

Once things began to settle, he sent out people to gather their dead and wounded. The medic tents were buzzing long into morning, pained groans filling the air. Fortunately, modern medicine was far superior than in his day, so he had high hopes for those who survived.

Ryan stood in the middle of the battlefield just staring at all the bodies of the Risen that were left behind. Men and women that were led astray by one man's personal revenge caused such a waste of human life. The energy he felt during battle quickly began to subside.

He lowered his head in respect, but a woman with wide-open glazed eyes caught his attention. Her dark hair was plastered to her bloodied face with a long gash down her cheek so deep that he could see her teeth. He barely noticed when Damian and Cato waltzed up beside him.

"Lost around five hundred men and women," Damian reported. "Most were killed while they slept. It was an ambush."

Ryan nodded but couldn't force himself to look away from the corpse that stared through his soul. Cato must have followed his line of sight because he crouched down to the woman and with two fingers, gently closed her eyes. Taking a deep breath Ryan forced his gaze towards the rest of the fallen.

"What do we do with their bodies?" Cato asked.

"Burn them?" Damian suggested.

Ryan shook his head. "We will bury them properly."

"That will take some time," Damian called after him when he marched back towards the tent.

"Then have everyone get started." Ryan didn't look back.

Damian caught him by the elbow and pulled him to face each other. That familiar worried looked plagued his eyes. "Are you okay, Ryan?"

"Marc used those people to test our defenses. He knew they wouldn't win."

"I'm not talking about that right now." Damian crossed his arms.

"When we leave, we need to make sure that our commanders are skilled enough to recognize strategy when they see it." Ryan continued, "Had we not been here our men would have chased them down leaving the rest of the camp vulnerable without being warned of the threat."

"Will you quit talking battle strategy and answer me?" Damian's jaw clenched. "You're acting strange."

Cato let out an exasperated laugh. "Of course, he is acting weird. You saw him out there. It was freaking magnificent. Slice here, cut there, dismembered head here, flying arm there. It was like it was symphony."

"Adrenaline was just rushing," Ryan admitted. "I miss fighting like that. It felt so natural." He shook his head letting himself smile. "Man, am I messed up or what? How is it I can enjoy killing our enemies and not feel anything but excitement for the next battle?"

"Years of practice." Damian smirked.

"It's not normal. Most people would be appalled."

"We aren't most people."

Ryan was getting ready for a broadcast over the TV after their fight. He had done this every so often over the past three months even though he hated it. Caleb assured them it was a good idea to let the people know who their leaders were and that they were still fighting for them. 'Reassurance for the cause,' he called it.

Damian and Ryan knew nothing about TV and even less about the technology behind it but thankfully they managed to get a crew for the job. A man named Liam, was some sort of computer hacker and managed to live stream them on every TV.

The camerawoman was a petite little thing named Lee that had previously worked at a news studio in New York.

"Are we almost ready?" Damian asked. "We need to get a move on."

"Just about, give me a sec." Liam's dark head of hair bobbed from under the desk.

Ryan stood in his usual spot in front of white drapes dressed in his all black gear. He was heavily armed, apparently a sign that they were well equipped for the war, and still dirty from their battle as a sign they were fighting the good fight. It was all propaganda.

Damian tiredly made his way to Ryan. He hated doing these things too.

"You ready?"

Ryan placed his helmet under his arm. "Seriously, I feel like I just keep repeating myself. Besides that, I feel like an idiot making a speech to a machine."

"Well, you aren't. You're making a speech to the whole world."

"Yeah, well it feels like I'm talking to myself."

"Okay, we are ready to go," Liam said and sat down at his desk. His fingers were working wildly against the keyboard typing Zeus knows what. It was actually quite amazing to watch.

Ryan huffed when Lee attached a microphone to his collar. She never took his moods personally. She was fully aware he hated doing this and she quickly became one of the only women that could put up with Ryan.

"Quit your bitchin' and just wear it." She patted his cheek a little too hard.

"You're not a nice person," Ryan muttered like a child.

"Then quit being a puss because you know you gotta do it."

"So mean," Ryan teased.

"Suck it up buttercup and let's put that ugly mug to work." She got behind the camera directly in front of Ryan.

Damian loved watching them together. Their brother sister relationship was refreshing, especially coming from a mortal with a short, dark bob and big doe eyes. She was significantly shorter than Ryan yet commanded his respect.

"As you wish." Ryan cracked his neck from side to side, took a deep breath and waited to be cued.

Damian stood beside Lee with his arms crossed. Watching Ryan give a speech wasn't something new to him but watching Ryan do it without a crowd present was awkward. He was so uncomfortable that it made Damian almost laugh.

"We are live in five... four... three..." She held up two fingers and then one, then pointed at Ryan to start talking.

"Good evening everyone. I am here once again to reassure you that our efforts have not ceased against our adversaries. I want you to realize you are not alone in your labors, for the danger is not limited to a single nation, a single race, or sex but for all mankind."

Damian gave him a thumb up when Ryan started to shift from side-to-side. For everything the man could handle, speaking to a camera made him nervous. Who would have thought?

"We shall never surrender to the sinister fury of our enemy no matter the cost. For they will bring with them an era of pain, suffering and despair. We must remind ourselves of our light, compassion, and honor. Such things are foreign to the Risen.

"Nothing worth defending is ever easy but if we all carry out our duties, if we all persevere and remain ever faithful, then all of our suffering will bring us closer to this historic end. For the first time, men and women from different faiths and backgrounds have joined together, not as enemies, but as allies in the world's darkest hour."

"He is doing remarkably better than the last time," Lee leaned towards Damian speaking lowly. "A few more times and he will be a pro."

Damian had to agree. Ryan's confidence was brightening after every sentence, his voice was more intense, and his face had a fierceness to it. No one could ever doubt his leadership purely by the way he held himself.

"I'm glad he still has blood on him," Liam added. "According to my statistics the people feel safer seeing proof that the Risen is being wiped out."

"How could you possibly come up with any statistics?" Lee grumbled.

"I have my ways." Liam winked. "Pay attention, he is almost done."

"Never forget that I willingly stand with you until my last breath and beyond."

"And we are clear." Lee turned the camera off and made her way towards Ryan. She removed the microphone from his collar before she patted him on the cheek, this time softly. "You did good, kid. Real good."

"Gee, thanks." He trudged towards Damian. Quite frankly the man looked exhausted, as he rightfully should. "Let's get our officers up to speed on our plan and leave for the Domus. We will leave capable Warriors here to command them instead of train them for the time being."

Damian led him towards the entrance to the tent. "We need to get you cleaned up."

"What is the point? I'm just going to get covered in blood and mud again."

"Yo, Ryan," Liam called over to them. "You did damn good, man. Everyone is buzzing about how glad they are they have you as their leader."

"How could you possibly know?" Lee grumbled again.

"I'm a hacker. I have my ways."

"Thanks," Ryan said as they left the tent before they could get pulled into another Liam and Lee argument.

They walked through the camp and back to their tent. The sounds of the wounded were nearly gone which was either a good or bad sign. Damian could barely make out the trench from a distance that was being dug to lay those who had fallen to rest. A large group had volunteered to dig it, so the work was going by quickly with Cato's guidance. The deceased wouldn't rot above ground at least.

"It's an unfortunate thing to bury bodies without a proper marker," Damian finally said.

Ryan looked in the direction of the mass grave where Cato was directing men with shovels. "We can't leave them above ground. I won't chance disease spreading throughout the camp and at least they will not be buried on top of one another."

Damian wasn't questioning Ryan's intentions, yet the man always acted as if he needed to explain his actions. Or, perhaps Ryan had to convince himself of the right path.

"I'll call in the officers to execute your plan. Then back home to shower, okay?"

"I told you there is no point in it. We cannot waste time on trivial things when we have a war happening. I will wait no longer. I want this over with."

"I understand that, but a shower can take you five minutes. Freshen up and feel—"

"Quit arguing with me over a damn shower, Damian." Ryan's voice raised momentarily but as he looked around the camp filled with people he regained his composure. "Let's just get this done."

"What is going on with you?"

"I don't know."

"Is it all the bodies?"

"I don't know," he repeated.

"We've killed thousands, Ryan. Why is this getting to you?"

They entered their empty tent and Ryan practically fell into a folding chair. "I liked fighting like that. Loved it, actually. I'm conflicted by it, I guess. It felt so good to be in hand-to-hand combat and I want to do it again."

"Go on."

Ryan rubbed his hands together, looking down at them as he did so.

"What if I become addicted to it again? To me, that kind of combat is intoxicating and what if I want it to continue? What if I make it continue? What if I try and conquer the world and rule it myself just as Marc is doing? The thought terrifies me."

Damian pulled another folding chair in front of Ryan and faced him as he sat down. Both of them rested their elbows on their knees with their heads nearly touching. He could understand what Ryan was feeling. It was a worry he always had about Ryan, just knowing how much he craved the feeling of a blade ripping through flesh with warm blood staining his skin. Only a man bred into that type of life could understand the weight of it and Damian did.

Alexander the Great wasn't just a military genius. He was a warrior, a soldier, a killer. He enjoyed defeating his enemies with their blood covering his hands and the triumphs that followed. Things like this were so immoral in this day and age, but back then it was life. It was Ryan's calling. It was glory.

"I know it is difficult. It is for me as well and I was nowhere near your level when it came to warfare so I can't even imagine how hard it is for you." Damian grabbed the back of Ryan's neck and pulled their foreheads together. "What I do know is that you are a good man. You will only do what you must in order to save the mortals as well as any god. You are not filled with selfish ambition anymore. You are better."

"It feels so… exquisite though."

"It does. It really does, but that is the past. We must look towards the future, in all things."

CHAPTER VII

Ryan

AFTER CONDUCTING THE MEETING with the commanding officers and Warriors, Ryan, Cato and Damian went back to the Domus to face Aden. Ryan hadn't seen him since the scum Alois had gotten his hands on him and he could only imagine the state Aden was in. There was hope that nothing overly brutal had been done, but knowing Alois, Ryan could only think the worst.

The three of them marched down the dungeons towards the room Aden was held in. With each step his heart raced, pounding fiercely within his chest at the thought of what state he would find his son in. What evil had he allowed to happen?

Once the door was opened, he had his answer. His very breath caught in his chest and his knees felt weak at the sight before him. Ryan didn't realize Damian and Cato were holding him up until he felt their hands squeezing his forearms.

Every ounce of his being trembled with anger and guilt at what his people allowed. Ryan had inflicted such things on others but to see Aden like this... it was unimaginable, inexcusable regardless of the situation. It felt personal.

"Ryan, you should go," Cato spoke lowly into his ear. "You don't need to see this."

Ryan tried to speak but he was without words. His eyes were glued to the mutilated body before him. Aden hung from chains with his arms pulled out wide, his feet not even allowed to touch the ground.

His fingers and toes were either chopped off or skinned down to the bone. A single ear lie on the floor while the other hung from a thin string of cartilage against his neck. Pieces of his skin were peeled back revealing the bloodied muscle below.

Ryan gained his footing but nearly lost it again when Aden raised his head, revealing metal spikes driven into his eyes. "Aden..."

"Who's there?" Aden's voice was hoarse, probably from screaming so loudly while he was torn apart so savagely.

"You need to leave." Damian tried to push him out the door but Ryan stood his ground.

Cato tried to force him away. "Now."

"No." But Ryan should have listened as the color drained from his face when Aden tried to speak louder.

"Ryan?" Aden's dry voice croaked while his body quivered.

Ryan took a step within the room. Death hung in the air but thanks to the priests magic it would never come for Aden. He was stuck in an eternal suffering and it was every bit Ryan's fault. Alois would pay for this.

"Aden," Ryan's voice shook when he spoke his son's name again. "I..."

"What?" Aden tried to laugh but it set off a coughing fit instead. Blood dripped from his mouth to the ground until he could speak again. "Come to add to your legacy of misfortune?"

"We've come because we want to end this war and in order to do that, we need your help," Damian spoke up from behind him. "If not, I am fairly certain you know what will happen."

"What else could you possibly do?" Aden cocked his head

to the side as if he were seeing them. "I've just been hanging in here and that animal comes to play with me for no reason. He doesn't even ask questions anymore. I'm already in hell."

Ryan's fists clenched tightly at the thought of Alois hurting Aden for fun. That man was going to die a slow and painful death.

"Then we will make sure you never leave this room for the rest of existence. If we lose the war, then we will bury this room in the rubble leaving you to hang without any hope of dying or escape," Cato answered. Ryan knew Cato was bluffing but the thought made Ryan see red.

Aden hung in silence for some time before he finally asked, "What do you want?"

"We need to know the General's exact location. He is commanding his forces from somewhere and after the wild goose chase you sent us on trying to find him, I have a feeling you are keeping something from us."

"Of course I am keeping things from you." Aden tried to raise his voice and failed. "What do I get out of this if I help you?"

"Freedom," Ryan answered.

He would no longer allow Aden to stay within these walls regardless. Not at the mercy of Alois or any other that had laid hands on him. If Ryan were to meet him in battle then so be it, but it would be a fair fight. Not a man hanging by his obviously broken wrists for other's amusement.

Cato stood in front of Ryan and spoke lowly. "Is that wise?"

"It isn't up for discussion." Ryan kept eye contact with Cato until he backed down.

"Freedom?" Aden hung his head. "What is the point when I'm like this? What life could I possibly have?"

"If you help us, you will be healed completely and allowed

freedom. However, you must accompany us to make sure you keep your end of the bargain." Ryan tried to sound as stern as he could manage. "If you lie to us even once, you will be put back in here and all those under this roof will be allowed to have their way with you."

"Deal." Aden seemed almost relieved at Ryan's promise.

"Well that didn't take much convincing but there is one problem. How do you expect to heal him?" Cato countered. "Look at him. We have magic but we aren't gods. We can't even try to heal part of what was done to him."

"So, we will ask a god," Ryan answered plainly.

"You can't be serious?" Cato asked.

"Why not? If one god doesn't then we will ask another and if they refuse, we will ask another. So on and so forth until one agrees to help us." Ryan left the room to pray away from Aden's torn body.

> *Kind Asklepios, son of Apollo, hear my prayer.*
> *I seek your favor so that you may cure my son.*
> *Healer of broken men and women, renew his health.*
> *Judge not his misguided ways, I beg of you.*
> *Asklepios, your compassion is needed in the dire time.*
> *I ask for your blessing so that his vitality is returned to him.*

Ryan waited with his eyes closed, repeating his plea until a firm hand gripped his shoulder. Behind him stood a kindly, pale man with a long white beard. He wore a blue sweater vest with a long white sleeved shirt underneath and khakis.

"Alexander. A pleasure to make your acquaintance, Uncle." Asklepios smiled warmly. "I never thought I would be awarded the honor of meeting you."

"Please, there is no need to call me Uncle." Ryan thought

it was rather odd given the man looked like he could be Ryan's grandfather than his somewhat related nephew.

"Given you are half siblings with my father I feel the need for a proper introduction."

"Just call me Ryan and leave it at that please." Ryan bit the inside of his cheek. "I am begging you for your help with Aden. He needs to be healed desperately."

Asklepios looked within the room, the winkles in his face crinkled together at the grisly sight. "My cousin has done terrible things to many innocents. I understand your need, yet I cannot provide it. I am forbidden to do such things."

"Please, I beg you."

"There are limitations to even gods. I am nearly forgotten— therefore I am weak because of it." Asklepios truly looked unhappy about the circumstances.

"You asked the wrong god for help, dear Alexander," a voice came from behind them both.

Asklepios closed his eyes without even turning around but Ryan's attention was fully on the man before him. He was wearing white board shorts with a black V-neck shirt. His skin was tanned darker than Ryan's. What else would you expect from a sun god?

"Father, must you always intervene?" Asklepios asked crossly.

"Why must you always ask questions you know the answer to?" Apollo grinned brightly. "Now, Alexander, what can I do for you that my feeble child cannot?"

Ryan looked back and forth between Apollo and Asklepios. It was humorous to see them together given Apollo appeared to be the son of the older Asklepios, yet it was the other way around.

"My son needs healed." He stated simply but when Apollo

knit his brows together. Ryan wanted to scream at Apollo's hesitation. "What?"

"I've healed you before and for that I was punished by our father. I'm not sure I can do that again without even harsher consequence."

Ryan threw his hands up in the air. "Then why the hell are you even here? Are you going to tell me that the two of you, the gods of healing, cannot do their damn job and heal someone?"

Apollo and Asklepios exchanged ashamed glances. "Alexander, we exist purely because there are still believers in the Greek and Roman gods. Our power has dwindled significantly. We must—"

"I've heard this all before but it's bullshit and you know it. You have the power, now do it."

"You don't understand. If we do this then Zeus—"

"Screw him!" Ryan resisted clapping his hands over his mouth at his blasphemy. "Show a little backbone for once and help me. We need Aden's help and in order to maintain that he needs healed. If he leaves that room he will die instantly otherwise."

Never had Ryan seen one god, let alone two, with gaping mouths and stunned eyes. He had to admit, he rather enjoyed their discomfort for some strange reason.

"Fine then. I will do it." Apollo grimaced. "But if Father hears of this little brother, I will blame you. Just forewarning."

Ryan slapped Apollo on the back. "Let me know when you actually grow a pair." Apollo shot him a nasty look before Ryan added, "Gratitude for your help. It means the world to me."

"Are you sure about this, Father?" Asklepios looked even more aged than before.

Apollo wrapped his arms around both Ryan and Asklepios' shoulders leading them towards the room Aden was in. "I'm one hundred percent regretting this already but if I want to keep existing, I better do what I can."

"You know we are supposed to save our strength for—"

"I am aware, Son. Yet, we do what we must."

"Then I shall help lighten the load."

"Much appreciated." Apollo smiled but it melted off his lips once he saw Aden hanging in the middle of the room. "Holy Hades! Poor child…"

Ryan could barely look at Aden in his condition, but his heart swelled at the thought of it soon being over with. Cato and Damian were cleaning his bloodied body with rags when they entered the room. Cato's mouth dropped and Ryan could see relief wash over Damian's face.

"You will need to leave the room." Apollo's face was set in stone instead of his cheerful demeanor. "This will take some serious power on our part."

"I won't leave him," Ryan said firmly.

"That wasn't a request. Get out now and shut the door," Apollo snapped.

Before Ryan could argue, and he would have, Damian and Cato dragged him out the door and shut it loudly behind them.

"I need to be there for him," Ryan insisted.

"And do what exactly? You weren't there to protect him from this and now that you've seen what was done you feel guilty?" Cato blocked the door with his body. "You know very well we could have put an end to his suffering. We could have broken him out, but you knew we needed him."

"Are you saying I don't care?" Ryan's eyes narrowed. "That I wanted this to happen?"

"All I am saying is you knew it would. We all knew about it, yet we did nothing."

"By all means Cato, tell me how you really feel."

Cato lowered his head and spoke to the ground, "I'm sorry. I don't know why I said that, but it's the truth. I'm just confused by how you feel about him I suppose. It doesn't make sense to me."

"Nor I," Damian added.

Ryan crouched down, running his hands through his hair as he spoke. "I don't either. I care about him, I do, yet I know what needs to be done. I'm walking a fine line between father and Warrior." His guilt was feasted upon him. "Hypocrisy at its finest."

Before either man could say a word, a dim glowing light came from under the door. It grew brighter and brighter, almost blindingly so even with the door closed that Ryan had to shield his eyes from it. The earth rumbled beneath their feet and he could hear things within the room crash to the floor, breaking upon impact.

Merely a minute went by and the painful brightness disappeared leaving the dim florescent light in its wake. Asklepios, who looked ten years older and ready to collapse, leaned against his staff as he opened the door.

"How is he?" Ryan asked impatiently as Asklepios blocked his view.

"Come in," Apollo called from inside the room.

Ryan squeezed past the old god and nearly hugged Aden when he saw he was untarnished and whole. "This is unbelievable."

"No, Alexander," Apollo yawned. "It is magic."

"How can I ever repay you?" Ryan stared at his son, who stared back with clear yet irritated eyes.

Apollo said, "You can rid the world of evil scum like the ones that did this to my nephew for starters. What was done to him wasn't done for answers. It was done for recreation and fun. It was a horrendous evil regardless of what he has done."

"As if you gods are known to be such prudent and upstanding beings," Aden hissed. "Or have you forgotten all the rotten things you have done to not only each other but to the mortals?"

"I would tread carefully with your words, nephew. Though your blood runs with our own, it will only grant you so much leniency."

"I'll be sure to remember that." Aden rolled his eyes.

Ryan really wanted to slap him across the cheek for his disrespect but part of him knew Aden must have gotten his attitude from him. After all, Ryan basically called Apollo a frightened child with no backbone. The apple truly doesn't fall far from the tree.

Apollo placed a warm hand on Ryan's shoulder. "We must leave now and rest. It took a lot of our energy, but he is full of health now. Don't waste our efforts and don't be a fool even with your own blood. That boy is dangerous."

"Have you seen his future?" Ryan grew suspicious. He always did when Apollo spoke to him.

Apollo's lips firmed into a thin line before he spoke. "I have seen what the future may hold but there is uncertainty there. The paths each of you take haven't yet been preordained by the fates. Proceed into your future with caution, Alexander. For the fate of us all rests on your very shoulders."

"No way. No way are you going to a shark infested island in the middle of the Atlantic." Julia pulled her fist back to punch the bag once more.

She was sweaty and angry and totally sexy. Wearing nothing but spandex shorts, a sports bra, running shoes, not to mention the ponytail—he was in heaven. "What else should I do? Attack his forces until he comes out of hiding?"

"Yes!" Another hit to the bag pushed the air out of her lungs.

"If we take out the leader, show his true nature to the masses, then we can win this. Those who are following him out of fear will join us in our efforts to wipe out his forces. Continuing to fight in small skirmishes will only lessen the lives we can save and diminish both armies slowly. We need to hit them at the heart of their cause. We are lucky this hasn't become a nuclear war yet."

"Yes, but all of that is at the expense of your own life." She jump kicked the bag before her fists connected once again. "It's a suicide mission. He must have hundreds of men protecting him."

"Damian and I can handle it."

Julia stopped her assault. "You're only bringing Damian? What about Cato?"

"Cato will stay here with you."

"What? You'll need him. Two people can't do this."

"Aden is coming with us." Ryan looked down at his feet to avoid the anger he felt radiating off her body. "Cato doesn't need to see his father being assassinated and neither do you."

"You are going to bring Aden?" She was seething. "You can't trust that snake. He is evil, Ryan. Pure evil."

"He knows that place inside and out."

"And he will betray you the first chance he gets."

"What other choice is there, Julia?" Ryan asked heatedly. "Fight until the human race goes extinct? Things are terrible out there right now and people are losing their faith rapidly. We must do this."

Julia crossed her arms, looking like she was ready to let him have it until she sighed. "I don't like this. I think, no, I know it will end badly."

"Like it or not this is our only option as of now. He is gaining power every day from the mortal's beliefs. We can't afford more battles on land without victory in sight. Marc needs to die."

Her breath visibly hitched in her chest, yet she nodded in agreement. "He does."

"It's for the best."

"Is it what's best for the world or for your inability to combat your addiction?" she asked, her eyes opened wide at her outburst. "I'm sorry. I don't know why I asked that."

Ryan wrapped his arms around her waist and pulled her body against his. Kissing her sweaty forehead, he forced a small smile. "Someone has been telling you my confessions, haven't they?"

She wrapped her arms around his shoulders. "Yes, but to be fair Damian worries about you all the time."

"That he does." Ryan pulled back to look at her, even though his arms remained firmly around her. "When did he have time to talk to you?"

"He was up here while you were taking a shower. I wasn't supposed to tell you, he was just warning me about your infatuation with slicing up people again."

"You make it sound like I am some sick killer with a fetish," he grumbled.

"Sorry. He warned me that you are becoming addicted to your old ways. Hand-to-hand combat in large groups."

"That's better." He tried to relax his muscles, but he couldn't help tensing up. Just the thought of battle had him on edge. It was an addiction that had resurfaced and it made him want to relapse for the pleasure of it.

Julia pulled away from him and started to unwrap her gloves. "Don't tell me you are going to revisit your old plan to conquer the world."

Ryan's laugh echoed throughout the room. "Damian really did put a lot of things in your head, didn't he? That is far from my mind. Believe me. The only thing I want is to put an end to Marc's foolishness and bring order back to the world."

"The world has never had order." Julia grunted. "There will always be war and death."

"You sound like your father now."

"Don't you dare compare me to him." She glared. "It's just the truth."

Ryan knew he was digging himself a hole, so he decided to change the subject. "So, what are we going to do tonight before I leave?" He wiggled his eyebrows and became satisfied when her angry brows smoothed out and her mouth curved into a smile.

"I'm thinking some champagne, light a fire, and take everything off until we—"

"Hey, Damian told me I'd find you two up here." Cato burst through the door.

"Cato, as always your timing is terrible." Ryan bit the inside of his cheek. "What is it?"

Cato grinned wickedly knowing he must have interrupted something he wouldn't approve of. "Yeah, I was listening outside the door for the best moment to interfere. Anna wants us all to get together tonight before you and Damian leave. Get your smelly asses down to her room ASAP."

"What in the name of Zeus did we just watch?" Ryan's mouth hung open.

Anna sat beside Damian, hiding her amusement behind

her hand rather poorly. Her entire body shook with fits of giggles.

"What?" she managed to snort out.

Damian shifted uncomfortably in his seat. Anna and Damian were on the bed while Julia, Cato and Ryan sat on their couch. He just stared at the TV screen as the names of actors scrolled by on a black background.

Ryan was having a hard time trying to comprehend and process the movie they just watched. "How did... Is that what people... Oh for the love of creation." He smacked his hand against his forehead.

Cato burst out laughing making everyone that wasn't Damian and Ryan join in. Even in the darkness of the room Ryan could see Damian blushing. This had to be the most awkward moment of their lives. And Anna was loving it.

"How is this amusing?" Ryan spoke loudly through their laughter. "Does reminding me of my past hell amuse you?"

"It's not that." Cato wiped tears from his eyes. "It's just... you and Damian."

Ryan and Damian locked eyes. Both men had avoided reading books and watching movies about their lives but this... this was almost insulting. "I was never that blond nor did some of that even happen."

Anna managed to quiet her fits of laughter.

"It's a movie, it's not like it is a documentary or anything."

"Why is this so amusing?" Ryan demanded. He had agreed to watch the damn movie as a way to help him move on from his past. Instead of moving on, it'd made him angry at how he was being depicted. "They made me seem so soft and dramatic." *Why did I agree to watch this damn thing?*

"So, it was completely off?" Anna asked.

"Some parts were close but not what I remember exactly," Ryan answered.

"What about the parts where you kept kissing men?" Cato laughed and shoved Ryan's arm.

"Sure. Let me try it again and see if it still pleases me." Ryan leaned over to Cato who pushed him away with a horror-struck expression. Julia pulled Ryan away from her brother and slapped his leg. "What? I'm just playing."

"I mean seriously, the guy they picked for you seemed weak. Not to mention that it wasn't that hard to bed your wife," Damian countered.

"I gotta admit, I'm surprised you wanted to watch it." Anna's grin towards Ryan was sickeningly mischievous.

Ryan had always been curious at how people viewed him and the movie made him feel insignificant upon all levels. He was now fully convinced the mortals believed he was a pathetic drunk with woman issues. "I thought it would be healing to watch, but in all honestly it felt like some moments of my life were mixed with some bad Shakespearian dialect and terrible acting."

"As long as you don't have any horrific flashbacks anymore, I think it was a good experience," Cato managed to say with a straight face, but a lingering smile wanted to crawl its way up. "Did your mother really kill your father?"

Ryan wanted to sink into the couch and make the questions stop. After his wife visited him in his dreams, he had begun to heal old wounds that should have long been scarred over. Yet the constant need of others to ask about his life made him uncomfortable. Why couldn't they just live in the present like he had decided to do? Why must his past be a constant annoyance?

"I cannot and will not confirm nor deny," Ryan spoke clearly. "I will however acknowledge the fact that her and I both had our fair share of blood on our hands that I am not proud of. It was merely a necessity to survive in a time were death lurked around every corner, waiting to drag my soul to the depths of Tartarus."

"What a happy thought to end our night on," Anna grumbled as she tried to sit herself up.

Her belly grew more each day. It was a wonder the woman hadn't popped open yet. From what he calculated she was in her eighth month now. Even worse, he realized Aden had been their prisoner for nearly a month.

Damian helped her sit up, giving her a loving smile that warmed Ryan's heart. "Not much longer and my boy will be here." Damian kissed the back of her neck.

"Yeah, and no more butterball Anna." Cato grinned before a smiling Anna threw a pillow at his head.

Her smile faded quickly as she sat back on the bed clutching her stomach. A look of pain tightened its grip on her face with her teeth clenched and eyes squinted shut.

"Oh God," she muttered.

Damian leapt off the bed and Ryan ran to her side. Both men kneeled before her holding her hands, rubbing her arms, and made calming shushing noises. Julia pushed them both out of the way and Ryan fell back on his ass.

"Will you two quit it?" Julia shook her head at them. "Are you okay, Anna?"

Anna nodded but the look on her face was anything but okay. "It hurts."

"It's tightening?" Julia asked and Anna nodded. "I'm sure it is just false contractions. It will pass I promise."

Just as Julia promised, the pain seemed to pass from Anna's face and she laid back down in relief. Pointing a finger at Damian she growled, "You aren't doing this to me again. Get me the damn pill, hell, the shot or a freaking hysterectomy. I don't care. This blows."

Damian kissed her damp forehead with a look of pure happiness on his face. Ryan could see Damian was planning on future children by the look in his eyes but for now he would accommodate his hormone riddled fiancé.

"So, what's next on our list of fun activities to do before we send Ryan and Damian into the lair of the beast with the treacherous spawn Aden?"

"Nice, Cato." Damian inhaled deeply. "Real nice."

"Well, you should let me go with you. I don't care if that man gave his sperm to create me. As far as I'm concerned my father is dead." Cato had insisted upon mentioning his grievances against Ryan's decision every chance he got.

Unfortunately, Ryan had his reasons for it. Watching your father take his last breath in front of you isn't anything he wished on any man. He knew that firsthand and he'd be damned if Cato had to experience that.

"Cato," Damian groaned.

"I mean seriously," Cato continued speaking, but Ryan stopped him.

"It isn't up for discussion. That's final."

Chapter VIII

Damian

R YAN AND DAMIAN CASUALLY walked down the hallway
with one another before turning in for the night. Neither
were in a hurry and both probably wanted to discuss what they
just witnessed. When Anna had brought up the movie about
Alexander, he had to admit he was curious. He was even more
surprised when Ryan agreed to watch it.

"Julia is going to meet you in your room?" Damian asked
trying to break the silence.

Although he could tell Ryan was in deep thought he still
answered, "Yes, she stayed back to speak with her brother."

"I see." Damian studied the lines in the marble as his feet
walked across them.

"Was I really that unbearable?" Ryan's head snapped towards Damian, catching him off guard. "I don't remember losing myself like that."

"Well, I recall a man with an appetite for greatness that
treated his men with respect and love. You had your downfalls
though towards the end, but I feel like that started when you
became Immortal."

"From the beginning it seemed as if no one could stand me
though."

"Your ambitions were higher than they thought possible and it made them anxious. They loved you. I am sure of it. But their own desires outweighed that admiration."

Damian went back into deep thought as they strolled down the halls filled with paintings. There was Tlahuicole from the Tlaxcala Tribe in Mexico. He was a fierce Warrior that was only Immortal for a short time. He was captured and instead of the dishonor of betraying his people he chose death.

Next came the Gallic chieftain, Vercingetorix who now went by the name of Torin. Then there was Triệu Thị Trinh, who knocked Ryan out when he tried to make a move on her. Tecumseh, Shaka, and then Cuauhtémoc. All men and women worthy of becoming Immortals.

They continued down the wall, Damian recalling the names of every person in the portraits they passed. Ryan stopped abruptly, his brows furrowed.

"I wasn't that blond either."

Damian tried not to laugh but he couldn't help it. "You are fixated on that aren't you?"

"Of course I am! They made me look ridiculous."

"No, your hair wasn't that blond. It was more dirty blond but not that yellow. Feel better?"

"Yep." He nodded but just as they were about to keep walking, Ryan stopped suddenly.

Zee's portrait was in front of them. She wore a Zapotec warrior's headdress that was fashioned painstakingly with bright feathers and colored leather. Her dark hair hung in a single braid over one shoulder with the tip of a spear leaning against the other. Her face was set in a serious tone that didn't resemble the woman at all in life.

"How are you doing about that?" Damian asked.

Ryan studied her for a moment. "It doesn't feel great, but

I've accepted it. She deserved a better death but at least she is with her husband and child now."

Damian made his way over to the portrait next to Zee's. "Remember Khutulun?" He smirked knowing full well Ryan did.

Removing his eyes from his former lover, Ryan looked to the portrait of Khutulun. "Oh yeah..." He bit his lip with a smile which made Damian split a grin. "That woman was a ball buster."

"Still is." Damian patted him on the back. "Last I heard she had retired and now works teaching wrestling and other fighting techniques to prospective Warriors."

"Well, not retired anymore since this damn war. That woman can fight." Ryan sighed. "So damned beautiful too. Too bad she wouldn't have me."

"I thought it was Triệu Thị Trinh that wouldn't sleep with you."

"It was both." Ryan smirked. "They practiced self-control on a daily basis and would never let a man like me near them. Too proud and too smart to fall for my tricks." Laughing, they moved on towards the next portrait. "Artemisia. Now there was a woman who knew my tricks yet seemed to use me instead of the other way around."

Artemisia's portrait seemed to stare back at them with her dark brown eyes. Her long dark hair parted neatly in the middle and she wore black clothing against a reddish background. Her skin was golden honey color from days upon days voyaging on the seas.

"Broke your heart if I recall." Damian smirked.

"That she did." Ryan clicked his tongue. "Oh well, worked out in the end. I have Julia now and that's what matters."

"Ryan!" someone yelled from down the hall. Both he and

Ryan turned to see Alois marching angrily towards them with Aden towed in chains behind him. "What did you do? How is this scum perfectly healed?"

Damian took in Aden's appearance when Ryan said, "Judging by his swollen eye I'd say he isn't perfectly healed anymore, Alois." Aden smirked at Ryan's comment to his surprise. "Was it necessary to chain his ankles, wrists, and neck? You could have just collared him."

"It is necessary," Alois spat. "You have yet to answer my question. This just goes to show your true loyalties, Ryan. You should be held for treason for your sympathies to your little pet."

Alois pushed Aden towards Ryan, but Aden tripped over the chains and fell into the wall that held the portraits. The impact knocked Artemisia's picture off the wall landed upright on the ground thankfully.

"You disrespectful little shit." Ryan grabbed Alois around the throat and slammed him up against the opposite wall. "I should kill you, Alois. For what you've done to Aden and for what you continue to do to those that are loyal. You are scum of the earth."

"I did what you couldn't. I got answers."

"You tortured him for fun, regardless of asking questions." Ryan gripped his throat a little tighter so he couldn't talk. Although Damian agreed Alois should be punished, it would come at the expense of Ryan's command of the Immortals.

Damian gently put his hand on Ryan's shoulder drawing him out of his anger. "Ryan, you cannot kill a member of the council. Calm yourself."

Ryan looked between Alois and Damian then back. Wheels turned within his best friend's head as his anger began to ease ever so slightly along with the grip of his hand. "He deserves it," he gritted out through his teeth.

"That he does, yet this isn't your decision." He leaned in to whisper, "Don't give him anymore ammo than he already has."

A growl escaped Ryan's throat as he tossed Alois to the ground. "Get out of my sight if you know what's good for you."

"I will take the prisoner—"

"No, you will not." Ryan lunged towards Alois as he quickly stood up and ran off like a frightened chick and out of sight.

Ryan

Going against what Damian thought best, they tied Aden down to his bed in his own room for the night. After all the torture, the kid deserved a good night's sleep in his bed even if it included chains. Once the task was complete, they returned to Ryan's room and lounged on his couch in silence.

Alois was scum. There was no doubt about it. But Ryan knew his temper needed to be reined in. He couldn't help but want to pulverize that little prick for what he did to Aden. It was odd how parental instincts seemed to kick in even after such a short amount of time knowing the truth.

Could Aden ever change? Was there any possibility he could make up for the hell Aden went through as a child? So many questions ran through his mind and none of them could be answered.

"Why is it that when things start to look up, some force rears its ugly head and obliterates it?"

Damian had his head lying back with his eyes closed as he answered, "One day it will be over and return to how it was. Minuscule missions and parties lasting into all hours of the night, vacationing on an uninhabited island for months without a care in the world."

"You will have a child though."

"He won't be a child for long. Soon he will join our ranks or live peacefully in Urbs. Maybe become a butcher or something."

"Your son, a butcher?" A laugh escaped him. "I hardly think so."

"Would it be so bad if he were? A life of peace and a family he wouldn't ever have to worry about dying. It'd be a utopian state of being."

"More like a tediously dull state of being," Ryan countered.

Cato surged through Ryan's door making both Ryan and Damian jump. If Cato were closer, Ryan probably would have punched him for scaring the hell out of him. Caleb came running in after him, both out of breath with sweat upon their brows.

"What's going on?" Ryan groaned.

"We need to reinforce the edge of Italy. The General is trying to bring his ground forces in by the thousands," Caleb answered.

"What happened to our plan with Austria, Switzerland, and France?"

"Not sure but the Risen's men are equipped with ancient warfare and our army isn't handling it very well. It's nighttime and arrows are raining down on our men unseen. They have ballistae and scorpions." Cato looked impatient with Ryan, standing in his gear and ready for battle.

Damian patted Ryan on the shoulder as if he already knew Ryan's answer. "I'll go get ready." And with that he was off.

Ryan's heart beat faster. Not because he was nervous but the thought of fighting another battle made him eager. Marc was pulling out ancient Roman warfare and his insides jumped with excitement. This was what Ryan was made for and what he excelled in.

After they quickly got ready, the four of them jumped into a portal and into a sea of blood. Men and women lied all over the countryside. Some crying out in pain and others never to move again. Ryan went from nervously excited to commander mode instantly.

"Take men through the tree line and attack from behind. The night will keep you hidden but don't light anything to give away your position," he said to Caleb before he ran off to carry out his orders. "Take another group on the opposite side and do the same, don't allow them to outflank us, Cato."

Explosions broke through the blackened night illuminating the dead sprawled across the field. The green grass was painted red with blood. Arrows littered the fallen bodies as if pinning them to the ground. The light flickered across paled faces contorted into hauntingly pained expressions.

With a cry from ahead he could barely make out their men falling one by one to swords and spears before they could get a shot off in the dark. They were equipped with swords due to Ryan's insistence, but their experience lacked. Ryan ran with Damian as fast as he could toward his men.

"Hold the line!" Ryan yelled at the terrified faces that turned to him. He clutched his sword tightly in his hand as the other flexed nervously. "Push forward. Do not retreat! Do not forget what we are fighting for!"

His mind gave out flashes of his past as another explosion went off. Men in armor. *Flash.* Their heads falling from their bodies. *Flash.* A spear penetrating a black horse.

He didn't want to fight this raw anger building within. The lust to kill was much too strong as his mind warped to a time before firearms tainted humanity.

His breathing was heavy and he was drenched with sweat. No, not sweat. Blood. Red-hot blood dripped down his cheek as if they were tears leaving streaks of crimson down his skin. It was an all too familiar feeling, but he could barely remember how he had gotten this way.

Ryan stared down at the body in front of him. The man was penetrated through the chest with Ryan's sword and on his knees, yet the life was long gone from his eyes. Ryan yanked his sword out of the man's corpse, and it fell to the ground with a soft thud on the damp earth below.

The daylight had broken through the long night and their battlefield was illuminated to reveal the carnage left in their wake. Bodies were strewn as far as the eye could see. Many were already being plucked at by birds relishing in their hefty meals.

"Ryan?" Damian's voice came unsteadily from behind him.

Ryan nearly tripped over an arm as he tried to turn around and managed to catch his balance. He could somehow feel the hand he stepped on through his boot as it pressed deeper into the dirt. Both Damian and Cato looked at him with apprehensive eyes and took slow balanced steps towards him.

"Ryan?" Damian echoed. "It's over. You can put your sword away."

Looking down at his drenched sword, he realized his hand was trembling, yet his nerves felt at ease. He studied the blood flowing slowly down the blade, dripping off the tip like water from a leaf after a fresh rain. *Drip. Drip. Drip.*

"What happened?" Ryan continued to stare at his blade.

"You don't know what you just did?" Cato was hesitant.

His brows drew together in confusion. In truth he had no idea what happened. Flashes of him using his sword came in and out of his memory but other than that he was at a loss. Last thing he truly remembered was telling his men not to retreat.

"I don't." He looked up at Damian to see his face harden.

"You just…" Damian gave Ryan a once-over. "You killed all of these people."

"That isn't possible." His face contorted as he watched their men gathering their dead and wounded. "There are too many."

Cato and Damian shared uneasy glances to one another. "Our men helped a little but Ryan, you were unstoppable. Quick. Our men took theirs by surprise from behind like you ordered but you pressed into the front."

"There isn't even a scratch on you." Damian looked him over and even through all the blood on him, Ryan knew he was right.

"So, what are you saying?"

"What I am saying is, you couldn't be touched. No one in your path even stood a chance. You overpowered every mortal out there and cut through them like butter." Damian chewed on his bottom lip. "Maybe… maybe you just got back in the groove of it?"

"Maybe."

"Yeah, his groove. Sure." Cato rolled his eyes. "Let's get back. Now that Ryan killed everyone."

Chapter IX

Damian

"IS IT REALLY NECESSARY to collar me?" Aden gritted out.

Damian smiled wide as he locked the seemingly harmless black leather collar around Aden's neck. With a press of a button by either Ryan or himself, the leather would begin to constrict tightly until Aden's head was severed from his body. A safety precaution put in place to ensure Aden didn't betray them.

"Very." Damian slapped Aden on the back.

With Aden collared, they were finally able to make their way out to the ocean in search of Marc's lair. They rode on a boat as far as they would dare without giving away their intentions to the Risen but the ride there was impossibly heart-wrenching.

Ryan wanted the girls to stay behind in the Domus but they both raised hell until he finally succumbed to their demands. More so, they marched their way on the boat without giving a damn about what Damian nor Ryan said on the matter.

Damian knew Anna wasn't going to like the boat too much and it didn't take long for her to realize it too.

"I'm going to throw up," she mumbled.

He rubbed small circles on her back. "I told you to stay—"

"Finish that sentence one more time and I will blow chunks

all over you." Anna grimaced but her threats only made him smile. That crass charm of hers would never get old to him.

"Maybe I should get her a bucket?" Ryan asked thoughtfully, amusement shining in his eyes.

Anna flipped him off without even looking at him and finally threw up over the side of the boat. Julia nudged him in the shoulder giving him her motherly, 'quit being a jerk' look but Ryan simply winked at her. Julia had taken Anna's side more often than not, which Damian was thankful for. The women in his and his best friend's life got along and that made it so much sweeter.

"The dumbass says this is as far as we should go!" Cato called from the helm.

"Is he ever going to quit calling Aden that?" Ryan rolled his eyes noticeably.

This time Julia winked at him. "I highly doubt it." They all walked to the bow of the boat and looked out at the water. "I don't see anything."

Aden walked up next to her and Damian could see her body tense up at his proximity. "It's hidden but it's there. If you look out there long enough, the sun will hit it just right and you can see a ripple of it."

Ryan maneuvered his way in between Julia and Aden, wrapping his arm around her waist showing off his newly found possessive tendencies with her. "I'll take your word for it. Let's get ready to go." Ryan led Julia towards the stern for a private moment.

"My, my, isn't he a sight." Aden's eyes nearly rolled out of his head. "It's a wonder he has maintained a relationship this long and hasn't ditched her for something better."

Damian clenched his fists, not from what Aden said, but just being around the man made him sick to his stomach with annoyance.

"He was been burned many times before as well. It hasn't been just one sided."

"I highly doubt a woman has ever hurt him. It's in his nature to feel nothing and only care about his own fulfillment," Aden said.

"And was one of those women your mother?" Damian urged for information. "Is that the reason you are so fucked up?"

Aden's smirk tugged at the corner of his mouth as he looked out into the ocean to the hidden fortress that lay ahead. "Is this your way of trying to get me to open up? Because if so, it's a terrible tactic. You're not very good at trying to butter me up."

"Oh, I couldn't give a damn about buttering you up. But if I am capable of helping Ryan's mind rest at ease then so be it," Damian said. "Maybe if you actually told him who she was, he would remember her and could explain things."

"There is nothing he can say that will change how I feel. Also, I doubt he would remember her."

"Or maybe you should just grow a pair and quit blaming your parents for your shitty attitude," Anna groaned as she leaned her head against the metal railing. "You are seriously annoying. Let's all throw a tantrum and act like a piece of shit because Mommy and Daddy didn't love you."

Anna knew what it was like to have bad and absent parents. She was a foster child, never adopted and hated her real parents. She told him about them once but refused to speak of them again. Given her own upbringing she managed to become such a lovely person and he couldn't help but beam at her. His grin quickly died once Ryan made his way back to them absent Julia.

"Ready?" Ryan asked.

"Always." Damian kissed the top of Anna's head. "I will see you soon love."

"Be careful." She managed to push herself up from the

railing and wrap her arms around his neck for a hug. "Come back in one piece."

Damian squeezed her as tight as he dared with her stomach so round and when he let her go, he kissed her gently on the lips. "I will, love."

"Don't kiss me, my breath is disgusting."

"I don't care." He kissed her again.

"Alright come on, we need to get off the boat so the girls can take a portal back home." Ryan called up to Cato, "Don't forget to keep your ass out here for when we come back."

"No shit, it's not like you haven't told me a thousand times already!" Cato called back.

Ryan flipped Cato off, who returned the sentiment before they both dragged Aden to the edge of the boat.

After dressing in their diving gear, Aden reached for a knife until Ryan swatted his hand away. "Do you really think I am going to trust you with a weapon?"

"There are dangerous creatures in these waters. Are you really going to leave me unable to protect myself?"

"That is exactly what we are going to do," Damian answered for Ryan. "All you need is a rebreather and your diving intercom. Deal with it."

"You have your stupid little button that can kill me in ten seconds if I stab you. Just give me a knife."

Ryan dug into his pockets and gave Aden a knife. "There, happy?"

"This is a pocket knife." Aden held up the small chunk of metal. "A freaking pocket knife."

"Very observant. Now let's go."

Once they were all under the water and swimming in the direction Aden provided, Damian's nerves began to spark. The water was extraordinarily comfortable but the farther they swam the more clouded the water became, almost to the point he could barely see five feet in front of him. They swam side by side for a few minutes before Aden stopped.

"There is an entrance down below for underwater crafts to enter through," he spoke through his intercom. "It's about three hundred yards from here."

"Okay, so let's keep moving." Ryan tried to swim but was caught with Aden's hand to his chest.

Damian gripped his dagger and swam quickly towards the other two men until Aden spoke, "We need to be careful. The water has changed."

"So, what do you suggest? We float here until you decide to grow a pair or until our tanks are too low to breathe?" Damian spat out.

"What the hell is up your ass, Damian?"

"Fuck you, Aden."

"I don't like my father's sloppy seconds."

"Could have fooled me when you raped Julia."

"Enough!" Ryan yelled through the intercom making Damian's ears ring. "Both of you shut the hell up, quit bitching, and let's get this done."

"Son or not, that little prick raped your woman, killed our friends, and refuses to tell you who his mother is which is driving you insane."

"Is this really an argument to have under water?" Ryan asked.

"Guys…" Aden muttered.

"Why shouldn't we have this discussion?" Damian ignored Aden.

"Where is this anger coming from all of a sudden?" Ryan asked.

"Guys…" Aden muttered again.

"Am I not allowed to blow up once in a while? Or is that just something you can do?"

"It's not something you do normally."

"Well being around your bastard makes me irritable."

"Guys!" Aden yelled.

"What?" they asked together.

"I thought maybe you'd like to know we are being watched."

He spun around as quickly as he could in the dragging water and barely made out a form floating in the distance. Damian was treading as he kicked his legs and moved his arms so he didn't sink further down. Unfortunately, as the creature moved closer, he forget to move until his brain caught up.

"What is it?" Ryan asked.

Aden merely stared out towards the creature ahead and said, "Swim as fast as you can. Do not let your eyes fool you." Ryan tried to speak but Aden wouldn't let him. "Move. Now!"

It didn't take much to convince either Ryan or Damian to swim as fast as they could. If Aden was even the least bit nervous, they should be too. Damian kicked his feet as fast as he could, slicing his arms through the water until they burned from the effort.

"We are getting close," Aden panted through the intercom. "Don't slow down."

Damian's muscles protested but he pushed through the pain. Ryan was paddling right beside him but as soon as he turned to look at Aden, Ryan was gone. Damian glanced back at Aden just in time to watch his blurred image being dragged into the murky abyss by an unseen force.

There was silence on the intercom except for someone's harsh breathing filling his ears. The clouded water was becoming nearly impossible to see through. He turned and turned in the water looking every direction, but not even Aden was near him.

"Aden? Ryan?" he called out but there was no answer. Nothing but the sound of breathing filled the silence.

Anna

Stepping back into the Domus was a huge relief. Being on a rocking boat that made her lose everything her stomach contained and then more, sucked. She still felt weary and her forehead glistened with sweat but the cool breeze blowing through the open windows made her nausea cease rather quickly.

"Boats don't usually make me sick like this." She covered her fowl smelling breath. "I need a toothbrush."

"I have a feeling the baby was the culprit." Julia rubbed her lower back like a damn miracle worker, making her instantly ready for a nap. "Let's get you to your room for some rest."

She didn't have to tell her twice. Anna waddled along while Julia drifted perfectly across the marble floor like some damn ballerina.

"You make me feel like an elephant."

The corners of Julia's mouth tugged up. "Be lucky you aren't. You wouldn't even be half the way done with your pregnancy if you were."

"I don't even know why or how you know that."

"I read."

"Yeah, boring crap," Anna said smugly.

"After a few centuries you will grow bored and read many random things too. Besides, elephants are rather fascinating creatures," Julia added

"I love you, Julia, but I really don't care." A squeezing pain engulfed her entire abdomen. She drew in a quick breath, stopping in her tracks and causing Julia to give her that usual worried look she adopted. Anna shut her eyes tight until her stomach loosened from its grasp. "I hate those stupid things."

"False contraction?" Anna nodded to her. "We really need to get you to bed. Damian should have never allowed you to get on that boat in your condition."

"I'm pregnant not a glass doll. I can get on a damn boat if I want," Anna snapped. "Damian doesn't *allow* me to do anything. I do what I please when I—" Another pain shot through her stomach making her double over.

Julia put her hand on Anna's stomach while holding her steady with the other. "Anna?"

"I'm fine." She took deep breaths like the midwives had been teaching her. "It's gone."

"Sit down for a second, okay?"

"Why?"

"Just do it." Julia helped her sit against the wall and ran off towards the male dormitories.

Anna leaned her head back against the cold stone, clicking her feet together as she waited for Julia to return. She should just get up and continue to her room, but if she were being honest she probably couldn't push herself up at this point. Being pregnant was not her thing at all. Women were insane for doing this.

After a moment she realized how much she liked sitting here with a view of the outside. The breeze tousled her hair and the smell of fresh bread from the bakery down below in the city made her taste buds water with hunger. She loved Natalia's bread shop. The woman knew how to bake, that was for sure.

Cinnamon rolls and some sort of sweet bread that Damian introduced to her flooded her cravings. Just the thought made her stomach grumble. She had no problem with the food cravings this baby made her have. She relished in eating a lot when it was socially acceptable to do so.

"Damn I need food." *Even after throwing up.*

"Here she is." Julia panted as she ran back to Anna. "Help me carry her."

Anna looked up at Julia and Caleb, laughing at how worried Julia looked and how clearly uncomfortable Caleb felt.

"I can walk you know."

"Walking is causing you pain," Julia scolded. "Grab an arm and a leg Caleb."

Poor Caleb shifted from side to side. "I could just carry her myself."

"Or I could walk."

"Fine, pick her up and bring her to her room please. I will get the midwives." Julia ran off before Anna could object.

With one easy swoop, Caleb had her in his arms and they were off to her room. She really hadn't spent time around the man and had absolutely nothing to say to him. It was awkward and the feeling was definitely mutual because he looked around trying to avoid eye contact with her.

It was rather surprising how easily he carried her. He wasn't the biggest Warrior by any means, but he was in shape enough not to seem to mind her weight. Damian would occasionally pretend she was massively heavy just to tease her. He would breathe heavily and fake wipe sweat off his brow when he put her down. Needless to say, he got a punch in the stomach every time, but he maintained it was worth it.

"Sooo…" Anna smiled forcefully and Caleb did the same as he briefly made eye contact. "Julia is gone, you can put me down you know."

"I think I better just follow her instructions. That woman can get vicious."

"Even when she isn't brainwashed." The both nodded in agreement.

He walked like it was nothing and made her feel even better about her weight. Anna couldn't help but stare at the Star of David necklace around his neck and he was quick to realize she was staring.

"What?"

"Didn't know you were Jewish." She shrugged.

This time he actually grinned. "The curly hair and exaggerated nose didn't give it away already?"

Anna bit the inside of her cheek to keep herself from laughing. "Your nose isn't big. Don't try to make me racial profile you."

"I think I inherited my mother's looks a little more than my father's. She was born in Russia long after him."

"She wasn't Jewish I take it?"

"Not originally, but my father was apparently so charming he managed to convert her." Caleb grinned. "That was about the only thing he could make her do though. She was a lot like you actually. Strong and independent, never taking a command from a man. Probably what my father liked about her so much. One of a kind."

"I believe you gave me a compliment." They reached her bedroom door and somehow Caleb opened the door with ease. "You are well practiced at opening doors with a woman in your arms." She teased him and she swore his cheeks turned red.

He laid her down in bed and she started to keep going with her teasing, but he managed to cut her off.

"No, I am not well practiced in laying a woman in bed. In case you were wondering." He genuinely looked amused by her and sat on the love seat across from the bed.

"Really? Because it seems to me like you got this damsel in distress thing down pat."

Caleb's shoulders went up and down. "Every time I was interested in a woman either Jesse or Aden or both would 'try her out' as they used to call it. There were a few I managed to keep secret but then they would catch wind and ruin it for me."

"That's terrible." As if Anna needed any more reasons to hate Aden. Caleb's confession was definitely giving her more.

"It's fine actually." Caleb leaned against his knees. "It showed me who actually cared about me. If those women were so eager to ruin what we had for a one-night stand with them, then they were not the ones for me. Though, it has made me rather cautious of who I approach."

"You don't look the type to sleep around," Anna admitted out loud.

"I'm not." Caleb was far sweeter than Anna could have imagined. Especially after being around Jesse and Aden for so long. "I can't see sex as just sex. For me it has to be personal and with someone I care about. Otherwise, I don't see the point."

"You are being very open with me." Anna smiled.

"I apologize. I haven't had many people to talk to since this all happened. Not many people trust me anymore and besides that, my team was the closest thing to family I had." God, she wanted Caleb to find the love of his life and be happy forever. He was so damned sweet. "But you can't always agree with family and here we are. Jesse is dead and Aden turned insane."

Julia ran through the door in a hurry with a midwife rushing behind her dressed in all white. Seriously, why do these people wear white when it's going to get nasty from some sort of bodily fluid?

"Okay, here she is. She keeps doubling over from pain and I think it might be real contractions, not false labor," Julia blurted out. "It's still not time for the baby."

The midwife came to Anna's bedside and checked her pulse

and temperature and pushed along her stomach, all without her permission. It wasn't until the nurse was done checking her inside and out that she proclaimed, "She isn't ready yet."

"Told you." Anna rolled her eyes. She noticed that Caleb had disappeared at some point, probably when the nurse decided to pull down her pants. "I haven't even felt anything since you went to get Caleb."

Julia made a silent prayer and started to tuck Anna into her bed. "You are getting rest and so am I. This child is stressing me out and I am not even its mother," she said sadly.

CHAPTER X

Ryan

ONE MOMENT HE WAS swimming next to Damian and Aden and the next he was being dragged at an alarming speed through the ocean. He had no idea which direction, but it felt like he was being tossed around like a rag doll. Ryan wasn't one to get sick from spinning, yet he could feel bile rising in his throat.

The weight of the water pushing against his body made it hard to reach the knife strapped to his boot. If he had any chance of getting out of this situation, he had to stab the thing holding onto him. That was proving easier said than done though.

His arm flew backward while the thing twirled him roughly through the water by his feet. After his third attempt he managed to grab hold of the knife. His ab muscles felt like they were on fire. Thankfully he was able to maintain his grip on his weapon and slashed at whatever had ahold of him.

He stopped moving in an instant, leaving Ryan kicking his legs fiercely to float upward instead of ass-end up. His vertigo was starting to balance out when the sight of his captor came into view. It wasn't a monster exactly, but the very depiction of Julia in front of him was startling, nonetheless.

Her blonde hair floated beautifully in the water like a piece of art from a master painter. She wore light, sheer robes as if they were made from mist showing off every curve of her body leaving nothing to the imagination. The biggest difference were her eyes. They blazed green even in the water and lacked pupils making her look entirely unnatural.

This wasn't Julia. Just a trick by another monster trying to lead him to a horrid fate just like the sirens. The picture of her in front of him only caused a momentary lapse in judgment but he knew better by now.

"What do you want?"

Without moving her lips, she answered him as if her voice echoed into his mind.

I want you to die.

"You can try, but your tricks won't work."

You see what you wish to see.

"Right, I wish to see you out of my way, so get moving."

You are not far from your destination. However, you shall never reach it.

"Who's going to stop me? You?"

No, the hungry beasts I have led you to will.

Ryan looked around him seeing nothing but the creepy version of Julia in front of him. She didn't move towards him at all and when he tried to swim near her something unseen blocked his way. He smacked at the hidden wall preventing him from moving forward but to no avail.

"What is this?"

Something to make sure you as well as those beasts in there with you do not get out.

"I don't see anything."

You will. They are quite hungry after all. Their last meal was a few days past.

"What kind of sick fucking creature are you?"

This time monster Julia smiled revealing pearly white teeth.

An angry one. The General has promised us all a life we could have only dreamt of. Be sure to pray to your gods while you die. I doubt they will answer though. They never do.

The beast swam off, leaving him alone in the deep ocean with a damn invisible wall blocking his path. It wasn't an ideal situation at all. At any moment he knew some man-eating monster was going to attack.

"Damian? Aden?" Ryan called out but there was nothing but static on his end. "Shit..." He swam the opposite direction of the hidden wall and had yet to run into any beast.

He gripped his knife tighter in his hand and his nerves began to set in. Maybe the monster was just trying to make him scared. If whatever beast were hungry for meat, they wouldn't wait this long to attack prey. He was an easy meal left alone in the sea with nothing but his knife as protection under the water.

He continued to swim until black rocks were visible under the water. That had to be the island the General was on, but he couldn't go any further without Damian or Aden. If they were eaten by some ocean dwelling kraken or something, he would never forgive himself.

His wish seemed to be granted as two bodies were dragged viscously through the water near him. After depositing their victims, the two creatures quickly swam away before he could see who they looked like. Damian and Aden were kicking furiously in the water to float upright and Aden held up his little pocketknife to defend himself.

"Guys!" Ryan called. They both looked around until they caught sight of Ryan swimming towards them.

"What in the hell were those things?" Damian asked windily.

"Rusalkas," Aden answered. "Be lucky all they did was drag us here."

"They said something about hungry beasts," Ryan added. "What sort of beasts?"

Aden's eyes narrowed. "Sharks. Great whites that the General keeps starving to drive them insane with hunger anytime a trespasser gets near. We need to move and fast."

Ryan didn't need to be told twice. In fact, he really didn't need to be told at all because as soon as Aden said 'great whites' Ryan took off swimming in the direction of the island. The water was not as murky here thankfully, but his anxiety was spiking to an all-time high. He wasn't a fan of water and the main reason was sharks.

The three of them were so close to the rocks underneath the island, but as luck would have it, Ryan spotted a small speck swimming closer to them from the corner of his eye. The speck quickly grew into the size of a coin and then into the size of plate. Bubbles quickened up around them as they sliced their arms through the water at a quicker pace.

"It's coming, it's coming, it's coming," Ryan kept repeating the useless mantra.

"Shut up, shut up, shut up," Damian countered, his voice going an octave higher.

He could feel the current of the water twirling behind him but when he looked nothing was there. They were so close to the rocks now and he felt another current, and then another. The damn things were toying with them and it was working. Fear was elevating within himself so much that his swimming was becoming erratic and less graceful. If there was one creature on this planet that made Ryan lose all thoughts of his training, it would be a shark.

His relief when they reached the rocks promptly disappeared

when he couldn't see an entrance anywhere. "What the hell, Aden?"

"There's a switch somewhere. I'm pretty sure."

"Pretty sure?" Damian shouted.

"Yep."

As Aden looked, Ryan and Damian faced out into the waters to watch his back. He gripped his knife so tightly he doubted he could open his fingers after this was over with.

"Anytime would be a good time, Aden." Ryan's voice shook.

"Shark!" Damian pointed to Ryan's right.

He looked almost too late when a giant head with sharp teeth came charging towards him. He barely had any time to push his body away using the sharks head before it clamped down on him. It may not be manly, but he shrieked as soon as it came back for him. The sheer size of the thing could shallow him whole and he doubted he could dodge it again.

"Aden?" his voice broke. "Anytime!"

"I think it's down a little lower." Aden kicked his feet, pushing him further down along the rocks.

"Two! There are two now!" Ryan screeched. "Poseidon get your animals in check." The second shark charged at him and was able to nick Ryan's arm before he stabbed it in the eye.

Somehow, Ryan now found himself clinging to the creature's fin and riding it like a bronco trying to buck him off. His arm was leaving a small blood trail through the water and it wasn't until he had the air knocked out of him that he realized the second shark had barreled into his ride. The animals started to fight, giving Ryan enough time to escape towards Damian and Aden.

"How in the—" Damian began.

"Found it! Get in now!" Aden swam through a large entrance in the rocky foundation that had appeared. How he got it open, Ryan didn't care at this point. The important thing is that he was away from the carnivorous sea monsters.

Once they were all safely inside the cave, the wall behind them rumbled. It dropped down, closing out the open water behind them along with the Ryan-hungry sharks. An underwater tunnel was lit with runway lights that didn't help illuminate any of their surroundings.

"That. That right there is exactly why I hate the ocean!" Ryan growled in frustration.

"As soon as we reach the end of this tunnel there will be a pool of water that has stairs leading into the castle. More than likely there will be guards so we need to take them out before they can radio for help." Aden ignored Ryan per usual. "Let's get going."

Ryan was still rattled from his shark experience, but they swam about fifty feet before he could see lights above the rippling water. He could faintly make out two dark shadows standing on either side of a stairway. Now was when stealth was required.

"Get against the wall. We will go on three," Ryan told Damian.

Ryan and Aden swam to the left side of the room and stopped about five feet from the platform. Once Damian was in position, he unholstered his rifle, slowly raising it up above the water. The darkness of the tunnel helped conceal them nicely but, in all honesty, the guards didn't seem like they were paying much attention anyways.

"On three. One... two... three."

Both guards collapsed in a heap on the platform. Heaving himself up out of the water, Ryan flopped on the edge like a dead fish.

"I hate swimming," he said after pulled off his rebreather.

"We are all well aware of that fact." Damian pushed one of the guard's body into the water. "Even with a suppressor, I hope no one heard us."

Aden pushed the other body into the water leaving swipes of blood along the platform. "I doubt it. The stairs above shouldn't be guarded."

"Hide the diving gear in the corners," Ryan said. The corners of the platform were hidden in shadows, hopefully it was dark enough to mask their gear. "After we kill Marc, we get the hell out and if we get split up at some point just meet down here. Cato will be waiting for us on the boat. Make sure you have the camera ready to record so we can show the mortals, Damian."

"Again, Ryan. We know," Damian grunted as he took off his diving gear.

"Okay, what did I do?" Ryan practically pinned Damian against the wall.

He wouldn't meet Ryan's eyes for a moment as if contemplating the right words to use. Knowing Damian that was exactly what he was doing. Words out of anger could wound a person and Damian wasn't the type to be that cruel.

"You didn't do anything, Ryan," Damian started. "I am just stressed."

A laugh escaped Ryan. "We all are."

"I know we are." Damian finally met his eyes. "I'm sorry I am being ridiculous. It's just being around Aden is rather aggravating and leaving Anna behind…" Ryan started to speak but Damian cut him off at the start. "I know, I said I would come, and I am glad I am here, but I feel torn leaving my pregnant betrothed alone in the middle of a war."

"She isn't alone, Damian. I would never put her in danger."

"I know." One side of his mouth went up in a crooked

grin. "I'll calm down. I'm sorry. I can't promise I will be nice to that idiot over there though."

"Nor do I expect you to."

"Uh, I can hear you." Aden crossed his arms. "Can we get a move on and quit worrying about each other's feelings? That would be great."

"Lead the way." Ryan held out his arm for Aden to lead them up the stairs.

"I don't know how you two have accomplished anything when you constantly bicker like women."

Ryan patted his back. "Behind every great man is a bickering woman, my son. We get the job done for each other."

"Seriously, get a room."

Julia

Hard rapping on her door made Julia shoot right up in her bed, her heart raced in her chest. After Anna's false contraction scare, Julia decided to close her eyes for a bit but according her clock she had been sleeping for hours. If Anna was having her baby without her, Julia was going to feel awful.

"Julia!" The person continued to knock fiercely.

"For god's sake, just come in!" she yelled back. Running her fingers through her hair she was somewhat horrified it was a massive mess.

Caleb burst into her room wearing only gym shorts, a back holster and pistols sticking out of his pockets.

"Get up, we need to evacuate."

"What?" She didn't even bother acting embarrassed by being in her nightgown with messed hair. She rummaged through her dresser and pulled on pants. "What's happening?"

"The Risen are here. They are raiding the Domus."

"Why would they bother? There are barely any Warriors here."

"I don't know, but we need to get as many of us as we can and use a portal out of here." Caleb handed her a pistol from his pocket and they ran towards Colette's room. Julia knocked on the door and was greeted to a fully geared up Colette. She rolled her eyes at Julia and ran back into her room, tossing Julia a flak jacket.

"You will never learn, will you?"

"We are sort of in a hurry," Julia countered.

"You can take two seconds to insure you don't get shot in the chest. Put it on and go get Anna. I will find whoever I can."

Caleb shook his head. "No, we need to stick together Lettie."

Julia looked between the two of them while they had a silent stare down. Neither looked as if they would back down and it grew a little awkward standing here.

"What's going on?" she finally asked.

"Nothing," Colette said decidedly. "I'm going. Tell everyone to meet in Yate, England."

Caleb was obviously not going to back down.

"We are sticking together. I don't want you running around in here alone."

"We are wasting time."

"You are wasting time."

"What the hell is going on with you two?" Julia nearly stomped her foot like a child trying to get some attention.

Colette smiled grimly but pulled both Julia and Caleb into a run. Julia briefly made eye contact with Caleb as they ran and he had a satisfying sort of smirk on his lips. She had little time to ponder the implications because gunfire went off down the hall hitting portraits of Warriors past.

Holes ripped through the paintings, mutilating them to the point they were not recognizable. She threw herself into a doorway as did Caleb and Colette and dared to peak around the wall. Three men in black gear and cloaks marched their way towards them with their guns held ready.

As soon as she tried to move, bullets ricocheted off the wall beside her and she pulled out of view with her back against the door.

"On three?" Julia called over to Caleb and Colette.

"Yep."

"Yeah."

"One… two…" Julia took a deep breath. "Three!"

All three invaders went down from a shot to the head in an instant. Julia jogged over to one of the men and stripped him of his weapons before they made their way to Anna's room. If they had any chance of making it out of here, she would need more than just one pistol.

Her feet smacked painfully against the floor as she walked barefoot over the fallen debris. She hoped they weren't bleeding but as soon as she turned a corner, she tripped over a body lying on the floor. The midwife that had checked on Anna earlier was motionless, her white uniform bloodied from being riddled by bullets.

Julia scrambled to stand but slipped in the blood that puddled on the floor. Caleb caught her arm and hauled her up.

"Oh, my gods…"

Shots began to fire throughout the building.

"Keep moving," Colette grunted.

As soon as they got to Anna and Damian's room, she shoved the door open and locked it behind them. Tears streaked down her cheeks silently, just knowing that more of their friends were being murdered right now and there was little they could do about it. Their numbers were stretched few and far between with most of the Immortals in the mortal world.

"What the hell is happening out there?" Anna's voice came from her wardrobe closet. The poor woman was clutching her swollen belly as she stepped back into view and her brow was drenched in sweat.

"We need to go, now." Caleb guarded the door.

Anna crossed her arms which was less than intimidating given she used her belly as an armrest.

"Again, I ask, what is going on?"

"The Risen are attacking the Domus." Colette rummaged through Anna's clothes. She found boots and tossed them to Julia. "Get those on. Let me help you get dressed, Anna."

To her surprise, Anna let Colette dress and arm her as much as she could stand. Julia changed into Anna's gear after Colette practically chucked it at her. Looking Caleb up and down, Anna waddled her way to the armoire and tossed Caleb, Damian's spare gear.

"Might be a little big on you, but it's better than you running around in your shorts."

Caleb quickly began to get dressed while Julia laced up her boots. "I don't get it, why are they attacking us here? There is no advantage anymore."

"Tear down morale? I don't know." Colette shrugged. "What I do know is that they don't care who is in their way. Not even women and children are safe."

"We need to get Anna out of here. Colette, you take her to Yate and we will try to help the rest of the Immortals." Caleb tried to take charge but the look on Colette and Anna's face gave no indication they were going to listen.

"We are going to help." Anna crossed her arms again.

"You are with child," Caleb said.

"I'm not made of porcelain."

"You are not staying here and that is final." Unfortunately, Caleb didn't have a very demanding presence, so Anna just laughed and shook her head at him.

"Let Anna come, we are wasting time and that means more people are dying," Julia huffed. "We are all dressed and ready to go so let's get going!"

Apparently, Julia had the demanding sort of voice that rallied the troops because they all filed up against the wall by the door. Caleb opened the door and peaked out, waving everyone on once he made sure the coast was clear. They went down the hallways, knocking on each door they knew to be occupied.

"Janett?" No answer.

"Rosa?"

"Luca?"

Door after door and a few skirmishes later they had at least ten people in tow. Once they piled safely into an empty room, Julia threw a crystal in the air.

"Yate, England."

The portal opened and they herded their people into it. "Luca, look after them." The tanned dark-haired man nodded and led the last woman through the portal as it closed.

"That can't be everyone?" Anna heaved.

"Either they fled already, or we saw them on the ground." Caleb scowled. "I'll do one more check and meet you back here."

"I'll go with you." Colette followed him out the door leaving Anna and Julia alone.

"How's the baby?" Julia asked after she locked the door.

Anna rubbed her belly. "Well, he is kicking his heart out and putting his foot in my ribs but other than that he's okay."

Julia could only imagine what that would feel like. Having

a little human body moving within, so innocent to the evils of the world yet awaiting the endless possibilities and wonders of life.

"Do you think Ryan will ever want one?" Anna asked unexpectedly.

Caught off guard, Julia fumbled with her words. "Well… uh… I'm not sure. I mean, I think so."

Anna grinned. "Yeah, once he sees this kid, that boy is so gonna knock you up."

"So crude."

"So I've been told."

"Check in there!" voices from outside the door yelled.

Julia blocked Anna's path from in front of the door with her gun held ready. The banging from outside the door grew louder and she could tell the frame was giving way. Anna's hand was gripping her shoulder tightly, but she didn't notice the pain of it. The continuous banging set her nerves on fire.

"What are we going to do?" Anna whispered.

"Just stay behind me."

Splinters of wood floated to the ground as the door burst open tearing the frame to shreds. Her finger squeezed the trigger and the bodies began to fall.

Chapter XI

Ryan

"WHAT IN THE WORLD?" Ryan gasped once they reached the top of the steps.

"It looks like Alexandria," Damian said as he stared in shock.

Tall columns with elaborate floral capitals were brightly painted, the walls were covered with religious and mythological scenes. White marble floors stretched throughout the building with tall open windows making the atmosphere light and airy. It was a close replica of a palace long lost to the bottom of the sea.

Ryan walked to the nearest carved and painted scene in the wall, running a gloved hand over the etches. It was a scene depicting the Gallic Wars.

"Portraying Roman wars in an Egyptian fresco. Odd."

"Well, the Roman's did a mosaic of you," Damian pointed out.

He couldn't argue with that. The Romans were always taking the best of other civilizations and calling it their own. Still, it was odd to see Roman legions with their plumed helmets and shields painted in the flat stylized tradition.

"I think we better get moving unless you feel the need to gawk some more?" Aden tapped his foot impatiently.

They moved along the floor as quietly as possibly. Regrettably, they stuck out like sore thumbs with their black gear against the vast light colors that adorned the entire building. His boots were thankfully made for stealth, otherwise he was afraid he might squeak his way down the hall.

"Where is everyone?" Damian asked quietly.

Aden merely shrugged as they continued down the hall. Ryan kept an eye out for anybody, jumping slightly when he heard a large crash come from within a double-doored room. The three of them hid behind a massive column just as the doors burst open with Marc marching out of the room. Ryan clenched his teeth. Just seeing the man he once considered as a brother brought a flush of fury throughout his body.

"How were they not there?" Marc yelled. "You continue to fail me over and over, Phillip."

"How can I possibly control where he is?" Phillip roared back. "The bastard is probably off drinking in excess."

"You are heavily mistaken about his character." Marc flipped over a bear-clawed table. It crashed down near their column but drew no further attention. "The man has changed in all ways since we knew him. He's no longer self-absorbed or overindulgent. He is stronger than ever. A man of his stature with an important mission is dangerous."

"I am fully aware of how dangerous Alexander can be. It doesn't change the fact that he wasn't in the Domus and nowhere to be found though," Phillip said.

"Find him or I will send you back to the depths of Hell where I found you." Even from here Ryan could hear the tension in his words. As the silence built up between the two men, Ryan grew impatient. He wanted to attack now but Aden pulled him back and shook his head.

"Make your threats all you want, but the fact of the matter is, you need me. Be mindful of your disrespect."

"It is you who must be mindful," Marc spat. "Now get out of my sight."

Phillip stomped down the hall with his back to Ryan. It was a miracle he didn't look back at Marc, otherwise they would have been spotted. Once the man's cloak swiped past a corner Ryan tried to come out from his hiding spot until he was held back once again by Aden.

"What are you doing?" Ryan whispered through clenched teeth.

"The General is guarded at all times. There are members of his elite force in that room." Aden nodded towards the doors that were open.

"So?" Ryan asked.

"You may be exceptionally skilled, but you are no match for ten men that have been brought up from childhood purely to protect their master."

"Wanna bet?" Ryan wagered.

"No," Damian answered. "So, what do we do?"

"I know what to do." Ryan embraced Damian quickly before stepping out from behind the column. "Hello, Marcus. So good to see you."

Marc had his back to Ryan but he slowly turned around with an unnerving smile that made Ryan's heart drop.

"Hello, Alexander. I see my plan was executed perfectly." His eyes shifted to Ryan's side.

Ryan turned around to see Damian thrust to the ground with his hands bound behind him. Aden stood triumphantly with his heel digging into the middle of Damian's back, a gun pointed down towards his head. His smile infuriated Ryan to no end but when he moved for his gun Aden clicked his tongue at him.

"I wouldn't do that if I were you."

"You evil little bastard," Ryan sneered.

"Right on all counts," Aden agreed. "Though, I don't know why you are so surprised. The trick was not letting you know until the last moment, so this damn collar didn't kill me. Now hands up."

Ryan reluctantly put his hands in the air as a heavily armored man marched straight towards Aden and removed his collar. Damian's cheek was pressed against the ground, but he managed to look at Ryan. The guilt he felt from that look almost overwhelmed him. Damian knew not to trust Aden in the slightest, but he'd hoped his son could change. He was utterly wrong and it may cost him and his friend's life.

"So, what was that little show we just saw?" Ryan asked.

"Something to make you feel as if you were actually succeeding. The trick was to separate you and Damian to prevent you from killing Aden. I knew you wouldn't resist attacking me as soon as you saw me. I wasn't kidding when I said you changed, yet you are still as vengeful as ever."

"How did you know I was even here?"

"I put a tracker in Aden's arm. New technology is so convenient."

Ryan's cheeks became warm from the embarrassment of being out maneuvered. He let his feelings for Aden cloud his judgment. How could he be so stupid? He knew he captured Aden too easily and the clarity of it all made him feel like an idiot.

"You planned for him to be captured and tortured, didn't you?" Ryan grimaced at the thought.

"Aden was willing. He was to give you information of my whereabouts after we planned when we would destroy each site. I wanted to break your spirit and I think we did well."

Ryan wanted to scream at it all. Not only were all those innocent people killed because of him, but Aden willingly let himself be mutilated just to get him here.

"You played me," he said to himself.

"And you fell for it so easily. It wasn't difficult to play off your emotions," Aden answered.

Before Ryan could retort, his hands were captured behind his back and put into cold metal chains. Guards flanked him from behind. He tried to struggle against them until Aden couched down over Damian and put the gun flush to his head.

The smile on his lips was sinister. Ryan stopped resisting. He wouldn't be the cause of Damian's death no matter his pride. Besides, the hall had begun to fill with about twenty members of the Risen leaving them completely at their mercy.

"A little excessive, don't you think?" Ryan glanced around the armed men that caged him in.

"You are someone that should never be underestimated," Marc said. "Bring him."

They were led back into the room Marc had been and as soon as his feet stepped through the threshold, Ryan was hit with panic. The room was dark with chains and devices of torture lined the walls. It looked almost identical to the room they had tortured him and Damian in.

He struggled against the men that held him.

"No."

The memory of those days would never fade. It was probably one of the many reasons he couldn't do the same to Aden. He knew the pain all too well and it scarred him deep within, like a wound that would never heal.

Ryan slipped a pin out of his back pocket that he carried for situations like this. Picking at the lock on the shackles around his wrists proved difficult as the men pushed him towards hanging chains. Once he was free, he elbowed them both in the nose. He barely had time to pull out his gun when it was knocked from his hand by a swift kick from Marc. Before he could react, he was met with a strong blow to the head that turned his world dizzy.

Countless boots ravaged his body as soon as he hit the ground until they abruptly stopped. "And that is why I have so many men to guard against you."

Rolling to his back with a metallic taste in his mouth Ryan said, "If you are going to kill me just do it. There is no need to torture me, Marc."

Several men heaved Ryan's weakened body up, raising his hands above his head and chained them up in the air. He was effectively and completely at their mercy. Judging by Damian's busted lip, he must have tried to fight them off while Ryan was getting stomped to oblivion but neither prevailed.

"I have no intention of torturing you." Marc stood directly in front of Ryan. "I have other plans."

When Marc turned his back to him, Ryan brought his feet up and wrapped his legs around Marc's neck. He squeezed as tightly as he could until another blow struck the back of his head. At this point, he was sure he had a concussion or something, but it was damn worth it.

Even through his coughing Marc managed to croak out, "Chain their legs down!"

As his men scrambled to follow orders, Ryan took great satisfaction watching Marc's anger grow. They stared one another down until Marc forced himself to regain his composure. He had a role to play in front of his men and by being vulnerable to attack threatened that role.

"Are you okay, sir?" Aden asked.

Ryan couldn't help but laugh.

"This is who you see as a god?" Ryan looked at the men around the room. "Nearly choked to death by a chained man. Not so invulnerable, are you?"

"Merely caught off guard," Marc muttered as he smoothed down his cloak.

"Wouldn't be the first time," Damian muttered.

"You two are quite the pair." Marc glared between them. "Never serious, are you?"

Ryan and Damian both scoffed at the remark. "Do you not remember yourself? The mortal man known to be wild in his affairs and a free spirit? Untamed?" Ryan shook his head with a smile.

"Many lifetimes ago. Many loved ones taken from me as well."

"A fact known to us all yet the madman before us broke instead of fighting through it," Damian interjected.

"I've watched my family die time and time again, even those who were kin to you as well."

"Once upon a time we were tied by blood, but all of those we shared are now part of this earth. Your wife and children, my ancestors, were laid to waste due to your selfish ambitions," Ryan spat.

"It wasn't only my ambition." Marc glared. "My wife wanted it too."

"I no longer care about your reasoning for losing your shit," Ryan growled.

"That's fine." He heard a door open, leaving Marc with an unsettling grin on his lips. "I have a few surprises for you."

"I'm sure you—"

Ryan's mouth went slack as a figure came into view from behind and stood before him. A woman he hadn't seen in years. One of the only women to break his heart.

"Artemisia?" She was a chained captive as well. Her dark hair hung meekly around her face yet that same look of regality remained in her eyes. Ryan didn't take his eyes off her to speak to Marc.

"Why is she here?"

"Take a wild guess." Marc's voice dripped with satisfaction.

"I don't know." His voice grew smaller.

Aden placed a hand on Ryan and Artemisia's shoulders connecting the three with his touch. "Father, meet my mother."

"You said your mother died." Ryan swallowed the bile threatening to rise from his throat.

"She did," Aden mused. "We brought her back from the Underworld."

"How could you possibly do that?" Damian spoke quietly.

"She was reincarnated physically and we called upon her soul to enter this mortal's body," Marc answered. "We don't shy away from dark powers here in order to get what we want."

"Then raise your wife from the Underworld and let this madness end," Ryan pleaded.

"That requires a direct descendant who is her doppel-ganger. You know what? I'm not going into details with you. It was purely chance that this woman existed for Artemisia to take over."

"Okay, you did all of this and for what? To make me squirm and uncomfortable?"

"Basically," Aden chuckled. "But also, because I wanted you both to see what you've created out of me."

"Aden pledged to do as I told him with one request—to make you suffer as much as he suffered. Bringing back Artemisia was part of his vengeance." Marc shrugged.

"What did I ever do to make you, of all people hate me?" Ryan nearly yelled. It was a question he had wondered for some time now. "We were as brothers for hundreds of years and then you fake your death. Now you take pride in my suffering?"

Marc clasped his hands behind his back as he paced before them. "My only negative feeling towards you is the fact you are not on my side. I tried to get you to join us and you refused."

"This justifies you torturing me and Damian? By putting your daughter at the mercy of your pet who relished in raping her over and over again just to piss me off?"

Marc's eyes widened at his last comment and his attention immediately fell on Aden whose face paled in an instant.

"You didn't know?" Ryan shook his head. "You left her at the mercy of an animal without a soul. What did you expect?"

"You have no room to talk," Artemisia said breaking her silence.

It took Ryan a moment to answer her and when he did the shakiness in his voice was apparent, "I had no idea."

"Would it have mattered?" she hissed.

"Yes. I would have been there for you both." Ryan's voice trembled.

"Like you were there for your other children? Your wife? When they were murdered by your own friends?" She fumed.

"Do you have any idea how I felt about you? You weren't just another woman to me." He hated that she never truly saw it. "I would have done anything you asked of me. I loved you, Artemisia. I would have been there for both of you both, but you left me without a word as to why."

She looked taken aback and confusion flashed in her eyes as if studying her memories for any sign of his truth.

"It doesn't matter what you would have done. He was always cruel, even as a child."

"Maybe because you beat him." It hurt saying the words, but her actions weren't forgivable when it came to Aden's upbringing.

"Beat him?" She looked genuinely shocked as she glanced between her son and Ryan. "I never beat him."

Aden snorted trying to hold back his laugh. His amusement grew until he started to laugh so hard that he clutched his stomach.

"Oh, Ryan. Are you so thick in the head to have believed anything I've said?"

Everything was a lie. The little bastard played with him how he knew best. Making him believe he had a terrible childhood. Making Ryan believe it was his entire fault Aden had turned evil.

"You are sadistic." Ryan hung his head back and smiled. Not out of amusement but he was so annoyed with himself for being fooled by Aden, that he couldn't help but smile.

"I did everything for him. Loved him and cherished him. Tried to get him help for his impulses and what thanks did I get?" Artemisia asked. "I get smothered in my sleep by a pillow."

"Aden." Ryan brought his head up to look him directly in the eyes. "I swear to all the gods, I will end you."

A syringe went into Ryan's neck and he began to get drowsy in an instant. The last thing he saw was Aden's blade thrust into Artemisia's belly and her body collapsing to the ground.

"You will never get the chance."

They rolled around the grassy hill, each trying to find dominance over the other as their lips clashed in feverish passion. He never gave up the chase for this woman until she finally blessed him with her attention. He vowed he would never hurt her. Not that he could even attempt to try.

She was too strong to let a man break her down. That strength is what drew him to her in the first place. Still, he would never tire of her stubbornness or ability to take him down in a spar.

He found himself pinned to the ground. Arms raised above his head with a goddess upon his lap. There was no way he would fight her. She wanted the high ground and he was willing to give it to her. There wasn't a single thing he wouldn't do for her.

"You aren't even trying now," she pouted playfully before adjusting his pinned hands to rest on her hips.

"I find myself enjoying you in control of my body." He squeezed lightly on her hips and relished in her eyes fluttering closed in pleasure from his touch. So many years had passed since he felt his heart open to a woman, but he would gladly give her his soul if she asked for it.

Running her hands down his bare chest, she clicked her tongue.

"I doubt you relinquish your control often."

"Never, in fact."

"Why now?"

He sat up with her still siting upon his lap, brushing her long dark hair over her bare shoulder and out of his way. There was no helping him, he was smitten by her. He kissed along her collarbone until her hand in his hair yanked his head back, forcing his chin up.

She tasted his neck, nipping every so often while she took what she wanted, and he let her.

"Answer me." Her breath was heavy with want.

"I admire your strength." He groaned when she took his bottom lip between her teeth. Slowly he was released from her grasp and it sent a chill down his spine. "I will never make you surrender that strength to me and I won't ever take you for granted. You've captivated me and I hope you never forget that, Artemisia."

Chapter XII

Damian

He awoke completely unaware of his location. The room he was in was like a cage from the past. Dirty stone walls on three sides with bars acting as the fourth. He was trapped in a hell he thought was long gone.

Sitting up on the hard-wooden bed in his cell, his back ached from the discomfort. He realized what he was wearing when his feet hit the ground. Armor, from days past when he and Ryan called themselves gladiators.

"What the hell?" Even his shoes were replaced with sandals from ancient times.

"Damian?" a voice called out from a cell next to him.

He stiffly stood up and wrapped his hands around the cold bars of his cell.

"Ryan? Is that you?"

"No shit," Ryan laughed but there was no humor behind it. "Are you wearing the lovely ancient attire as well?"

"Unfortunately. I thought our days of man skirts and loin-cloths were over with." Damian held his wrists up. They were each wrapped with leather on top of cloth. A wide leather belt covered his waistline with metal plates for extra protection against an attack.

Additionally, metal shoulder guards were strapped on, as well as leg guards that ran from his knee to above his ankle. Cloth was placed under each to provide padding from chafing although Damian had to wonder why his captors cared so much about that. He was dressed for battle. One he knew they wanted him to lose.

"My thighs look great." Ryan was trying to break the tension, but Damian couldn't find the humor in this situation.

"We are obviously meant to fight today. I highly doubt the odds are in our favor."

"Where do you suppose we are?" Ryan asked.

"I can answer that, gentlemen." The unmistakable voice was overly ecstatic.

"Aden," Damian hissed, "what is the meaning of this?"

"Damian, I know you are smarter than that. You both are going to fight in the old style. Swords smashing, blood flying, all for the entertainment of the General and our followers. I have always wanted to see gladiators in action. I hope to bring it back as a favorite past time of our people. Watch our enemies fight to the death for sport. Good times."

Damian's grip on the bars tightened. He could feel his pulse thumping in his neck. This was not something he missed although he knew Ryan did.

"You little shit."

Guards in modern gear walked into the dungeon. "Open the gates. It is time to begin." Aden grinned from ear to ear. "I will see you both from the VIP section. Ta."

As Aden walked away, he and Ryan were forcefully yanked from their cells.

"Get your fucking hands off me," Ryan growled.

"Move." One of the guards pushed Damian towards a long dark hall lined with stone.

"This is a freaking nightmare," Damian said quietly. It was almost as if they went back in time two thousand years.

He looked at Ryan. His metal armor was colored black with designs of Zeus etched into them. Damian's armor gleamed bright silver, decorated with scenes of Poseidon. Two brothers fighting side-by-side.

"I don't believe my armor was this fancy back then," Damian declared.

"Nor mine," Ryan agreed as they both looked down the hall to their awaited fate.

They were both pushed from behind. "Move."

It wasn't a long walk, but the roar of a crowd grew louder as they made their way towards what Damian figured to be an arena. How it was made, he was unsure. All he could speculate was that the General had a lot of manpower to do what he wanted. If he wanted a gladiatorial arena, he was going to get one.

Reaching the end of the hall, they were met with tall metal gates with guards on each side of the doors. As soon as the men saw Damian and Ryan, they began to pull the gates open with excited grins on their faces. Before he could get a word out, they were pushed out onto the sands and came face to face with a nightmare.

"We are in the fucking coliseum." Ryan gapped as he looked around the grandly lit arena.

"How is this possible?"

"Marc must have restored it."

"Or built a new one." Damian looked at the thousands of people that filled the stone seating. They seemed to be the only ones wearing ancient attire and it felt odd to be so exposed to the masses.

He and Ryan walked towards the arena seating where the

most important people watched from. The imperial box was filled with Aden and a few others but one man towered above the rest. Marc. Even from a distance, Damian could see the look of triumph on his face as the crowd roared with approval.

Marc held up his hands, effectively silencing the crowd with just a gesture.

"Today is a day we have all waited for." He grinned as the crowd clapped but continued once it went silent. "Tonight, we shall witness the fall of our enemy and find ourselves rid of those who would fight against us. These men, these leaders of the rebellion have been captured and brought here for one purpose. To die in the arena and provide warning to all those who would see our cause obliterated."

Damian watched as thousands of people cheered. Could he really have swayed these people into believing him? For the longest time he thought it was fear that drove them to betrayal of the gods but as he looked out into the crowd, they seemed… excited.

"These men once fought on grounds such as this. Purely for entertainment of those that enslaved them and now, today, they shall repeat the past and become nothing but a distant memory. May this be a warning to those who fight against us. Even their strongest will fall to the power of the Risen!"

More cheers filled the arena, louder than before. Damian looked to Ryan who didn't meet his eyes. Instead, Ryan's gaze was fixed on the imperial box with his fists clenched and fury in his eyes.

"And who would be our opponents?" Ryan yelled at the General. "Who would so boldly claim our lives before even making the attempt? I would love to see what amazing warrior you have come up with that could possibly take us on."

Marc grinned widely as the crowd went dead silent. Even

as he stood a prisoner to the General, Ryan elicited fear from those who opposed him. His celebrity had grown immensely, even to the Risen it would seem.

"Ryan, the leader of the rebellion, would like to know his opponent." The General laughed loudly but no one joined in his amusement. "Look to your right and you have your answer."

Damian felt like his heart just dropped from his chest, into the sand and was then stomped on as he looked over at his brother. Ryan's head dropped for a brief moment until their eyes connected. The look Ryan gave him was unreadable, yet one thing was certain, his life was about to be ended by the sword of his best friend.

"Oh, yes. You will fight one another to the death." The General grinned. "It will be a sight for the ages."

"What makes you think we would do this? Fight brother against brother purely for your entertainment? You are insane!" Ryan yelled angrily. His eyes were once again fixated upon the man they equally hated.

"I knew you would be against such a spectacle, yet I am a man that always gets what he wants." He clapped his hands and there was a brief scuffle in the imperial box until his purpose became clear. "Consider this your motivation."

Anna, heavy with their child, held onto her belly as she stood next Julia. They both had knives at their throats. An anger like he never felt raged within him. Pure hatred coursed through his body just looking at Marc's triumphant face.

"You would murder your own daughter and a woman heavily pregnant for sport?" Ryan yelled.

"My daughter has proven to be a disappointment," the General yelled back. "This other one holds no meaning to me, but to you both, they hold the world. You will fight each other to the death or see both of their lives slowly and painfully ended in front of you."

Two men appeared in the arena from behind them carrying swords, which were quickly thrust into their grips. Ryan and Damian turned to face one another but neither could strike. Damian's hand started to hurt from gripping the sword so firmly from his nerves. It felt like his body was seizing up from anxiety.

"What's the plan?" he asked.

"There isn't a plan, Damian." Ryan looked up at the box and back to Damian with a heavy breath. "There isn't a way out of this one."

"There is always a way," Damian urged. "Someone will come—"

"No one is coming," he interrupted.

"They will."

"They won't."

"I cannot fight you, Ryan." Damian's face felt red. "I couldn't kill you even if I tried."

"Have you two come to a decision?" the General yelled down at them. Damian could see the look in his face from here. He was victorious. "Either you fight and save your women, or all of you will die. Leading to the annihilation of your rebellion once and for all."

"Why don't you just kill us and end it yourself?" Damian yelled for the first time. "What is the point of this?"

"The point is to see my enemy destroy themselves. The point is to have your followers watch as their leaders kill another and to prove that I am superior. I have the power and you two are nothing compared to me. Even the resistance's strongest cannot survive my wrath."

Damian finally noticed a large screen hanging on one end of the coliseum showing them standing in the arena. He and

Ryan were being broadcasted live for everyone to see. Marc planned to show their execution, just as they were going to do to him. Ironic.

"If we do this," Ryan yelled, "the victor and the women are set free?"

"You have my word." The General smiled. "Is that your answer?"

Ryan's eyes met Damian's. There was an intensity that wasn't there before.

"I am sorry, brother."

"What? No!" Damian shouted.

Without warning, Ryan swung his sword down hard towards Damian's head. He was barely able to block it until Ryan once more thrust his weapon at him. Damian thwarted him, shuffling his feet to escape his friend's blade. The clashing of steel echoed throughout the arena over the roaring crowd as they fought.

"Ryan!" His sword thrust towards Damian's chest. "Don't do this. Don't let him win."

"Our choice is taken from us," Ryan grunted between attacks. Damian swung his sword at Ryan's midsection, but he jumped back out of his reach. "If we don't do this, he will kill them. I will not have more blood on my hands, Damian."

Ryan twisted his body using his leg to take Damian's feet from under him. Landing on his back, the air was knocked out of his lungs before Ryan brought his sword down on him. Damian blocked it just in time and swung his leg as Ryan did, effectively knocking him to the ground.

Hurriedly they both scrambled upright with their blades in hand as they danced around each other slashing. A cut here and there. The crowd roared in approval every time blood appeared.

Damian grew tired, he knew Ryan could have taken him at

least five times already, but he never did. He was biding his time or making enough of a spectacle that Damian didn't look completely inadequate at the task. Either way, he was giving Damian an honorable death and he would be forever thankful for that.

Fighting Ryan was exhausting. He had to take a second to catch his breath and he merely held his sword out in front of him instead of provoking more action. He was mistaken to think that Ryan would grant him such leniency so instead of a break he charged at Damian. Before he could fully react though, Ryan had run straight into Damian's sword.

The crowd went silent.

Ryan dropped his sword, standing impaled in front of Damian and making no attempt to fight.

"No!" Damian roared.

Ryan's eyes went wide and his breath hitched in his chest. Placing his hands on Damian's shoulders, he pulled their bodies closer together until the sword's hilt was against Ryan's belly. Damian tried to pull the sword from his body, but Ryan stopped his hand.

"What have you done?" Tears spilled down his cheeks.

Ryan grinned. His teeth no longer white, but instead stained with his own blood. His hands fell to his side, no longer having the strength to stop Damian as he pulled the sword from his body. The sound of Ryan's flesh giving way to the blade made Damian sick to his stomach.

"You won." He collapsed to his knees and Damian dropped down with him. Ryan cupped the back of Damian's neck, their foreheads pressed together. "Take care of your son... take care of Julia."

"Ryan!" Damian pulled back to look at Ryan, blood dripped out of the corner of his mouth and Damian tried to wipe it away. "Why? The world needs you. I need you and so does Julia."

Ryan tried to laugh but it turned into a cough filled with blood.

"No," he choked back, "they need you… Raise that baby…" He coughed again. "Raise that baby to be good. To be just."

"Ryan!" He fell over but Damian caught him in his arms.

"Take care of her."

"Ryan!"

"I have always loved you Hephaestion… above all others." Ryan's hand tried to reach up towards Damian's cheek, but it never made it. The life slowly ebbed from his eyes as he looked up at Damian, a small smile playing on his lips.

"Ryan!" Damian screamed as Ryan's body went limp in his arms. He shook him, begging him to wake up but he wouldn't. "Alexander!"

CHAPTER XIII

Damian

H IS STRENGTH WAS DIMINISHED. His eyes grew heavy from weeping for what seemed like hours, yet only minutes passed. The limp form of Ryan was hugged against his chest and all Damian could think was how this had to be a trick. This couldn't be real.

But when he pulled his face from his best friend's shoulder and looked at his stilled face once more, he knew it to be true. Damian had witnessed thousands of men dying and the way Ryan looked mirrored them all. Lifeless. He was gone for real.

The other half of his soul was destroyed. Though Damian held the sword, Ryan had taken it upon himself to ensure Damian lived for the future. A future Damian couldn't imagine without his best friend in it and yet it would have to be.

Ryan's blood warmed Damian's legs as it dripped down to his bare skin. He couldn't remember where he was until Marc's booming voice came into earshot. As if the sound returned to him to the present, the roar of the crowd blasted his ears until it dimmed at the sound of Marc's voice telling them to be silent.

Damian looked up at the man he once held dear. He was cocky, surprised, and ultimately triumphant as his grin spread from ear to ear.

"Well, that was unexpected. I hardly pegged Ryan for a martyr. Self-preservation was something even I could admire in the man."

Damian's body shook uncontrollably. He had been angry before and sad many times, but this feeling was what Ryan described as 'seeing red'. His levelheaded tendencies were out the window and all he wanted was the death of Marc. A long, slow, painful death. Marc would die by his hand for this and he would relish in it.

"Silence?" Marc laughed with actual joy. "You have finally defeated him, Damian. Sure, he practically took his own life, but you held your own. I suppose he knew he was on the losing side and took the easy way out." The crowd roared in approval, clapping and hollering at the insults Marc threw towards Ryan.

"You are the coward!" Damian yelled. "Putting brother against brother for sport. Not facing either of us yourself and threatening to murder your own daughter and a pregnant woman. Why would anyone follow someone so callous with life? Who's to say you won't kill every follower you have if it pleased you to do so?"

"If I so wished it, I would. But what would be the point in it? This was a lesson." Marc looked out into the crowd with his arms raised high. "A lesson to those who oppose us. You will not survive this war, especially now that the one man who could deliver you from my grasp is lying in a pool of his own blood. Give up, as Ryan gave up and maybe, just maybe I will spare you all from a fate worse than death."

Damian laid Ryan's body gently on the ground. His eyes were still staring off into the sky in a frozen gaze, his lips still parted from his last breath. A piece of Damian was lost from this moment on and he knew it wasn't for the better.

"We will never give into you. You have shown nothing to the rebels except a reminder of what we are fighting for. Ryan gave up his life so others may live on. He showed us there is still good in this world and as long as it remains, there is a chance you will be defeated."

"Enough of your dramatics." Marc gave a signal with his hand and armed men emerged through the gates, surrounding Damian in the arena. "Toss the body into a river and kill that pitiful excuse of a man. After that, make sure his women follow the same fate."

Julia must have managed to free herself from her captor because she punched her father in the side of the head.

"You said he would be freed!"

Marc regained himself from his attack and grasped Julia's throat with his large hand. Leaning into her ear he spoke to her quietly but neither father nor daughter looked pleased. She tried to swing at him again, but his reach was too long for her.

"Let this be a warning," Marc roared at the silent crowd. "No one, not even my daughter, is safe from treason against my will. Feed her to the lions below. I will not have my future defiled with pathetic offspring any longer."

Damian ran towards the imperial box as men began to shove Julia and Anna away from the arena. Both fought tooth and nail refusing to follow the orders of their captors and thank the gods not one blow was landed on Anna's stomach. When he got closer however, he could see the agony on Anna's face as she clutched her abdomen.

Men rushed towards Damian. He was pulled every which direction and he briefly caught a glimpse of Ryan's body being dragged away by chains that were now clasped around his ankles. He clawed and fought to get to Ryan's body but the people around him grew too thick for him to move. He couldn't do anything to help anyone. Ryan killed the wrong man.

The crowed was screaming wildly at the sight of them

unsuccessfully fighting to get free. Someone grabbed a handful of Damian's hair and yanked him painfully towards the gates away from where Ryan's body was being dragged. Fists landed against his body and his minimal armor wasn't helping at all.

Damian finally fell to his knees from the blows that rained down upon him. He looked up into the eyes of a light skinned man that held confliction in his eyes, yet his fist raised high for another blow. There would be no escaping this fate.

He prepared himself mentally for the hit until a loud explosion resonated throughout the night sky followed by a blinding flash of light that filled the entire arena. Once Damian was able to see again, he was sitting alone with Ryan's body in the fighting arena. His attackers were nowhere to be found and the crowd was in complete silence.

Marc's jaw had visibly dropped as he looked towards the skies. In fact everyone was. Damian looked up to see the floating forms of five gods decked out in their finest attire. He knew the gods rarely showed themselves in their divine form. He only ever saw them as men and women that could be mistaken as mere mortals, but right now the awe and beauty of the beings before him was arresting.

Zeus was in front of the other gods, his eyes fixated on Marc. His presence making the man seem minuscule. Then there was the Archangel Michael, who looked out at the crowd as a displeased parent would with his child. Next to Michael was Oden whose angered expression mirrored that of Zeus.

Horus, the Egyptian lord of the sky was on the other side of Zeus wearing his traditional face of a falcon and next to him was Buddha. Every single god was decked out in golden armor except of course Buddha who sported his large belly and minimal cloth. Never in all of his lifetime had he seen the gods come together like this before.

Damian looked towards Marc once more and he could tell words escaped the man. He had made a career of convincing the masses that the gods were no longer there for them, that they could care less about the people of the world, and that he was their one true god. Yet, the sight of so many divine beings before them had silenced all within this place of death.

"You will no longer taint my son with your evil," Zeus' voice boomed out within the stone walls. "The body of Alexander the Great will be given a proper end that a man of his caliber deserves. You have opened a very dangerous door, Marcus. One that will never again close."

Ryan's body began to lift in the air by an unseen force towards the gods.

"What are you doing?" Damian panicked as he watched helplessly.

"Fear not, Damian." Zeus used his modern name for some reason. "The mortals have you to lead them now. A decision your brother made and therefore must be respected in kind. I have faith you will prevail against this veil excuse for a human being."

Marc finally gained his voice and spoke with more authority than appeared on his face. "You see, the gods only care about those that are exceptional. They don't care about the common man or woman. Once these so-called gods are defeated, I will show kindness and compassion to all of my followers. I will not put those with wealth and affluence above the common—"

"Do shut up, will you?" Michael rolled his head in annoyance. "You care for no one save yourself."

"That, is where you are very wrong." Marc glared towards the angel.

"Enough," Buddha called out. "What we have proven here tonight is that we are indeed real. That our followers will reap proper rewards and that you, Marcus, are nothing but a child having a fit."

Before Marc could speak another word, the five gods raised their arms up high. Ryan's body floated above them and with another blinding flash of light they were all gone. Specks of black clouded Damian's vision and as he blinked them away, he took in his surroundings. He was back home in the Domus with Anna and Julia at his side.

The three of them took in the sight of one another before collapsing into each other's arms. The weight of their loss was too much to handle alone, even for a moment. They all instantly felt the void of not having Ryan here. Damian's body was wrapped tightly in the embrace of Julia and Anna. Ryan was forever gone from this world because of him.

His body shook from the emotion battling within him but when he looked at his hands the reality slapped him even harder in the face. The evidence of the deed clear as day with Ryan's blood still staining his hands. He'd killed him.

How could I do this?

His breathing grew ragged. He couldn't take his eyes from the blood on his body that didn't belong to him. This couldn't be real.

Julia took his head between her hands, but he could barely see her through his teary eyes.

"I am so sorry, Damian."

"Why?" His voice cracked. "You lost him as well and because of me."

"You lost your other half." She wiped away a tear with her thumb.

Damian collapsed into another mess of emotions. He felt tired and weak. His mind felt distant and he couldn't focus on anything around him. The pain of this loss was too much for his mind to handle.

So, he screamed. Screamed as loud as he could but he couldn't hear the sound through his inner turmoil. His throat grew sore and his chest heaved as tears rolled freely down his cheeks. Not a soul could make him stop wailing and he didn't want to even if he could. The pain was too much.

He was hardly aware of the frightened eyes of the women in front of him. Their hands tried to calm his broken soul to no avail. It would never be healed. He'd been by Ryan's side for thousands of years and now he was gone. Julia was right, he lost his other half and it was his own fault.

When his vision started to dim he welcomed the darkness as he black out.

His eyes fluttered open to the feeling of water being poured gently down his cheek. The smell of soap invaded his senses bringing him back to reality from the nightmare he kept reliving in his mind.

"Cato?" Damian's throat felt like he swallowed razor blades.

They were in an old-fashioned bathing house that was the size of a pool. The water was heated from below and provided much needed comfort to his aching body. They were alone in the bathhouse and Cato was at his side with a sponge, washing away the blood from Damian's cheek.

"I thought you lost your sanity for a while there," Cato said lowly.

"How did I get here?" Damian's hoarse voice was barely a whisper.

Cato came in front of Damian, silent tears flowed steadily down his cheeks but other than the tears his face lacked emotion.

"I found you screaming in a ball. Anna and Julia tried to comfort you, but you wouldn't stop screaming. Caleb and I tried to calm you down and we thought it worked once you went silent but then you didn't respond. You just sat there like a statue staring off into space as if you couldn't hear us. So, we brought you down here to wash the... to get you cleaned up."

Damian held up his hands, they were cleared of any sign of the deed and yet he could feel the sting of his betrayal. "My sword should have never been that close to him."

"The choice was taken from you."

Was it really though? He could have stood there and let Ryan cut him down. Ryan could have lived on to save the lives of everyone in this world and the women they both loved. "If I would have not fought back, he would be here instead of me."

Cato was silent for a moment, rinsing off Damian's body without complaint.

"Ryan did what he had to. Not only for us but for himself."

"What do you mean?" Damian felt anger rise within him. He didn't know if it was directed towards Cato or Ryan. "His death did nothing but doom us all."

Carefully mulling over his words Cato finally spoke, "Ryan knew you could live on to fulfill our mission. You are strong enough to get past this loss to save us all. I don't think Ryan could get past losing you."

"He is... was, stronger than me."

"Not in that sense." Cato lathered Damian's arms in soap. Dirt washed off into the pool showing scratches on his body he didn't realize were there. "Ryan would never, ever be able to lose you. He would kill himself before he even knew how to cope."

Damian knew Cato was right. Ryan nearly took his life for hitting Julia and although Ryan was a force to be reckoned with, he was so very vulnerable to heartache. Yet, Damian knew he could never accomplish what Ryan was meant to do.

"I cannot win this war without him."

"You don't have a choice," Cato said plainly. "This is your destiny and I will follow you to my death if I must. It is worth it and Ryan knew that."

I can't do this.

Damian wasn't a leader. He never was and never could be. He followed Ryan because he knew what to do even if Damian never agreed. Ryan was the strength of their people, even if he didn't want to be. There was no way in hell Damian could ever match up to him.

"Quit second guessing yourself." Cato gave his shoulder a gentle squeeze.

Damian tilted his head back while Cato washed out his hair. The grime of the day could be washed away. The evidence of his deeds could be sucked down the drain, but his soul would never feel clean. His body would never again feel the strength Ryan gave him. He was a shell of a man that no longer existed.

Damian understood why Ryan would never be able to get past this loss. Thoughts of death rolled around in his mind. A gun to the head. A knife to the heart. His damaged body spread across the train tracks leaving him unrecognizable.

It was almost soothing to think of the many ways he could end his life. He deserved it for what he had done. He deserved worse.

A man erupted into the bathhouse breaking Damian from his thoughts of suicide. He watched with detached interest as the man dropped to his knees at the edge of the pool with quick breaths.

"Damian, you must hurry, it's Anna."

CHAPTER XIV

Julia

"ANNA YOU MUST BREATHE." Julia urged her but Anna's brow was damp with sweat as she clutched her belly in desperation. "Let's get you on your bed."

"No. I need a healer and lots of pain medicine. Preferably some that doesn't let me feel a damn thing." Anna grimaced as another contraction must have hit her. They were getting closer and closer together and Julia knew that the baby was on its way very soon.

"I have already sent for them in Yate. I'm sorry Anna, but you are going to have your child naturally. It's too late for medicine."

Anna grabbed Julia's hand and squeezed it to the point of extreme pain. Surely her hand must have broken.

"Immortals can't die from medicine, get me the damn epidural."

Julia smiled weakly knowing very well what could happen to her.

"Sweet Anna, childbirth for us is exactly how it is for the mortals. My mother died from childbirth when she was on a mission but I will make sure the both of you will get through this safely."

Julia stripped Anna of her clothing and helped her into a long white gown before helping her lay down on the bed. Healers rushed in the room with their equipment and got to work on prepping for the new arrival. All the while, Anna kept glancing at Julia nervously and all she could do was give a reassuring nod and massage her back to ease some of the pain.

"Where's Damian?"

"I sent for him," Julia assured her but his state of mind might not be all there right now. Her own mind was holding on by a thread for Anna's sake. The reality of it was she wanted to collapse into a ball and cry. She hadn't been able to feel the entire force of Ryan's death due to the circumstances and it was eating away at her sanity.

She watched from above as the blade slipped so easily into his flesh like butter. There were so many times she had seen his skin pierced and marred, yet this was different. She could see even from afar the look in his eyes accepting death. It was obvious he stepped into the sword, even to her. Yet she didn't think she would ever be able to forgive Damian for holding that blade in place.

Anna cried out loud from another contraction and her eyes overflowed with tears. Julia grabbed a cloth and dabbed her cheeks and forehead.

"It will be over soon. Just breathe," she cooed.

"Where the fuck is he?" Anna screamed. As if answering her call Damian and Cato ran into the room.

"Anna." Damian ran to her side nearly pushing Julia out of the way while Cato remained in the doorway. "My love, I'm here."

Julia moved around to the other side of the bed and stared down at Damian's bent over body as he leaned his cheek against Anna's hand. His eyes were swollen and red with trails of tears that still flowed steadily over the brim of his lids and onto the white cotton sheets.

"I didn't think you would—" She cried out again and the female healer spread Anna's legs and her hand disappeared up Anna's gown.

"Anna, your water just broke and you're already fully dilated. It's time to start pushing."

"It's too early." Damian paled.

"The child is coming now. It will be fine. She is far enough along." The healer responded sullenly. "Now bare down and push with the next contraction."

Anna gritted her teeth and began to push with everything she had. Her body shook from the pressure and she held her breath until she couldn't push any longer. Julia desperately wanted to help her, but Damian was doing that for her. He kissed her forehead, wiped away her sweat and held her hand as she pushed and pushed.

"He's tearing me apart!" Anna cried.

Damian whispered in her ear, speaking words only meant for them to hear. Anna's eyes fluttered as he spoke and once it was time to push again, she looked determined.

"You can do this, love." Damian kissed her temple while smoothing back her untamed hairs.

After thirty minutes of screaming agony and encouragement from everyone, cries sounded throughout the room from the plump child that finally made his way into the world. Owen's dark hair was plastered to his head and his toothless mouth cried out in frustration from leaving his comfortable home inside his mother's belly.

Anna lay back limply against her pillows exhausted but as soon as the healer placed Owen in her arms, her eyes lit up like the sun. She cradled his little body against hers, kissing his head and looking up at Damian with pure love resonating from her eyes.

A stinging pain erupted in Julia's chest as she realized she would never be able to experience this with the one she loved. Ryan was lost to her and she would never give him a child. She would never see the love in his eyes as Damian had for Anna right now. Her breathing started to quicken as she felt anxiety build within her chest.

"Julia," Cato rubbed her arms from behind and spoke softly so the new parents wouldn't hear. "It will all be fine. I've got you."

"I can't..."

"You can." He took a ragged breath letting her know he was trying to hold himself together. "You are not alone in the pain of his loss, baby sister. We will get through this together. I promise you, but now is not the time." He hugged her tightly against his large body and she wanted to cry more than ever now, but Cato was right. Now was not the time.

She closed her eyes trying to contain her emotions for the sake of this moment. Her throat felt like a rock had lodged in it on its way down and her knees grew weak. She had to get it together.

"How is he?" Julia choked out as she looked down at little Owen. Somehow the baby was already cleaned and cuddled into a blue blanket leaving Julia wondering how long she had been silently standing there.

"He is perfect. Not a thing wrong with him," the healer said as she wiped her hands on a towel. "The gods had this little warrior in their hearts."

"As do we all." Damian kissed Owen's head as the babe suckled at Anna's breast greedily. "Already hungry, my little Owen Alexander." Damian's eyes teared up once more as he caressed the newborns head.

"I need to leave," Julia whispered to her brother. "Please."

Cato nodded. "Anna, I am sure you are tired and want time alone as a family. He is a beautiful child and I cannot wait to get my hands on him, but he seems rather fixated on his dinner. We will leave you two until you are ready for us to kidnap your son for some Aunt and Uncle time."

Anna smiled weakly at him as she tried to stay awake.

"Thank you both," was all she could manage to say before she drifted off to sleep while Owen still ate his fill. Damian propped the baby up against his mother while she slept, never once taking his eyes off his son nor saying a word.

Julia quickly made her way out of the room and ran the short distance to Ryan's. She burst through his door half expecting him to be standing there with a smile and to tell her 'it was all part of the plan', but no one was there. The room sat empty with everything as he had left it, never to be moved by him ever again.

She collapsed to her knees, her body was too weak to stand. Not able to contain it any longer she cried out in agony from the loss of him. Her body shook violently and she couldn't stop it. She quickly became aware she was followed when her brother dropped to the ground and pulled her into his arms as she broke down.

It was rare that Cato cried but he was crying almost as hard as she was and for some odd reason it gave her comfort knowing she wasn't alone in her pain.

"I can't live without him," she said between sobs.

Cato pulled his face back enough to look her in the eyes. His eyes were sad, but he tried to smile at her with his boyish grin.

"Yes, you can. He died so you would live. He saved my sister by giving his life and it is a debt I can never begin to try and repay. All we can do is make sure his death means something."

"So what? I just forget and move on?"

"No. You remember him every day. You make sure all those we try to save have the chance to find such a love in their lives because without us, they will live in darkness for the rest of their existence."

"As I do now."

Cato

"Fuck!"

Cato flipped over the table in his room spilling all the supplies from his locomotive model he worked years on perfecting. A slew of curse words followed the destruction of his model but instead of picking it up he grabbed his signed Jackie Robinson bat. Pieces popped in the air from hit after hit to the model supplies. After that he went to work on his collection of coins he'd collected throughout his long life.

Glass sprinkled the floor from the display he meticulously made for his collection. Coins of every size now littered his floor until his bat broke from impact.

"Fuck!" he yelled again.

The splintered bat fell to the ground as Cato dropped to his knees. Once the news of Ryan's demise hit him, he tried to choke back the tears that threatened to fall but he couldn't hold back. He wasn't here when his sister and Anna were taken and he wasn't there when Ryan was killed. He waited on that damn boat for them to return only they never did.

Once he returned to the Domus to try to figure out why they hadn't come back to the boat he was met with debris and bodies. Anna and Julia were gone. Caleb and Colette were frantically searching for them and other survivors but to no avail.

And then the news came. More so, he watched the news. It was broadcast on every fucking channel and there was nothing he could do about it. He had to watch as the life left Ryan's eyes while dying in Damian's arms.

It was plain as day that Ryan maneuvered himself onto the blade. Cato's heart felt like it was ripped from his chest seeing the tip of Damian's blade sticking out of Ryan's back. Caleb consoled a hysterical Colette while he sat in silence.

It couldn't be real. Especially when the gods showed up with all their divine bullshit. One would have thought they could have shown up just a few minutes earlier and saved Ryan's ass from being ran through. But no. Of course they didn't, because that would have been too easy. Too good.

"Cato?" a small voice came from his bathroom as Amara's face peaked around the corner apprehensively.

He couldn't form words to comfort her from his mood. Sitting still with anger pumping through his veins seemed the best option at this point. Last thing he needed was to go off on a woman, an oracle at that, when he wasn't in the right state of mind.

"Cato?" Her voice was closer, but he didn't look in her direction. He just stared ahead at the broken pieces of his stupid hobbies. "I'm so sorry."

"Why didn't you see it happening?" His voice was small. "You could have stopped it."

Amara lifted his chin to look her in the eyes. Her dark hair was wet from being freshly showered, a towel still wrapped around her body. "He had to make his choice. It wasn't certain what he would choose, but he had to make it. Apollo wouldn't have it any other way no matter how much I wished I could stop it for you."

"How long have you known?"

"Since my vision in the temple. I told Alexander he would do the right thing. That he would do what he had to and he wouldn't second guess it." Her palm rest against his cheek but he didn't relish in the feeling of it. "Do not be upset with me, my love. I was not permitted."

"The one man in this world that treated me as a son and not a disappointment is now dead. The woman I love could have prevented it, but she stood back and watched the carnage in her dreams became a reality. Of course I'm upset."

"But Apollo—"

"Fuck Apollo!" Cato yelled in her face. "Fuck all of this shit! It's all bullshit, Amara!"

"Shh…" She leaned over and placed a kiss on his forehead. "If I was capable of telling you I would have, my love. Every time I tried the words wouldn't form. Since the day I met you long till I came back to your arms."

Cato's mind flashed to images of her looking conflicted while lying in bed. Even after they had sex the confliction was there, but he didn't know why. Even the day she showed up at his room wearing the white chiton that hugged her curves he could see the apprehension in her eyes.

"How did you get off that island?"

Amara took hold of his hand, pulling him to his bed and straddled his lap. Automatically his hands rested on her hips, but he couldn't look her in the eye. His head leaned against her shoulder and he didn't give a damn if he looked pathetic. Because he damn sure felt like it.

"I've told you how, my love." She leaned her head against his. Her fingers drew small circles on his back. "A god took me from there and brought me to you."

"Who? Why?"

He could feel her smile against him, but she just shook

her head. "These things will reveal themselves in time. Unfortunately, some information is out of my control to give just as it was with Alexander. Look at me, my love."

Cato took a deep breath before pulling back. "What?"

"Forgive me and forgive him. He made an impossible choice and you should be proud."

"What's there to be proud of? He took the easy way out of a hard fight and died."

"Because he chose his family over himself. Without hesitation. Had it been you down there he would have done the same." That struck his heart in a new painful way. "He loved you. More than you ever knew. That much I can tell you at least."

He didn't realize his eyes were wet again until her thumb brushed the tears from his cheeks. With a small smile she brought his lips to hers. A hunger turned in his stomach for her when her hips accidentally rubbed against his groin. He wanted to get lost in her body. He needed to forget even if it were just for a brief time. Cato deepened the kiss until she pulled back.

"We shouldn't be doing this." She bit her lip, which only turned him on more.

"I need you," he growled against her neck. Nipping it a little harder than he meant. He could feel her body give in to him. Once a little moan escaped her lips, he flipped her on the bed and ripped off the damn towel that hid her body.

Amara scrambled to undo his belt, but he was already ahead of her. Cato swatted her hand away and was naked before she could pull herself up his bed. He didn't bother easing his way in her. His need was deeper than being a gentleman at the moment as he thrust in her, drawing out a deliciously sharp breath from her lips.

Dick move? Probably. But he really didn't give a fuck right now.

His thrusts grew more urgent as his thoughts tried to break through. Cato couldn't even focus on Amara. Not the shape of her lips as they opened in pleasure, nor the look in her eyes filled with want. What he needed right now was to fuck his demons away and that's exactly what he was doing with her body.

Knocking came at his door and he yelled, "Not fucking now."

"Cato!" Julia's voice yelled from behind his door.

He didn't stop pounding out his frustration. "Fuck off, Julia!"

"You have thirty seconds to open this door before I shoot the lock out."

"Mother fucking shit," he mumbled and reluctantly removed himself from Amara. "Hide."

"Must I still?" Her chest rose with heavy breaths.

"Now is not a good time to bring you out of the shadows. It raises too many questions and no one needs another bomb thrown at them right now." He kissed her lips as she crawled off the bed. He watched her hips sway as she walked to his bathroom.

A deep groan vibrated through his chest and he grabbed the towel, wrapping it around his lower body. Swinging the door open, despite all his emotions, he smirked seeing his sisters' eyes get wide.

"Are you sleeping with someone?"

"No, I'm jacking off." He rolled his eyes. "Of course I am, you cock block. What do you want?"

She cocked her hip and crossed her arms in obvious disapproval.

"Do you really think now is the time for that?"

"Not one bit but I don't know how else to keep my mind from…" He took in a deep breath as the emotions threatened to build. "I don't know what else to do."

Julia's face softened. "I get it." Her eyes teared up, but she pushed them away like the lady she was. "Who is it this time?"

The saint that his sister was, she was trying to change the subject from Ryan. "You don't know her. Hell, I barely do." Not a complete lie.

"When will you ever find the one, brother?"

"Maybe I have."

"Right. Anyways, I just thought I'd let you know that Anna and the baby—"

"Are they okay? Is she okay? Is the baby okay? What about Damian?" Cato nearly dropped the towel covering his fun bits.

"Calm down." Julia's smile was small. "Everyone is perfectly fine. Health wise anyways."

Relief flooded his system before he began to think of Ryan again. He could see the pain in his sister's eyes. She was tired, they all were but he couldn't even imagine how she was feeling. She finally came back from the hell Aden put her through and happiness was just in reach for her until the love of her life was snatched away.

He didn't like the thought of his baby sister with Ryan very much. Not after all the shit Ryan and Cato did together. Women mostly but that was some time ago. If he had to choose anyone to steal her heart it would have been Damian, but Ryan was a close second. Regardless, he was happy Julia and Ryan found each other and now all that had turned to shit.

"Is that all you wanted to do? Give me an update on the baby?"

"I don't want to be alone," she admitted.

"I get it." Cato kissed his sister's forehead. "Let's go shoot some shit in the practice arena."

"Love you, Dearest."

"Back at you, Sweetest."

Chapter XV

Anna

"WELL, ISN'T THIS RAD." Anna hopped out of bed and landed on her feet without trouble. "Gotta love Immortal healing meds."

"Take it easy, Anna." The healer shook her head at her. "You may be healed but you still need to rest. It isn't as if you can just waltz about as you wish."

"To hell with that, I feel great." Anna smiled at Damian but faltered as soon as his forced smile turned into a grimace. "I'm sorry."

Damian ignored her and stared into Owen's sweet sleeping face. Anna knew this wasn't an easy moment for him. His truest friend was dead, yet his son was born. She could only imagine the mixed feelings he had swirling around in that head of his.

"Those in the Domus want to offer our deepest sympathy to you all for your loss. We all watched the broadcast and it was terrible, but very brave of him. Please tell Damian he is in our prayers," the healer whispered to her before leaving Damian and Anna alone with Owen.

She slowly walked back to her bed and sat down next to Damian as he continued to stare down at the tiny ball of perfection in his arms.

"He looks like you."

"He has your hair," Damian croaked. "As well as your lips."

Anna caressed Owen's tiny head and he sneezed but never woke from his deep slumber. "Sweet baby."

"He would have made a great uncle and godfather." Damian's voice was small. "He was so excited for you, Owen."

"Damian…" She couldn't figure out what to say and was pretty sure there was nothing she could say to make this any better.

"I wish you could have met him."

"Please don't do this to yourself."

"We must reassure our troops we are still in this. I cannot let them think I killed Ryan and gave up on them."

"No one thinks that. It was obvious what Ryan did to save us. The whole world saw his sacrifice for the greater good. Hell, the gods even showed up and—"

"I am well aware what happened, Anna." Damian growled at her rather uncharacteristically. "I need to get out into the field. I will see you both later today. Please don't leave the Domus. I need you both safe."

"You're leaving so soon?" Anna wanted to protest when he handed Owen to her and climbed off the bed. "Our son isn't even a day old and you are leaving me here by myself?"

"Anna." Damian's eyes pierced her in a way that was foreign and made her want to sink deep into the bed. "Ryan martyred himself and I will not let that go to waste. I must rally our troops and maintain our goal. With any luck his death will aid in their reaffirmation against the Risen."

He was upset and he had every right, but none of this was her fault. Anger spewed out of her mouth before she could contain herself.

"You know what Damian? Fuck you! I just had our baby. A

baby you wanted by the way and now you are leaving me here like some sort of carpetbag or something? Hell no. I am going with you and both of us are going to prove to the world that we will never give up." She looked down at Owen's sleeping face. "And we need to show them why life is worth fighting for."

"Anna, don't."

"No, Damian. You don't. I am not going to stand by anymore. Your ass needs my help and you are going to get it whether you like it or not so lead the fucking way to make a damn broadcast to the world."

Oh my, this was a bad idea. Anna shifted back and forth on her feet while holding Owen. Lee and Liam were setting up the microphone on Damian's shirt. Both had tears in their eyes but never said a word about Ryan. It was the elephant in the room and the feeling of loss was felt more intensely as each minute passed.

"Now I understand why he hated doing this. It's unsettling." Damian's face lacked any emotion, but his voice was filled with a hint of malice. The man beside her was no longer the man she grew to love. He'd been replaced by a shell of his former self. She hoped it was only temporary.

"We can do this." Cato stood next to Damian's right with Anna on his left.

"There is no longer an option." Damian scowled. "Let's begin."

"We are on in three… two… one."

Damian looked at his feet for a moment before he began. Anna watched him in the corner of her eye until he finally spoke to the ground.

"Good evening to all of our allies. As you all know by now, our leader was killed. The General made sure it was a public spectacle for his enemies to see. You saw my blade pierce his body, you saw as he collapsed to the ground, and you saw that the moment he died I lost control.

"What you might not have seen was him pushing himself onto my blade willingly. You didn't see the sacrifice he made for the ones he loved to be spared. The General wanted to kill our spirit with either the death of our leader or with my death by our leader. He wanted us to turn on each other, but what he really did was show us all why we are fighting.

"He showed us a man giving his life for those in need. Not even for a moment did Ryan think of his life, but instead the lives of us all. He spared me so that I could lead you to victory over those who do not find the beauty in life. He proved that there is still good in this world and when the Gods finally appeared for the first time in centuries? Well, it proved their existence to you all. The General can no longer say the Gods are false. That they are not around and do not care about us because they just proved they are very much here."

His voice was growing far more intense as he spoke. Anna's eyes were clouded with tears as he spoke, while Owen remained oblivious to the world around him. He slept peacefully as his father's anger began to rise to the surface and take control of his usually calm demeanor.

"The end is near. We may win or lose, but I assure you we will not go down without a fight. I will risk my life for each of you, even if it means my death. So that our children," he said as he looked to Owen and then Anna, "will not live in fear. So that our loved ones can live freely in a time not ruled by a mad man with a personal vendetta.

"Most of you know our leader by the name of Ryan. But

that was not who he truly was. His name is… was Alexander. An Immortal Warrior chosen by the gods to protect you all till his dying breath. It may be hard to believe but it is true. The man known as Ryan, the one we all looked to for guidance was none other than Alexander the Great. One of the greatest military minds to walk this earth. I did not kill him, as the General wants you to believe. Alexander saved me and I promise I will do the same for each of you."

Chapter XVI

Ryan

RYAN AWOKE TO A sliver of bright light peeking through a curtain. Propping up in his bed he recognized the dark silks to be of ancient origin but seemingly new. Was he back in the dream he had when Roxane came to him? Was he in a coma or hallucinating from blood loss in the coliseum?

Tossing his legs over the side of the bed his feet dug into a sable fur rug. The soft fur brushing against his toes felt too real to be a dream. His body surely ached from battle but as he stood, he felt nothing. No sore muscles or aching bones. Not even thirst consumed him. He looked down at his hands and they were clear of blood or any signs of bruising.

Thank the god's he was still wearing his black briefs, but other than that he was naked. On a carved wooden couch filled with pillows there was a robe laid out neatly for him.

What the hell is going on?

He awoke in a palace of sorts judging by the white walls and elaborately decorated furnishing. The couches were carved, precious wood decorated with ivory and gold, mosaics decorated the walls and floor. One showed a man in a Greek helmet battling a lion with a spear. Familiarity struck his memory, but he shrugged it off.

"He's awake. I will bring him too you shortly," a voice came from outside of his room and he rushed to mask his bare body with the robe. It was red silk embroidered with golden designs that caressed his skin with each movement he made.

"Greetings, Alexander."

There was a man standing in the doorway wearing a tunic and sandals. His hair was darker than Ryan's and his skin was a light copper but something about the man made him feel hesitant. He smiled warmly at Ryan suggesting familiarity, yet Ryan could not place the man in his memory.

"Do I know you?" Ryan asked.

Locking his hands behind his back the man casually walked further into the room.

"Depends I suppose."

"I'm not in the mood for games." Ryan's eyes narrowed into slits. "Do I know you or not?"

"No need for hostility, Alexander. I am your son and my mother is Roxane."

With knees ready to buckle, he sat back down on the bed.

"Excuse me?"

"If I may be candid, Father? You are dead and this is Elysium. I am also named Alexander but for the sake of simplification I go by Aegus. My mother is here as is your mother. If you would follow me, they along with many others, are anticipating your arrival."

"I'm dead?" Ryan rested his elbows on his knees. "This can't be."

After two thousand years of battling death it finally happened. The clutches of Hades finally dragged him from the world he cherished. It didn't feel real to him. In fact, it felt the same as being alive. He was breathing and could feel the beating of his heart within his chest. He still had to blink and move his limbs the same.

"None of those things are actually needed here. It is a habit from the mortal world that will slowly begin to fade with time." Aegus seemed to read his mind. The thought was not comforting. "Breathing can have its affects. The scent of something you once loved like rain or a woman's perfume may be enticing yet not a necessity for survival. Closing your eyes is only needed if you actually feel the need to sleep or nap. A favorite of mine." He smiled warmly.

"This is fucking insane." Ryan rubbed the back of his neck. "I cannot be dead. There is way too much shit for me to do. Now I am stuck in the underworld with a man claiming to be my son and going to visit the two biggest ball busters of my life."

"If I may be so bold, Father. You are not the image of the man my mother painted in my mind."

"Yeah, I'm sure that's true," Ryan grunted.

"She described you as ambitious with a higher intellect than the average. From the way you speak I beg to differ." Aegus added, "With no offence to you of course."

"Believe me, a lot has changed up in the real world and language was definitely something that was downgraded to the lowest degree."

Aegus almost glided towards him as he spoke. "I am sure this is difficult, but Mother is anxious to see you. If you could come with me—"

Recognition suddenly popped into his mind causing Ryan to stand up before Aegus could finish talking. Ryan bolted out of the room with his son quickly at his heels. He was indeed inside of a palace and a familiar one at that. Every twist and turn he recognized. The mosaic and furniture so familiar it was as if he were here yesterday. He was back in Macedonia or at least a replica of the place he once called home.

He hadn't been back here since he left for his conquest of

the known world not even when he married Aegus' mother or when Damian and he had become Immortal. This place he never thought he would see again was exactly as he remembered.

"Where are they at?"

"The gardens." Aegus' sandals slapped against the marbled floors from behind.

The halls were lined with statues on pedestals that were painted bright green and red. A mosaic depicting Dionysus riding a cheetah brought unpleasant memories of his father to mind. His father had thrown his cup of wine at the mosaic during a fight with Ryan's mother. He couldn't recall what was said exactly, he was only seven or so, but the memory dug itself into his mind unwillingly.

As soon as he reached the gardens, he was overwhelmed with the scent of herbs that grew in neat rows down the long winding dirt path. Colorful flowers surrounded an area closer to the palace with marble benches and statues. A table was set up within the flower garden and two women sat underneath a red cloth tent on couches.

Ryan stopped in his tracks as soon as he saw the two women. Even from a distance he would recognize both of their faces. Both were young but while one had hair as black as night the other had reddish brown.

Roxane tossed her long black hair over her shoulder as she turned to lock her gaze upon him. She smiled brightly as if pleased to see him, but he couldn't imagine why. His mother, Olympias rose slowly from her cushioned couch and beckoned him towards them.

He couldn't seem to make his feet work so Aegus gave him a gentle shove from behind to put him in motion. As he got closer, he recognized his mother's favorite black snake wrapped around her forearm like a bracelet. He kept his eyes on the snake instead of the two women before him which lifted its little black head up as he came within touching distance.

"Alexander?" His wife's voice wavered. "Will you look at me?"

He stared at the snake unsure of what to say. His focus was turning blurry from the tears building up in his eyes, but he knew he had to restrain them in front of his mother. She would never approve of such emotion, but a stray tear betrayed him as it wet his cheek.

"I'm sorry." His voice cracked through the lump building his throat. "This is too much."

Roxane's delicate hand lifted his chin, forcing his eyes to meet hers. Her skin was smooth to the touch, her hair fell like luscious silk as she tilted her head to the side. There was no blemish or sign of age on her. No signs of how she died by the hands of those he called friends. He didn't even realize he was cupping her cheek until her tears wet his palms.

"This cannot be real."

"It is." She smiled through her tears. "You have been missed."

"As have you." He kissed her forehead and felt her skin beneath his lips. She was actually here with him. Her body and soul were in the afterlife with him and the sorrow of the mortal world begun to melt away. "This feels wrong."

"What does?" Roxane wrapped her arms around his waist.

"The both of you here... smiling at me." He shook his head. "The three of you should hate me for what I did."

"We were all bitter when finding out the truth." His mother pulled on his arm to sit down on one of the cushioned couches. Roxane and Aegus sat opposite of him on the other couch. "I was furious at you for leaving your empire to be ripped apart by those jackals and leaving us to fend for ourselves. But after we were murdered, and many years had passed we started to realize something."

"That you were changing into a man beyond just selfish ambition and were now fighting for a greater good," Roxane finished.

"I abandoned my pregnant wife and unborn child for my ambition. I didn't join the Immortals for any reason other than for the glory of it. I didn't think twice when leaving you three."

"Perhaps it started off that way, but you are changed now and we are so proud of everything you have done." Olympias patted his hands after taking them in hers.

"If I am at all honest, I think you saved me from a lifetime of living in fear," Aegus added. "I was barely twelve when I was taken from the mortal world and already knew fear beyond imagining. Mother didn't help with her constant fretting."

"Quiet," Roxane scolded.

Ryan studied Aegus. He was lighter than his mother and his hair was not quite as dark, but their eyes were the same. He looked like a grown man in his twenties with a strapping build to boot. "How are you so much older now?"

Aegus blushed ever so slightly when he answered. "Here, you can be who you want to be and I wanted to be like my father. A youth in his prime ready to take on the world, as I would have undoubtedly been forced to do whether I wanted to or not. It's sad we had to meet in death, but it was always destined to be so."

"No wonder you look so young, Mother." He sideways grinned at his disapproving mother. "So now what?"

"There are many others waiting to meet you. Friends and family that were allowed passage thanks to your long service to the gods. After that you do what you wish. You are free from all burdens, my love. You have proven your worth and can now be at peace," Olympias said.

"Seems too good to be true."

"Usually it would be. But not now." Olympias smiled warmly. "You are finally at rest my son. Enjoy your well-deserved reward."

Julia

Julia felt drawn back to Ryan's room after watching Damian's speech on TV. She entered his room and looked at his belongings. Never to be touched by him again. Never would she make love in that bed with him again. His sweet kisses forever gone, never to return.

She remembered one night he surprised her with enough roses to fill his entire room and candles on candelabras lit the night like twinkling stars. He'd surprised her from behind with a single white rose in his hand, wearing a buttoned-up shirt and slacks. So handsome and so sensual.

They made love for hours after that and laid in bed talking as he caressed her bare skin. The memory was so vivid in her mind even though the room was so cold and lifeless now. Ryan would never move a book in here again or clean another gun. His swords would go unsharpened and his clothes would never touch his skin.

"Alexander sent me with a message," a voice said and pulled her to awareness.

"Hermes?" Julia was rather shocked by the appearance of the Greek god but what shocked her even more was the mention of Ryan.

"A message? Is he alive?"

"You are mistaken I am afraid. His soul is alive if that helps you?" Hermes was a lanky man with curly brown hair. He usually looked rather mischievous. Right now he wore a mask of sorrow, for Julia's benefit most likely.

She couldn't hide the disappointment in her tone.

"How can he give a message then?"

"I am a god and he is in the underworld in the land of the heroes. He asked a favor of his father so here I am, delivering the favor."

Knowing Ryan still existed in some sense helped, but the fact he was totally unreachable except in death hardened her heart. It was as if he were barely out of her reach.

"What is the message?"

"He had one for each of his friends. The other messages I have delivered but this one is for you." Hermes cleared his throat. "Julia, I am sorry I left this world without a goodbye. Apollo has assured me we will be together again. Please don't do anything to hasten that reunion because your life isn't meant to end for a long time. Until then, my love, I will wait for you in the fields of Elysium. You were the greatest gift in my life and I can honestly say I died a happy man knowing the love of a goddess. Goodbye, my love. Until we reunite for the rest of eternity."

A mix of feelings played through her mind. She was crying from happiness knowing how much he loved her, and she was angry because hearing those words were almost torturous. It was like dangling himself in front of her then pulling himself out of reach before she could touch him.

She could feel the moment the god left her alone in her sorrow. Hermes was far too carefree to deal with a crying woman and there was no way she could gain control of herself right now. It hurt. All over.

It wasn't long before Damian and Cato joined her in Ryan's room. Hermes said the others received a message as well and it must have been for them. The most important people in Ryan's life were given what most people were not allowed. A final goodbye.

Damian pulled Julia into his lap on the floor.

"Did he come?"

She nodded against his shoulder. Her brother had joined them on the ground and held her hand, not meeting her eyes but the rising of his chest told her he was struggling to keep it together. She needed them just as much as they needed her right now.

"Are we ever going to get past this?" she mumbled. "It feels like a constant pain."

"We will." Damian sighed. "We don't really have a choice but to accept it."

"Sucks," Cato grumbled.

"Big time."

"At least we have you though." Damian rubbed her back as the tears fell silently. "Can't express how thankful I am that Anna, Owen, and you survived."

"Did you know he wanted to become mortal?" she asked. Damian's breathing hitched once the words left her mouth and her brother's grip on her hand loosened. "He told me in one of our quiet moments together. One night we were in bed and he told me all about what he wanted to do. How he wanted to become mortal and to finally grow old like he was supposed to. He was sick of this life, I think. Sick of losing everyone to death while he still lived."

"He finally wanted peace," Damian added.

Cato stood up from their spot on the floor and started to pace. He was wearing nothing but grey sweatpants, all she could hear besides his growls of frustration were the soft pads of his feet against the painted floor. The large eagle tattoo on his back rippled from his muscles contracting and she knew he was angry. Cato never hid his feeling well from her, and her brother was about to explode.

"Peace!" he finally laughed out. "Alexander the fucking Great wanted peace?"

"He lived for an unnaturally long time. Even for an Immortal." Damian helped Julia stand up before standing himself to meet Cato face-to-face. "Don't you feel the same sometimes?"

Cato's jaw clenched. "No. I am a Warrior until the day I die in battle."

"Why are you so upset about this?" Damian's voice softened.

Cato ran his hands over his short hair leaving his hands clasped behind his head. He looked older than normal. She desperately missed her carefree loving brother, this was a side she hated to see. Lately, it was all she saw.

"I'm upset because he wanted to leave us. Well, he got his fucking wish, now didn't he?" Tears were brimming in his eyes as he tried to blink them away, but he couldn't stop his pain from showing as they rolled down his cheeks. His chest heaved while he tried to control himself. She wanted to hug him, but she knew better than that. He was angry, hurt, and she knew her brother better than anyone. "I'm sorry."

"Don't be." Damian smiled sadly.

"I shouldn't have said that." Cato gently squeezed Damian's shoulder before he was pulled into a big bear hug by Damian. "I love you, brother."

"Ditto. I get your pain, but you aren't alone in this. None of us are." Damian pulled back and put his forehead to Cato's. "So, let's make that fucker proud and kill some assholes."

Chapter XVII

Anna

DAMIAN STOOD OVER THE large world map painted over the entire floor area in the library. Bookshelves were pushed to the walls. Some were doubled up making it impossible to reach a book without moving the entire shelf, but Damian had told her there was no need to read about romances at times like these. He was walking along the area of Australia when he suddenly stopped.

Shaking his head, he started to pace again. Anna could hardly stand his silence, but she wanted to be near him. Owen was fast asleep in a crib she'd hauled in the room, but Damian was too fixated on the map to pay them any attention.

Cato silently sat cross legged on the other side of the room staring at the map. He hadn't said a single word since Anna came in here thirty minutes ago.

"Hello." Cato looked in her direction merely giving her a wink, but Damian remained silent. "Hello, anybody fucking home?"

This time Damian turned slowly towards her with his arms crossed.

"Yes?"

"What are you doing? We've been in here for a while and no one has said a single word."

"I am determining a plan," he said simply.

"I get that. But a little attention would be nice." Anna knew she sounded needy. Hell, even bitchy. But she was still hormonal and craved his comfort.

"I love you both dearly." Damian smiled weakly. "However, I have a duty thrust on me that I didn't wish and now I have to formulate some sort of plan."

"What about strengthening our hold in the mid-west? That's a good portion of our food supply." Cato was turning the subject around much to Anna's annoyance.

"But then we would be leaving the east defenseless. There isn't enough numbers on our side and the west coast is already taken by the General. We would be trapped."

"We could—"

"Thought of it."

Cato pointed at the North. "What abo—"

"Gone."

"Well fuck me, what are we even trying to do now?" Cato laid on his back staring up at the ceiling.

Damian looked old and tired. She hated it. His eyes were rimmed with dark circles and his hair was a mess. He looked so worn.

"Please just come get some sleep?" she begged him.

"I can't. Not till it's done."

Just breathe, Anna.

"It isn't only you that can do this, Damian. There are seasoned Warriors here that can take it for a while."

"It has to be me. I have to do this."

"You are losing it. Painting maps on the ground and ignoring those around you. Doesn't this ring a bell to you?" She instantly regretted her words.

"Don't you dare insult him. Ryan knew what he was doing even if we didn't see it that way." Damian's eyes seemed to stare through her. "It's easier to see what must be done on a large-scale map and I have to win this."

"So, it's you against the entire world? How can that possibly be done?" she asked.

Cato let out an exaggerated sigh. "We can't. If we keep going the way we are, then they will pick us off slowly. Our numbers are dwindling lower and lower because he is recruiting our POW's for his side out of fear. With Ryan gone our troops are in confusion even after Damian's speech. Ryan was the face of our leadership. They trusted him. Worshiped him even. They saw Damian sure, but they need reassurance."

"So, what are you going to do?" Anna asked.

"Propaganda films," Damian muttered. "With me leading our troops into skirmishes. Show our troops I will die for them just as Ryan would."

Anna didn't think that would work. Ryan fought with the troops in hand-to-hand combat, visited their hospital tents, and held the hands of those he knew weren't going to make it. These men saw him in action for how real he was. If Damian did films, it would only look forced. No, he needed a different approach.

"You can't build that sort of trust up with films and we don't have enough time for you to mingle with the soldiers. We need a solution right now."

She had Damian's full attention now. "So, what do you propose?"

"First off, screw all these battles. We are done fighting and losing our men. We need one last stand against the General with all the troops we have. Bring both of our armies to one location and end it all. It's final battle time."

Damian took slow calculating steps towards her. His eyes were directed toward her, but she could see he was somewhere else in his mind. Just as he stood next to her, he placed a gentle hand on top of Owen's belly as he slept in his crib.

"You want me to declare a battle to end the war? Is that it?"

"It's time we finished this shit once and for all," Cato agreed.

"And how would this rally our men behind me exactly?"

"Shoot another speech. Call out the General with a time and place for the battle and stress that we want to end this. For Ryan. For everyone. Don't play games with the public. Be honest. You can't try to turn yourself into Ryan for them. Be who you are. It's enough."

Damian's thumb caressed Owen's cheek. He smiled at the touch in his sleep and her heart felt like a gooey mess. She wanted this to end for Owen. There was no way in hell she would allow her child to grow up in a shit world.

"Well, let's start planning then."

"What the fuck do you mean I am sitting the battle out? It was my idea!" Her raised voice echoed in their room.

She was fuming. Livid. Damian was not going to be able to father any more children if he continued to stand so close to her because her foot was about to head right towards his junk.

"Owen needs at least one of his parents around, Anna. If we both die, then what? He will grow up never knowing who we are. Do you really want that?"

"Of course I don't, you dumbass. But I am not sitting this fight out!" She was not going to back down. Her hip was cocked and her arms were crossed over her chest. Typical stance for a woman not going to give in. "You will not stop me, Damian. I have flying experience and I am going to use it."

Granted her flight experience was limited but still. When she knew she was joining the Marines, she had enrolled in a flight school so she could get a jump on becoming a pilot. She knew that she had to work her way up to it in the Marines but she wanted an edge.

"I will not have my future wife and the mother of my child flying around in the air!"

Anna cocked her head to the side and watched Damian's breathing become heavy. His fists were clenched, as was his jaw. Everything about him screamed tense and worried.

"Are you afraid of flying?"

"No," he said quickly.

"You are."

"No, I am not."

"Yep, you so are." She couldn't help but grin. "Interesting."

Damian practically growled at her when he said, "So what if I am? It's high up and…"

"And what?" She tried to hide her borderline giggling from him.

"Nothing. I don't like it that much. Okay? I fly when I have to, but I don't pilot, ever." He shook his head and his voice raised higher. "The point is, it's not happening. You are staying here with Owen and that's final."

That's it. Her leg aimed between his legs.

Sadly, his reflexes were quick and he caught her foot before she made contact.

"That's not okay, Anna."

"Neither is you trying to control my life." She glared making his eyes soften.

Foot in hand he pulled her towards him making her hop or fall on her ass. His arms snaked around her waist and he nuzzled against her neck. Bastard didn't play fair, but her anger started to dissipate.

"Please, Anna. Just listen to me this one time and after that I am yours to command."

She pulled back from him and planted a kiss on his lips.

"Nope, I am going. End of fucking story."

Delicate kisses trailed along her neck. Her eyes fluttered even as she tried to keep herself composed.

"What do I have to do to convince you?"

"Umm." She was borderline incoherent when his hands trailed up the back of her shirt leaving goose bumps against her skin from his touch.

The bastard had the nerve to smile.

"Tell me, Anna. What do I have to do?"

How in the world did they both go from mad to turned on in a matter of seconds? Damian knew how to play her like a fiddle that was for sure.

"You are not playing fair."

"I don't intend to." His hand slithered into her hair, gripping it just right making her jaw drop and breath hitch.

"What's wrong, Anna?"

The controlling jerk was annoying, but damn he was sexy when he talked all deep and growly like that.

"You aren't going to change my mind with sex." Her slack-jaw self managed to sound stronger than she felt inside. Hands explored her body and the look in his eye was feral.

Oh hell. Oh hell. Oh hell.

"How about you stay." He kissed behind her ear. "And you plan our wedding for when I get back. That way your mind will be preoccupied."

Anna rolled her eyes. "Or we could just go ahead and do it. Don't need to plan anything. This isn't ancient Greece you jerk. I'm not going to play house while my man goes to war."

Damian stopped his blissful torture and looked at her with those serious eyes of his.

"You want to get married right now?"

Anna, you're an idiot.

"I'm just saying…" She fumbled with her words. "I don't need to plan anything. It's not like we need a big ol' ceremony. I mean it can wait if you don't want to do it now."

Word vomit. Worse than real vomit. Now the man wanted to marry her right away. She could see that clear as day in his eyes. The hope was there along with the giddiness of making it happen sooner than she expected. But what the hell, why back out now? He was everything to her.

"Fuck it. Let's do it." She shrugged.

"Seriously?"

"Yep. Tonight."

A smile as wide as his was contagious. He picked her up and twirled her around like in the movies and just like in the movies she giggled.

"I thought you'd want a traditional Catholic wedding." His cheeks reddened.

"I mean, I probably should but I don't think the same rules apply for Immortals as they do for mortals." His head hung a little. "What?"

"I've been having Colette teach me about Catholicism. I was trying to figure out how to get baptized and even talked to priests about marriage preparation programs."

Yet again her jaw dropped, but not from being turned on.

"Are you serious?"

"I thought I needed to change religions for it to be valid in the eyes of your god. I want us married for real and that's part of the reason I haven't been sleeping much. I wanted to surprise you. Yeah, I've been planning war, but I've also been studying."

With a big kiss and a pat on the head she left him standing in the middle of the room confused.

"You silly man. You don't need to do all that for me. Let's get hitched." She turned to leave their room and called over her shoulder, "Oh, and this doesn't change anything. I'm still fighting."

Chapter XVIII

Julia

"DO I SERIOUSLY HAVE to wear a fucking monkey suit?" Cato groaned as he pulled on the collar of his shirt.

He looked handsome, and she couldn't help but laugh at his discomfort. Cato could dress nice, but tuxedos were definitely not his thing. He'd said repeatedly he'd rather wear a toga over this crap. Julia lucked out when Anna said she could pick whatever she wanted to wear but she stood firm on tuxedos for the guys.

"Will you stay still?" Julia adjusted his tie for him and once she was finished, she patted his chest. "Perfect."

"Yeah, yeah, yeah. Whatever, sis," he grumbled.

Julia continued to fidget with his jacket, smoothing out lines that weren't there and trying to keep her mind off the one person she would never be betrothed to. It was hard realizing Ryan and her would never experience marriage or children together.

She didn't hate Damian and Anna for being happy together. Their love was beautiful and she was happy for them. Unfortunately, the ugly green monster of jealousy ripped through her chest and went straight to her heart.

Cato must have sensed her distress because his fingertips gently pushed her chin up to meet his eyes.

"It will be okay, Sweetest."

"Only days after his death and we all move on like this. We haven't even had time to grieve." She shook her head. Maybe jealously was a tiny bit there.

"Maybe this is what we need? Some sort of happiness in our lives in order to keep us off the brink of despair." He kissed her forehead. "I know I need it."

His strong arms wrapped around her body making her feel small and protected. Cato was an asshole a lot of the time, no doubt, but she knew he hated seeing her suffer. After all the things going on, he was her rock now. The one person she could count on in the world.

Tears threatened to fall again but once Damian walked into the room she pushed them back with trained composure.

"You ready?" She smiled brightly. This was their day, not hers.

Damian looked just as uncomfortable in a tux as Cato did.

"This thing is worse than our gear."

"Grow a pair, the both of you." Julia shook her head.

They were in the Great Temple and a priest was standing in the center. Julia took her place by Colette who held a sleeping Owen in her arms. Both women were wearing blue strapless dresses that flowed down to the ground. Zarah was able to get them all hooked up with wedding clothes rather quickly, one day to be exact, which helped calm Anna's nerves.

"It's time." The priest named John smiled in his black robes with the little white collar popping out. He was bald with a large burn mark on the back of his head. An ex-Warrior that retired and chose another path to serve his god.

Colette and Julia stood on the bride's side with Cato and Caleb on the groom's side dressed in all black tuxedos. Caleb looked at ease wearing formal wear and Julia noticed, Colette couldn't keep her eyes off him. His unruly locks were long gone, replaced with a high and tight cut matching Cato's. He looked sterner and less boyish now. It suited him.

Anna didn't want a large wedding. She just wanted the six of them there to keep it simple. Sure, the people in Urbs that remained could probably use some sort of good news, but this was private for them. The last thing they needed was to be hounded by the public. Damian was a celebrity of sorts so the news would travel rather quickly.

Once the violin player started to play a sweet tune, Anna came around the entrance wearing a simple white gown with a lace bodice that draped neatly to the ground. Zarah had worked her magic and it was absolutely perfect for Anna. Her hair was half up in loose wavy curls that were held together in the back by a diamond-encrusted hairpiece.

Julia could see her hands trembling but as soon her eyes locked onto Damian, she ran to him. Julia's eyes went wide, but her brother had a shit-eating grin as they watched her rush to her groom. As soon as she got to him, Damian swept her up and they kissed each other without a care to who was around.

Cato finally had to clear his throat to get them off each other.

"Not yet guys. Almost to that point."

"Oh yeah." Anna was placed back down on her heels and she handed over her bouquet of blue flowers to Julia. Turning to John she smiled.

"Let's do this, Padre."

With a chuckle John asked, "Do you take Damian as your husband, to have and to hold, from this day forward, for better or for worse, for richer or for poorer, in sickness and in health, through war and through peace, to love and to cherish until death do you part?"

"I do." Anna pulled a ring off her finger that was far too

big for her and placed it on Damian's ring finger. "I give you this ring as a sign of my love and faithfulness. I am forever yours."

"Do you take Anna as your wife, to have and to hold, from this day forward, for better or for worse, for richer or for poorer, in sickness and in health, through war and through peace, to love and to cherish until death do you part?"

"I do." He produced a ring from his pocket. "I give you this ring as a sign of my love and faithfulness. I will be yours only, in life and death. Forever my love. Forever my heart."

With a big grin and a clap on the back, John said, "I now pronounce you man and wife. You may kiss your bride."

Anna's usual tomboy exterior shed as soon as she was married to Damian. She squealed and jumped in his arms smashing their lips together in haste. Cato and Caleb clapped and laughed while both Julia and Colette cried. Not once had she seen Anna so happy. Her usual gruff exterior was replaced with someone as giddy as a schoolgirl.

"My love, I can't believe you actually did it," Damian laughed through his happy tears.

"Thought I'd back out?" she laughed as she kissed Owen on his head as he slept peacefully in Colette's arms.

"Actually, yeah." Damian grinned and kissed her softly.

"To be fair, I did too," Cato chimed in with a nodding Caleb behind him. Both men sported huge grins.

Anna elbowed Damian in the ribs and the giddy school-girl was gone but her smile wasn't. "Jerk."

"Let's get fucked up!" Cato held his hand up for a high five to Caleb, who awkwardly slapped his hand back.

"Come on wife. You heard the man." Damian picked Anna up, tossing her over his shoulder.

"What about Owen?" She playfully hit his back.

"Olivia is going to watch him. You ma'am, are all mine." Damian smacked her butt as they walked out of the temple.

Julia smiled as they retreated back towards the Domus. They were adorable but her heart ached. Large arms wrapped around her from behind and she received a breath halting bear hug.

"You did great. Let's get shitfaced," Cato grunted.

"Let's."

Cato

Cato changed into sweats before joining the rest of their crew in the parlor room. Formal wear was ridiculous, but Anna's hormones must still be kicking because she flipped her shit when he told her he didn't want to wear a tux. Cato knew better than to fuck with a woman on a mission, so he did as he was told because Julia threatened his manhood otherwise.

Amara wasn't too pleased about him leaving her in his room, but he still didn't know how to tell the others about her. Sure, it shouldn't be a big deal, but right now there was no point in adding more questions to their already fucked up universe.

How did she get off the island? Who took her? Why is she here?

Things he could avoid, he would.

"So, bride, groom, shots?" Cato walked in carrying a box full of alcohol followed by his sister. His plan? Get slammed. Life was a mess and he needed to numb it.

Anna hopped from Damian's lap and ran to the drinks.

"Vodka please!"

Damian pushed himself up and snaked his arms around

Anna from behind. He leaned and whispered something probably dirty in her ear judging from her giggles.

Jupiter give me strength not to hurl all over them.

"Who did you say was watching Owen?" Caleb asked. He was sitting right next to Colette with his hand on her knee. She smiled at him but as soon as Colette made eye contact with Cato she pulled away from Caleb.

Drama. Drama everywhere.

"He's with Olivia tonight. She offered to watch him since we were getting married," Damian mumbled between his kisses on Anna's neck.

"Ahh, Olivia." Cato closed his eyes and grinned. He remembered Olivia. Short petite thing with brown hair and bright eyes. She helped put him back together a time or two. In many different ways.

Lining up six shot glasses he poured vodka in each to the brim. Everyone now stood around the table with a glass in their hand. Colette looked hesitant about the liquid but didn't complain. He liked that about her. Anna was more interested in Damian's lips at the moment, so Cato cleared his throat. After the third time and a lot louder, he finally got the newlyweds attention.

"For the love of Jupiter. Pull yourselves together." He smiled wide. "A toast to the new couple. Stuck together for eternity with no way of escape."

"Cato!" Julia slapped his chest.

"I suck at toasts obviously!" He continued and raised his glass, "Love each other every damn day like it's your last."

The glasses clinked together before they all downed the shot. Cato opted for another as soon as possible but Colette looked on the verge of spitting it out. Taking a step back out of the possible splash zone, he opted to give another to Anna, but she declined.

"I probably shouldn't have anymore." She sighed. "Or you could convince this caveman I can bottle feed if I want too."

"It's better for the baby if his mother feeds him." Damian's look was serious, but he softened when Anna grabbed his butt.

"He will be fine either way, but whatever. If it is so important to you than fine." Anna opted for water.

Leaving the lovebirds to paw over each other, Cato made it his personal mission to get his sister drunk.

"You've been awfully quiet, Sweetest." He poured her a glass of whiskey.

With a sniff of the liquid her nose wrinkled. She tried to set it down, but he lightly pushed the glass to her lips and she didn't fight him much. After the first sip and a very amusing scrunched face, Julia downed the whole glass and held it out for more.

"Just thinking."

"Well, quit that and keep me company. Too much love in one room for the likes of me."

"One day, Cato."

"You always tell me that." His adult beverages were starting to kick in. He couldn't help but smile wide at the thought of Amara sitting on his lap in a white dress.

What the hell is wrong with me?

Julia loudly set down the glass and took his whiskey from him. He was about to protest to give it back until the bottle went to her lips and she took a big swig. With wide eyes he took the bottle from her, shaking it slightly while giving her the eye.

"Not much left, sis. Need some more?" With her hand over her mouth she nodded. "Just… don't throw up. It'd be a waste of perfectly aged whisky."

With more of a skip in his step he made his way to the table full of booze. Seeing Julia drunk was a rarity and he loved it. It was the little things.

"She is going to be throwing up soon." Damian nudged him from behind.

Large grin in place Cato nodded. "Yup!"

"You are an evil man." Damian laughed throwing his arm around Cato's shoulders. "How are you?"

"Not as good as you but working on it," he admitted.

"I am beyond happy right now but when it settles down," he paused, "I will probably be overcome by my personal hell."

Cato knew Damian wanted nothing more than to marry that sassy little Latina, but Ryan's death was close to all of their hearts. If anything, he was happy Damian got married this quickly after the incident. They needed to bring some light into the darkness. There was a high chance they would have lost Damian otherwise.

"No matter what you need, man, I'm here for you. Don't you fucking forget it either." Cato one arm hugged Damian.

Anna's waving arms caught both their attentions as she sat next to Caleb and a very uncomfortable Colette.

"She's grilling them about their relationship. Woman gets one shot in her and can't keep her questions to herself," Damian said chuckling.

"She's opened up a lot more since the first time she got here. That woman isn't shy about anything anymore." Cato smirked. "Even grabbing your ass in public now."

Damian tried to hide his smile, but couldn't. The man was stupid in love. Not that he could blame him. In all honestly, Cato thought Anna was hot as hell when he first met her. Even with the dirt on her cheeks. But as soon as Damian's affection became one hundred percent clear, that woman over there became a sister to Cato. No doubt about it.

"Oh yeah, they are totally boning." Cato roared with laughter seeing Colette bury her face in her hands while Caleb rubbed her back. He on the other hand had a wide smile on his face while Anna made some rather unladylike motions indicating sex.

"Why is she acting out the motions?" Damian shook his head. "That isn't water she's drinking, is it?"

Cato honestly didn't know if Anna pulled a fast one on Damian or not and he really couldn't help but laugh.

"It's her damn wedding, man. I think she can do whatever the hell she wants. Owen isn't gonna lack for shit so let her have fun."

"True." Damian sighed.

A few other Warriors showed up to the party after getting Cato's invitation. They all needed a break before they died so why not celebrate with comrades? Damian gave him a side-glance that was somewhat disapproving but Anna smiled and waved at the new party guests.

"I figured she wanted it to be a secret." Damian couldn't help but grin by his wife's acceptance of their companions. "But apparently I was wrong. Thanks for inviting them."

"We all need a little happy my friend." Cato nodded. Zachary, Malakai, Otis and Juniper all ended up with cups in their hands thanks to Anna.

"She didn't waste any time," Damian mused.

"Drink?" Cato offered him.

"Fine, let's all get wasted. It appears your sister is already there."

Cato watched in horror as Julia sat on Zachary's lap. If this wasn't a cry for help, he didn't know what was.

"What the hell is she doing?"

"She's numbed herself, Cato." Damian sighed. "My guess is she has no clue as to what she is doing."

"Do I intervene?"

"Nope, she is a grown ass woman," Anna said coming out of nowhere like a damn ninja.

Cato didn't fully agree with that statement even though it was true. His sister was a grown woman, but she also needed someone to watch over her during this shit time in her life. Making mistakes like sitting on another man's lap while the love of her life had recently died was a big one.

"To hell with that." Cato yelled over to Zachary, "Hey, get your fucking hands off her before I cut them off."

Zachary did as he was told and took his hand off Julia's waist. His sister was far too drunk to even give a damn at this point. She didn't even look in his direction when he yelled across the room, instead she took another drink.

"You should put her to bed." Damian tried his hardest not to laugh. "I think she is about to pass out."

"Freaking light weight," Cato muttered. "Alright, hold my beer. I'll be right back."

Stalking over to his sister and the dumb man that refused to push her off his lap, Cato swept his sister up in his arms, her head falling backwards. Damn woman was like a ragdoll.

"Wha?" she managed out of her comatose mouth.

"You are way too drunk, little one." Cato laughed as her eyes fought hard to stay open.

"Am not."

"Let's get you to bed." Cato began to walk away. "Oh, and Zach?" The man sheepishly faced him. "I'm coming back to kick your ass."

Satisfied with his look of terror, Cato made his way towards his sister's room. Was he going to kick Zachary's ass? No. It wasn't his fault Julia sat on his lap. He probably had his hand on her waist to keep her from falling. It was just fun making people squirm.

They walked in silence only for a few moments before Julia made heaving noises.

"Fuck."

He set her on the ground and ran for a trash bin. Luckily for him one was near and he made it just in time to catch this graceful creature's vomit. Cato rubbed her back until her body stopped convulsing.

"How do you all do this all the time?" she grumbled.

Trying to avoid vomit breath he answered, "Well, you just grow accustomed to it I suppose."

She leaned against his shoulder while he propped her up. Maybe drunken Julia was less fun than he thought. Still, he couldn't help but wish he were on her level of inebriation.

"I will never marry him. I will never have a child with him. I am forever alone in this world, Cato." Julia sniffled. "What's the point anymore?"

He hated seeing her like this. She was the purest human being on the damn planet and didn't deserve to be feeling this way.

"You will find someone I promise. He will take the hurt away and make you whole again. Then you can pop out a bunch of little shitting machines."

She shook her head, which resulted in the continuation of vomiting into the trash.

"At Zee's funeral Zeus pulled me aside to talk to me. He said my path could only lead two ways depending on what I choose to follow. I would either be seduced by the darkness surrounding Aden or the bright flame of Ryan but one of those paths would end in tragedy. Looks like I picked tragedy."

"No offense to Zeus but that's a load of bullshit if I ever heard one." Cato picked her up and started back off towards her room. "We have plenty of years left in us to find our perfect someone."

"I did find him and he was taken from me."

"Look here missy. When Hermes came barging in my room giving me Ryan's message, I was given a very clear set of instructions. And that was to not let my sister give up on life and to never ever let her hasten her way back to him. I intend on keeping that promise to him."

"Good luck."

Chapter XIX

Damian

L YING IN BED NEXT to his beautiful wife with their baby in
his nursery was by far the best feeling in the world. He had
never known such peace in life. The steady breathing of the
woman next to him was therapeutic. Owen sneezed in the other
room but didn't awaken. He loved it. The two of them calmed
the pain in his heart more than they could ever know.

Ryan was gone, but Damian wouldn't let him down. He'd
sacrificed himself so Damian could move forward and that was
what he intended to do. He truly hated being a leader. It was
never something he wanted, and he still didn't. If he could pass
the reins to someone else, he would but there was no one else he
trusted enough to succeed, except Ryan.

It was time to gather his forces together, to challenge Marc
to a final battle and get this over with once and for all. He wanted
to begin his life with Anna and Owen. A life with no worries of
their survival or fear.

But this quiet moment in bed was too good to interrupt.
Anna was passed out from a night of drinking, her hair wild.
The small amount of eyeliner she had worn the night before was
slightly smudged. She was still the most beautiful creature he
had ever seen.

She must have sensed someone staring because her eyes lazily flickered open.

"What?" Her voice croaked.

"Good morning beautiful." He kissed the tip of her nose.

Anna stretched her arms and legs out as far as she could and yawned. She squealed as she stretched her body and didn't give a damn if she was taking up all the bed. Damian couldn't help but chuckle. She was such a different type of woman and he thoroughly enjoyed it.

"Where's Owen?"

"I asked Olivia to bring him back last night while you were passed out." He laughed at her horrified features. "He was fast asleep and so were you. So, I put my two babies to bed."

"You weren't drunk?" she asked.

"No, I think you had enough for the both of us." Damian pulled her body towards his. "I liked seeing you happy."

"That I am." She grinned wide and ruffled his hair. Crawling out of bed she looked over her shoulder at him and winked. "I'm going to take a shower, care to join?"

"Yes ma'am." He jumped out of bed, but a small knock came at the door.

"Go ahead and get it," she called from the bathroom.

"Damn door," he grumbled. Pulling on some underwear he marched his way to the door, ripping it open. "Yes?"

Brianna stood in the doorway looking irate. He was keenly aware of her hand on the hilt of her sword and noticed two other Warriors flanked each side of her.

"We need to talk."

"What's this all about exactly?" He gestured towards her sword. "What the hell is going on?"

"Alois is dead. Ryan made a threat on his life and Ryan is no longer here. So well, we are taking precautions." She frowned.

"Are you insinuating I killed him?" Damian wasn't all that sad to hear the news. Crossing his arms, he leaned against the doorframe. There was no way he was going to cower down to them.

Brianna shrugged her petite shoulders that were weighed down by heavy gear.

"Can't say either way."

"You're shitting me, right?" Damian wanted to laugh at the notion.

"Look, I don't like it either, but I was assigned by the council to come get you and Cato."

"And go where exactly?"

"To the crime scene." She sighed heavily and Damian could tell she was getting agitated. "So, like, could you put some pants on because I am seeing a whole lot of you right now."

He looked down at his boxers and rolled his eyes at her. "No, I would love to see a dead body in my underwear while being accused of murder."

"We aren't accusing. At least I'm not. The council is just a little on edge as of right now with everything going on."

"Could have fooled me with the gear you're sporting and the hand on your blade but whatever." Damian closed the door in Brianna's face to get dressed but turned to find his smoking hot wife totally naked and crossing her arms.

"What's going on now?" she asked.

His brain failed to function for a split second.

"Alois was killed so Cato and I have to check it out apparently. I will be back soon, I promise."

"Always something." Anna turned on her heel and walked back towards the bathroom. "Have fun," she called over her shoulder.

He stood there staring at her body while she walked away

and was broken out of his trance when a loud knock on his door came again. Hurriedly, he tossed on sweats, shirt and shoes. By the time he opened the door, Cato was already standing there with Brianna. He looked like he was going to pass out.

"Hangover from hell and now a dead asshole." Cato yawned. "Good freaking morning."

Brianna flicked his forehead. "Man up and shut up if you don't want the damn council thinking you two did this."

Cato rubbed his forehead but did as he was told. Brianna was a little spitfire and would probably kick him in the balls if he said the wrong thing. It was one of the many reasons Damian loved her. Even if right now he was pissed.

"Lead the way." Damian held his hand out.

Brianna glared but didn't say anything. Damian expected a long walk to the Great Temple or outside of the Domus, instead they came to a stop in front of Ryan's door. There was blood smeared from further down the hallway leading under the doorframe into the room.

He felt his body freeze up. Not from fear, but from excitement. Could Ryan be alive? Did he come back and give Alois the revenge he promised him?

Damian exchanged glances with Cato and they both pushed into the room. Looking around everything was in order from the last time Ryan was in here except the hanging corpse of Alois. No, it wasn't Ryan, because the sight in front of him was done by a monster.

Alois was hanging in the air by his arms which were stretched out in a t-shape with rope. His skin was cut away from his spine and his ribs were separated and pulled backwards away from his spine. The brutality didn't stop there though. His lungs were pulled out of his body and spread over his protruding ribs to create a pair of crude wings.

"Damn, blood eagle." Cato whistled. "That's a shit way to go."

Damian walked around to the front of Alois' body and nearly slipped in the blood dripping from the corpse. A look of agony was painfully frozen on the man's face, but Damian wasn't sure how he felt about it all. Alois was a horrible person—there was no denying that, but so was Aden. After all that had happened, Damian had a hard time feeling bad for either man at this point. But this? This was brutal on so many levels.

"You actually think I could do this to another human being?" Damian's jaw clenched. "This is…"

"Disturbing," Brianna muttered.

"Yet here he is," a man said as he entered the room.

It was Eric, another council member. He was far less pompous than Alois had been. Damian actually liked the man but if he thought for a second that Damian or Cato had anything to do with this, his opinion of Eric would be changed drastically.

He was about as tall as Damian with a stocky build and black hair. One thing Damian liked about him was his ability to avoid drama. When they had their meeting in the Great Temple, Eric ignored Alois' rants accusing Ryan and Damian of treachery.

Damian recalled seeing him lounge back in his chair just studying the floor with disinterest. It wasn't that he didn't care, it was he knew to fight with a ticking bomb was pointless. It was just the type of man Eric was.

Damian noticed that two more council members entered Ryan's room. The woman beside him paled and looked on the verge of vomiting. Her dark hair fell in curtains over her face trying to hide her disgust, but it was plainly on her face.

"Don't puke on the floor, Katina." The Reborn named Jian rolled his eyes at her. He was of Chinese descent and could have easily been a Warrior but had a different calling in creating art.

Jian won many competitions in mixed martial arts and swordsmanship but as far as Damian knew, he never wished for this life.

Katina's small frame shuddered but she tried to straighten herself. She was the daughter of one of the council members that was murdered by the Risen and had never even applied to be a Warrior.

"I assure you, I won't." She shot Jian an annoyed look.

Coming further into the room with the other council members, Eric looked up at Alois' body with disgust plain on his face. "Well, if you two didn't do this than who did? The only grudge Alois had was with Ryan and given you two are the only ones left, well, it's a difficult circumstance."

Cato huffed. "You honestly think we would do this?"

Eric merely shrugged. "I believe you capable, but I really don't think you would be so barbaric."

"Then what the hell is with the armed guard over here?" Damian motioned towards Brianna and other two Warriors. "Seems like an accusation to me."

"One of the council members was just murdered in the Domus. We are a little bit on edge if you didn't notice. The last faction of the council was murdered and strung up, then Ryan and now Alois," Katina practically yelled at him. "They aren't there to arrest you. They're there as a precaution, to protect you."

Eric placed a hand on Katina's shoulder and she took a deep breath to calm down. Her nerves were obviously heightened and Damian really didn't blame her given she was part of the very organization that her father died for being a part of. Hell, knowing someone was murdered in Ryan's room while his wife and child slept next door made him uneasy.

"We do have a question though." Jian stepped in. "Given Ryan's promise to Alois and seeing as he is strung up in Ryan's room…"

"What?" Damian glared.

"We were wondering if Ryan may have faked his death as part of some plan?" Eric finished.

Damian felt the heat rise in his face. He had wondered the same thing before coming into Ryan's room, but it was difficult to believe Ryan would stoop so low as to perform the Viking blood eagle on someone purely for vengeance. Torture for information was one thing but this?

"I felt the blade slide into his flesh. Saw the life drain from his eyes and his blood drenched my body. We were on a mission to kill the General and were caught. So no. It wasn't a plan at all. Our plan to survive failed miserably and resulted in his death. So, did Ryan do this? No. Neither did Cato or I because honestly, we have more important things to worry about than the damn fool that tortured Aden beyond recognition. So, don't you dare belittle his sacrifice with baseless accusations."

"We didn't mean it that way." Katina's face softened but Damian wasn't having it.

Damian held up his hand to silence her. "How about you do a little detective work and see if there are any signs as to who did this?"

Cato pushed past Brianna who remained eerily silent and began patting down Alois' body.

Damian went through Alois' pockets and pulled out a note.

"Was that so hard?" He rolled his eyes at the council members as they looked sheepish.

The front of the paper said, 'Payback', and inside was the crude writings of a deranged man.

"What does it say?" Cato looked over his shoulder.

i KEPT mY FATHER'S PROMiSE.

Cato

"How that little fucker got in here is beyond me. We have guards constantly patrolling the hallways and cameras placed everywhere. Yet, not even a glimpse of Aden coming or going into Ryan's room with a dead body in tow." Cato chucked a shoe across the room and sat down on his bed. Rubbing his hands over his face he fell onto his back and groaned. "I'm going to kill him. I swear it to all the god's, I am going to kill Aden."

Amara plopped herself down on his bed, running her fingers over his short hair making him sleepy.

"Don't fret, my love. He will get what is coming to him. They all will."

"Have you seen something?" He sat up quickly almost knocking her over.

Sadly, she shook her head. "Not for some time now."

Cato fell back into his bed again and closed his eyes. Apollo must have it out for Amara because she said she hadn't had any visions for a while. The one bonus about your woman being an oracle and it was taken away.

"This makes no sense. Why risk being seen or captured just to viciously murder a guy that tortured you and then claim you did it for your father who you hated?" Cato looked up at Amara and watched her eyes slowly meet his. "What are you thinking?"

"Nothing."

"Want to tell your face that?" He smirked

"Alright then," she started. "I am thinking that you need to introduce me finally to your family. All I hear is what's going on out there but never get to help."

"Whoa, what brought this up?"

"I'm sick of hearing about the distractions you all seem to encounter. So much complaining when you lose sight of the big picture. I could help keep you on track."

"How in the world are we being distracted?"

"They do something bad to one of you and you lose sight of what really matters. Every time you fall for it. The religious places, murder in the Domus, being separated by a woman at the chariot races, even Aden played off your emotions to get what he wanted."

"How did you know about that?"

"How about when Julia needed you to help save Colette and Grace when she was brainwashed? What reason was there to keep them alive other than to distract you from your main course of action?"

Cato stood up from his bed and made a beeline to his fridge. Pulling out the nearest bottle of alcohol he could find he took a long swig.

"So, what you're saying is we are a bunch of idiots falling for their games."

Amara came from behind him and wrapped her arms around his waist.

"That's not what I meant. But perhaps if you all stopped to think about what was going on around you, you'd see that the Risen is purposely tearing you apart to weaken you."

"And Alois' death is just another ploy to weaken our resolve?"

Amara kissed between his shoulder blades and he sighed at the contact.

"See, I can be helpful to your cause."

"I don't understand how you know all this."

"I watched in my visions of the outside world." She turned

him around by his waist to face her. Amara leaned up on her tip toes and kissed his lips gently. He didn't find any comfort in it though.

"And those visions were concentrating on me and my family?" He tilted his head to the side. "Are you a distraction as well?"

Her eyes snapped up to his and she hurriedly unwrapped her arms around him. "No. God's no. I want nothing more than to be seen by everyone. I want to meet people and go places. My entire existence has been in a prison. I wish nothing more than to meet Anna and Damian, the people closest to you. It just hurts and I have too much time to think on things."

Tears spilled over onto her cheeks and he pulled her body close to his. This whole Risen thing made him wary of everyone around him and he was casting suspicion on her where it didn't belong. He hated seeing her like this. She came into his life quickly and his heart was already becoming hers and hers alone.

"You truly want to meet them?" He kissed the top of her head. Nodding into his chest he backed off a bit and held her at arm's length. "Your wish is my command."

Leaving the room, he knocked on Damian's door which felt odd given it used to be his door before he gave up his room for the baby. Damian answered looking sweaty and gross, but he was wearing clothes, so it was a little less traumatizing.

"What's up?" he asked breathlessly.

"What are you guys up to?" Cato couldn't help but smirk.

Rolling his eyes Damian said, "I was rearranging this damn room because Anna doesn't like it the way it is."

"That is far less entertaining than I thought."

"Sorry to disappoint. What's up?"

Cato bit his lip. "We need to talk."

"Okay?"

"My room."

Without another question, Damian followed Cato back to his new room down the hall. Cato hated keeping Amara from everyone. There just never seemed to be a good moment to bring her out into the world. There were too many questions surrounding it, most of which he couldn't answer himself. However, the woman had him wrapped around her little finger and he was sick of seeing her cry.

Once they made it to Cato's room, he shut the door quietly and turned to face a confused Damian.

"So, I have a confession."

"Is everything okay?"

Cato nodded but then shook his head. "I've been hiding things from you guys. Well, one thing but it's a big one."

"If this is some sort of euphemism…"

"Gods no." Cato nervously laughed. "That's funny though."

"What is it, Cato?"

He rubbed the back of his head and looked around for the purpose of this little meeting, but she was nowhere in sight. "It would probably just be easier to show you but I don't seem to see her anywhere."

On cue, Amara poked her head out from the bathroom. Cato motioned for her to come forward and she sheepishly did so. Damian followed his indication and Cato saw his jaw literally drop. He looked between Amara and Cato.

"What the hell were you thinking?" Damian demanded. "She isn't supposed to be here."

"Why not?" Cato closed the distance between Amara and himself. "We said we would get her off the island."

"Yes, but we didn't. So how in the ever-loving underworld is she here?"

Cato looked down at Amara who mirrored the woman he first saw. She was scared, timid and looked like a damn flight risk. Some sort of caveman instinct kicked in within Cato that said, 'protect my woman' and he grew angry.

"A god rescued her and brought her to me."

"Don't get all pissed off with me." Damian's laugh didn't reach his eyes. "You're the one keeping secrets."

"Oh, as if you haven't?" Cato spat out.

"What the hell does that mean?"

"It means I am always out of the loop with everything." This was not how he envisioned this conversation going. He imagined bad but this was worse. Damian looked hurt and angry. Amara looked scared. He felt all kinds of crap that he couldn't explain. He needed to tone this down a bit. "That's not the point. The point is, is that Amara is here now and I wanted her to finally come out of hiding."

"Which god brought her here?" Damian crossed his arms. "I doubt Apollo did."

"I don't know." Cato looked down at Amara. "Who was it?"

"I cannot say." Her voice was barely above a whisper. "I was instructed not to."

"Well that seems awfully suspicious," Damian grunted.

Cato rubbed his face in frustration and placed his hands on Damian's shoulders.

"Look, I get it. It's odd but she's here and dammit I love this woman."

Damian's eyes widened and Cato could see the anger transform into worry.

"Love her? You've never said that about anyone."

"Yet here we are." Cato sighed. "I trust her. She picked me up when Ryan died and I can't thank her enough for it. I just... I love her, Damian. I want you to love her too, like I love Anna."

Damian took a step back and locked his hands behind his head. He was thinking hard. Damian hard. Which was basically over thinking, but Cato admired that quality on most occasions.

"Can we speak alone?" Damian looked to Amara and smiled slightly. "Please."

Amara nodded and practically ran back into the bathroom. Once the door was shut Cato waited for all hell to be brought down upon him.

"Okay, let me have it."

Damian about sat down on his bed but changed his mind. "Yeah, I'm not touching that." He went over to the couch but by the look Cato gave him, changed his mind and decided to just stand with his arms crossed.

"This doesn't bode well, Cato."

"How so?" Cato knew what he was talking about, but he wanted to believe the best of the situation.

"She showed up out of nowhere after being on an island for hundreds of years. Rescued by a god she can't name. She has penetrated the inner circle of our group, no offense. It's a tad bit suspicious."

Cato had these thoughts all along, but he couldn't help but give her the benefit of the doubt.

"She seems sincere."

"Has she pushed for information? Been acting strangely?"

"If you are asking if she is a spy, I highly doubt it."

"Do you really believe that or is your heart speaking for you?"

Cato didn't care what Damian thought of his furniture. It was perfectly safe to sit on and so Cato did. Resting his elbows on his knees and couldn't help but shrug.

"I really don't know. She listens to me. Makes me feel like

I am actually worth something more than I am. I feel fucking great when I am with her. I can't explain it."

"I get it one hundred percent because Anna does the same for me, but Cato, this isn't a typical situation. Please, I beg you just be careful with her. I hope to Zeus I am wrong, but I don't trust her presence." Cato was about to interrupt but Damian went on. "I would love nothing more than for you to have found your soulmate and I hope and pray this will turn out amazing for you."

"Thanks." Cato took a deep breath. "I'm not an idiot. It's super sketchy and the way she was talking earlier got me a little messed up but damn, it's hard to see past my feelings."

Damian nodded. "It's a shit storm. It's exactly how Ryan felt with Julia."

The both took deep breaths and felt the air grow heavy around them. "I miss that fucker."

"Understatement of the century."

Chapter XX

Anna

"I DON'T CARE HOW YOU do it, get hold of that son of a bitch so we can have a meeting!" Damian yelled into a cell phone. "Find a damn way then."

Anna wasn't quite used to this side of Damian still, but she had to put up with it for just a little longer. He was making plans to meet with the General for a final battle to end the war and it didn't seem to be going well. Caleb was on the receiving end of her husband's tantrum right now and she felt bad for the guy.

She cradled Owen in her arms and kissed his little forehead. He scrunched up his face at her touch but didn't wake up. He was a tired little thing. Eating and sleeping were his specialties.

After laying him in his crib she turned to find Damian leaning over the railing of the balcony. His head in his hands and shoulders hunched. It hurt her heart to see him like this. Her man deserved so much more than to be tormented.

Coming up behind him, she wrapped her arms around his waist and laid her head between his shoulder blades. She could feel his body relax and it brought a slight smile to her face knowing she had a calming effect on him. Giving him a tight squeeze, he turned in her arms to face her. His pathetic excuse of a smile flitted across his lips before resting into his never-ending frown today.

"Breathe," she cooed.

With a groan, he pressed their foreheads together. She could feel the frustration radiating off his body and she wanted to calm his soul. To let him know it would be okay and she believed in him, but she said it so often she was fairly certain he tuned her out.

"This is frustrating."

"Well, yeah." She smirked up at him, but he kept his eyes closed.

"I don't know how to handle this. I wasn't born into this type of leadership and honestly, I hate it. This isn't me."

"You are just as capable as anyone, Damian."

Shaking his head, he made his way back into their room and out of Owen's. "That's not what I mean. I know I am a damn good Warrior and damn good in battle but being the man everyone is counting on... I hate it. This isn't what I want at all. I feel no need to prove I can do it and I feel no pleasure in it."

"That's a good thing. You won't get all power hungry like the General."

"You don't get it. I don't want this responsibility. I want to advise my leader and do what I can to help."

"Unfortunately, those aren't the cards we've been dealt right now." He rolled his eyes at her. "We all trust you, so you need to trust yourself."

"I need to get hold of Marc." He changed the subject. "Caleb doesn't know how to. It's not like we have a damn phone number for him and I sure as hell am not going back to his damn fortress."

Anna walked to the bed and laid down, crossing her ankles and put her hands behind her head. "I love you but sometimes you can be super dumb."

"What?"

"Call his ass out." She shrugged. "Get on the damn TV and tell him to meet with you to end this. Call him a coward or whatever if he refuses to see you."

Damian leaned over her body, hovering just above her on the bed in a mouthwatering sort of way. He pressed his lips roughly to hers and that familiar spark in her belly ignited. She would never get tired of this man's touch.

"See what being a leader has done to my intelligence?" He smirked. "I can't even see the simplest solution. Thank you, my love."

"Just promise me you bring that smart little brain of yours back to me when this is all over."

Their lips touched again before he moved down to nuzzle her neck. "It isn't little but yes, I will. I think stress has taken its course on me."

"What can I do to help?"

A wicked grin flashed along his lips and his body leaned down against her. "I can think of one thing."

Anna rolled him onto his back and straddled his hips. The stress and frustration seemed to leave his body and was replaced with the happy man she loved so much. His hands massaged her thighs, all the while she was forcing herself not to attack him right then and there.

A little whine came from the other room and they both sat still not making a noise. Anna looked down at Damian and bit her lip waiting to see if Owen would go back to sleep. It seemed to pass and Damian opened his mouth to speak but instead of his words, Owen's little cry muted him. They waited to see if it grew and sure enough it did.

"I'll get him." Damian picked her up off his lap and deposited her onto the bed.

"It's okay, I can do it." Anna started to get up, but Damian stopped her with a kiss.

"Let me take care of my boy." Damian grinned and practically ran into Owen's room.

"Fucking adorable," she mumbled to herself.

Damian was sitting at a table with a camera directly in front of him. Lee was putting a mic on his shirt while Liam fiddled with his computer. They weren't allowed in the Domus, so Damian decided he wanted to broadcast from a church in Tennessee where Liam and Lee were working out of right now. It was a last-minute decision, but Damian was determined to get this war over with.

Anna was determined to be the rock Damian needed in the most difficult time in his long life. It was the least she could do given how he pulled her out the ashes of her mortal life and bought hope and love back into her heart. There was no way in hell she was going to let him fall into a dark abyss.

He was nervous, it was painfully obvious by his continuous tapping on the table and his leg bouncing up and down. Unlike most of their broadcasts, he was wearing a white V-neck and jeans. His hair was freshly buzzed on the sides leaving the top longer and slicked back. Anna had also convinced him to clean up his heavy stubble, so he didn't look ragged and solemn.

"Looking good, Damian." Lee playfully smacked his shoulder. "Got that whole male model thing going on."

The exasperated look his eyes begged Anna to save him. She couldn't help but giggle at how he took compliments.

"Super sexy." She grinned.

"Zeus, protect me from these women," Damian muttered.

Cato walked into the tent and hugged Damian from behind. "Well aren't you just a cutie pie?" He squeezed Damian's cheeks.

Swatting him away, Damian couldn't help but show a smidgen of a smile.

"Yeah, yeah, shut up everyone and let's do this."

"Got the speech ready, Liam?" Lee turned towards the man madly typing away.

"Yep." As soon as he said it the speech appeared on a teleprompter by the camera.

Anna took a deep breath and watched as Damian did the same. He gave her a quick smile and she returned the favor. "You got this."

Damian nodded to her then to Lee. "Ready."

Lee counted down with her fingers from three to one and pointed at Damian to begin speaking.

"We are in an age where human capability knows no bounds. Technology exists that our ancestors couldn't even fathom. And yet even with our technological advancements, we are still fighting for the basic right of religious freedom. It is a fight our ancestors have fought before and it's one we wish to end once and for all. Do you think our ancestors would have given up their fight because the head of their revolution sacrificed himself for the greater good? No. They would not have given up. They would have kept their cause firmly planted in their mind, and hope alive in their hearts, as they became examples for future generations of what it means to fight for what you believe in." His face grew sullen as he continued to speak.

"Friends and family have died. Been torn from your arms for one malicious man's plan for personal revenge. We will no longer allow the Risen to continue their reign of terror. For months they have waged a war against us and our different religious beliefs. Much like our faith in our deities, we have never lost faith in our cause. Not once have we ever thought about giving up. Now is the time to stand and fight. For once and for all. A final battle to end the war against the dictatorship of the Risen." Damian's eyes glanced towards her briefly before he went on.

"So now I call on you, General. Choose a place and time and we shall stand and fight. If you really are the god you claim to be, come and face our armies. Come and fight those you think are yours to rule over. Unless of course you'd rather remain hidden in your little fortress, forcing your pawns to fight for you?

"If you do not take my challenge, the whole world will be forced to see you for what I already believe you to be—a coward who hides away because he is too scared to finish what he started. You have until tomorrow evening to give me your answer."

Damian paused for a moment, the intensity in his eyes was gripping. "Long live Alexander's memory."

The camera light flickered off.

"And we are out." Lee grinned widely.

Damian took a large breath and sat back in the chair.

"That was fun."

"Yup, you called his ass out for sure." Cato grinned at Anna's side. "Biggest puss ever if he doesn't answer you."

"Oh, he will. I know he will." Damian stood from his chair and made his way to her. Anna looked up into those brown eyes of his and kissed his nose. He scrunched his brows, but a smile crept on his lips. "You sure know how to make a guy less stressed, you know."

"I bet she does." Cato grinned widely and was then punched in the shoulder by Anna. "Ouch."

"You deserve it." She tried to hide her smile. "That was perfect, Damian."

"Now we wait." Liam was typing away some more. "It's on repeat, broadcasting around the world as we speak."

Anna pulled Damian's body to hers as she closed her eyes listening to the heavy beating of his heart.

"Nervous?" she asked quietly.

Damian merely nodded yes and held her body against his before leading her to sit down on some chairs. They watched Damian's speech on repeat for at thirty minutes until it flicked off and was replaced with the large frame of Julia and Cato's father. His eyes were serious, his jaw tense. Yep, he looked pissed.

"It appears I have no choice but to answer," the General started. "So, you wish to end this war? That is fine by me. My people have died enough for your petty attempts to defend those who have brought us injustice. Our armies will meet head to head two weeks from today. We will further discuss the location privately. I won't apologize for being so short but I don't need inflated speeches to rally my followers."

With that, the screen went blank and they were left with the sounds of the wind whistling outside.

Damian

His fingers were tapping madly on the phone to the point where he knew what Anna was about to ask.

"What the hell are you doing?"

"Texting Marc," he answered simply.

Cato took his eyes off his computer screen and huffed.

"You're texting him?"

"Yep."

Damian could see Anna and Cato exchange glances in his peripheral, but it didn't stop the constant banter he was having with Marc. The damn man couldn't agree on shit. Location was never good for him and the time frame seemed nearly impossible but given the masses heard it, they didn't have a choice.

"What about?" Anna decided to sit next to him instead of cuddling with Owen on the ground in the Garden of Isis at the Domus.

"Nothing"

Owen sneezed and Cato left his laptop on the ground and army crawled over to Owen. "Are you allergic to your dad's bullshit too? Yes, you are. Yes, you are!" His voice went up high to make Owen smile wide.

"Nice baby talk." Anna rolled her eyes at him. "How did you get his number and why are you texting?"

"A phone was sent to me earlier today by a messenger and we are discussing the battle." Damian was already annoyed with the conversation on the phone, he didn't feel the need to repeat it out load as well.

"You're discussing the future of humanity via text message?" Cato asked.

"Yep." Damian's phone buzzed with a reply from the General.

Rome

Home field advantage? I don't think so.

Besides, you've put that city through enough turmoil.

Hasn't been my home for hundreds of years.

There is plenty of farmland there.

Not happening. What about New Zealand?

Very secluded and less likely to get civilians killed.

No.

This isn't working.

You might as well draw a country's name out of a hat and decide that way.

England.

Too many people are there.

On farmland, free of city life and isolated.

Rather poetic, don't you think?

"Will you please show me what the hell you two are saying?" Anna tried to look at the phone but Damian kept moving it out of the way.

"I'm trying to concentrate."

"Please?"

"I will tell you when I am done."

You want to perish where your wife died?

I prefer to see it as the beginning of an uprising.

Where it all began.

Fine.

Damian turned the phone screen off and looked up to Cato and Anna's curious eyes.

"England."

Cato's mood changed in an instant, but Anna didn't look much bothered by it. The bliss of not knowing the significance must be freeing. However, like Cato, Damian wasn't exactly excited about England either. He knew Marc's wife well and it was a hard time in all their lives when she passed.

"So now what?" Anna asked.

"Now we prepare for war. The stage is set and we must gather our troops."

"Is there going to be land large enough to hold both of our armies there?" Cato looked like he tasted something nasty. "It isn't exactly a large country."

"It will be perfectly fine." Damian said a little more forcefully than he intended. "Get word to the Warriors, our troops need to start moving towards England. Our North American troops need to get the hell over there now. Those protecting Rome, Washington D.C., and Notre Dame will remain as well as other significant sites. I refuse to leave those unguarded. We need to begin getting armor and weapons for those heading to England."

"That's a lot of people to mobilize." Anna looked sheepish as she spoke.

Damian stood up from the ground and walked among the flowers. "It can be done. Just get word out. A camp needs to be set up as soon as possible to house our soldiers. Just make sure we move people out as quickly as possible okay?"

Cato nodded, grabbing his laptop he kissed Owen's head and ran off to get things done. Damian felt odd giving orders like this, but he needed to man up at this point. It was nearing the end. Less than two weeks to go and there was far too much to be done.

He started to walk off to deal with the armor issue when Anna coughed from behind him.

"Yes?" He couldn't help but be amused.

"And what the hell am I supposed to do exactly?" She crossed her arms.

Damian walked with purpose towards her, pulling her body to his and kissed her deeply until her heart beat rapidly under his touch. "Isn't it obvious?"

"No," she said breathlessly.

"Get me a damn squadron of fighter jets."

Chapter XXI

Damian

"JULIA, ANSWER THE DOOR." Damian stood outside of her room but there was no answer.

From what Cato had told him, she had been in her room since getting drunk. Cato had tried to get into her room but she kept it locked. He'd almost snuck in when food was brought to her but she was too quick for him. Damian decided enough was enough. Besides, they needed her to help prepare for war.

"I swear to the god's, I will break down this door, Julia." He kept knocking continuously. The door flew open and there stood a Julia he had never seen before.

"What the hell do you want?"

She was drunk. He could smell it on her. Whatever eye makeup she had on was now smeared in tear-stained tracks down her cheeks. That wasn't what was most shocking though. She was completely naked.

He turned away from her as quickly as he could muster.

"We need to talk."

"Talk?" She laughed behind him. "Sure, why not. Let's talk."

He could hear her feet pattering away from the door, so he walked backwards into the room, closing the door quickly behind him in case anyone were to walk by and see her.

"Do you mind?" he asked.

"Mind what?"

"You're naked, Julia."

"Oh, yes. I sure am." She didn't sound the least bit phased, but he could hear her rustling through her closet for clothes. "It's safe."

Damian turned around to find her in pink silk pants and a blue cocktail dress.

"Sweet Athena…" he mumbled under his breath.

"So, what is it you want?" She reached for a bottle of whiskey, but he stopped her in her tracks. "What the hell, Damian?"

"You need to get it together. This isn't you."

She looked herself up and down and laughed at her appearance. She smiled at herself then tears began to fall down her face and her body began to tremble. Damian pulled her into him and wrapped his arms tightly around her small frame. She heaved heavy cries, gasping for air as her grief and sorrow ravaged her mind and body. All he could do was hold her and soothe her because he knew he was on the brink of feeling the same way.

"Deep breaths." His voice was as soothing as he could muster. "In and out. Good job. Again."

Her ribs expanded and deflated repeatedly until she seemed to calm down. But the weight of her body grew and he caught her before she collapsed to the ground. Making a quick decision, he carried her to her bathroom, cradling her body to his as he started a bath with lavender salts.

She didn't protest when he peeled off the odd combination of clothing from her body, nor did he shy away from her. There was no awkwardness from seeing her exposed like earlier. He was merely taking care of a woman he considered his sister when she needed help the most.

Once the tub was full, he placed her in the warm water and

the crease in her brow smoothed out. Her eyes remained shut while he worked. With a rag, he wiped her cheeks and under her eyes until any trace of makeup was gone.

As soon as he washed her hair out, she opened her swollen eyes and placed a wet hand on his cheek.

"Thank you."

"Don't mention it." He forced a smile. "Really, don't. Cato and Anna would kill me."

To his surprise she laughed at his joke.

"It still hurts so much."

"That it does."

"I don't get how any of you can carry on and be happy. Weddings and parties, all good times as if the world didn't crumble the moment his heart stopped."

Taking a deep breath, he counted to ten before he could answer her.

"May I be honest with you?"

"Yes."

"I am happy with my son and Anna. More than I have ever been. I would be lying if I said I wasn't using them as a distraction though." He took another deep breath. "Yes, I wanted to get married. That wasn't a secret. But getting married helped me hide how devastated my soul is. If I didn't have them, I would feel as you do right now. Seeing you like this… I can feel myself falling apart just talking about it."

He hung his head and tears threatened to come. The intensity of mourning Julia had was close to taking him over until she placed her forehead to his. They breathed deeply together, inhaling the soft lavender fragrance with no sound but the air they took in.

His soul was tattered, almost beyond healing, but Anna and Owen were helping him heal. Julia, well, she simply didn't have it as easy as he did. The torment she was going through would probably cause him to end his life if he were in her position.

"How do I survive this?" She pulled her head from his.

Her eyes were so sad he couldn't help but kiss her forehead.

"We go on. Make sure we avenge the hell out of him and never give up. I don't know about you but if he ever found out I was giving up he'd kick my ass."

Her tearful eyes twinkled with amusement. "Then we will kick some ass."

"Atta girl."

Cato

"Let the fucking countdown to hell begin."

"Nice outlook," Damian grunted at him.

Cato had called on the Urbs' armorer and weapons master to meet in the training arena at the Domus. Both were the top men in their fields in Urbs and in Cato's opinion, the world. They brought with them the different options for Damian to choose from to arm their soldiers.

"So, what are you wanting to assign each foot soldier? Short sword, long sword, dagger, axe, I could go on and on." Tyler's enthusiasm was apparent.

Cato watched Tyler's black Mohawk sway when he moved his head. It was like watching weebles wobble, but it never fell down. He liked that about him, dude didn't care what people thought and did his own thing.

Damian walked up and down the tables that were set up with different weapons displayed.

"I'm thinking AR-15."

Cato crossed his arms. "I'm more of an AK-47 kind of guy."

Tyler shrugged. "Could do both and add some SA80 Carbines in there while we're at it."

Damian nodded in agreement. "That's fine. I need at least two handguns."

Tyler walked over to the table with handguns.

"Glock 19, Sig Sauer P226—"

"Both," Damian interrupted. "And one of each for each solider."

"Jupiter, why both?" Cato asked.

"Just in case." Damian walked towards the swords and knifes. "One of each of these as well."

"Short sword or long?" Tyler questioned.

"Short."

"Any specific knife?"

"Just make sure it is a fixed blade and not folding. Whatever you believe the best to be. Make sure the swords come with scabbards on the hip as well."

"Can do." Tyler saluted.

Next was Jason the armorer. He wasn't quite as tall as Cato but then not many people were. He stroked his beard while waiting for Tyler to finish up with Damian, so Cato walked over to the man. Nudging Jason to the side he was returned with a shove.

"Fucker," Cato laughed.

Jason's lip quirked up. "You guys are really going to put him in a hell of a bind, aren't you?"

"You mean with all the shit Damian wants for thousands of people?" Jason nodded. "Yeah, but I'm sure you guys have your ways."

"You're lucky we horde the hell out of shit and know where the warehouses holding this stuff are."

Jason picked up a tactical vest and smacked Cato in the stomach with it. Cato held the vest at arm's length.

"What?"

"It's military grade. Only type I have vast amounts of. I've tweaked it and was expecting to present it to the Warriors as their new go-to vest, but here we are. It's a light weight, multi threat proof vest against both bullets and knives."

"Don't we already have that?"

"Yes, but this covers a larger area of the torso and shoulders than normal while still keeping easy mobility. Not to mention the steel plates are far superior in strength than what you have now. It's way better, trust me." Jason took the vest from Cato's hands and placed it back on the table. "I can provide enough tactical helmets as well."

Damian came closer to them with Tyler at his heels.

"Good, we need full body armor for one million fighters. Think it can be done?"

Jason nodded as did Tyler.

"What in the name of Pluto are you guys doing with a stockpile that large?" Cato was partially impressed and shocked.

"It was inevitable in my opinion. From the first day the Risen attacked the Great Temple we sort of started to gain more and more supplies. We didn't know exactly what you guys would want but we figured Ryan wouldn't want anything cheap." Tyler squeezed his eyes closed catching himself. "Sorry, I didn't mean to..."

Damian held his hand up. "No need to apologize. You're totally right and I intend to do the same. Just let me know the cost of it all once you figure it out."

"There isn't any need for that." Jason looked somewhat offended at the notion of being paid. "I'm happy to provide whatever is needed."

"That isn't how that works." Damian smiled lightly. "You both will be paid. These things weren't free to you and I have no intention of taking a handout. We will do this the right way."

Tyler and Jason both looked as if they wanted to argue but knew better. Hell, Cato knew better at this point than to argue with him. Damian's tone was always friendly before Ryan's death but as of late, it became more serious. You can see the weight of his new role as leader weighing on him. Being somebody that you really weren't had to be draining for the soul and it was definitely taking its toll on Damian.

"We will have the supplies ready as soon as possible and meet you at the camp." Jason held his hands over his heart as did Tyler before they turned to gather their things.

Cato and Damian left the arena, both quiet and deep in thought. Damian was probably thinking about the war but Cato had other things on his mind.

"Thank the god's for fanatics that prepare for the end of the world."

"No shit." Damian amazingly cracked a smile. "I don't care how or where that shit is as long as we have it. I just hope we aren't bringing too small of an army. I can't risk taking more fighters without giving up our strongholds in case shit goes south."

"We will make it work. An English farm can only hold so many people." Cato put his arm around Damian's shoulder as they walked back to their rooms.

"You and the damn English." Damian smirked.

"Me and the damn English."

"Who the hell is this again?" Cato watched his sister look Amara up and down like she was some sort of dirty rodent.

"Amara," she reintroduced herself. "The Oracle."

"You mean former Oracle?" Julia crossed her arms over her chest.

"I thought you didn't remember who I am?" Amara shot back.

Cato felt his eyes widen and he looked to his left at Damian. The damn man had the nerve to look amused by the two women. Not that Cato was opposed to catfights, but when it included his sister it most definitely lost the hot value.

"Did you tell Julia about Amara?" Cato whispered into Damian's ear. His response was his shoulders shrugging and high-pitched hum.

"You fucker."

Damian slapped him on the back. "It was bound to happen. Besides, she needs the distraction."

"You thought the best way to distract her from Ryan was to piss her off?"

"Better angry than sad."

"That literally makes no sense," Cato grumbled.

The two women were hardcore staring each other down in the middle of the library. Since Ryan's death, Damian had turned it into a sort of control center for planning. Everything was pushed against the wall and Cato was precariously standing in the middle of Russia on the world map painted on the floor.

He needed to escape this awkwardness as soon as possible. He slowly took steps backwards while the women bickered. Something along the lines of Julia not trusting her presence and so on. Unfortunately, he only made it a few steps before he got called out.

"Get your sneaky, lying, ass back in here," Julia spat at him. She was in full-on mom mode.

"Look, I know this is weird."

"Oh, we are beyond weird. There is no way in hell a god

would go behind Apollo's back to free her. And for what reason? It's not as if the Siren's Island is a hot spot for vacationing gods."

"She has a point." Damian shrugged.

"Who is to say I don't have connections with other gods? Ones that aren't as cruel to leave a woman all alone on an island full of monsters?" Amara shot back.

Cato nodded. "She has a point too."

"Her point is calling the gods evil," Julia countered. "Something a traitor would say."

"You would know." Amara smiled wickedly.

Cato was about to have a damn aneurysm or something. He knew his sister would be just as cautious as Damian was, but he did not expect Julia to go all crazy on her. If anything, he thought she would be happy he'd found someone to settle down with.

"Okay, let's just stop insulting each other and try accept the fact Amara has promised to keep her savoir a secret." Cato tried to smile at everyone, but no one looked amused. "I literally have no idea what to do here."

"You could start by interrogating her," Julia scoffed. "She's probably a damn spy!"

"How dare you accuse me of betraying Cato." Amara was now in Julia's face, but his sister didn't back off at all. "I love that man with everything I am. When he found me I was scared, dirty, and defeated. He brought me up from the ashes and treated me as someone more than a tool to be used."

If he were a sensitive man, he may have had tears in his eyes, but Cato merely felt his heart beat faster. He wanted nothing more than to attack Amara with his mouth, but he restrained his urges in front of his sister. It was the polite thing to do. Still, he couldn't see the suspension falter in Julia's or Damian's eyes at all.

"Let's concentrate on the upcoming war instead of who I am seeing. Seems like a better use of our time." Cato grabbed hold of Amara's hand and squeezed. She gave it a squeeze back before wrapping her arms around his waist. "When are we heading to the camp?"

Damian cleared his throat before speaking. You could see he was glad for the change of subject.

"Well, it's been a week since Marc declared that we have two weeks. I say we head there tomorrow. Caleb and Colette are already there and have been organizing the incoming troops. Some are setting up tents, assigning gear and weapons as Tyler and Jason bring them in and others are making sure food lines are stocked. About half our men have arrived so far."

"The Immortals have already brought their horses there for the cavalry. We should get ours as well." Cato hated the thought of his beautiful creatures getting hurt but unfortunately there wasn't any other options. Supplies were becoming few and far between.

"Agreed." Damian side-eyed Julia who was still staring at Amara.

Cato hated seeing his sister fuming but then again, he did the same with Ryan and Aden. One turned out to be a raging psychopath, so he was hoping that didn't turn out to be the case with Amara. Far as he knew though, she wasn't drugging him.

"Cato, I need you to come with me if you don't mind." Julia stalked towards the stairs. "Now."

Kissing the top of Amara's head, he rubbed her back. "I will see you back in a little, okay?"

"I'll be here."

Cato decided to avoid Damian's reaction to this entire meeting and ran to catch up with Julia. She was already making her way out the doors of the Domus. Where was this woman going?

"Yeah, if you could wait up for me that'd be great!" Cato shouted at her back.

"Hurry the hell up," she shouted over her shoulder.

Cato did as he was told and made his way down the steps to her. She didn't say anything but the fury in her eyes said it all. Was she pissed with him? Most assuredly.

The crazy woman didn't say a word, just kept walking down the streets and looking over at him to make sure he still followed. It wasn't until the familiar twists and turns registered in his mind that he knew where they were headed. The one place he hadn't stepped in for many years.

Once they were outside their family's estate, Cato looked up at the house with disdain. He hated it here. His father had made life miserable. Whereas his mother did everything in her power to make life enjoyable. After she'd passed, Cato had refused to come back. The place was a prison without his mother's presence.

"Why are we here?" he asked, stopping in his tracks outside of the house.

He looked up at the three-story home that had roman and colonial influence—his mother's design. It was made from limestone and covered with marble. The statues of Greek and Roman heroes were placed evenly between the shrubbery in front of the house for as long as he could remember. Multi-paned windows with shutters were evenly placed on either side of the columned front door giving it a White House sort of vibe.

"I need to grab something. It's important and I am afraid to come back here alone." Julia looked up at their parents' home.

Cato was a sucker for his sister, there was no doubt about that. After their father drugged her with the tonic, she said this was the meeting place of the Risen. She had described many occasions of watching Ahmose and others tortured to obtain information. It chilled him to think of such horrors happening in his mother's home.

"Alright, lead the way." Cato held out his arm for her which she linked hers into.

He opened the unlocked door and took a very difficult step inside. There was no doubt about how odd it felt being in this house right now. It looked so similar since the last time he was here that he felt like he was in some sick creepy movie was invading his memories.

After a few hundred years he figured it would have been sold and remodeled but that was obviously not the case. Even as they walked up the left side of the double staircase he was overcome with the familiarity. His hand skimmed the black banister that was a stark contrast to the white marble flooring, his thumb brushing over the small niche he carved in the wood as a child.

"Is that the same chandelier?" Cato was in utter shock.

"Yep. Black crystal illuminated by candlelight."

Although it wasn't lit right now, he could make out the semi-melted candles still in place.

"For the love of Mars, update it a little."

"Mother loved that chandelier," Julia spoke softly as they reached the top of the staircase.

Cato kept his mouth shut. She was upset with him and more than likely whatever was going to come out of his mouth would just upset her more. So, he stared at the long red, carpet runner in the middle of the marbled floor.

"Didn't you say Maggie, the housekeeper, was still around?" Cato ran a finger along one of the many framed pictures of past Warriors. "It's dusty."

"I guess she must have finally moved on." Julia sighed as she turned towards one of the empty closets in the hallway.

All that resided inside the closet were two blankets sitting on shelves. There was enough room to walk in but for Cato it was still a little difficult. Julia fit in easily and knocked on the side wall next to the door. The hollowed-out sound made him laugh out loud.

"You little shit, hiding things from me."

Julia smiled up at him from her crouching position. "I had my little spots in this house. I'm sure you did too."

"Too true. Most of mine fit two people comfortably though."

"Such a pig." She smiled and returned to her little hiding spot.

She unstrapped a blade that was sheathed on her thigh and wedged it between the boards. One of the boards came loose and Cato could see something long and wrapped in linen. Okay, now he was definitely curious.

"What is it?"

Julia grabbed the object and after replacing the board they scooted out of the closet. She carefully unwrapped a small sword that gleamed in the sunlight shining through the windows. It was a petite woman's sword decorated with swirling designs along the blade.

Cato took a step back from Julia.

"What are you doing with that? I thought it was destroyed."

"Hardly. I hid it from Father. He wanted to destroy it, but I couldn't bear the thought."

"Why would you want to keep the very blade that took our mother's life?"

"It's a good thing I did." She covered the blade back up. "So I can take our father's with it as well."

Chapter XXII

Damian

"It's time to go, my love." Damian hugged Anna from behind as she held on to Owen.

His little brown eyes were alert and he was cooing at his mother as she made silly faces. It was hard to leave him here but there was no way in hell he was going to allow Owen in the camp. Zeus knows what Marc could possibly have up his sleeve and Damian didn't put it past him to attack without warning.

"Just five more minutes." He could hear her try to suppress her sobs and, in all honesty, he was trying to as well.

"You said that about an hour ago."

"I can come to the camp the day before," she said for about the tenth time.

Damian gently rubbed his thumb over Owen's brow. His nose scrunched up, and his toothless smile melted his heart. How in Hades is he going to be able to leave him here?

"We need all of our Captains there for the planning. You have command of the air."

"We aren't Captains, Damian. I haven't earned that rank. Besides, I have found more decorated individuals than myself to fly that are more deserving."

Damian gently turned her around to face him. Tears were

running down her cheeks and he couldn't help but to smile at her.

"I thought you wanted to go. That there was no way in hell you were staying behind."

"Well, look at this cute little butterball in my hands," she groaned.

"You didn't want to be a mother either," he mused.

"Well, look who changed her damn mind." She was visibly upset but her expression softened once he kissed her with a grin. "Yeah, yeah, yeah. I'm a damn liar, hypocrite, whatever the hell you want to call me."

Damian took Owen from her arms and kissed his little head. Little fingers found their way into his hair and held on for dear life as Owen accidentally pulled his hair. "Easy there, strong man."

Anna helped released him from the death grip of a baby's grasp.

"See, he doesn't want you to go either."

"I yield. You can stay with him." Damian smiled down at his little boy.

With one last kiss he handed Owen back to Anna. Her eyes started to tear up once again and his heart sank into the deepest depths of the earth. He was determined to make it home to the both of them. There was no way in hell he would allow his son to not have a father if he could help it.

"I will see you when it's done, my love." He kissed her lips softly, passion quickly taking over. Damian tried his best not to squish the little body between them, but he wanted nothing more than to bring her closer to him.

"Take care of him, okay?"

"Damn it all to hell," she growled. "Olivia!"

Olivia came running into their room from Owen's and

tossed a washcloth over her shoulder. "What's up? Y'all ready to go?"

"Actually, Anna is—"

"Ready to go." She kissed Owen's head and gave him a small squeeze. "I love you little one."

She handed Owen off to Olivia who smiled down at their child with loving eyes. "No worries, we will be waiting at the safehouse for his bad-ass mom and dad to come back." With that she walked Owen off into his room leaving Damian and Anna staring after their son.

"What changed your mind?" He laced his fingers between hers.

"I can't sit by and let everyone else fight for him. I would never forgive myself and I will not cower down to those assholes. I was there when this shit started and I intend to finish it for his sake."

Damian pulled her body against his and grinned when her breath hitched. His hand wove into her hair while the other pulled her closer by the small of her back. Lips crushed against each other and frustration for closer contact itched at his insides.

"Be careful," she breathlessly whispered against his lips. "Don't start something you don't intend on finishing."

Pulling her earlobe between his teeth he relished in the sharp gasp he caused. "Don't worry, tonight we will have a tent all to ourselves."

"You frustrating man." She pulled away from him with amusement on her lips and lust in her eyes. "Let's get our ass to the camp before I change my mind."

It wasn't as hectic as he imagined it would be. Multi-colored camping tents were set up in neat rows and there was a line of people waiting in a chow line. Horses for the Warriors were kept in a fenced pasture and were grazing the green earth under their feet.

Damian looked down at his feet and could tell the grass was starting to die from being pounded into the dirt by thousands of feet preparing for the end. The smell of campfires filled the air and the familiar atmosphere was intoxicating. He stood for a moment with his eyes closed, enjoying the sounds and smells from remnants of his past. Ryan would have loved this.

The buildup to a confrontation on a massive level had his adrenaline in overdrive and he craved battle. He was never one to fully enjoy it. He didn't realize till just now how much he missed Ryan's campaigns to conquer the known world. He just wished Ryan were here with him.

"You okay?" Anna squeezed his hand.

"Yeah." He slowly opened his eyes and scanned over the military machine the Warriors had pulled together through their camp.

"Your tent is this way, sir." A man with curly black hair ushered them to what was obviously the biggest personnel tent in the camp.

Damian walked inside and noticed the tent had a communal area with three separate rooms branching off. He was thankful to be surrounded by those he trusted most. He was especially thankful to have Anna by his side. However, it posed a problem with keeping his promise for privacy to her.

"Tent to ourselves my ass." Anna looked around but she didn't seem all too bothered about it.

"What up roomies!" Cato burst out of one of the curtained offed rooms. "We fixin' to get this shit started or what?"

"Fixin'?" Damian's eyebrow raised. "Who the hell have you been around?"

"May have done a few shots with some southern boys before I came up here. Possibly. Not sure. It's hard to tell."

"Could you perhaps set a higher example for us?" Damian sighed. "We are their leaders. They look to us for guidance."

"They also need to see we are still part of them and not stuck up assholes that think they are better than them." Cato's smile didn't falter. "A lot of them only have a few days left on this damn planet. Might as well make the most of it."

"Just make sure they are able to fight when the time comes." Damian smirked. "Otherwise, have at it."

Cato exaggerated a salute and left the tent just as Caleb and Colette entered. Damian saw Colette's eyes widen and her cheeks redden when she saw him and he had no idea why. Anna, however, was as giddy as she could be.

"Are you two in the other room?" Anna smiled from ear to ear.

Colette nodded and Caleb had to answer for her in actual words, "Yes."

Colette made a beeline to their room leaving Caleb behind.

"What's with her?" Damian felt his face look just as confused as he felt.

"Oh, she used to like you," Anna said nonchalantly.

Damian's eyebrows shot up. "What?"

"That's not why." Caleb laughed. "She's old fashioned. I think she feels odd about people knowing we are sleeping together, in the same bed that is. Not to mention I'm Jewish and she's a die-hard Catholic."

"Why the hell would we judge?" Anna laughed. "Mr. Pagan over here is with Mrs. Catholic."

"I don't try to change her feelings. I just try to be there for her while she works through it." Caleb shrugged. "We are going to get some sleep though. Been up all night getting that damn horse fence up."

Caleb patted Damian's back and disappeared behind the curtain to their room. Damian led Anna to the last room. It was small but with a bed and nightstand in it. Their gear and weapons were displayed on wooden mannequins in the corner of their room and looked brand new. Thank the gods Tyler and Jason pulled it together in time.

"How are you holding up?" He pulled Anna into his arms.

"Better than expected. It just became super real that this shit is about to go down."

"You still have time to back out." He kissed the tip of her nose, watching it scrunch up after he did so. "Owen gets that from you."

"Well, I ain't leaving so quit using his cuteness to get what you want."

"Can't blame a guy for trying." He kissed her temple, then her cheek as he worked his way to her lips.

Backing her to the edge of the bed with his lips still on hers, Damian held her close to his body as he lowered them down to the bed. Pulling herself further up on the mattress he climbed between her legs and moved his hips against hers. Frustration built up in his core and he growled when she nipped at his bottom lip.

Pinning her arms above her head she grinned up at him with lustful eyes. His hips ground into hers and it was his turn to grin when her eyes became hooded with want. As much as he enjoyed teasing her, he needed her more. He sat up between her legs, taking his shirt off and tossing it to gods know where.

"For the love of Jupiter! Is everyone in this tent getting laid?" Julia exclaimed as she walked into their room.

Damian quickly climbed off Anna and sat on the edge of the bed. Julia was standing with her back to them, bouncing on her heels and probably felt just as awkward as he did. She had a bag clasped in her hands behind her back that looked rather heavy.

"Need help?" He was breathless but he tried to tame his voice. It didn't work very well.

"Nope. Judging from the fact that I just walked in on two different couples about to get it on, it's safe to assume the third room is for Cato and I?" Julia shook her head, probably in embarrassment. "I'm somewhat frozen from humiliation so if you could just push me out that would be fantastic."

Anna jumped out of the bed and gave Julia a smack on the ass.

"No problem. Love ya, now get out."

Julia laughed and called out, "Glad I brought freaking headphones!"

Julia

They had been in the camp for too many days arguing about what approach to take and who to put where. Julia was sick of it. She loved every damn person in this tent, but this was too much time in close quarters with them and her patience was hanging on by a thread.

It wasn't just the battle talk either. Colette and Caleb were at least discreet about things. Damian and Anna on the other hand tried to be quiet and failed miserably. Damian was too much like a brother to her for her to want to hear those kinds of noises.

After the second day, Cato had brought a massive package

of ear plugs but they both quickly found out they didn't work too well.

"Listening to people doing it while lying next to your sister was never something that ever even crossed my mind of things that would ever happen in our lives," Cato said one night.

"I guarantee it never crossed mine either."

Cato ended up sleeping on the floor because in all honesty, it was just awkward as hell.

So here they were, on the brink of war and in this damn tent for two more nights. How in the world Ryan, Damian, and Cato did this for years on end was beyond her. Then again, it was a man club back then, so no one probably gave a damn about what they heard.

"After tonight we just have tomorrow to prepare." They all knew it, but Damian still felt the need to remind them.

Julia was absolutely terrified. Reading about head on warfare was one thing but the actual participation? She never thought she'd have to do it.

"So, we have tanks?" Cato asked.

"Yep," Damian answered.

"And horses."

"Yeah," Anna said.

"And freaking jets, swords, and guns. This is all kinds of mixed the hell up." Cato groaned.

Julia had to agree to an extent. "The world wars were fought with all of those."

"Sort of," Cato mumbled. "It wasn't everyone in one place and charging at each other on horses with swords and shit though."

"So, it's a little different." Anna shrugged. "We got this."

Julia looked down at the map and tilted her head to the

side. It was sort of a chaotic set up. It definitely wasn't modern warfare.

"If we are going to meet them in hand-to-hand combat, we need to bring what we have available to us. Do you really think the General isn't going to bring guns to this fight? Or tanks or swords or any of it? He will be just as prepared as we are."

"If we are meeting on the field, we need swords for when guns run out of ammo, which they inevitable will. We can only hold so much ammo on ourselves so we take what we can get," Caleb said putting his two cents in.

"Yeah, yeah, yeah. I get it. It's just weird. A horse will get shot before it can even make it to the other side," Cato grumbled. "What sort of artillery are we expecting them to use?"

"Marc and I came to an agreement on that." Damian looked exhausted. "The only one we are allowing is tanks. However, I highly expect him to bring jets too, so we have Anna prepared for it. She will head out tomorrow with the other pilots to get ready."

"How do you know he will have aircrafts?" Colette asked.

"I just know how he thinks. We'd be able to see ground weapons from a distance and call it off, but an aircraft can come from miles away in the middle of the battle. He isn't exactly known for playing fair." Damian sighed. "This is chaotic. There's no rhyme or reason to any of it but it's what we have to work with I suppose."

"Only way to end it is one great battle," Anna agreed.

"Let's hope he sticks to his deal of winning this by strategic gridlock rather than pulling out cutting edge technology. I was hesitant to even agree to guns and tanks at this point," Damian sighed.

Julia had to admit to herself that this was nowhere near

anything any of them had experienced. It was as if someone took bits of every type of warfare and tossed it in a blender.

"So many people are going to die."

"We just need to follow the plan." Damian looked back down at the map of the landscape.

Scouts brought back what they saw and so did drones but there was no way to be sure exactly what Marc had in store. She knew her father probably had something hidden up his sleeve and it was frightening. He was never a man to cross and here they were, crossing the hell out of him.

"Are we all in agreement how this goes down?" Damian looked around the table.

Everyone nodded, but Julia was still skeptical about it all. Her brother was right, it was a mess to look at and there was no way of predicting how it would turn out. Guns, jets, tanks— it complicated the hell out of everything.

"Well, I can't wait for this cluster-fuck of a fight." Cato rubbed his hands together. "I plan on getting shitfaced tonight since Dad over here won't let me tomorrow. Any other takers?"

Everyone shook their heads no at him, including Julia. So with a sarcastic bow, her brother left the tent to gods knew where. Colette and Caleb took their leave to their room as did Anna, leaving Julia alone with Damian.

"There is no organization here, Damian."

"I need Ryan." Damian closed his eyes, she watched as his fists clench until his knuckles turned white. "I have no tact for this. I can lead others to a solution. Yet I can't make one though."

"You made the best call you could given the circumstances."

All she could do was picture people running towards each other. Guns firing and bodies dropping to the ground before they could even reach the other side, until everyone ran out of ammo. They would have to climb over the slaughtered bodies to keep the fight going with swords.

"Everyone in the front line will likely die." He sighed in defeat. "All those people out there probably don't even realize it either. I have to send them to the slaughter."

"We do what we must for the greater good, Damian. It's the hand we've been dealt."

"One I may or may not have to live with for eternity."

Chapter XXIII

Julia

"THIS IS IT," DAMIAN muttered from on top of his horse.

Julia merely nodded. The beast below her was growing restless standing still. Cato was on the right side of Damian and his horse pawed at the ground from impatience as well. Damian had offered to let her ride one of Ryan's prized horses, but she couldn't do it. She would never forgive herself if it died in battle.

The Warriors made up the cavalry whereas the mortals were firmly planted on the ground. Damian had spared no expense when it came to their safety. They wore the best body armor money could buy. Every single person was equipped with a sword, a rifle, two handguns, a knife and more. They wore all black gear but with blue armbands with the Immortals symbol to tell the difference between the enemy and them.

"Do you have any money left?" Cato asked.

"Doesn't matter as long as they are well protected." Damian's face was serious.

Julia knew he'd spent every cent he'd saved since becoming Immortal on their army. So she made sure that in her will, all her assets would be transferred to him and Anna if she were to die. Anna needn't worry about money with Owen and he deserved a good future.

She looked out past the long field separating them from the Risen. The enemy was large and well equipped but so were they. Their infantry was in front of Marc and his personal cavalry to protect himself from the Resistance forces. Julia cringed at the thought. Ryan always rode first into battle and his men had to catch up to protect him from getting overran.

"They have a similar formation," Cato grumbled.

"The Romans valued Ryan's military tactics. It's not a surprise." Damian looked to the left and right. "We have more cavalry at our flanks, but their heavy infantry is vast."

Cato popped his neck. "Let's get this over with.

Caleb commanded the left cavalry and Colette the right. Their purpose was clear, but Julia grew nervous. She had never been in a battle such as this. Damian looked at ease, as did Cato. Her heart dropped at the sight of so many people ready to kill her.

"I don't know if this is going to work," Cato mumbled. "They know your tactics."

"They know Ryan's tactics," Damian said.

Which is exactly what Damian planned to use, but Julia kept her mouth shut. Marc knew each way Alexander the Great confronted his enemies, but Damian also knew how her father would too. Tactics and formations might not be enough, it may just come down to who is the strongest out of the two.

"Here we go." Damian raised his hand in the air and dropped it swiftly to his side.

The troops lurched forward at a slow pace with men yelling orders to keep in line. The sound of thousands of feet marching filled the tension as the gap slowly closed between them and the enemy. Julia's horse was glad to be moving but fear was starting to take its toll on her as her heart pounded rapidly in her chest.

She could hear Caleb and Colette barking out orders and she jumped when Cato called out, "Keep your position!"

The front of their row was completely made up of heavy infantry with the cavalry at the sides. Behind them was more heavy infantry, archers, and light infantry. There were tanks following besides the cavalry, which made the horses somewhat skittish, but they persisted.

The front row held spears and as soon as Damian yelled, "Ready!" the spears lowered towards the marching Risen infantry.

"Steady!" Damian yelled with all his might.

The men around her started to yell as soon as they could see the faces of their enemy clearly and Julia found herself yelling right along with them. She didn't know what overcame her but the need to fight surged through her core bringing out a fierceness she didn't know was there.

Both armies sped up in their haste to reach the other. Adrenaline coursed through her veins as her horse kept up with the running infantry. It wasn't long until shots were firing off and the spears of those still standing drove into the marching infantry. Within seconds, the gasps and groans of dying men had begun.

Julia thrust her sword at the onslaught of enemy that surrounded her while her horse whined in protest. Vain attempts to stab her were made from those bellow and she thwarted every one of them as she sliced them across their throats. Blood drenched her stallion, but her adrenaline didn't mind when the reins became slick with crimson.

Soon she found herself unhorsed as a burly man with a long beard yanked her down and held a pistol to her cheek. She quickly took his feet out from under him and stabbed down hard into his belly. His eyes went wide open but she didn't have time to feel any empathy towards her would-be killer as the chaos around her took over.

There was no way of knowing if they were winning and she didn't have time to survey her surroundings. The only thing she could do was to defend herself over and over again. Threats never ceased and her arms protested from their weakened state. Multiple times she had to wipe the blood out of her eyes with the back of her sleeve and her sword slipped from her hand.

A man ran at her with a dagger and she barely removed her gun as he swiped the blade down the left side of her face. Instinctively she covered her eye with her hand and shot him in the head before he could have another go.

Suddenly, someone grabbed her shoulder and twisted her around. As she let off another shot her brother jeered out of the way just in time, to her relief.

"Watch it!" He grimaced as he pulled her hand from her face. "Fuck," he muttered and removed gauze from one of his many pockets.

"We don't have time for this!" she protested as he pressed the cloth against her wound.

"Bullshit. Watch my six," Cato grumbled. He dabbed at the wound quickly and coated it with some type of liquid that burned. "That'll keep the blood from getting in your eye."

"Thank you." She opened her left eye and was relieved she still had it. Cato smiled until he pushed her head down and swung his arm out above her. As soon as she stood, she saw a woman behind her with a large gash across her throat. "Thanks again."

"Don't mention it." Cato nodded in front of her. "Damian is bringing the cavalry around to trap them in. The middle is falling back."

"Father knows that maneuver," Julia groaned.

"But his men don't. Father is still at a safe distance and his men will think we're retreating."

Julia was unsure but who was she to say otherwise. Heavy artillery started to go off around her and mounds of earth flew up into the air from the impact of the tank's missiles. Hell was raining down all around them and her ears rang from someone shooting off a round much too close to her ear.

Cato let out a few curses when a bullet grazed his arm and Julia tried to help him but he shrugged her off.

"Stay focused, Julia. It's just a scratch." He gave her a charming smile and sliced off someone's arm as they tried to kill one of their soldiers.

The person wailed like a babe and fell to the ground as the blood loss began to take its toll. The carnage was building so quickly that she had no choice but to step on the dead bodies to move forward with the rest of the line. The men to her far left were successfully pulling back and the Risen's troops were actually falling victim to the trap.

Cato hollered with his fists in the air in triumph, but the victory was short lived when the enemy ran into their ranks with grenades strapped to their bodies. The heat from the explosions could be felt from were Julia stood and she had to crouch down to protect herself from the debris. An outburst of bloodcurdling screams erupted in the air.

"Fucking suicide bombers?" Cato yelled towards their father who probably couldn't hear him. "You coward!"

"What now?" There was a massive hole filled with unrecognizable body parts. Their numbers had been painfully decreased. "We are outmaneuvered."

"We can still do this." Cato urged but the fear in his eyes was all she needed.

"We must retreat. Regroup."

"No." Cato cut down a man that ran towards him. "Where's Damian?"

It was tough to see through everything. Smoke was filling the air from the tanks. Fires were starting to spread throughout the forest they were near and men were still fighting one another tooth and nail.

"We need to find him." She decided.

They ran through the crowds, cutting down men and women as they went along.

"Damian!" Cato yelled at a man dripping in blood and sweat.

Damian turned around and he was hardly recognizable. His hair was plastered to his head with thick amounts of mud and blood. His eyes were wild and his mouth was set in a tight line. The kindhearted man Julia had always known had transformed into a fierce animal with his eyes bouncing around the battle waiting for the next strike.

"What are your orders?" Cato yelled to him, but Damian looked panicked and defeated. His silence was terrifying. "Damian!"

"I don't know..." he mouthed quietly. A man lunged at him with a spear but Damian deflected it with ease and shot him in the stomach close range. "I don't know."

"We need to get to the General," Julia said. "Take the fight to him and if we defeat him then we have a chance."

Cato nodded but Damian was stuck perpetually killing people left and right muttering, "I don't know."

Julia slapped him in the face as soon as she reached him. "Snap the fuck out of it and let's kill the General!"

Damian blinked at her for a moment before his senses started to return. He looked towards her father and nodded solemnly. "Let's."

They had almost taken the right, but spears buried under the ground found their horses being punctured to death and Damian had barely made it out of the death pit alive. He was stupid to think Marc wasn't prepared for such maneuvering.

He was quickly rushed by the Risen and had to defend himself before he was able to make his way back to his army. His mind had gone blank after the first few kills as if he were watching himself from a distance slicing appendages off his enemy. The feeling of warm blood dripping down his face didn't bother him in the least.

It wasn't until he heard Cato yelling at him that his mind came back to the present and he watched bodies falling left and right.

"What are your orders? Damian!"

"I don't know..." Damian said mostly to himself. He had no idea what to do. He dodged a spear and shot the man in the stomach without so much as a second thought to what he was doing. He was on autopilot. "I don't know."

A sharp pain flashed across his cheek as Julia struck him.

"Snap the fuck out of it and let's kill the General!"

Finally looking at her, he realized she had a massive cut down her face and his blood began to boil thinking about what Marc was allowing to happen to his own children. "Let's."

They fought through the carnage and despair of those perishing around them. For the most part they were just trying to push through the crowd to reach the bastard that started this whole war. As they grew closer Damian saw Marc sitting upon his horse gazing out into the hell he had created. A look of triumphant was plain as day on his face until Damian managed to lock eyes with him.

"Marcus!" Damian yelled in a battle cry—his sword raised high.

The man he once loved dared to grin at him with amusement. Stepping down from his steed he disappeared in the crowd as Damian tried to fight through the enemy's line of infantry. He thought perhaps Marc had tried to get away until the line spread apart to let Marc waltz towards him. Looking to his sides, Damian became keenly aware that Julia and Cato weren't with him.

"Don't you miss this, brother? The smell of blood and leather, and the cries of your enemy being sliced to bits. Ah, I feel young again."

"You are no longer my brother," Damian growled. He was still cautious of Marc's troops around him, but none of them made a move as they stood waiting for instructions from their commander. Marc closed the gap between them until he was standing five feet away.

"You know you can't win. I can see it in your eyes." Marc gripped the hilt of his sword that was still sheathed. "Give up and I may allow you to live."

"That's not an option."

"I thought as much. It seems Alexander killed the wrong man."

"Don't you dare mention him." The vein on his neck began to throb and heat seemed to fill his chest.

"Don't fret, Hephaestion. You will join him presently." Marc grinned wide making Damian want to punch those perfect white teeth out of his skull.

A small noise came from the skies like the rumble of an old car. The sound escalated quickly until it became a ferocious thundering and crackling roar. Enemy jets screamed overhead dropping missiles in their wake. The noise was deafening and the men around him began to scream even louder.

"Anna, it's time," Damian spoke through his headset. Within thirty seconds the roar grew louder as more planes drew nearer. Marc's face went from smug to shocked.

"Didn't think I would take aerial warfare into account, Marc? I knew you wouldn't keep your word."

Blue painted fighter jets burst overhead shooting rounds of ammunition from their Gatling guns at Marc's infantry. Dirt and body parts burst in the air from the impact. The shooting abruptly stopped once the Risen's jets realized they had company and started to return fire.

Now the massive machines began to attack each other from up above while the fight continued below. Marc was bellowing orders to his men, but the chaos had ruined his formations. It was now a free for all without any command.

"To hell with this!" Marc yelled and pressed on his own headset. "Send them all in!"

An actual roar burst into the already loud setting with such rage that it promised death. Men stood still and looked up towards the sky as the ground trembled when the sound resonated again. A heaving mass of flesh and scales came out of nowhere and flung itself on one of the blue jets.

The amber colored beast ripped apart the jet with its claws and teeth while in the air, sending debris tumbling towards the ground. People ran to avoid the shredded plane, but it was just about to get worse. Black smoke filled the air as another onyx colored dragon engulfed one of their jets in a stream of fire igniting from its jaws.

"Shit..." Damian nearly fell backwards in shock. Dragons and jets filled the skies. "How?"

"You have those that follow your beliefs and I have those that follow mine."

"A fucking dragon has beliefs?" Damian yelled over the sounds of plane parts falling like hail.

"No, but their masters do."

"Anna, get out of there now!" There was no answer. Dragons were breathing fire at Damian's troops leaving men and women screaming until they collapsed immobile to the ground as their flesh burned away. "Anna!"

"Will you shut the hell up and let me get away from this flying death machine?" Anna's voice blared in his ear. "Fucking hell! Fucking Falkor over here is fast!"

Damian's eyes darted to the sky until he found a blue jet being tailed by a white dragon. Weaving in and out of flying debris, Anna banked making the dragon fly headfirst into the rear of the amber dragon. Damian pumped his fist in the air but had to dodge a fist headed for his face.

"Okay, I am landing this bird," Anna heaved out. "See you in the field."

Damian was about to protest until Marc tackled him to the ground knocking all the air out of his lungs. The back of his head smacked against a piece of shrapnel and his vision went hazy. He needed to move but once his sight started to return, a razor-sharp pain erupt in his shoulder.

"Scream some more." Marc twisted the spear he thrust into Damian and he unwillingly complied. "Like music to my ears."

Damian looked out into the field and saw mythological creatures had joined the fight. His army was being ripped apart by man's worst nightmare and there was nothing he could do about it.

"You brought demons here?"

"They were glad to be of service. Sick of the god's rule over them, just as I am."

As the cries grew louder around them, Damian saw people falling dead at an alarming rate. "You're killing your own men," he managed to choke out. "Your beasts can't tell the difference."

"I don't care who dies, as long as the Warriors are wiped out of existence! There are plenty of people left on this planet for me to command."

Another twist of the spear brought tears to Damian's eyes. He tried to kick Marc off him but was rewarded with another sharp pain to his ankle. "Fuck!"

"Oh, I didn't mean to stomp on you. Looks like it may be broken." Letting go of the spear, Marc dropped a knee into Damian chest and placed his sword directly over his heart. "Once you are gone, there will be no one to lead the rebels. You should have kept yourself in the Domus. Safe and sound with that little woman of yours, but pride got the best of you. Say your prayers Hephaestion."

"Don't do this." Damian tried to feel for a knife or something with his good arm until Marc trapped it under his other knee.

"No other option, brother. I'm truly sorry it turned out this way." Marc scowled as he raised the sword up and brought it swiftly down to his chest.

Damian closed his eyes as he accepted his fate. Flashes of Anna and Owen flooded his mind as he waited for his end, but the pain of the sword never came. It wasn't until the spear was yanked painfully out of his shoulder that he opened his eyes. He screamed in agony. It felt as if his entire arm was ripped off.

"Fucking hell," Damian clutched his wound.

"Can you get to a healer?" The man that pulled the spear out asked as he tossed the weapon aside.

Damian cocked his head to the side as he stared up at a man with dirty blond hair decked out in Ancient Greek military armor. He was a built man. A powerful man. A man that looked dangerous.

"Ryan?"

Chapter XXIV

Damian

"I T's NOT POSSIBLE."

"Alas, here I am." Ryan helped him stand up.

"How are you here?" He reached out towards Ryan. He had to be imagining this.

"I just pulled you up, Damian. I'm not fake." Ryan forced a smile. "We need to get you out of here."

"I'm fine, I'll just use my right arm." Damian tried out his ankle and despite what Marc said, it wasn't broken. He could put weight on it, but his left shoulder pulsed with heat.

"Good because someone is charging at you."

Ryan yanked Damian behind him and in a flash, cutting down his attacker before Damian could react. It was a blur of movement and the man's head landed on the ground long after Ryan was once again facing Damian.

"How did you do that?"

"Do what?" Ryan pushed Damian's dropped jaw up with his finger.

"I barely saw you move." Damian's eyes widened. "And you're alive. How the hell are you alive? Have you been this whole time? What the fuck, Ryan? Do you have any idea the hell I've been going through?"

"Whoa, calm down." Ryan casually threw a dagger at a man landing it square between his eyes. "I will explain, but right now we have a war to win."

"We are outnumbered and heavily overpowered with all these creatures joining their ranks. We need to retreat."

Ryan stood his ground looking Damian square in the eyes. "There is no way in hell that is ever going to happen."

Ryan's fist connected with a man's jaw, the impact clearly shattered the bone and his head twisted around unnaturally. He then sliced cleanly through body after body as if they were butter. Damian just stood there slack jawed once again after Ryan grabbed a man's arm and tossed him like a ragdoll through the air.

"Damian, get moving!" Ryan yelled at him through the screams.

He knew he needed to move but the shock was still too much to process for him. It wasn't until Anna came running towards him followed by some beast that he snapped out of it.

She was breathing heavily with scorch marks smeared across her face. Sliding along the mud she picked up a sword and slashed at the beast in one movement. Her blow did no good as her blade struck its sallow, yellowish skin. Patches of matted hair peeled off its skeletal figure, but the Wendigo didn't seem to mind. Instead, it flashed its yellowed fangs at Anna, dripping with saliva.

Damian ran to help her but was beat to the punch when a winged lion landed on top of the Wendigo with such force that it was smashed it into the ground like a pancake. The lion looked down at Damian who had fallen over from the impact with curious eyes. It cocked its head to the side before it nudged him with its muzzle to get up.

Anna yanked Damian up, but he never removed his eyes from the lion. *For the love of Zeus, this is insanity!*

"What is happening?"

"Reinforcements," Ryan yelled over his shoulder as he

decapitated what looked like a gargoyle. "You can thank me later!"

"Reinforcements?" A griffin flew overhead with its wings spread wide, a loud piercing shrill came from its eagle head while its lion tail smacked a soldier in the skull knocking him over.

A horse sized wolf pounced on one of their soldiers. She screamed as the wolf bit down on her arm like a chew toy until it ripped it clean off. Suddenly, the beast was struck by a large lightning bolt, instantly reducing it to burnt flesh and Damian could smell the singed fur from where he stood.

Damian looked up to the sky seeing a familiar bearded man riding on Pegasus.

"Zeus?" Damian asked more to himself but obviously loud enough for Ryan to hear.

"Yes," Ryan answered.

Damian's senses kicked in as he sidestepped a knife and knocked a gun away from its owner. An explosion nearby went off and he could feel the heat on his skin. They tried their best to keep moving but the dead were thick over the ground like a graveyard of the unburied.

"Where is Marc?" Ryan jogged gracefully beside Damian as he and Anna shifted through the debris.

"You tell me. You pulled him off me," said Damian.

"He scurried away when I freed you of that spear." Ryan grimaced as he looked out into the scene before him. "The centaurs are having at it with the manticores… Thor is zapping creatures left and right. Where is he?"

"Is that Ryan?" Anna stared in disbelief before she jumped into Ryan's arms and hugged him tight. "You're real? And blond? What the hell?"

"I missed you too squirt. Now focus," Ryan laughed.

Julia

She and Cato got separated from Damian as they tried to make their way to the General. They had gotten caught up in a crowd of men pushing forward as they battled one another until she couldn't help but join in. Fire bellowed from the bellies of dragons and narrowly missed her and Cato several times. It was a wonder her hair hadn't caught on fire yet.

"Did I just see Horus fly by?" Cato asked.

It had to be a trick, but she had seen it too. A figure, taller than a man with the head of a falcon and wings had just flown overhead followed by what seemed to be a harpy. Looking further up into the sky she saw a man riding a flying horse and a lightning bolt erupting from his fingertips.

"Jupiter," she mumbled.

"Hellhounds, hippogriffs, dragons, and a bunch of weird ass shit I've never seen before. What in the name of Pluto is going on?" Cato asked.

"We need to get our people out of here!" Julia yelled over the noise. "They are getting slaughtered by creatures, not men."

Barely any soldiers on either side were fighting at this point. They were either running away from flying beasts or getting their entrails spilled over the blood-soaked mud. A few maintained their stance, but it was pointless. The heavens were pouring out creatures left and right matching their numbers in men. This was now a war of the gods, not of men.

"Back to the camps!" she yelled to her allies.

"Damian didn't order that!" Cato protested.

"Let the gods and creatures fight their war. As they should have done in the first place."

Julia's eyes dared him to argue but instead he turned to relay the order. With no shame, their men began to retreat while the creatures ripped each other apart. Gods were flying overhead doing what they could to even the odds.

Cato ran back over to Julia with green blood splattered on his cheek.

"Our men are retreating and it looks like theirs are too. We need to find Damian."

"We need to find the General." She took off towards the enemies ranks.

"Stubborn ass woman!" she heard her brother yell behind her.

Her boots were being sucked into the mud as she trailed along after her father's guard. She had tripped over multiple body parts and each time her brother was there to help her out of the muck.

How could Ryan, Damian, and her brother miss this? Ever since she became a Warrior all she heard was about were the glory days of battle. The blood-stained ground and deafening cries of the enemy seemed to be a common sense of pride between her brother and friends.

All she felt was sorrow.

"I see Damian." Cato started to run to meet him, but Julia had different plans.

She had spotted her father. He was barking out orders to his men to stay and fight, but most weren't listening. The sight of mythological creatures scared them more than their commander and she couldn't blame them.

Running towards him she drew out a pistol from her belt. This had to end now if they had any chance of lessening the carnage. If it had to be done by her own hand then so be it.

She was within feet of her father when he whirled unexpectedly around to catch her gaze. Slowly he unsheathed his sword, never taking his eyes off her.

"A gun?" her father sneered. "Fight like real Warrior."

Reluctantly, she tossed her gun in the mud. Her eyes never left his as she unsheathed the sword that belonged to her mother. Her father's eyes made a quick glance at the blade before returning to her.

"Beautiful, isn't it?" she asked. "I remember running my little hands over the filigree on the blade. Such pretty designs that never seemed to fade. Mother would smile down at me but whenever you caught me, I was scolded. I never knew why."

Her father's jaw clenched and his grip on his sword tightened. "A Warriors life wasn't what I wanted for my daughter."

"Yet you seem to think I am more capable than your son."

"I was tough on him to make him stronger. I wanted you to find a good man and settle down. But seeing you now, I am prouder of you than I ever was of Cato. Such talent and skill in someone so nonthreatening to look at. It's your greatest weapon."

"You've always underestimated him." She hated that her father thought so little of her brother. Cato was a force to be reckoned with.

"Perhaps. Yet here you are. The one to face me while he is off who knows where." His eyes darted back to the blade and he visibly flinched.

"I feel like this sword bothers you more than it should. You can't seem to keep your eyes off it."

"She took her life with that." His eyes clouded remembering another time. "She laid in bed after giving birth to that damn king's son. She was bleeding out slowly for days and in so much pain. The gods wouldn't heal her no matter how much I prayed. They wouldn't let me go to her." He shook with rage. "But I stole into her chambers, saw her lying there in that bed with her skin paler than I've ever seen it. Her lips cracked and her body too weak to walk.

"Death was knocking on her door and no matter how much

she begged for me to end her life I couldn't. And then she did it. Her weak hand rose as high it could go and she dropped that damn sword on her heart when I was too far away to stop her."

Julia's heart felt like it stopped. She never knew her mother killed herself and the thought brought no comfort. "You let her suffer. You lied about how she really died."

"It's not something I wanted my children to know."

"This whole time we believed she died giving birth to our half-brother. I despised that child because of you."

"It was because of him she died. Had that little vermin never been created she would be alive. If the gods didn't send her on a mission to be some kings saving grace for a son she would have been at home with her real family." His anger was taking over his calm demeanor. "Enough of this. It changes nothing."

"You know, it's almost poetic." She tried her best not to concentrate on the truth of it all. "The blade that killed my mother will also kill my father."

"You cannot beat me."

Her father almost sad. It was almost enough to make Julia second guess herself. Almost.

"We shall see." Julia raised her sword towards him.

Her father shook his head at her but did not fall back. Instead, he stepped forward, closing the distance between them. The screams and clashing bodies faded away in that moment as she faced this man. The bringer of death. The enemy of her people. Her father.

Chapter XXV

Ryan

"**H**OLY-FUCKING-SHIT! IT'S RYAN!"

That was the first sentence to come out of Cato's mouth. His jaw was agape, much like Damian's was when he first saw him. Only Cato seemed excited rather than shocked.

"It's me." Ryan couldn't help but laugh.

Cato threw his arms around Ryan's shoulders in an extremely tight bear hug, picking him up and then swinging him around like a child before letting him go. "Fucking hell, man. Death did you good. No scars, flowing locks of luscious hair and nice ass armor. I'm jealous."

"Don't be." Ryan smiled weakly. "Are the troops retreating?"

"It seems both sides are. The mortals are terrified of the mythological creatures." Cato looked around at the carnage. "Julia ordered them to fall back. She said it's the gods war not theirs."

Ryan agreed to an extent. These men and women chose to be here, but they also didn't think a dragon was going to burn them alive.

"Where is Julia?"

His nerves tingled at the thought of seeing her. Even in Elysium a huge part of him missed her and now that he was back, well, the thought of her reaction was almost frightening. Would she be happy? Sad? Angry? Knowing her as he did, it would be a mixture of the three.

Cato craned his neck looking out into the battlefield.

"She was with me just a second ago." He kicked aside a small skinless creature that was hell bent on biting his ankles. "I'm about to shoot this thing."

"Anna, why the fuck did you bring your cat here?" Damian picked up the feline who magically appeared by their side.

"I didn't." Anna took the cat from his arms. "Calypso, what are you doing here?" The cat meowed looking up at her with bright eyes.

"Never mind, just don't—" Damian took a large fist to the chest that left him sprawled out in the mud. "Shit."

Ryan's breath was knocked out of him as he landed on his ass next to Damian. He looked up and saw an overgrown humanoid with weathered gray skin and wild hair sticking up every which way. It took a step towards Cato, swatting him away just as he did to Ryan and Damian. A variety of curse words could be heard over the beasts heavy breathing.

It stomped towards Anna's frightened form and his instincts took over. Ryan pushed himself up from the ground and ran towards her, sliding along the mud he sunk a dagger deep within the troll's leg.

Anna cowered down with Calypso in her arms when the troll erupted in a head splitting roar. "What. The. Hell. Is. That?"

"Don't worry about it just run." Ryan stood between Anna and the monster. "Go!"

"I can't." Calypso hissed up at the troll, baring her teeth at it while trying to wriggle out of Anna's arms. "Stop it. It will kill you."

The cat didn't give up until it broke free of Anna's grasp

and landed on the ground putting her body between theirs and the troll. She arched her back in defense to look bigger, but her body didn't stop growing. Calypso's frame grew longer and wider until it was larger than the troll. Her fur had disappeared leaving behind smooth olive skin as it transformed into a woman's body.

She wore a diadem over her long black hair that held the image of Bastet, the Egyptian goddess. Her nails were as sharp as knives and she had the eyes of a cat. Fine sheer linen clung to her body in a very intimate way that sparkled in the light with every movement she made.

"Your cat… is super sexy," Ryan muttered.

"That's really weird." Anna nodded.

"I know."

With one swipe of her hand Calypso sent the troll sailing through the air before landing on a tree that collapsed under its weight. The large woman bent down to Anna, placing her cheek against hers, a soft purr resonating from her chest. Anna merely stood in shock as Calypso marched off into the battle cutting down larger enemies in her wake.

"This is without a doubt the weirdest day of my life," Anna grumbled.

"Ditto."

Cato and Damian limped over to them holding their stomachs.

"Holy hell that troll got it's ass kicked." Cato watched Calypso strut off. "Your cat is a hottie, Anna. Introduce me."

"Pretty sure your cat is the goddess Bastet and I highly doubt she would like you Cato." Damian leaned on Anna. "Something is definitely bleeding inside me."

Cato started to look around the chaos again.

"I need to find Julia."

"Oh shit." Anna's eyes widened.

Ryan followed her gaze to the General's lines. He squinted

his eyes trying to see through the smoke and fighting until bright blonde hair caught his eye. Standing right across from her was none other than his enemy. Marc took a step towards Julia and she stepped back. Her sword rose to defend herself.

"No!" Cato yelled and he took off towards his sister.

Ryan took off alongside him and pulled ahead. Julia lunged away from her father's sword but he kicked her in chest knocking her to the ground. She rolled out of his advances, but Marc was quickly on her. Ryan pushed people out of the way with all his might trying to reach her before it was too late.

Julia

Her father kicked her in the chest landing her flat on her back. Her ribs screamed in protest. She may or may not have broken a rib. Either way it hurt to breathe. As she rolled away from his sword coming down towards her, Julia crawled in the mud to retrieve her sword.

"Get up, little one." His tone was as blank as his face when she turned around to face him. Slowly she pushed herself up but was kicked back down again. "I told you to get up."

"Fuck you."

His body dropped down on top of her, sitting on her waist making it impossible to move away from the weight of him. He blocked every attempt of her desperately trying to get free. Her strength was nothing compared to his.

"I wanted more for you than this. I wanted to give you the world. All you had to do was see the truth, but you were blind from the start. I am sorry, little one, but I have to do this. They must be stopped."

Pounding her fists against his chest, he grabbed them and

tucked them under his knees at her sides. She was officially trapped with no means of defending herself. As he placed the tip of his sword to her chest, she could actually see the sadness in his eyes.

"Don't do this Father." Her eyes went wide. "Please."

"Tell your mother I love her. That I'm sorry I couldn't save you."

Before she could tell him that her mother would hate him for doing this, a knife lodged itself in the back of her father's hand. His body was ripped off hers the instant he turned his head to look at his assailant. Cato's hand shot out to her while a man in white armor wrestled with her father on the ground. Fists were thrown but her attention was drawn back to her brother as he checked her over.

"Are you okay?" His eyes reflected more anger than she had ever seen.

"I was stupid to think I could take him." She grimaced while trying to breathe.

"Luckily we have your back." He pressed his forehead to hers.

Damian came running up with Anna at his heels. Both were wide-eyed and breathless. "Thank the gods he got to you in time." Damian quickly wrapped his arms around Julia before running off to help the man in white.

"Who is he?" Julia asked her brother.

"No time for that. We are going to finish this little sister and then he will explain."

Julia was dragged behind a boulder by Anna. They had a clear view of the men that came to protect her. They were standing, conversing with her father until they leapt into action. Cato swung his sword at her father but lost his footing in the slippery mud. Seeing him fall, Damian ran to help him just before her father lunged at them both.

The man in white quickly jumped into action as he blocked

the advance. He was now wearing a helmet with a red plum going down the center with two white feathers on the sides. Who was that man with a body like a god? His movements fluid, quicker than a normal man and his style so familiar. Her father was barely able to keep up.

A lion with large white wings dropped down on a massive serpent in front of her and took its body between its teeth. The lion shook it until the snake went limp, tossing it to the side like a rag doll and went on to the next beast.

Soldiers were still running out of harm's way from the fighting creatures. Every sight around her was like a horror movie come to life with monsters running all around ripping each other to shreds. Most didn't pay attention to the people—they were the least of their concerns especially when the gods were up in the air fighting off dragons and demons.

"Are you hurt?" Anna's voice broke her concentration on the fight.

"I'm fine, but we need to help."

"Sorry but Damian told me to keep you away."

Julia glared. "I don't give a damn what Damian says." And with that she ran towards the fight, bending down to pick up her dropped sword as she made her way.

Damian had just tripped over a fallen body with his ass landing in the mud. Before her father's sword reached Damian's head it was once again blocked by the man in white.

Who the hell is that?

Ryan

Marc's sword was drawn over Julia's heart. He didn't have time to think, he just threw his dagger at Marc's hand and tackled him to the ground right after. The man growled in frustration when Ryan struck him in the nose with his elbow. Their bodies entangled with one another, each trying to get the upper hand.

"Get off me!" Marc hissed.

Ryan wrestled out of Marc's grip, the both of them now stood with their chests heaving with glaring eyes to match. It wasn't instant, but he could tell when Marc figured out who he was. His eyes went wide and the veins in his neck popped.

"How?"

"Does it matter?" Ryan asked.

"It isn't possible."

"Yeah, I've been hearing that a lot."

Damian and Cato now flanked both sides of Ryan. Their swords were drawn, eyes filled with hatred. "You may want to cover your face," Cato said lowly. "My sister can't keep her eyes off you. It's only a matter of time before she figures out who you are."

Ryan nodded and slammed his fist against the lion embedded on his chest plate. A golden helmet materialized over his head bearing a deep red plum with two white feathers on either side. Marc's jaw went slack and he could hear both his brother's groans of approval.

"Holy shit, that's cool," Cato mumbled.

"So, the gods have gifted you." Marc's eyes wondered over Ryan's armor. "Yet it takes the three of you to try and defeat me."

"No, we just don't want to let Ryan have all the fun." Cato spit on the ground at his father's feet.

Marc smirked before lunging toward his son. Cato blocked it but when he tried to swing back, his foot slipped in the bloody mud and he fell on his ass. Ryan quickly blocked the deadly blow Marc tried to land on Cato's skull and pushed him backward with a shove to the chest.

Before Ryan could try and help Cato up, Marc came at him in a hurry. There were signs of hesitation in his movements but only slightly. Ryan blocked him easily enough, his body quick and nimble but he was sideswiped by a creature's tail that threw him off balance.

Damian jumped in but quickly found himself landing on his backside.

"Shit," he yelled as his legs lay over the dead body that tripped him. Marc's sword tried to attack Damian, but Ryan was too quick.

He had caught Marc's blade with his own as they battled their strength. Pushing their swords towards one another with all their might until they were face to face. Sweat dripped down Marc's face but Ryan didn't feel the least bit tired. His energy was at an all-time high and he couldn't help but smile in the face of his enemy.

"You have no way of winning this." Ryan grinned wickedly.

"I have more strength than a normal man. The beliefs of my people have risen me to newer heights of capabilities. I am a god to them!"

"Just wait until they see me." Ryan grinned. "Now, Lee."

A helicopter carrying Lee flew overhead until it hovered over Ryan and Marc. A camera was in her hands shooting directly at the scene below. The sound of the machine drowned out Marc's roar of frustration, yet Ryan was still able to hear him when he said, "This will do nothing."

Ryan could see the fear in his eyes coming to the realization about what was going to happen. "Oh, we both know that isn't true."

Ryan thrust Marc away from his body before walking towards the lowered helicopter. The blades started to slow down and the noise was replaced with the sounds of the monsters around him. Turning back towards Marc with a smile, his triumph quickly ended when he saw Julia lunging towards her father.

Marc twisted under her advance and held his sword to her throat with her back to his front. Ryan froze. Damian and Cato weren't in a position to come to her defense and neither was he. It was as if he were reliving the nightmare before his death all over again.

"Let her go, Marc. You don't want to do this."

"Oh, we both know that isn't true." He mimicked Ryan's words. "Tell them to leave and don't you dare take that helmet off."

"Afraid of what the world will see?" In all honesty, Ryan was terrified to take his helmet off now. Julia's reaction to seeing him was horrifying to think about but Zeus made it clear this needed to happen. He wanted their reunion on his terms but it wasn't meant to be.

Marc laughed against his daughters' ear. "Not as much as you are apparently."

Ryan saw a droplet of blood roll down Julia's neck. Her chest heaved and her hands were empty at her sides. Cato and Damian stood by one another looking between Ryan and Marc, unsure what to do but prepared to spring into action.

There wasn't an option. He had to finish the job he was given and being selfish for one soul wasn't part of that plan. Millions of lives were at stake, so he reluctantly pushed the lion on his chest plate that dissolved the helmet off his head. The recognition didn't hit Julia right away, but Ryan knew the exact moment she realized it was him. Her eyes widened and her knees threatened to buckle as her body visibly weakened.

"I love you," he said more to himself than to her.

He forced himself to look away, to walk towards the

camera without a second glance as the red light was already shining telling him he was live. He raised his arms to his sides and kept his face lacking emotion.

"To all the followers out there who believed me dead, here I stand before you alive and well. My mortal life was stripped from me and I have been born again."

Ryan turned out towards the chaos around him. Beasts killing beasts and men still fighting to get away. "This is what the General's war has done to us. Killed fathers, mothers and children for power over mankind and the gods that gave us life. The reign of the General has been nothing but mayhem and death.

"When I died in that arena, gods of different faiths came together to carry me to the afterlife. The General made you all believe they were gone, that they didn't care anymore. But look around as proof that they do care. They are fighting for you even if it means they fall, letting mortals escape to safety while their existence is threatened."

A centaur galloped by throwing his spear into a large Camazotz, a humanoid bat creature with slobbering fangs. His victory was short lived when he was impaled by a spear welded by a Nuckelavee.

The monstrous beast had a man's torso attached to a horse's back as if it were a rider. Its skin appeared flayed off both the horse and man's body with blood coursing through its yellow veins. The single red eye of the monster was barely able to focus on Ryan before he ran towards it decapitating both man and horse with one blow.

"Is this what you want your world plagued with? These are the troops in the General's army." Ryan held up the skinless head of the Nuckelavee man.

"Follow the Gods, the real Gods, into victory against

those who would destroy us. Because creatures like this," he tossed the head to the ground with a look of disgust, "are what the Gods have been protecting you from. This is what I have vowed to do for the rest of my existence, not as Ryan leader of the Resistance, but as Alexander, God of Salvation."

Chapter XXVI

Damian

ONCE RYAN'S BACK WAS turned to them and looking in the camera, Damian could see the anger on Marc's face. Julia looked on the verge of having a breakdown. Her lip quivered and her body was being held up by her father. Damian had a feeling that the knife to her throat had nothing to do with her distress.

Unfortunately, he was in no position to get to Julia without Marc seeing him. What was also unfortunate was his wife was sneaking up behind Marc with a small knife in her hand. He glanced nervously at Cato who looked just as panicked as Damian felt.

Anna crouched low, shuffling her feet along the ground until she was right behind him. Marc seemed to feel her presence as he turned his head to look over his shoulder, but Anna was too quick. She quickly swiped her knife across the back of his knees, and he could only imagine the pain of it.

Marc roared out load as he dropped his daughter to the ground to face Anna. Thankfully, she had ran to Damian's side before Marc's sword could meet her neck. His anger towards her was short lived though, as he made a beeline for Ryan whose back was facing them.

Damian was right at his heels until he heard Ryan say,

"Alexander, God of Salvation." He stopped in his tracks nearly sliding in the mud.

Damian was close enough he heard Marc exclaim in disbelief, "No!"

Alexander turned to face them.

"Oh, yes. I have been brought back from the dead by Zeus himself. My responsibility is simple—save the world from the destruction of mankind." Electricity begun to dance around Alexander's fingertips. "It seems my believers have already given me the strength I need to defeat you."

"Alexander?" Damian called over to him but was met with a shake of the head.

"I need you to stay out of this, Damian. All of you need to remain clear of us and let me finish this once and for all."

Anna's hands grasped his arm, pulling him a fair distance away from Alexander and Marc. Cato and Julia followed suit giving the two men plenty of space, but he couldn't back down now. Damian pulled his arm from Anna's clutch and stood his ground.

"What are you doing?" She tried to grab him again, but he dodged her touch.

"I can't leave him."

Cato came from behind him and yanked on his arm to get moving further back. "If you didn't fucking notice, Alexander is a god now. There isn't shit you could do to help."

"I can distract Marc. I can't let him die again." With a quick kiss on Anna's lips he took off. Alexander and Marc were stuck in a silent stare down when Damian jogged up to Alexander's side.

"I told you to leave." Alexander's voice was rough.

"Can't do that."

"Don't be a fool." Alexander's eyes met his. "I will not see you die."

"And I won't watch you die again. So deal with it." Damian swung his eyes back to the bane of their existence.

He was bloody, muddy, and super pissed but Marc didn't show any sign of giving up. His sword was ready in his hand, eyes shooting daggers at them both.

"So, you were made a god. Seems we aren't different after all."

"Except my people love me and yours are ruled by fear alone," Alexander retorted.

"This will not end in my death," Marc vowed. "I will not be the villain. The gods are the true villains."

"Hate and loss has driven you away from your true self, Marc. I hate that you have suffered so much. Truly, I do. I wish I could give you back your old life before hate consumed your soul. I must say if it were me in your shoes, I would probably be standing there instead of you. But I cannot let this continue. I am sorry it has come to this. I love you as a brother still. I want you to know that."

It was brief, but Marc's eyes seemed to show the pain that struggled within him. Damian hated it coming to this, just as Alexander did, but he had to die. He was too far gone in his vengeance that no one could forgive his actions.

"Enough talk. Let's finish this." Marc stood ready.

With a nod of his head Alexander took off towards Marc with Damian shortly behind. He couldn't help but flinch when Alexander's helmet materialized over his head. The gold flashed out of nowhere right before Alexander's sword was brought down towards Marc's head.

He deflected it over and over, even when Damian joined in on the offense. Marc was wielding two swords at that point, Alexander didn't even look like he was trying, yet Damian felt sweat dripping down his own back. With a swift kick to the stomach, Damian fell to the ground trying to catch his breath from Marc's hard knock.

"Stay out of this!" Alexander begged.

"I won't." He crawled to stand.

"Do what you master tells you," Marc chided.

Damian's wounds were throbbing, but he couldn't help but try and defend Alexander the best he could. With his body betraying him, his knees buckled after a few steps. He used his sword to prop himself up but was knocked down by Marc once again with a blow to his head.

He could hear Alexander and Marc's raging fight behind him, but he was too busy staring at the dirt until he gained the energy to turn himself over. Fuck, Marc had a harder hit than he thought. After his eyesight cleared, he sat up and made another attempt to stand.

As soon as his body would allow it, he rose to find Marc standing still and weaponless. There was a cut on his brow, but he didn't wipe the blood away as it rolled further down his face. His stare was aimed directly at the man in front of him.

"Don't do this, Alexander," Marc pleaded.

Alexander's helmet had disappeared at this point and even from where Damian painfully stood, he could see the misery in Alexander's eyes.

"I have to, brother."

Alexander's arms rose into the air and the electric charge between his fingers grew stronger than before. The brightness of it was blinding but Damian tried not to look away. Alexander's entire being was surrounded by the white sparks snaking through the air that ignited as he created a vortex of energy.

Moving quickly, Alexander pointed his arms out towards Marc as he stood before him. The sparks sped rapidly through the air connecting Alexander and Marc by electricity. Damian's mouth dropped watching as Marc's body spasmed violently while the blinding bolts danced around him.

His flesh begun to darken, the short-cropped hair on his head disappeared and was replaced by singed skin. Marc didn't make a sound. His body was too overcome with energy to let him breathe. Damian couldn't take it any longer.

"Alexander!" he screamed over the electricity weaving through the air. "Alexander, stop this!"

But Alexander wasn't there anymore. His eyes were pure white, his jaw clenched shut as the energy left his body and went into Marc's. Damian reached to touch him but was met with a tiny spark warning him not to. It hurt like hell for a split second and he couldn't imagine what Marc was going through.

He looked around for something to throw at Alexander. Anything to break the concentration he had on torturing Marc. "Fuck it." He took off his boot and chucked it at his friend landing it right against Alexander's cheek.

It worked. Alexander's energy faded until there was no blinding light between the two men.

"What… are you doing?!" Alexander's breathless voice rose. "He is still alive! Now he feels the pain!"

Damian's eyes widened looking over at Marc's fallen body. He could hear feeble groans erupting from his chest. They both ran to Marc's lifeless form, but what lay before them was someone almost unrecognizable. Bile threatened to rise in his throat at the smell alone, and the sight of Marc's burnt flesh would haunt him for all his days.

He was charred with small spots of pink flesh that remained on his face. One eye was blistered shut while the right still fluttered weakly open.

"Marc…" Damian's voice cracked.

A weak hand tried to reach out to Alexander but fell limply to the ground. Marc grimaced baring bloody teeth.

"Finish it. Just finish it."

Damian was nudged away by Alexander as he lifted Marc's shoulders off the ground. He rested the dying man on his lap and they just stared at one another for a minute.

"I'm so sorry, Marc," Alexander muttered. "Even after all you have done. I am so sorry."

Marc tried to smile but his skin tore as he tried.

"I just wanted to make it better."

"I know."

"Please, just do it."

His body started to spasm uncontrollably until Alexander slipped a dagger into Marc's heart, seizing the dying man's breath in an instant. His body didn't even flinch as Alexander pulled the blade from his chest.

"May your passing bestow the peace you sought, brother."

As soon as Alexander said it, the clash of swords died away along with the shouts of bloodshed being spilled. Silence cloaked the blood-stained ground that was littered with the bodies of the dead. Beasts retreated to where they came and those who survived the battle stood in awe facing Alexander and Damian. Even the enemy dropped their weapons without pause seemingly glad that the battle was over.

"It's finished," Damian muttered. "It's finally finished."

Alexander laid Marc's head gently to the ground.

"Almost."

Julia

The dead were being collected into truck beds along with make-shift carts pulled by horses. The sight was unbearable but the smell was the worst part of it. Limbs littered the ground and were already turning pale. Bodies were singed beyond recognition and every so often when a breeze came through specks of burnt skin flew through the air.

All the beasts were gone. No more mythological nightmares roamed the battlefield except the ones who were killed. There was no point for them to remain. It was all over. Her father was dead and with it his dream. His troops instantly laid down their arms when the word of the General's demise spread through the field. Thanks to the whole ordeal being broadcast around the world crews of people came to help with the dead.

She breathed in the heavy smoke-filled air before walking into the tent that held her father's corpse. Cato and Damian worked on cleaning his body. The bowl of water next to them had turned red and glistened from the lanterns throughout the tent. Cato was concentrating on his work, eyebrows tensed together and his jaw clenched as he gently patted their father's brow with the rag.

Damian looked to her and offered an apologetic smile, but she couldn't return the sentiment. She was still in shock at the fact her father was dead, again, but for good this time.

"He's terribly burnt," she muttered. Cato nodded but continued to clean. "Why are you doing this for him?"

There was silence for a moment before Damian answered, "It's the right thing to do."

"He was an evil man. He doesn't deserve your respect," she countered.

"He was doing what he thought was right no matter how misguided he was."

"He murdered thousands and thousands of people, yet you still treat him as one of us." She shook her head at the thought of her father's actions. All the lives lost and all the pain she endured and for what?

"We are not giving him a Warriors funeral."

Cato slammed his fist down on a wooden table, knocking over the bowl of bloodied water to the ground. "Tradition dictates he must be cleaned and anointed before we burn him on a pyre along with the rest of his followers and our soldiers. We cannot and will not sink to his level of disregard for life nor death."

"You are clouded by the fact he was our father."

"And if I am?" Cato countered. His cheeks grew red and the bloodied rag dripped on the ground.

"You both need to just breathe. It's been a hell of a day and we all need rest." Damian put a gentle hand on Cato's shoulder and Julia swore she saw her brother's body shiver.

"He tried to kill you more than once, he tortured your brothers, he drugged and brainwashed your sister and you still feel the need to give him a proper send off? Hell, he would have killed any of us to reach his goal. He didn't care about us at all!" she screamed.

His body visibly tensed but he didn't retaliate. Instead, her brother turned his back to her and continued to wipe the body of the man who gave them life and hell. She wanted to shake him and make him understand, but Damian's eyes stopped her in her tracks.

"We are preparing the funeral for all those who have fallen in two days. I've sent a broadcast out and have planes on standby for the families."

There would be joy from those who found their family alive and intense grief for those who found the body of their loved one on a pyre. She didn't think she could handle the sight of it. Grief was all too familiar with her at this point.

Yells rose from outside the tent effectively ending the argument.

"What in the world?" Damian dropped the rag and burst out of the tent.

Julia followed by Cato walked into the night air and came face to face with an angry mob. Men yelled at the top of their lungs and spit at a group of people being pushed towards their tent. She couldn't see over the massive crowd but whoever they were they, were not popular.

"Who the hell is getting the walk of shame?" Cato grumbled trying to peer over the crowd.

"Well, they are headed this way so I guess we'll find out." Damian crossed his arms over his chest, standing his ground with his eyes set on the group headed towards them.

The line finally burst open revealing a very bloodied Aden followed by rogue Immortals. Alexander shoved Aden forward with such force that he fell headfirst into the mud. Men spit on him and one even landed a kick to his ribs before Alexander backed them all off with a glare. The crowd gave them space but surrounded the group with anger apparent on their faces.

Still in his battle armor, Alexander lifted Aden up from the ground by the arm and led him closer to the tent. "I found him retreating with this group of Immortals."

Caleb pushed through the crowd with a crew of Warriors. "You told us to meet you here?"

"Yes." Alexander pushed one of the prisoners towards him. "Bring these men back to Urbs and put them in the dungeons. The rest of you get back to work."

Damian and Cato flanked Aden and dragged him into the tent as the crowd dispersed. Julia's breath hitched just looking at the man that raped her and when his eyes met hers, she could feel her pulse quicken from terror. She couldn't move from where she stood but her insides screamed to get as far away as possible.

Once Aden was out of her sight, Alexander was by her side in a heartbeat.

"I know this is difficult. But you need to be in there with us."

"Why?" she croaked.

"Because I need you to be." Without a word she turned away from the tent but was caught just as quickly by the arm. "Don't run from this. You've faced him before."

People looked over towards them but continued their work. She could feel their eyes on her as she fought to not have a mental breakdown. She couldn't show the weakness she felt. Being an example of strength was draining.

"I did but I cannot do it again. He has plagued me and now with you here… I can't handle this."

"We can talk about us later. Believe me I want nothing more than to do so, but right now we need to deal with Aden."

"You need to deal with him. Not me."

"Get in there, Julia." Part of her wanted to punch him for talking to her like that but another part of her knew she had to obey the new god in front of the mortals. As they walked through the flaps of the tent, he whispered next to her ear, "Thank you."

Aden was sitting in a chair next to her father's body with Damian and Cato glaring down at him. Their arms were crossed like angry bodyguards trying to intimidate their target. Aden looked rather pathetic covered in blood and mud with his gear hanging on his body like rags.

Did she feel bad for the broken man in front of her? Not one damn bit. She hated that little prick with every fiber of her being. His head needed to roll.

Alexander

He hated having to do this to Julia. He knew the last thing she wanted was to confront Aden, but he needed her in the tent. Not only because her presence calmed his soul but because she would be a deciding factor in Aden's fate. His instinct was to kill him without remorse but deep down there was some sort of fatherly instinct that wanted to protect Aden. He knew it was wrong. He knew that Aden deserved to die, but could he make that call alone? No.

Alexander stood between Cato and Damian, both of whom radiated intense loathing, while he tried his best to keep his emotions in check. He had to keep a level head with this and not let his emotions overrule him. Sometimes doing the best thing for the good of the people was the worst thing you could do for yourself. Now that he was a god, he could no longer think about what he wanted, but rather what the people needed. Something a few gods could use a lesson in remembering.

"What is your plan?" Damian asked between clenched teeth.

"His fate is not in just my hands. We will all decide this together."

"I'm sure you don't need to even ask what our vote is, Alexander. He dies. End of story." Cato reared back his fist for a blow when Alexander caught his arm. "What?"

"We need to think about this rationally." Alexander released Cato's arm and looked down at Aden. His chin was pressed against his chest, hunched over and pathetic in appearance but also in spirit. "He is broken."

"He is a master manipulator. You know this. Or did you gain some mind reading powers while you were off doing gods know what while we were down here fighting," Julia spat. "You left us to suffer. He dies. End of story."

"This is not about me and you know nothing of what I went through. We will discuss that later. Right now we decide his fate."

Unanimously the three of them said, "Death."

Alexander hung his head even though he already knew what the answer would be. Julia had every right to want him dead, there was no doubt about that and a big part of himself wanted Aden dead for the same reason. Cato and Damian had seen the evil Aden had inside him. The lies and deaths of all those who Aden's poison inflicted were countless.

"Why does it bother you? Because he is your kid?" Julia made her way straight for him and pushed her finger into his breastplate. "He may share your blood, but he was never your family. After what he's done to us all, he relinquished his right to call you Father. And don't you dare blame yourself for how he turned out. He could have told you so many years ago that he was your son, but not once did he try. He went down his own path and he deserves what is coming to him."

"He can't be saved, Alexander," Damian said softly.

"They're right." Aden raised his head and met Alexander's eyes. "I can't take back what I have done. I'm not sorry about it either. I know it's wrong to feel this way but it's the truth. Some people were just born monsters and I'm done fighting."

"This is another trick to save his ass," Cato grumbled. "Just shoot him in the head and be done with it."

"I don't want to be saved. I'm just fucking tired." Aden started to cough, and blood peppered his pants. "I'm done."

Chapter XXVII

Alexander

DAMIAN AND CATO TOOK Aden back to the Domus and locked him up in the dungeons. Alexander was glad to escape the presence of his savage child. He dreaded the explanation he now owed everyone. It wasn't a subject he intended to take lightly, so he waited with Julia for Cato and Damian to return.

They sat in a large tent in the rebels' camp. Marc's body was in tent next to theirs and the very thought had him on edge. Seeing someone he loved for so long in a charred and burnt state definitely messed with his mind. His intentions may have been misguided but Alexander knew that Marc was doing what he thought was best for everyone.

Julia sat across the table and stared at him with a suspicious look in her eyes as if he wasn't who he said he was. Not that he could blame her in the least. The whole circumstance was completely unreal even to him still.

Avoiding her gaze, he looked down at his white armor that was soaked with blood. The golden chest plate with a lion depicted on it glinted across the table towards the love of his life. As much as he tried to avoid her eyes, he couldn't help but look up at her.

"You're wearing linothorax armor." Her voice was less than friendly.

"Yes."

"A breast plate, shin guards, and a skirt."

"You know it's not a skirt." Alexander rolled his eyes.

"You really thought armor made from layers of linen and leather was the best thing to wear to this battle?" she huffed at him. "Just asking for death again or showing off your past?"

Alexander leaned his forearms on the table and looked her directly in the eyes. He wasn't about to allow her to make him feel bad for showing up, it wasn't something he had any control over. "I am dressed how people believed Alexander the Great dressed. It isn't how my armor truly looked, but it is close for the most part."

"Well, you are lacking Medusa on the front." Damian entered the tent followed by Cato and Anna. "But I suppose I understand why."

"Doesn't exactly feel right after she tried to murder me, so I put my foot down on that one," Alexander agreed.

"So, you have to wear that all the time or what?" Cato sat down in a chair next to Julia and leaned over to look at Alexander's legs. "It can't be comfortable."

"No, it's just for battle." Alexander sighed. "I rather be wearing our gear but since you outed me as Alexander the Great and Zeus made me a god, I have to play the part."

"Sorry." Damian looked somewhat ashamed as he sat down next to Anna at the table, their hands instinctively clutched one another's. "I don't know what came over me... telling everyone that."

"Zeus made you," Alexander explained. "He wanted me to become a god to end this. Which is why he let me die when he could have stopped it."

"Why the hell didn't he just kill Marc?" Julia's anger seemed to be growing by the second. "Why put us through this living hell?"

"You can't just kill the man, you have to kill the idea. Just killing Marc wouldn't have done much because his followers could still carry on his beliefs. We had to show the mortals the gods true power and intentions to change the minds of the Risen." Alexander could see their skepticism.

"This battle had to happen. They had to see the gods fighting for us against the monstrous allies Marc obtained because he recruited evil to his cause. By bringing me back to life as a god, they put hope back into the mortal's hearts. It gave more power to the real gods rather than Marc's false bravado."

"It doesn't make sense. How would they know we were going to have a last battle?" Anna spoke up. "They couldn't have predicted it."

"Where do you think you got the idea from?" Alexander sighed. "Look, I know it's confusing and you think it could have been done differently but this was the only way for us to prevail. We needed to show the evil behind Marc's forces and the good behind ours. By letting me die and return, they then had a face the people trusted and believed in."

The five of them sat at the table for quite some time without a word between them. Alexander watched their eyes glaze over in deep thought and multiple times one of them looked as if they were going to say something but never did. There was nothing else for him to say unless they asked because quite frankly, he felt out of place with them. They looked at him like he wasn't truly himself and it felt like he was run through with a sword all over again.

"So now what?" Julia cocked her head at him. "Since you're a god now does that mean you have to go to Mount Olympus or whatever? Leave us yet again?"

Her anger towards him was completely misplaced but there was no doubt in his mind he would feel the same if he were in her shoes. "I only agreed to becoming a god with the promise of being able to return to the Domus, to run the Warrior ranks as Ahmose did. That is, if you would have me?"

Momentary silence filled the tent again and his heart seemed to fall out of his chest. Did they despise him that much for what happened? It seemed so.

Alexander stood from his seat, his fists were against the table and his throat felt like a rock was lodged in it. "I see. Well, I will take my leave. Don't hesitate to call on me if you need anything." He turned quickly to depart because he couldn't stand sitting in here another minute.

"You talk differently," Cato said behind his back. "All serious and proper-like. Quit that shit."

Alexander couldn't help but smile at Cato. As he turned back around to face the group, he forced a serious expression on his face.

"Would you rather I curse a lot and make crude jokes?"

"Damn straight." Cato grinned up at him with that mischievous look in his eye.

"Well fucking hell, I guess I better nut up and get over this god bullshit." Alexander felt his entire being light up when Cato and Damian laughed. Both of his brothers stood from their chairs and the three of them embraced for what seemed like hours. "Missed you fuckers."

"This is so gay of us," Cato whispered in their huddle. "Does it give you two flashbacks?"

"Jackass," Damian grumbled.

Instantly the three of them let each other go and both Alexander and Damian rewarded Cato with a punch in his shoulders.

"Mother cracker!" Cato backed up from them and was holding his arm.

"What the hell?" Julia ran from her chair to Cato and inspected his arm.

"I'm good, sis." Cato smiled down at her through clinched teeth before looking at Damian and Alexander. "Bullet graze. No biggie. Better than getting a spear to the shoulder."

"You aren't wrong." Damian sighed looking down at his arm in a sling.

Julia and Alexander locked eyes. He wanted to hold her and tell her about everything that happened to him. Her eyes were furious and seemed almost full of hate.

"Julia, I—"

Before he could finish, she turned and left the tent without another word. Alexander was about to go after her before Cato put a hand on his chest to stop him. Slowly he looked down at Cato's hand. There was a part of him that wanted to break Cato's fist for doing such a thing but then his brain caught up to the situation.

"Give her some time to process. She's... this hasn't been easy on her." Damian put a firm hand on his shoulder. Alexander stared daggers at them both before they took their hands off him. "You okay?"

After a beat, Alexander shook himself out of his current pissed off state.

"Sorry, my emotions are magnified now."

"So, you got pissed I stopped you?" Cato laughed.

"Yeah, it's stupid. I haven't got it under control quite yet." Alexander let out a large sigh. "I didn't want this."

"So why did you do it?" Anna asked still sitting at the table.

"To save my family."

Julia

There was no way in hell she was going to sit in that tent for another minute or sleep in it again for that matter. She had to get away from the cries of the wounded, the smell of blood and death, and mostly she had to get away from Ryan. Or Alexander. Or whatever the hell he called himself now.

Back in the Domus, she peeled off her gear caked with mud and blood. There was no way in hell she was going to keep it in her room, so she chucked it over the balcony without giving a damn where it landed. She looked down at her almost bare body and felt like she was going to be sick.

Blood had soaked through her clothes and was drying to her skin. Quickly she ran into the bathroom, turned on her shower and got in without giving a damn about the temperature. The water below her feet instantly turned red.

She scrubbed her skin raw, trying her best to feel free of the death that clung to her but it was no good. Flashes of the battle took over her mind and she could see the horrors of the day clearly before her eyes. So many dismembered limbs littered the ground. It was impossible to tell who they belonged to. People catching fire, bullets dropping people like invisible assailants, and the cries… Gods she would never be able to forget the images in her head.

The blood was gone from her skin but no matter how much soap or scrubbing she did, it wasn't enough. She sat in her shower, pulling her knees to her chest and cried. Her father would be ashamed. What sort of Warrior cried after a war?

It felt like she was crying for hours before she finally pulled herself up and out of her shame. She towel-dried her hair and tossed a robe on before leaving the bathroom to find herself face to face with Alexander. He was no longer in his Greek armor but freshly showered in grey sweatpants and a white t-shirt.

Her mind raced and she couldn't concentrate on a single thought. He really was standing in front of her and he looked like himself but with a few differences. Shoulder length dirty blond hair, his body lacked any scar he once had, yet she could feel the power he radiated.

He left me. Abandoned me. She loved him but an unreasonable hatred filled her.

"Talk to me." His voice was pained. "I can't tell what you are thinking."

She opened her mouth to talk but closed it again. Repeating the process again, she probably looked like a fish, but she couldn't figure out what to say to him.

Hesitantly, he placed his hand on her cheek. She could tell he was uncertain how to act with her and quite honestly, she was unsure herself. But once her mind registered his skin against hers it sent butterflies into her stomach and she craved to be touched more.

"Julia, look at me… please," he begged her.

She didn't even realize her eyes had closed. She was in shock at having him here in front of her.

"You died."

He nodded solemnly when she looked at him. "I did."

"You left us. Left me." She felt tears pricking her eyes. "It hurt so much. I can't…" Her breath hitched and she started to sob again.

Her body was pulled tightly against his and he tried to soothe her, telling her loving nonsense that just made her angry again. She couldn't listen to another word of his 'love' for her so she pushed him away as hard as she could. Annoyingly he didn't stumble or move, and it felt like she was trying to push a boulder.

"How dare you leave us to fend for ourselves! You could have let us know about your damn plan." She tried to push him again, but he didn't budge. "I can't even push your stupid godly self."

"I can fall back if you want me to?" There was no humor in his eyes, only sadness.

"Did you get super strength or what?" She laughed coldly at him, but the shame in his eyes told her it was true. "Oh."

"Please believe me, I had no idea this was going to happen. It was so quick and sudden that I had no chance to get Hermes to send a message even though Zeus had forbidden it." Alexander held her head between his hands. "I thought I was dead for good. I truly did."

"So what? You just were lounging about in Elysium and Zeus comes down all, 'Hey Alexander, you're a god now. Let's go fighting!' or what?" She mimicked a deep voice but to her annoyance Alexander had the nerve to smile at her. "You sit there all high and mighty and forget about us little peons while you drink and party and—"

He kissed her. The son of a bitch had the nerve to kiss her. She backed away and slapped him as hard as she could. In reality, it probably hurt her more than him. He barely even flinched but it didn't lessen the satisfaction of it.

"Feel better?" he asked casually.

"No." She slapped him again. He took a step closer to her. Another slap and his body was pressed to hers. Raising her hand again he caught it in the air and kissed the inside of her wrist delicately.

Julia took a step back from him, he followed suit until her back hit the wall. She was officially trapped. The look in his eyes did nothing but turn her on at this point. His eyes were baring down on her with a hunger she hadn't seen before and it was frightening yet exhilarating at the same time.

"I missed you," he uttered. "I thought I'd lost you forever."

"Don't lie to me." Her strength was leaving her when his lips hovered over hers. "You knew I'd hasten my way to you."

A growl escaped his throat and he pinned her arms up above her head. The heat radiating off his skin was intoxicating, and she wanted nothing more than to feel him bare against her. He was like an animal on the prowl as his lips moved along her neck.

"I told you not to." His voice was stern and all that more mouthwatering.

"I don't take orders from you." She challenged, staring into his eyes daring him to say she should. "God or not, I don't have to listen to you."

"Which is infuriatingly sexy of you." His lips crashed against hers making her weak in the knees.

As if knowing this, he picked her up and she was quickly tossed down on her bed before she knew what was happening. He crawled over her body and they looked at one another while he slowly unfastened her robe sash.

His eyes raked over her naked body, captivating her with the look of hunger in his gaze. It made her bite her lip in anticipation. Alexander reached out, his thumb brushing over her bottom lip as he bit his own.

"That damn lip of yours," he practically moaned.

He leaned down to kiss her. It was gentle at first, but it grew into a fierce claiming as if her lips could save his life. She couldn't take it anymore, she needed to feel his skin against hers. She frantically pulled at his shirt. Obligingly, he just ripped it off his body and kicked off his pants.

Julia remembered his body clearly but it felt new to her this time. It felt as if years had passed and what was once familiar needed to be discovered again. Grabbing desperately at him she wrapped her arms around his neck and pulled him even closer to her. She relished in the feeling of his skin against hers even if it didn't quite ease the ache she had inside.

She bucked her hips against his, wanting more from him. Alexander pulled his swollen lips from hers, out of breath with a glazed look of desire in his eyes.

"Is this okay?" She could feel his heart beating in his chest.

Julia wrapped her legs around his waist and pulled his hips into hers. "Absolutely."

With a quick grin he kissed her hard, working his lips down to her throat and nipped at her neck. She moaned at the sensation and felt his body enter hers. Alexander wrapped his arms around her as he moved and held her close as if she would leave and never return.

His movements were frantic as if he couldn't decide what to do with her. Alexander's body was on top of hers, then she on top of him. They rolled around in bed not quite sure which way to satisfy this craving until her legs began to quiver. Alexander must have sensed her exhaustion and moved her firmly below him once more.

Locking her fingers in his hair she pulled back his head exposing his neck which she ravenously nipped and licked. A low growl vibrated in his throat and his hips dug deliciously into hers. It was as if his body showed her how much he hurt thinking he'd lost her.

She'd have delicious bruises from how hard he gripped her, silently begging her to stay as close to him in a desperate attempt to keep her near. He was anxious, scared, and she could feel it clearly with every touch of his hands.

Her mouth opened in a silent moan as his body put the pieces of her soul back together.

All the pain and torment since his passing was erased with the knowledge of how deeply he needed her too, something his body was able to express when his words couldn't. They were whole once again.

Chapter XXVIII

Alexander

"WELL, WHAT A PLEASANT *evening,*" Alexander groaned *into his overly jeweled goblet.*

"You mean you didn't enjoy reuniting with all your old concubines and wives?" His sister snickered into her own drink. Her reddish-brown hair fell back as she drowned the last of her wine with ease and a smile appeared on her lips. "Dear brother, even in death you are forever going to be plagued by the female population."

"So it would seem, Cleo."

"Will you please call me by my full name?" She rolled her eyes. "Cleo sounds like a cat."

He never understood his sister's distaste of it, but he intended to keep using it to annoy her. "It seems Stateira and Parysatis still hate Roxane."

"Well, she did kill them." Cleo lounged back on her cushioned dining couch. Her foot dangled above the ground as she stared up into the night sky.

Alexander couldn't help but stare at her. She was exactly how he remember, wearing her favorite long royal purple chiton dress with a silver breast band pulled tightly to show off her tiny waist. Even in death she felt the need to look her best and point out her figure. He loved her for that.

"After two thousand years you'd think they'd calm down." Alexander propped himself up on his left arm, turning himself more towards his sister on his own couch. "All of you are dead because of me. You know that, right?"

Cleo shrugged. "We died. Everyone does at some point. At least we have a claim to fame. Our names are remembered and will never be forgotten thanks to you. I couldn't think of a worse fate then dying in obscurity."

"You were murdered."

"I had an amazing funeral though." She winked at him. "Besides, this is better than life, dear brother. No murder here or lack of wanting. If you hadn't become who you did, who knows where all of us would have ended up? Your wives would surely be in the Field of Mourning. I would more than likely be in the Asphodel Meadows. What a disappointment that would be. And mother would probably be in Tartarus. If anything, you saved us from an eternal turmoil."

"You have a way of making me feel better, you know that?" Alexander felt his heart swell for the first time since his death. He never thought about the fates of his family, where they could have ended up had he not become Immortal. The thought of his mother in Tartarus, the hell of the Greek world, made his temper flare for a beat.

"I do what I can. Oh, and Aristotle was too hard on you at dinner. But I will agree, you've made some stupid decisions." Alexander laughed out loud and chucked a pillow at his sister. She caught it with ease and threw it right back with a big smile on her face.

"Aristotle will lecture me till the end of time. I have no doubt about that." He thought back on tonight's massive family dinner. His wives, his siblings, hell both of his children were there sitting side by side joking about something that made both of their faces light up. "You know, I always thought of them as hating me. Spiteful and waiting for my life to end so they could get their revenge. I surely deserve it, regardless of your praise but besides bickering wives, it was nothing as I expected."

His sister yet again rolled her eyes at him. "Roxane got her happy ass in your dream and told you to calm down about all that."

"Look who is talking like a modern woman." Alexander grinned.

"So, I eavesdrop on the mortals occasionally. Sue me." She sat up quickly on her couch and jumped off. Hurriedly, she sat next to him and took his hands in hers. "I can show you how to do it. You can see your friends, if you'd like?"

Alexander was about to open his mouth before a deep voice behind them filled the air with agitation. "He is not permitted to that and you know it, girl."

Cleo's eyes widened and she bowed her head down towards the man walking from the shadows. Alexander felt a tinge of anger build inside when he noticed the man standing before him was none other than Zeus. Instead of modern casual, he was in bright white robes holding a scepter with an eagle on his shoulder. His beard was longer, as was his hair and both were white and curly.

Zeus strode closer towards them which made Alexander instinctively hide his sister behind his back as they stood from the couch.

"What is it?" Alexander was less than pleased to see Zeus.

"Is that how you thank the god that saved you?"

"You let me die," Alexander countered.

"You had to." Zeus flicked his fingers at Cleo. "Leave us."

"She isn't…" But his sister ran into the palace without another word leaving him alone with Zeus under the stars. "Fine then. What is it?"

Zeus took in Alexander's attire. "Don't you strike a familiar appearance in your robes, Alexander?"

Against Alexander's wishes, his mother insisted he dressed in traditional robes, a fashion he truly did not miss throughout the years. "Get to the point."

Zeus's eyes flashed lightning. "Remember who you are talking to."

Alexander hung his head as his sister had and didn't look Zeus in the eyes. He was pushing his luck. He knew that but part of him was upset he was no longer with Julia or Damian. Hell, even Cato. He missed them terribly and knew he left them with a horrible burden in the mortal world.

"Apologies."

"I didn't save you for a reason, Alexander. There is a solution in the mortal world, one of which I gather you will not care for, but one that most come to be," Zeus started. "We needed a martyr. Someone the mortals trust wholeheartedly to lead them to salvation. They know of us, but for months your face has been their grip on hope."

Alexander couldn't help but sit back down on the couch. His mind was turning with what Zeus was telling him and what he could mean by it, but only one thing really stuck out to him. Something Cato suggested to happen and now he was wondering if his father was the influence of that thought.

"Okay?"

"What better way is there to show our existence and power than to bring their savoir back to life as a god among men?"

Alexander's face ended up buried in his hands. This couldn't be happening. He finally found peace in his afterlife with his missing family. Ones that didn't hate him and he wasn't ready to let that go.

"I wanted to be mortal. Why would I want to be a god?" he spoke through his fingers.

"Haven't you been paying attention to the world around you? What you want no longer matters. What matters is the continuation of our world. If we cease to exist, then so does the underworld and your family along with it. This is to protect everyone you love." Zeus took a brief pause. "I know the guilt you still feel for leaving them behind to join the Immortals. By doing this you will finally be saving them. Isn't that the redemption you have always wished for?"

His words sounded more like manipulation, but Alexander couldn't see anything but the truth behind them. He needed to do this for his family. To be selfless for his family once again so they could continue in their afterlife in happiness. He owed this to them more than anyone in creation.

"What do I need to do?"

"Then what?" Cato looked at him with fascination in his eyes.

Alexander couldn't help but laugh, dragging himself from the memory that seemed to play before his eyes. He needed to explain to them what had happened to him in the underworld and they were far too curious for his liking. Julia sat in his lap on his couch and Anna was feeding Owen while sitting next to Damian. Cato just lounged on his bed with his head propped up like a little schoolgirl getting juicy gossip. It was great.

"Then I had to make a big ass speech to the gods and goddesses of every damn religion about how we need their help to save our existence and theirs. So on and so forth and then they offered their help. They are the ones that called on the mythological creatures that weren't blood thirsty demons since those already worked for Marc."

"How did Lee and Liam know to come record you live at the battle?" Damian twirled a strand of Anna's hair around his finger while the other arm remained in a sling.

"Well, I had to show the world what we were doing somehow. So, I contacted them two days before the battle. Needless to say, they were both scared shitless when I showed up."

"That was far less entertaining than your sister and Zeus story." Cato sighed. "By the way, is your sister hot?"

Julia threw her shoe at Cato's head which landed with a soft *thunk* against his cheek. "You are with someone. Can you show a little couth?"

Alexander's head snapped up.

"What did you say?"

"Cato found someone." Julia shrugged. "Or her crazy ass found him."

The venom in Julia's words led Alexander to believe that they all knew who this woman was. Instead of asking, Alexander gave Cato a pointed look to fess up. This was definitely a monumental moment in history for Cato.

"So, did you and Roxane do it?" Cato blurted out.

Alexander wanted to sink deep into the couch at the mention of his wife while his girlfriend sat on his lap. "Don't change the subject."

"Or we can momentarily change the subject and then make our way back around." Julia raised her eyebrows at Alexander. "Did you?"

Wrapping his arms tightly around her, he looked into those worried blue eyes with shame reflecting in his.

"Julia, I am sorry." She elbowed him in the stomach and tried to get out of his lap. He tried his best not to laugh at her reaction but couldn't help it. "I'm kidding, love. Nothing happened between us. She knows about you."

Everyone sat still in his room just staring at him, all except Anna.

"Okay? So, he didn't bang her. Why are you all shocked?"

"Oh, I don't know. Maybe because that was his first love and wife and…" Cato looked at his sister and decided to take a better course of action. "Okay, so it's Amara."

"What!" Alexander jumped off the couch sending Julia toppling onto the floor. After many apologies and helping her up, Alexander turned back to Cato.

"Did you just say Amara?"

"Yeah, why?" Cato shrugged. "What the big deal?"

Alexander wasn't quite sure what to say. Something inside himself told him to be cautious and he couldn't explain it, but the dread was there. "Nothing. Be careful with that one."

Cato rolled his eyes at Alexander, a trait he noticed Cato had in common with Alexander's sister. "Yeah, I know. I've heard that like a hundred times."

"Listen to him," the voice of Alexander's annoying father came from the balcony. He was no longer the older godly version of himself but more of Alexander's age wearing a suit and tie. Apollo stood next to him wearing swim trunks with a straw hat and flip flops. Zeus looked Apollo from head to toe and shook his head at him.

"You couldn't change for even five minutes?"

"Sorry, surfing after this." Apollo flashed his bright white teeth.

"Anyways." Zeus gave up on the argument. "I want to thank you all for your part in our preservation. It wasn't easy and I know that, but we must discuss what will come next."

"What is there to discuss?" Damian looked on the verge of panic after he realized he just questioned a god. "Sir."

"I need to let you all know that this isn't the first time

something like this has happened." Zeus paused for his obnoxious dramatic affect. "One other time an Immortal did the same as Marc. He was tired of the gods and deemed it was time for mankind to take back what they created."

"How is that possible? I would have remembered that." It was Cato's turn to look nervous.

Zeus merely carried on with his explanation of events. "War raged leaving millions of dead. You all, with the exception of Julia and Anna, fought in it."

Alexander was told all of this already but the looks on Cato and Damian's faces probably mirrored his when he found out. It wasn't every day you were told you fought for years without any recollection of what the hell happened.

"Keep going," Alexander urged.

"The Black Death wasn't only about a plague, it also brought along with it a massive religious upheaval."

"There wasn't a plague?" Damian asked.

"Oh, there was one and it helped spark the rebellion against the gods. People blamed and turned from us easily and followed one of our misguided Warriors against us. Many Warriors fought on both sides to decide our fates and when they were finally crushed by our forces, we had no other option than to erase it from the memories of everyone. We couldn't risk the absolute knowledge of our existence because mortals thrive on faith and free will of belief. An absolute awareness threatens the soul of a mortal."

"Is that what is going to happen again?" Julia crossed her arms, almost glaring at Zeus. "You are going to make us forget again about the truth? As if all this hell didn't happen and it was just a sickness that destroyed so many lives?"

Zeus walked up to Julia, his eyes glaring down at her with such intensity that Alexander felt the need to get between them.

"It will be a war in the mortals minds without the gods or creatures' involvements. However, the Immortals will remember. You see that's where we went wrong last time. Had we let you remember, perhaps history wouldn't have repeated itself."

"Well, hell." Cato whistled.

Zeus didn't turn his eyes from Julia and either did she. "Is there a problem?"

"You make me angry," she said simply. "You made me think he was gone forever, put me in a living hell and you could have said something. You practically told me if I chose to be with Alexander instead of Aden, I would be miserable forever."

To Alexander's amazement, Zeus's eyes softened. "My dear girl, I told you either you would be seduced by the darkness surrounding Aden or the bright flame of Alexander. That one of them would end in tragedy for you." Zeus took Alexander's hand in his and placed it on her stomach. "Is this tragedy to you?"

Julia cocked her head to the side. "It's not even possible."

Apollo jumped into the conversation with another bright grin on his face. "Actually, it is. I sort of saw it as soon as it happened." Alexander's eyes went wide. "No, I didn't watch! Gods no… but I saw the outcome."

"Wait a holy-fucking-minute." Anna stood up from Damian's lap with a now sleeping Owen in her arms. "Does that mean—"

"You're pregnant!" Apollo threw his hands up and the air and wooed loud. "Uncle Apollo and Grandpa Zeus at your service."

Chapter XXIX

Anna

NEVER IN A MILLION years did she think she would have to witness thousands of bodies being burnt on hundreds of pyres. The troops must have worked day and night gathering the bodies and finding enough wood to burn. Whatever families could make the funeral had helped along with the process in a massive effort of unity, unlike anything she had ever seen.

"When do they lose their memories of the war?" Damian asked Alexander as they stood and watched the people gather together to begin the funeral.

"Once the dead have had their proper send off and their families return to where they came from." Alexander was dressed in his Greek armor again. It stood out big time but according to Zeus, he needed to keep up pretenses until the mortals forgot about him again.

"We better grab him." Damian put a hand on Alexander's shoulder and both the men retreated to the tent that held the General's body.

Within minutes they reappeared with a stretcher that held the body of enemy number one. Alexander, Damian, Cato, and Caleb each held a handle and led the way to a single pyre built for one man. Thankfully, he was covered with a thick black cloth that hid his terribly burnt body from the crowds.

People must have realized who was under the cloth because curses filled the air and the crying grew louder than before. They were angry with this man and she understood why. However, the pain she saw in the eyes of her loved ones was like a knife to the heart.

Cato's jaw was tense with anger and Julia had tears rolling down her cheeks uncontrollably. Damian and Alexander on the other hand looked stoic even if their eyes gave away the intense sorrow they felt for their old friend.

Her husband's chest swelled with heavy breaths as he tried to contain himself in front of the crowds of mourners. Anna could have sworn that things would turn violent until Alexander stared them all down with a flash of bright light igniting in his eyes. The shouting begun to settle down and became whispers among the people around them.

Placing his body on top of the wood, Alexander pulled back the cloth that covered the General's face which sent even more whispers among the people. Her family didn't falter though, Cato continued to place a coin over each of his father's eyes and recover his face with the cloth. She was so proud of their strength in having to do this in front of people who hated him so deeply. Regardless of what he had done, they all loved him in their own way or another at some point in time.

Alexander couldn't help but address the angry crowd. "I know you all don't understand why we are showing our enemy respect. Allow me to make myself clear. This man served you all for hundreds of years. He risked his life to protect strangers around him and raised a family all the while.

"He was a father, a friend, and a brother before he let despair misguide him. He was a man once so very loved by others until his heart was broken beyond repair. So, I beg you not to stoop to the level of our enemy and instead recognize the pain his family feels this very moment. Funerals are for the living, not the dead. And even though it is hard for you to understand right now, his family needs this closure, just as you need your own."

The crowd grew silent as Alexander spoke and remained so after he was done. While Alexander, Caleb and Damian returned to their women's sides, Cato remained by his father's body. He leaned down towards his father's ear and said something before taking a lighter out of his pocket and lit the pyre.

The heat of it was almost instant as the flames grew quickly from the accelerant used to help the fire quickly gain strength. One by one the pyres began to light up against the night sky. Anna didn't realize how vastly wide the pyres covered the land until it lit up the battlefield for at least a mile wide.

The families moved back quickly once the fires began. The heat became intense and too much for their bodies to withstand. Anna was glad she left Owen back home because the smell that wafted through the air was something she would never forget. It was overwhelming compared to the few Warrior's funerals she had gone to. This was almost too much to bear.

"Are the fire brigades on standby?" Alexander looked over her head to Damian.

"And aerial firefighting planes," Damian added. "They will keep it from spreading until the fire dies out on its own."

"What if it doesn't?" Anna looked up at them.

"We have it handled." Alexander walked away from the pyre while nestling Julia against his body. Cato retreated as well along with Colette and Caleb leaving Anna standing with an unreadable Damian.

"Are you okay?" She wrapped her arms around his waist and relished in the feeling of him pulling her against him.

"I'm not sure." He kissed her head before leading them towards the tents. "It feels odd, because when we thought he died the first time it was as if he truly did. From that death a new man was born as someone different. I feel as if I already mourned my friend many years ago and that this is a stranger."

"It's like an inferno," Cato said as they stood in front of their tent.

Alexander had his arms wrapped securely around Julia as they both faced the fire and Caleb merely held Colette's hand. Anna felt Damian's arms rest around her shoulders from behind and the seven of them watched the fires burn brightly in the night. It was a sight for the ages.

Without warning, wisps of thick snake-like smoke began climbing out of the pyres and up into the stars. It was as if a massive and thick fog rose from the ground and reached into the sky until it disappeared leaving bright stars in their wake. Anna looked at her companions and noticed they were in total shock at what just happened.

Following their gaze, she looked at the burning body of the General and let out a gasp. A single thick line of smoke escaped the fire and made its way up into the heavens on its own until a new star was created where is stopped. She was still very new to this Immortal thing but even she could take a guess as to what happened.

"Did all of them…" Cato tried to get the words out.

"Even Marc?" Damian asked.

"Yes." Alexander smiled through his tears, genuinely happy. "The gods forgave them all. They showed mercy. He can finally rest in peace."

"So, the entire world now thinks it was a world war and that it's over?" Damian asked Alexander.

"Seems like it. Our faces are no longer in their minds or hearts. Just like old times." Alexander smirked while he continued to clean up Ahmose's old office.

With a broom in hand, Damian couldn't help but hate that fact. "It doesn't bother you? That you died for them and now you won't receive their prayers or even remember the truth of it?"

Alexander stopped picking up papers from the floor and leaned against the large wooden desk. "No. For the sake of their sanity they can't know about what happened. The truth would consume them and if they believe it was just a typical war it would be easier for them to rebuild. Their loved ones still died heroes and that's what matters."

"Okay, but it doesn't bother you that no one knows about you?"

"Not at all. Besides, it meant I could chop off my hair again." Alexander ran his hand through his freshly cut hair. "Does it bother you?"

Damian had to laugh and shook his head. "Not at all. I hated being in charge so don't ever do that to me again."

"You were able to handle it. I knew you were capable." Alexander looked at him as if he couldn't understand why Damian felt insignificant. "You are stronger than you believe, Damian. You aren't my second in command, you are my equal and always have been. You've just refused to see it yourself."

"Well, thanks for that but seriously. Don't do that shit to me again. I don't like it and never will." Damian walked over and pat Alexander on the shoulder, probably a little rougher than needed. "So, does that mean you will cease to exist since no one remembers you?"

It was a thought that worried the hell out of Damian. If Alexander was a god now that meant he needed people to believe in him for him to exist. The thought of losing him again felt like a heavy burden.

"Well, that's the beauty of the Immortals not getting their minds wiped clean. They already know who I am and they live forever." Alexander rubbed his face looking as if he were exhausted. "This is all just insane."

"The being a god part or becoming a father part?" Damian was beyond happy for Alexander. Having a child brought a joy in his life that he never knew possible. Owen was his heart and soul, as was Anna, but there was just something about his son that made him feel utterly at peace.

"Both." Alexander crossed him arms and didn't look the least bit happy. "I was ecstatic in Elysium, Damian. It felt like I was at peace for the first time in my existence. Surrounded by the ones I lost and forgiven by them. It felt great."

Damian wasn't quite sure how to feel about that in all honesty. He wanted to understand how Alexander felt but the fact was it seemed like he didn't miss his Warrior family at all. Whatever look Damian had on his face it must have registered with Alexander.

"That doesn't mean I didn't miss you all. It felt different down there though. It felt as if everything was going to be alright with you guys." Alexander looked conflicted in his words. "I just wish I had more time to spend with them I suppose."

"I get that, but I think being a god you can do whatever the hell you want, right?" Damian grinned when Alexander had a mischievous smile on his lips. "Knew it."

"Besides my confliction of where I want to be, yes being a father is terrifying me," he admitted. "I spent time with my two sons in the Underworld and they hold no ill will towards me. What if I ruin this child like I did Aden?"

"You listen to me, you big pain in my ass." Damian faced

Alexander head on, putting his hands on his shoulders and staring him in the eye. "You love Julia. You love your family. That kid isn't going to lack for anything, including your love."

Alexander hung his head, but Damian thumped his forehead to look at him. "Ouch."

Ignoring his fake hurt, Damian went on. "You are going to be a badass dad and our kids are going to grow up together. Who the hell would have thought that would ever happen?"

"It still doesn't seem right. I mean, Julia and I barely just had sex and now she's pregnant? Pretty sure egg implantation doesn't even happen that soon."

"Apollo saw it you moron. Quit trying to second guess it and let's move on with our lives. The war is over and we saved the damn world. Be happy."

"I am happy you idiot." He backed off the desk and looked out the window of the office.

Damian followed right behind him and they both leaned against the open windows, listening to the sounds of Urbs coming to life once more.

"You hear that?" Damian asked. "That is the sound of peace. Of our people finding their way back into a normal life of bliss."

"I'll admit, I had my doubts it would get back to this."

"It did though. Thanks to you."

"Thanks to you as well, you fool. You kept the hope going and led a bigger army than I ever had. Don't diminish your accomplishments."

"I do believe I failed until you saved that day actually."

"Oh, Hephaestion." Alexander shook his head at him. "Will you ever know your worth?"

"Don't get me wrong, Alexander. I know I'm badass." Damian sighed. "But no one will ever be Alexander the Great, God of Salvation."

Chapter XXX

Alexander

T HERE WAS NEVER A moment in his life that he thought he would have to murder his own child. The fates of Aegus and Herakles were undoubtably his fault, but Aden never stood a chance in this life. Insanity had taken its toll on him from a young age.

He walked alone down the hallway towards Aden's cell. There was no need for a big spectacle of his death and quite frankly, Alexander wasn't about to allow it. Marc was one thing. People needed to see that happen, but Aden was just a pawn in Marc's plan.

Unlatching the door, Alexander stood outside of the room for a moment trying to collect his thoughts. He was about to end the life of his own flesh and blood. It wasn't something he took lightly. He would never be able to shake the grief of it either.

As he stepped inside, he saw Aden lying on the small cot in the room with a thin blanket covering his body. His face was bruised and scabbed over from wounds of the war and his body shivered as if freezing. He was a far cry away from being the strong Warrior Alexander knew for so many years.

Once he softly closed the door, Aden's eyes slowly opened and they met in a silent stare. He wasn't sure what to say to him.

There wasn't anything that could make this situation better for him and Alexander wasn't about to beat a man while he was down. Aden already knew his fate and dragging it out seemed cruel.

After minutes passed, Aden finally spoke with a cracked voice, "So, is it time?"

Alexander nodded as he took a syringe out of his pocket.

"It will be quick."

"It's more than I deserve." Aden tried to sit up until he started to cough violently. Pulling his hand away from his mouth, Alexander saw the blood spattering Aden's palm. "Doesn't look as if I had much more time anyways."

"I wish this was different." Alexander squatted down in front of Aden's cot coming face to face with his son. "I wish I knew about you and were there for you. I would have been. I hope you know that."

Aden abandoned his mission to sit up and laid back down on the cot. "I need to tell you something, but I need you to promise me you will go through with my death."

"What do you mean?"

"You are unpredictable when it comes to your emotions and what I am going to tell you is going to mess with your mind. I need you to promise to finish this with me because I can't go on like this any longer." Aden didn't look like the sadistic man Alexander had come to know at all. In fact, he looked down-right sympathetic to Alexander's feelings.

"I'm not sure what you could say that would change my mind, Aden. You've done everything possible to make everyone hate you."

"I don't want you thinking this is me trying to get you to care for me or hell even feeling sorry for me." Aden weakly smiled. "I just want you to know what happened."

"Okay." Alexander sat on the cold stone floor and waited for Aden to speak.

"When I was born, I loved my mother. She was my world and we did everything together but when I turned seven things changed. I grew angry for no reason and became hostile towards the one person that cared for me and I didn't know why." Aden took a breath. "She tried to get me help but nothing worked. I was losing myself and even at a young age I knew it. That's when Marc had started to come around."

"Go on." Alexander pushed when Aden took a long pause.

"Marc knew about my mother and you. She confided in him hoping he would help her, or something, I don't know. Instead, I became his experiment for the tonic Julia was given. He slipped it in my drinks without me or my mother knowing." Another coughing fit attacked him. Alexander quickly grabbed the small cup of water Aden was given and helped him drink. Once the fit stopped, Aden continued.

"It wasn't perfected at that point, but I was groomed to hate you and my mother without really knowing why. I had meetings with Marc every week. I now realize he was brainwashing me, but mother thought we were having Warrior lessons. My hatred and anger grew every day for years until one day I finally snapped when I turned fourteen."

Aden paused as if he couldn't continue but Alexander placed a hand on his arm gently, looking him in the eyes without an ounce of hatred behind them.

"Keep going."

"I killed her in her sleep. I don't know why I did it, but I did. I went to Marc for help but all he did was smile and pat me on the back. He told me I was ready to join him." Aden closed his eyes as if lost in a memory. "I was fucking fourteen and he made me a murderer. By the time I grew into an adult he no longer needed to give me the tonic. I was permanently made into the evil pawn he created."

"Why are you telling me this?" Alexander tried to swallow the lump in his throat. "You enjoyed every second of the misery you caused."

"I did enjoy it, a lot actually," Aden admitted. "But that innocent boy inside me never left, he was just subdued. I relished the pain I caused others but at the same time it hurt me just as much as my victims. I have two people in my head and the evil one always took over."

"Your personality is split." Alexander rubbed his face with his hand not knowing what to do with this information. His son was brainwashed just as Julia has been by the evil bastard he thought was his friend. "We can save you. Julia came out of it and so can you."

Aden smiled feebly at him and grabbed Alexander's hand. "I told you, don't try to save me. I took that shit for years and I will never be fixed. I deserve to be put down like a dog because that's what I am—an animal."

"It wasn't your fault." Alexander felt his eyes water, but he refused to cry. "This was done to you."

"All of it was still me though, just a different version of me."

"Is this the nice Aden or the evil one talking?"

"A little of both. We've both given up at this point. I'm serious when I say I just want it to be over with. I'll never stop hurting the people around me. I won't ever be able to control myself." Aden begun to cough again but his cup was empty. "Could you get me more water?"

Alexander quickly made his way to the sink. When he turned around Aden held the needle in his hand.

"Don't you dare do it, Aden."

"You're easy to steal from." His bloody smile sent chills

down Alexander's spine. "Don't feel bad for me and don't blame yourself. I am a monster and I know it." Aden stuck the needle quickly in his arm, pushing the liquid into his body before Alexander could stop him.

"No, Aden. Dammit, no!" Alexander ran to him, dropping to his knees unsure what to do.

His eyes connected with his sons but there was nothing he could do. He had to watch as Aden's chest rose and fell for the last time. A weak 'goodbye' on his lips.

The truth of it all drove him to scream at the top of his lungs as he pulled his dead child into his arms and began to cry. The only solace from Aden's death was knowing that he was no longer fighting a battle within himself. Like so many others, he was at peace.

Cato

He woke up to the feeling of his bed moving, but instead of opening his eyes, he kept them shut as if still sleeping. The sounds of bare feet padding along the ground let Cato know that Amara was sneaking out of his room. Which was confirmed by the click of the door latching shut.

"What the hell?" Cato sat up in his bed, rubbing the sleep out of his eyes.

There was no way he wasn't going to follow her. Call it curiosity or hell, even paranoia. Amara had been acting funny ever since he left for the funeral of the soldiers and his father. More to the point, she'd never left the room before without him with her because she was too afraid of running into people.

As he quietly opened the door, Cato peered down the hallway and jerked his head back into his room. Amara hadn't gotten far. In fact, she was standing outside of Alexander's room wearing a thin nightgown. His mind went straight to Alexander sleeping with her behind his back but then he remembered that Alexander had just found out about her.

Old feelings from times past quickly subsided because he knew Alexander wouldn't hurt his sister like that. More to the point, his sister was probably in there with Alexander. So, what the hell was going on?

He dared to peek his head around the doorframe again and saw the wisps of Amara's hair tailing behind her as she entered Alexander's room. Cato jumped into stealth mode and carefully made his way towards Alexander's door. It was wide open and as he looked inside, he saw Amara slowly prowling towards the bed with both his sister and Alexander in it.

She slowly and carefully crawled between their bodies, her knees digging into the mattress as she looked down at both of them in their sleep. Confusion filled his mind as she pulled up her gown from her thighs. The notion of a three-some quickly died when she produced two knives strapped to her body. Quickly, she pressed a blade to both Alexander and Julia's throat, effectively waking them from sleep.

"What the…" Alexander's voice could be heard from the doorway. "Amara?"

"Hello, Alexander." Her voice was laced with venom.

"What are you doing?" Even from a distance Cato could see the shock on Alexander's face. "Why are you here?"

With Amara's back to the door, Cato slipped into Alexander's room unnoticed. He looked around for anything that could subdue his damn woman from whatever the hell she was trying to do. All Alexander had were guns and knives and Cato really didn't want to stab the one woman he had ever loved.

"You killed the god that saved me." Her voice was full of sorrow now. He could tell she was crying.

"What?" Alexander tried to sit up in the bed, but Amara pressed the knife harder into his neck bringing blood up from under the blade. "I haven't killed any... wait. Do you mean Marc?"

Amara shook her head and her sobs became more apparent. "Aden. You killed him. My savior from an eternity of hell."

"Alexander had to," Julia spoke up and Amara rewarded her with a backhand to the cheek before placing the blade against her throat again.

"Do not speak to me." Her attention went back to Alexander. "You promised to save me and you didn't. You are a liar just like Apollo."

"That's no reason to kill us." Alexander held up his hands in surrender. "We can talk this through rationally."

"With Cato," Julia added.

Amara laughed coldly and started to cry again. Her emotions were ravaging her mind, Cato could tell. Thankfully, though, he managed to find a rope in the midst of Alexander's damn armory.

"Do you think he brought me here just to be nice? I was put here to keep an eye on you all." She looked down at Julia. "Yes, you were right. I was a spy for them."

"Why?" Alexander asked.

"I was supposed to gain everyone's trust. So, I started with Cato. It was rather easy. I saw how infatuated he was with me, so I took him to bed." Cato felt like he was going to throw up. "I was just bidding my time to get information for the true love of my life."

"You used him?" Julia tried to sit up, but the knife dug

deeper into her neck. Cato could see the blood dripping down her porcelain skin from where he stood.

His fists were clenched but he needed to hear the rest of what Amara had to say. He needed the truth and it began to consume him.

"Yes, of course I did," she said it casually without a care. "That man requires far too much attention for my liking."

"How did Aden even know about you?" Alexander laughed, which was probably not the brightest thing for him to do.

Amara took the blade from Alexander's throat and stabbed him in the shoulder. Cato nearly jumped into action, but Alexander caught his eye and shook his head at him. It took a lot of will power not to tackle her to the ground and wrap his hands around her throat till she passed out, but he managed.

"The General and Aden came to the island looking for mythological creatures to recruit. Fortunately for me, the satyrs captured them as they did with you, and told them of the oracle on the mountain. I was angry that you all left me there. Marc promised me freedom in exchange for my services." Her tense arms bent as she leaned over closer to their faces. Cato could barely make out what she was saying. "Apollo had cut me off since I helped the lot of you. So, I gladly accepted."

"Apollo said I shouldn't trust you," Alexander practically laughed in her face. "Seems he did the right thing by leaving you stranded on that island for centuries."

"You took Aden from me and my chance for happiness. I'm going to enjoy this." Her arms tensed, about to make her move when she was stopped in her tracks. She looked back over her shoulder at Cato. There was no sadness or despair from betrayal, just disdain and anger at him.

"I knew you'd protect him at all costs, I just didn't know how."

She fell forward landing between Alexander and Julia's bodies with a knife sticking out of her back. Cato barely saw his sister scrambling up in the bed towards him and he knew she was holding his face, but he couldn't tear his eyes off of Amara's limp body. Despite her not really caring for him, he'd just killed the only woman he had ever loved.

"Cato?" His sister tried to shake him out of his shock. "Cato."

A firm slap to the face from Alexander shook him from his current nightmare.

"Look at me, Cato." Alexander held his face between his hands, getting into his line of sight so Cato was forced to look at him. "Are you okay?"

"Yeah." Cato looked at Amara's body one more time before leaving Alexander's room to his own.

A few hours ago, he was having sex with her and now he'd just killed her. She was a liar and didn't like him at all. This is what he got for taking a chance on a woman.

"Wait up." Alexander chased after him. "You sure you're okay?"

"I don't know, Alexander. I just killed the woman I loved in my best friend's bed. Which sort of implies you guys were sleeping together. That would have actually been better than her using me."

"So, you're not okay?" Alexander's eyebrows rose.

"Everyone knew she was up to no good except me." Cato ignored Alexander's question. "That makes it suck even worse."

"We had suspicions, nothing concrete. Don't be so hard on yourself."

"It doesn't matter anymore. She's dead."

"You cared about her, so it does matter."

"I loved her." Cato shrugged. "A lot actually. Then I found

out the truth, and I blocked all of that out so I could save you guys from a Columbian necktie."

"You just blocked out your feelings for her." Alexander snapped his fingers. "Just like that."

"Actually, no. I feel like my chest is caving in and I want to beat the shit out of something. But I am better off knowing the truth now than in the Underworld with the rest of you wondering how the hell we all died."

Amara had left his life just as quickly as she come into it. The only thing that mattered to him at this point was his family and he would always put them first no matter what. He would just have to channel his current heartache into a bottle of booze and quick.

"Do you need anything? I'm here for you. You know that right?"

"Just time. I just need some damn time, man." He paused. "Besides, you're the one that got stabbed."

"I'm fine." Alexander shrugged his shoulders. "It was said you'd protect me at all costs. Sucks that this was how."

"I'd do it again. There isn't a damn woman in this universe worth letting my family die for." Cato shrugged. "If you don't see me for a few days don't freak out. 'Kay?"

"Please tell me you won't fall too deep again."

"Wouldn't dream of it. I have a niece or nephew on the way and I intend on being here for that."

Chapter XXXI

Anna

"MAN, THIS HAS BEEN the coolest vacation ever."

Anna propped Owen's chubby little body on her knees. He was nine months old and their vacation in Egypt was coming to an end. Julia was practically at her due date and there was no way in hell she wanted to miss the birth of that baby.

"I promised you Egypt and you got it." Damian leaned down and kissed her lips as he began packing their suitcases.

Owen wiggled until he was able to escape Anna's grasp on him and crawled quickly along the hotel room floor. It felt like most of her time was spent being his shadow and milk machine. She had to admit, she was a helicopter mom and was damn proud of it.

Damian stopped her in her tracks as she fast walked by chasing Owen. Pulling her body to his she tried to shimmy him off, but his grip was too tight.

"Let the boy explore. He will be fine."

"What if he jumps off the balcony? Hmm? Ever think about that?"

Damian's annoyingly cute laugh both infuriated and made her giddy. "He isn't even a year old yet and you are afraid he is going to climb up on the balcony railing and leap off."

"Stranger things have happened." She found her lips pressed firmly against his which made her melt into his arms like putty.

"You ready to go home?" He smiled against her lips as she tried to steady her breath. The damn man knew what effect he had on her even with just a kiss. "Three weeks without seeing Julia's round stomach must have been torture for you."

It was true. Ever since having Owen, Anna had some weird maternal love for all things baby lately. Damian thought it was amusing given how horribly she acted when she found out she was pregnant with her own kid.

"You better not play it up too much or I'll convince you to pop another one in this oven." Anna rubbed her stomach like a hungry man.

"I wouldn't need convincing." Damian stopped her rubbing and placed his hand over hers on her stomach.

Anna looked down at their hands and backed away from Damian in horror. "You want another one already?"

With a shrug he said, "I love you pregnant and I without a doubt am head over heels in love with our son. Adding another little person that is part of you into this world would make it even more like heaven for me."

"Just wait till he's out of diapers at least." Anna had a nervous feeling in her stomach at the thought of being pregnant again. In all honesty, that was the part she hated the most.

Damian took her head between his hands and kissed her. His voice was barely a whisper against her lips when he said, "I won't make any promises."

Pulling away from him, she smacked him on the back of his head.

"That's it. I'm going on the pill."

"Takes a while for that to take affect so good luck." Damian grinned down at her. "I'm kidding. I won't take that choice from you. When you are ready, you let me know. Just remember that I will never say no to having another child with you."

All she could do was grab his butt and start the packing process again. She really did want to get home. From the way Cato was talking, Julia was on the brink of giving birth. A new little baby Alexander was coming into the world and that was a miracle in itself.

"Ready?" She picked up her wiggling child and moved his light brown hair out of his eyes.

Damian held the bags in his hands, looking around in case the forgot anything. "Looks good."

Anna took a crystal from her pocket and tossed it in the air. "Domus."

After stepping through the portal, a feeling of relief flooded her. As much as she enjoyed seeing the pyramids and tombs of the pharaohs, along with secret places in Alexandria that her husband knew, she was ready to be home. He was like a walking tour guide in everything ancient and it was super handy.

"What's up lovebirds?" Cato uncrossed his legs as he got off the sofa in the parlor room. "I didn't know you guys were on your way back already."

"Anna was panicking about missing the birth." Damian kissed her head. "Besides that, this little nugget missed you."

Owen was jumping in her arms reaching for Cato. Without missing a beat, Cato had Owen up in the air making airplane noises. He was giggling uncontrollably as Cato dipped him up and down through the air.

"He's like a giant child." Anna laughed.

"And he loves it!" Cato said between plane noises. "Oh no, he's going to crash!" Cato turned Owen over and started to tickle his little body in his arms. The sound was music to her ears.

"Is Uncle Cato torturing my nephew?" Alexander came strolling in along with a very massive Julia.

"How'd you know they were back?" Cato blew raspberries on Owen's neck.

"Damian messaged me." Julia had a tired smile that didn't quite reach her eyes. "I'm so happy you guys are here."

"You look beautiful." Damian gave Julia a gentle hug and it made Anna want to kiss him.

Honestly, Julia was looking a little rough. Bags were under her eyes and her stomach was massive. Anna could tell she was having a hard time walking because her poor feet were so swollen.

"You okay?" Anna hugged her quickly. "Need anything?"

"Well, you are just in time because my contractions have started but they are still far apart." Julia looked on the verge of crying, but being the lady she was, she held it in as best as she could.

Out of nowhere, Alexander jumped back from Julia. Anna didn't know why until she followed everyone's eyes down to the floor. A sense of excitement flooded her entire body and she jumped up and down clapping her hands like some sort of cheerleader. Alexander on the other hand looked like he was in shock and just stood there looking at the now wet floor.

Cato handed Owen back to Anna quickly after giving him a quick peck on the cheek and grabbed his sister's hand. Alexander, still in shock, was now being shaken by Damian.

"Snap the hell out of it!" Damian was practically laughing now. "Your child is on the way."

Alexander

Alexander had lived through just about everything a person could in this world, but this was a new one for him. He'd never been there when his child was born, which was beyond painful to think about right now. For the first time, the life he helped create was about to make their way into the world and he was here for it.

He was in shock about it, there was no doubt, but mostly because becoming a full-time father was hitting him like a ton of bricks. Alexander would have given anything to be there and raise his other three children, but life didn't turn out that way. That didn't make them any less important though. Right now, was his redemption. One he wasn't sure he deserved.

He carried Julia to their room and laid her down on the bed as gently as he could even as a scream echoed through the room as her body contracted. Alexander felt helpless. He had no idea what to do or how to make it better. Julia's eyes were full of tears as they streaked down her cheeks.

"You damn son of a bitch." Julia glared at him. "This is your fault!"

Alexander looked helplessly up at Cato and Damian but they were more amused than worried about her outburst.

"Go get the midwives or something," he pleaded but no one moved. "Hello?"

"Anna is already doing that. Calm down, Alexander." Damian came closer to whisper in his ear, "I've never seen you look so scared. You have to pull yourself together so you don't freak her out too."

"What the hell am I supposed to do?" Alexander tried to whisper but it just came out as frustrated hissing.

"Your ass is supposed to be paying attention to me." Julia began to sweat, her cheeks bright red.

Another contraction hit her body and she was once again writhing in pain. Alexander's hands went behind his head, looking helplessly at his hurting fiancé and the tears started to flow.

"Tell me what to do."

"I don't remember you freaking out like this with Anna," Cato didn't try to hide his amusement when he spoke to Damian. "Give him a sedative or something."

"He's used to being in control and not being in control makes him panic." Damian put a hand on Alexander's shoulder, probably to comfort him, but Alexander felt like he was watching Julia die.

"She is going to be fine. Just breathe."

"Breathe with me, love." Julia grabbed his hand and she tried to smile through her pain at him. He didn't deserve her.

Alexander did as he was told and took deep breaths with Julia until she screamed again.

"Okay, where the hell is the midwife? Healer? Whoever?"

"It's time." Julia panted. "Alexander, the baby is coming."

"Oh hell no." Cato backed up and away from his sister's lower region. "Not going to witness this."

Alexander ran around to the end of the bed and lifted Julia's gown up. "For the love of Zeus, there is a head." He wanted to faint.

"Help me." Julia tried to push herself lower on the bed.

Alexander grabbed her behind her knees and pulled her to where her pelvis was close to hanging off the edge. Both her feet were digging into the edge of the mattress as another contraction coursed through her body. Damian quickly propped pillows up behind her and Cato held onto her hand as he swept away hair that was plastered to her forehead.

Alexander looked back down at his child and an anxious feeling coursed through him.

"My love, you have to push now. Can you do that for me?"

Julia shook her head with tears pouring out. "I can't, what if…" She looked up at her brother and Cato's eyes softened at her.

"Sweetest, you won't die from this. Mother is watching over you, I know it."

Julia, being the strong woman she was, nodded and bore down hard on her body. Alexander looked down as she pushed with every ounce of strength she had. The baby was just about here.

"One last push, baby. You've got this."

A growl came from deep inside of her as she pushed again. Cato looked like his hand was breaking. Alexander could do nothing but smile as his son made his way into the world. His strong little lungs cried out loudly and all Alexander could do was cradle the tiny body to his chest.

"Oh my." The healer and midwife both finally made their way in and his child was plucked from his hands as they began to clean him and Julia up.

The emptiness from being away from his son was immediate but Alexander knew they were just helping. He was about to follow his son everywhere those midwives took him until Julia's hand reached out for his. His attention quickly went to her and their smiles couldn't seem to go away.

Sitting next to her on the bed he leaned over her small body and brushed back her hair. "You did amazing."

"We did amazing." She smiled up at him. "So, we have a son?"

They wanted it to be a surprise but Alexander had a feeling it was a boy the entire time. "That seems to be a specialty of mine."

"Seems so." She laughed with tears in her eyes. They touched foreheads and didn't move from each other for a few minutes until Cato interrupted their moment.

"Here he is!" He placed their child gently into Julia's arms. "My future badass Warrior nephew."

"And mine!" Anna protested. Alexander forgot she came along with the midwife and healer, holding Owen on her hip.

"Me too." Damian looked down at the little bundle in Julia's arms. "What's his name?"

Julia bit her lip and looked up at Alexander with those damn beautiful eyes of hers. "I have a name in mind."

"Whatever you want, my love." He kissed her lips and then his son's head.

"Alec."

"Alec." Alexander put his hand on the bundle of blankets. Alec's little hand somehow wrapped around his finger and he didn't think his heart could be any fuller than it was now. "I will love you, my son. I will protect you till the end of my days and forever more."

Alexander

25 Years Later

"I swear to all that's holy, if you don't fucking leave Nadia alone I am going to cut off your balls." Alexander smacked Alec upside his dirty blond head. He had just caught him making out with Damian's daughter in their garden and there was no way in hell he was going to tell Anna about it.

"Dad, don't lecture me on who I play tonsil hockey with." Alec instantly regretted his words, which was apparent by his eyes seemingly bulging out of his head. "Sir."

"Anna and your mother are going to kill you if they find out. You know that right?" Alexander shoved his son through the kitchen door.

After the birth of their son, Alexander and Julia retreated to her old family home and made it theirs. Julia insisted on having a yard for their child to play in with less guns and sharp objects.

Alexander didn't understand her concern so much. He grew up learning to fight at a very young age but who was he to tell her no?

"It was just kissing. We are friends and were bored." Alec shrugged.

"She's basically your little cousin," Alexander groaned. "Do you know how weird that is?"

"No. She isn't my "cousin."" Alec did air quotes with his fingers. "We are not blood related whatsoever. Just because we grew up together doesn't mean we are related and she's a grown ass woman now. Besides, she started it."

Nadia grew into a ravishing dark-haired beauty with porcelain skin. Alexander had never pictured her as being that outgoing. She was strong, there was no doubt, as she usually put men in their place. Still, it was hard for Alexander to imagine her as anything but his little niece he used to play tea party with.

Alexander face palmed his head. "For the love of Zeus. Damian and Owen are going to have a heyday."

"Only if you tell him." Alec's grin reminded him a little too much of himself.

"Tell who, what?" Julia joined them in the kitchen. Seeing their son's far too guilty face she groaned. "Oh, for the love of Jupiter, what did you do now?"

"Why do you assume it was me?" Alec faked offense.

"Well, given this is your brother's acceptance party into the Warrior's ranks and he is mingling with our guests, I doubt it has to do with him." Julia gave him a pointed look.

Alec shrugged. "I don't know, Mom. Helios is pretty good at hiding his bad side from you."

"I love you, Alec." Julia put a hand on his cheek and patted it a little too hard. "But you get your personality from your father and he was the wild one."

Alexander shrugged. "I'm not going to deny it."

Alexander wouldn't change their sons for anything. They complemented each other well and looked out for one another without needing to ask. Growing up they only practice fought but never did so among themselves for real. Helios was the anchor for Alec's rebellious nature.

"I caught him in the garden, kissing Nadia." When Julia's jaw dropped, Alexander went on, "He said she initiated it."

"Oh, I don't believe that for a second. She's far too timid for that."

"That girl is wild. Hate to tell you guys." Alec had a goofy grin on his face.

"For the sake of your brothers party, keep your mouth to yourself and go mingle." Julia straightened Alec's tux jacket, turned him around, and pushed him out the doors.

Alexander followed Julia with their arms linked together and the hilarity of it all hit him like a ton of bricks when Alec awkwardly ran into Damian. His son and Damian's daughter. It actually made sense. The four of their children had been attached at the hip since they were born.

Damian's eyebrows rose at Alec's stumbling apology for bumping into him and Anna, before he ran towards Owen and Helios for protection.

"What the hell was that about?" Damian seemed more amused than anything.

"Nothing." Julia sighed. "Where in the world is my brother?"

Alexander tried to look over the crowd of people that had gathered in their house and found the tall bastard. "He's over there with Katina."

The council woman was Cato's latest arm candy. Katina's dark hair was pulled into a tight bun and a blue dress hugged her body. It was a little revealing for a young man's party, but she was the type of woman that flaunted her sexuality.

Once he caught sight of them, Cato made his way over with the little minx on his arm. Alexander tried not to feel uncomfortable, but his cheeks were flushed when Katina made eye contact with him. Little did he tell anyone, besides Julia of course, she had made a move on him recently and he'd had to pry her off his body. He may or may not have tripped her and ran as fast as he could just for good measure.

"Hello there, Alexander." Katina's eyes lingered a little too long on him before she turned to his wife. "And Julia, you look lovely."

"Why thank you." Julia plastered a smile on her face. Alexander knew what was coming. "Don't you just look absolutely slutty, I mean stunning."

"Why don't you get us some drinks." Cato squeezed Katina's hip as he nudged her away. As soon as she was at a good distance he asked, "What the hell was that?"

"I'll tell you later." Alexander was having a major problem containing his laughter. "Looks like our kids are ditching us."

Owen, the carbon copy of his mother, led his sister Nadia upstairs. Quickly, Helios and Alec followed right behind them. All of them were full of smiles and happiness. Alexander loved how much their kids adored one another.

"What in the world are they up to?" Anna tried to pull Damian towards the stairs but instead he pulled her body to his. "Let me go, you big bully."

"They are getting into mischief. Let them." Damian kissed the top of his wife's head.

"You sure that's wise?" Julia couldn't help but smile. "Knowing Owen and Alec, it isn't going to end well."

Cato shrugged. "I doubt whatever it is, is dangerous. Owen wouldn't let anything happen to his sister."

"She's a Warrior. She's used to danger," Julia countered.

"Aren't we all?" Cato one arm hugged a worried Anna.

Damian draped an arm around Cato and Alexander. "Whatever they are up to, I can't imagine it could be any worse than the hell we've gone through to get here."

And it was fucking worth it.

ACKNOWLEDGEMENTS

First off, I'd once again like to thank my amazing team of women who have helped bring my first series together. You ladies have gone far and beyond time and time again for every project you work on. I can see it in your work and in your amazing attitude towards creating the perfect outcome for every author you come by.

Jennifer, I can never thank you enough for all your help and understanding through all of this. You amaze me every day with your strength and positive attitude. Seriously, you rock girl.

I'd also like to thank a few of my military friends and their willingness to share their expertise. It helped a great deal when trying to make my characters complete and more accurate to their military background. So, thank you Randy Rome and Anthony Gardner.

Lastly, to my granny. My number one fan and the one person I wanted to finish this for. I miss you more than I thought possible. You were the one person that believed in me the most and I wish I could have finished this for you in time. THIS IS FOR YOU! I will always and forever love you more.

About the Author

Nicole Corine Dyer is an author from Kansas with a Degree in Liberal Arts. After many years of struggling to overcome writers block, she has finally finished her first series. Reading has always been a passion and to be able to become an author was a lifelong dream, finally taking form.

Writing has become an escape from the real world for her, coming back to characters that feel more like family. After a six-year journey, the Infinite Series has come to an end but Nicole cannot wait to continue on her journey as an author.

Contact Nicole

Website: www.nicolecorinedyer.com

Facebook: Author Nicole Corine Dyer

Email: nicolecorinedyer@gmail.com

Goodreads: Author Nicole Corine Dyer

OTHER BOOKS